HOW I
PAID
FOR
COLLEGE

A Novel of

SEX,
Theft,
Friendship &
MUSICAL THEATER

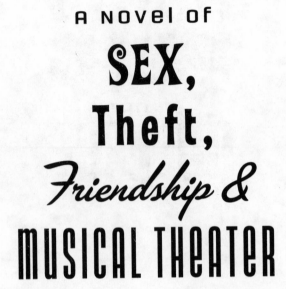

Marc Acito

HOW I PAID FOR COLLEGE

FOR

BROADWAY BOOKS
New York

PRINTED IN THE UNITED STATES OF AMERICA

BROADWAY BOOKS and its logo, a letter B bisected on the diagonal, are trademarks of Random House, Inc.

Visit our website at www.broadwaybooks.com

First edition published 2004

Book design by Mauna Eichner
Chapter opening illustration by Rex Bonomelli

Library of Congress Cataloging-in-Publication Data
Acito, Marc, 1966–
How I paid for college : a novel of sex, theft, friendship & musical theater / Marc Acito.—
1st ed.
p. cm.
1. Teenage boys—Fiction.   2. Acting—Study and teaching—Fiction.   3. College and school drama—Fiction.   4. High school students—Fiction.   5. Amateur theater—Fiction.   6. Fund raising—Fiction.   7. New Jersey—Fiction.   8. Friendship—Fiction.   9. Tuition—Fiction.   I. Title.

PS3601.C53H69 2004
813'.6—dc22
2003069742

ISBN 0-7679-1841-X

1 3 5 7 9 10 8 6 4 2

For Floyd, who makes it all possible . . .
and worthwhile

How I
PAID
FOR
COLLEGE

one

The story of how I paid for college begins like life itself—in a pool of water. Not in the primordial ooze from which prehistoric fish first developed arms and crawled onto the shore but in a heavily chlorinated pool of water in the backyard of Gloria D'Angelo's split-level ranch in Camptown, New Jersey.

Aunt Glo.

She's not my aunt, really, she's my friend Paula's aunt, but everybody calls her Aunt Glo and she calls us kids the LBs, short for Little Bastards.

Aunt Glo yells. Always yells. She yells from the basement where she does her son the priest's laundry. She yells from the upstairs bathroom, where she scrubs the tub to calm her nerves. And she yells from her perch behind the kitchen sink, where she stirs her marinara sauce and watches us float in the heavily chlorinated pool of water.

Like life itself, the story of how I paid for college begins with a yell.

"Heeeeeey! Are you two LBs gonna serenade me or what?"

Paula and I mouth to each other, "Ya' can't lie around my pool for nothin', y'know."

I roll over on the inflatable raft, giving a tug on my PROPERTY OF WALLINGFORD HIGH SCHOOL ATHLETIC DEPT. shorts so they don't stick to my nuts. (I wear the shorts ironically—a tribute to the one purgatorial semester I spent on the track team.) I reach over to turn down the radio, where Irene Cara is having a *Flashdance* feeling for like the gazillionth time today, and turn to look at Paula.

Shards of light spike off the water, so I have to shield my eyes with my hand to see her. Paula's poised on her floating throne, her head tilted "I'm ready for my close-up, Mr. DeMille" upright, her eyes hidden by a pair of rhinestone-studded cat-lady sunglasses, a lace parasol over her shoulder to protect her white-white skin. She wears one of Aunt Glo's old bathing suits from the fifties, a pleated number that stretches across her flesh like those folds you see on Greek statuary; it's more of a bird-cage with fabric, really, the desired effect being a Sophia Loren–Gina Lollobrigida–kind of va-va-va-voom sensuality. Frankly, though, Paula's a couple of vooms wide of the mark.

She takes a sip from a virgin strawberry daiquiri, then eyes me over her sunglasses to say, "What can we do? We've been summoned for a command performance." Then she throws her head back, unhinges her wide jaw, and lets flow the opening phrase of "Ave Maria" in a voice so warm and pure you want to take a bath in it. I join in, harmonizing like we did at her cousin Crazy Linda's wedding, our voices mixing and mingling in a conversation that goes on above our heads and into the thick New Jersey air. A pair of nasty-looking dogs on the other side of the chain-link fence bark at us.

Everyone's a critic.

But not Aunt Glo. Aunt Glo's a good audience and (since Paula's mother is dead and her father works so much for the highway depart-ment) a frequent one. "Such voices you two have, like angels." She al-ways tells us that. "Oh, son of a bitch, look at the time," she yells. "Now shaddap, will ya', my stories are almost on."

I can't see her through the screened window but I know she's light-ing up a Lucky Strike and pouring herself a Dr Pepper before waddling down to the rec room to watch *Guiding Light* and do her ironing.

Aunt Glo.

Paula deposits her glass on the side of the pool and twiddles her tiny fingers in the water to clean them off. "*Honestly*, Edward," she says, flinging a meaty arm in the air, "it is so *pat*ently un*fair*." (Paula has a *tendency* to *speak* in *italics*.) "I'm simply *wasting* my talent this sum-mer, *wasting* it!" Forever cast in the roles of postmenopausal women, Paula is continuing the trend this summer by playing Miss Lynch in the Wallingford Summer Workshop production of *Grease*.

I lay my head down on the raft. "You're right, Sis," I say.

She's not really my sister, but she might as well be. Apart from the difference in our complexions, we could be twins: Paula is the pure white twin; I'm the evil dark one. Otherwise, we're both all long curly hair, thick eyelashes, and high body-fat ratio.

I also call her Sis because she uses her nun costume from our production of *The Sound of Music* to buy us beer, on the entirely correct theory that no one would ask a nun for her ID.

Paula snaps her parasol shut and rows over to me using the handle end. "The problem," she says, "is that I've got a nineteenth-century figure. If I'd been born a hundred years earlier, I would have been considered *desirable*."

We've had this conversation before. Some of us are born to run, others are born to be wild—Paula was born to wear a hoopskirt.

I feel the tap of a parasol on my shoulder. "Look at *these*," she says, mashing her boobs together like she's fluffing pillows. "And *this*." She turns sideways to grab a hunk of her fleshy butt.

"In the case of an emergency water landing, your seat cushion may be used as a flotation device," I say.

Paula tips my mattress over with one of her thick nineteenth-century legs.

I bob up to the surface and try to capsize her by grabbing her tiny feet. "No, no, no, *please*, Edward," she says, "the hair, the hair, I've got to be at work in an hour."

"Fine," I say, backstroking to the shallow end, "but as far as the nineteenth century goes, I've got two words for you."

"Oh, yeah?"

"Yeah: No anesthesia."

I can hear her deep, chocolaty laugh as I look up at the high-tension wires crisscrossing the baby blue sky. I love making Paula laugh.

I step out of the pool. "You're looking at this *Grease* thing all wrong, Sis. Think of us as guest stars, like Eve Arden and Frankie Avalon in the movie." (Fully aware that I wouldn't make a convincing Danny Zuko, I opted to play Teen Angel instead.) "Let everyone else knock their brains out learning the frigging Hand Jive; in the end you and I are still going to come in and steal the show with our finely wrought comic interpretations."

Paula sighs. She knows I'm right.

"Besides, I, for one, have more important things to deal with." I'm speaking, of course, about my audition for Juilliard.

Juilliard.

Now in case you live in Iowa or something and don't know anything about it, perhaps I should explain that Juilliard is the finest institution for acting in the entire country, the Tiffany's of drama schools. Everybody famous went there—Kevin Kline, William Hurt, Robin Williams—and ever since I starred in *The Music Man* in the ninth grade I've known I wanted to go there, too. I've already got one surefire contemporary audition monologue (Mozart in *Amadeus*, a prankish man-boy I was born to play), but I need to come up with a classical one, too. So I've bought myself a brand-new *Complete Works of Shakespeare*—a really nice one, with a velvet cover and gold leaf on the ends of the pages—and I'm going to spend my entire summer reading it. Plus work on my tan.

Paula parks her inflatable barge in the shallow end and extends her hand for me to help her up. She frowns at me, like I'm a dress she's trying to decide whether or not to buy.

"What's wrong?" I ask.

She sighs and pats herself with a towel. (Always pats, never rubs. Rubbing is tough on the skin.) "Can you keep a secret?" she asks.

"Of course not," I say. "But when has that ever stopped you?"

She extends her pinky finger. "Pinky swear."

I link mine with hers. "Fine. Pinky swear. What is it?"

She looks around like she doesn't want to be overheard. "Do you remember how I told you about the night I let Dominick Ferretti take me behind the pizza oven?"

"Yeah."

"I lied."

"What? Why?"

"I didn't want you to think I was some kind of priss," she says. "You and Kelly have done practically *everything*."

This is an exaggeration. It's not like my girlfriend Kelly and I have gone all the way yet or even gone down on each other, but I guess compared to Paula's nunlike existence, we're something out of the *Kama Sutra*.

(Incidentally, I never believed that story about Dominick Ferretti.)

"You're not a priss," I say. "You're, uh . . ."

"Go ahead, say it. I'm too fat to get a boyfriend."

Let the record show: she said it, not me.

Paula flops down on a lounge chair like she's Camille taking to her sickbed. "What am I going to do? What kind of actress can I *possibly* hope to be if I'm still a *virgin*?" she says, grabbing me by the hand and yanking me down next to her. "Edward, you have to help me."

I adjust my shorts again. "Uh, listen, Sis, I'm totally flattered, but I don't think Kelly would . . ."

"Oh, don't be *daft*," she says, giving me a shove. "You've got to help me with Doug Grabowski."

Doug Grabowski? Doug Grabowski the football player I convinced to try out for Danny Zuko? Doug Grabowski who used to go out with Amber Wright, the single most popular girl in school? That Doug Grabowski?

"What about him?" I ask.

"Do you know if he has a girlfriend?"

Paula's capacity for delusion is astounding. It's partly what makes her such a great actress. "Uh . . . I don't think so," I mumble, as I try to figure out how to tell her she stands a better chance of being crowned Miss America than of landing Doug Grabowski.

"*Splendid*," she chimes, and she pirouettes onto the lawn in a manner that unfortunately calls to mind the dancing hippos in *Fantasia*. "I've got it all planned out: the four of us—you and Kelly and Doug and I—are going to go into the city this Saturday to see *A Chorus Line*. I can't imagine Doug's ever seen it and he must, he *really, really* must. If he's going to spend the *entire* summer hanging around us instead of those knuckle-draggers from the football team, then it's our duty, really, to expose him to the finer things in life, don't you think?"

"Well . . ."

"The poor boy must be positively *starved* for intellectual stimulation."

"But . . ."

"Oh, Edward, it's going to be a night we'll remember the rest of our lives," she says, thrusting my clothes into my hands. "Now all you need to do is drive over to play practice and ask him."

"Me? Why not you?"

Paula clicks her tongue. "I don't want to appear *pushy*."

God forbid.

"Besides, not all of us have rich daddies," she sniffs. "Some of us actually have to *work*." She slips her tiny teardrop feet into a pair of pink plastic jellies and sashays toward the house.

"I work," I call after her. "What do you call choreographing the kids' show at the workshop?"

She turns and points her pink feet, ballerina style. "I call it *play*," she says. "Making calzones in a 120-degree kitchen while Dominick Ferretti makes lewd gestures with a sausage—*that's* a job." With a regal toss of her head, she throws open the door. "Now get dressed and get over there," she commands, sending me inside to change. "My loss of innocence is *depending* on it."

two

Now outside it may be 1983, but inside Aunt Glo's it's forever 1972: harvest-gold appliances and orange linoleum counters in the kitchen, shag carpeting and wood paneling everywhere else.

I grab a Fudgsicle out of the freezer and pad down to the rec room where Aunt Glo is ironing and watching *Guiding Light.*

Imagine, if you will, a fire hydrant. Now put a black football helmet on top of that fire hydrant. Then wrap the whole thing in a floral-print housedress and that's Aunt Glo. She looks like the offspring of Snow White and one of the seven dwarves.

Aunt Glo is a MoP—Mother of Priest—and she expresses her gratitude for this good fortune by doing all of her son's ironing even though he's like forty or something. I plop down in the La-Z-Boy recliner, wrapping my towel around me so I don't get it wet. "Who's breaking up today?" I ask, trying to peel the wrapper off the Fudgsicle.

"Oh, baby doll, these poor, poor people," Aunt Glo says, ironing and crying, crying and ironing. (Aunt Glo calls everybody baby doll, partly out of affection, but mostly because she can't remember jack shit.) "I just thank the Virgin Mother that my Benny is dead, God rest his soul, so I'll never have to know the pain of divorce."

Even before her stroke, Aunt Glo operated according to a logic all her own. She is, after all, the woman who named her only son Angelo D'Angelo.

Sweat and tears mix on Aunt Glo's pudgy face and her crepe-y arm jiggles as she irons back and forth. Behind her, Angelo's collars hang clipped to a clothesline like severed doves' wings. "It's just so sad for the children," she sighs.

Oh, please, not this.

I know that sad-clown-in-a-black-velvet-painting look, that sympathetic tone, that warm washcloth of pity that grown-ups are always trying to wipe all over me. What she really means, what they all really mean is, "I'm sure your mom had her reasons, Edward, but what kind of mother leaves her own children?"

I'm fine, I want to say, I'm fine. I have my career ahead of me. My art. My friends. Besides, it's not like I don't ever see my mom. True, I never know when she's going to show up, but that's part of what makes her so cool: she's a Free Spirit. Our bond is more spiritual than temporal. But still everyone treats me like I'm Oliver fucking Twist.

Aunt Glo keeps crying and ironing, ironing and crying, and we're quiet for a moment, which, being Italian, is unusual for us. My bathing suit is giving me the itch and I want to leave, but I want to stay, too. There's something kind of comforting about watching Aunt Glo cry; I guess because I can't cry myself. It's probably my biggest failing as an actor, but I can't seem to do it. Sometimes I'll try to force the tears out, pushing and grunting like I'm constipated, but I just end up feeling trapped inside my skin and desperate to get out. So instead I sit like this with Aunt Glo, *Guiding Light* casting shadows on the wall behind us, while she cries for both of us.

✻　✻　✻

I back MoM (Mom's old Mercedes) out of Aunt Glo's driveway into the cul-de-sac. My mother gave up the car when she left Al because she doesn't really care about that kind of thing anyway. My mom is all about Personal Fulfillment, which is why she took off when I was twelve to find herself. Al may pay for all my training, but it's my mom who really understands me as an artist. She always said, "If you want to be a garbage man, *be* a garbage man, but be the *best* garbage man you can be." I wave at Aunt Glo's neighbor, an old Italian guy in Bermuda shorts and dark socks watering his tomato plants, then make the lethal left-hand turn onto Wallingford Avenue.

Now, when they make the movie of my life, this'll be when they begin the credits. There I'll be, breezing down suburban streets in my thrift-shop fedora while Frank Sinatra's "Summer Wind" plays on the soundtrack. It'll help establish the right mood of swagger and swing. Frank's all about swagger and swing.

What you see might surprise you. New Jersey may be the most densely populated state in the U.S. (or as Paula likes to say, the state where the population is most dense), but you wouldn't know it from Wallingford.

Colonial Wallingford.

Twenty minutes in any direction you'll find the Jersey you're thinking of—the toxic waste dumps; the wise guys who say *dese*, *dem*, and *dose*; the gangs, the ghettos, and the Garden State Parkway. But the moment you enter Wallingford the houses take a giant step back from the street, like they're too good to be seen near it, and expand upward and outward, sprouting things like turrets and gables and chimneys. Founded in 1732, Wallingford takes a disproportionately absurd amount of pride in its colonial heritage. The American troops may have camped at Camptown (or as we call it, Cramptown, because the food at the diner always gives us gas), and fought what was essentially an eighteenth-century version of a water fight at Battle Brook (the town over from that), but somehow Wallingford emerged as the epitome of all things traditional and quaint.

Wallingford is a bedroom community, which means that most people work an hour away in Manhattan and only sleep here. On the one hand, I find the term "bedroom community" sort of sexy, imagining that all kinds of otherwise respectable people are swapping wives and having orgies behind closed doors, but it probably just means that not much else happens in Wallingford beyond sleeping.

I get as far as Washington Street and sit for a moment behind the wheel, MoM's diesel engine chugging like a locomotive, while I decide which way to go. If I make a left and take it almost as far as the freeway I'll get to Oak Acres, the neighborhood I'm embarrassed to admit I live in. There are no turrets or gables or chimneys in Oak Acres; there aren't even any actual oaks, just sprawling ranch houses with circular driveways and phoney-baloney columns designed to appeal to people who possess more money than taste. Oak Acres is so full of Italians and Jews relocated from places like Hoboken and Bayonne that the Wallingford blue bloods call it Hoboken Acres. I turn right and head to the high school instead.

I pull into my usual spot, the one marked VISITOR PARKING ONLY, because I like to think of myself as someone who is just visiting a suburban New Jersey high school, rather than someone who actually attends one. When they make the movie of my life, this'll be where the credits end.

I duck in through a side door that only the Play People know about.

(Play People. Like we're not real. We're the realest people in this preppy prison.) Revolting Renée, the choreographer, is onstage teaching the Hand Jive while simultaneously grossing everyone out with her noxious BO and backne. Her excuse for not bathing is that she's like some ex-hippie or something, but personally I think there's a statute of limitations on body odor as an act of rebellion. Some little ninth grader sees me and points me out to the other kids in the chorus.

"Okay, people, that's right," Revolting Renée says, raising her scary Vulcan eyebrows, "the famous Edward Zanni has graced us with his presence."

I gesture to the cast with a *grand port de bras*.

"Let's show him what we've been up to while he's been lyin' around workin' on his tan," she says.

Did I get color? Cool. Without a tan I look like I'm jaundiced. I catch Kelly's eye and wave to her. She peeks up from under her blond bangs and waves back in that shy way that pretty girls do—wiggling her fingers, rather than actually moving her whole hand. She mouths "Hi," or "Hiyeee" to be exact, and smiles at me with both rows of teeth. She's wearing character shoes for dancing and the combination of high heels with tight terry-cloth shorts makes her look like a teen prostitute in a TV movie of the week.

It's a good look.

She turns her back and slides her thumbs under her shorts to pull them down over her Valentine ass, and I feel my cold, wrinkly dick stir in my pants.

Revolting Renée hollers "Five, six, seven, eight . . ." and leads the chorus in the Hand Jive, but they have a hard time following her characteristically inept choreography. Kelly, who's playing Sandy, spins across the stage, the muscles in her pale legs rippling like a colt's, and lands in the veiny arms of Doug Grabowski, who dances like someone whose foot has gone to sleep. (What can you expect when his usual mode of physical expression is knocking people over on a football field?) Doug wears a PROPERTY OF WALLINGFORD HIGH SCHOOL ATHLETIC DEPT. T-shirt, but since he's actually a jock it's not meant to be ironic.

He and Kelly look good together; so—I don't know—Northern Hemisphere, I guess. Kelly could easily date plenty of guys just like Doug, football players with necks thicker than their heads, popular boys who shout each other's last names in the halls and who mutter when they're called on in class. But for some unfathomable reason she chose *me*. It's like the high-school equivalent of Princess Di ditching Prince Charles to date a commoner. Like that's ever gonna happen.

I suppose I'm not bad-looking in my own way. My body's a little softer than I'd like it to be — my ratio of Twinkies to dance classes being unequal — but I look all right as long as I keep my shirt untucked; and girls have always liked to play with my curly hair and complain they're jealous of my eyelashes, which are long and thick, like a camel's or Liza Minnelli's. But still, Kelly is everything a high-school boy wants in a girl — she's thin, she's blond, and, most important, she likes to mess around. She was even a cheerleader back in junior high, but had some kind of falling out with the Rah-Rah's the summer before sophomore year and sought refuge with the Play People instead. Still, there's something kind of WASP-y about Kelly, despite her actually being Irish Catholic on both sides. After all, she does live in Wallingford Heights, a neighborhood so exclusive you practically need a blood test to get in or, perhaps I should say, a blue-blood test. I watch her do the Hand Jive and wonder whether we'll have time later for a hand job.

The chorus struggles with Revolting Renée's bizarrely Byzantine choreography, each frigging syllable accompanied by a supposedly appropriate hand gesture, the overall effect being less like a dance and more like a simultaneous sign-language interpretation for the hearing impaired, but I applaud loudly when they finish. It's important to encourage these chorus people.

"Okay, that's it, people, see ya' tomorrow morning," Revolting Renée says. I give her the thumbs-up sign and she looks grateful, as if my opinion meant something, which I suppose it does. After all, I have taken dance classes in New York City for nearly four years now and my voice teacher was in the chorus of *Sweeney Todd* on Broadway.

I hop up onstage in one swift move (I love being able to hop up onstage in one swift move) and greet Kelly by pulling her to me and grinding against her while some awed ninth graders look on. Kelly responds by wrapping her endless leg around my waist like a belt.

"You look hot," I say.

"I am hot," she says, fanning herself.

That's not what I meant, but I let it go.

"We had to do that number like a hundred times and Doug still can't get it right," she says. I glance over at him as he practices with Revolting Renée, flapping his arms like he's trying to land a plane. If I didn't know any better I would rush over and stick a pencil in his mouth to keep him from swallowing his tongue.

"He'll get it," I say. "You'll make him look good." I push back Kelly's bangs so I can see her eyes. From a distance they appear to be green, but up close you realize that they're actually two different colors; that the left favors brown, the right blue. She's self-conscious about it, but I think it's cool, like she's two people at once. I kiss her freckled nose.

"I'm telling you, Edward," she says, "he's, like, the horniest guy I've ever met. Just dancing with him makes me feel like a dirty girl."

"You're not a dirty girl," I say. "You're just a sweaty girl." Kelly laughs, a machine gun. I love making her laugh. Making a mental note to keep an eye on Doug, I grind against her again, like I'm marking my territory.

Doug spies me and saunters over, grinning like he's in on a private joke, and it's a dirty one. He may dance like a spaz, but I've got to admit he's got the Danny Zuko strut down perfect. "Yo, Teen Angel, hands off Sandy; she's my girl," he says, twirling Kelly around and dipping her. Then, chuckling at nothing in particular, he puts out his hand to give me five.

I hate giving five. I want to say, "Listen, it's 1983, not 1968, we're white and we're always going to be white, and if you're going to hang around with us this summer then you have got to stop calling us by our character names offstage because it is *so* junior high."

But I don't. I give him the requested five instead.

Wuss.

I can't help it. After all these years of being tormented by guys just like Doug Grabowski, I can't believe that I'm the person he actually wants to impress: me, Edward Zanni, a *Play Person*. He asks me to watch him and Kelly do the combination one more time and I can see that just saying the word "combination" gives him a jolt, like he's in on some cool insider theater lingo. I think back to the day last year when Doug shocked the school and auditioned for the choir, a football player of all people, and how he asked me to help him read music, and how I eventually convinced him he had exactly the right tough-guy quality to play Danny Zuko. And now I look at him, attacking a dance routine with unashamed enthusiasm—not in that fakey testosterone-y way that jocks usually have—but in a way that's, I don't know, joyful, I guess, like he's lit from within. I watch him as he grins and laughs at his own mistakes and I realize that Paula is right. He loves every minute of this. He feels more alive here than he ever has.

He's a Play Person.

There are certain pristine moments in your life when your destiny is made absolutely clear to you, like when I was nine and sang "Where Is Love?" from *Oliver!* in a school talent show and knew in an instant that there was no place I'd rather be than onstage, or when I was fourteen and saw the movie *Fame* and realized it was my destiny to live in New York City and wear leg warmers. I watch Doug tripping over his feet and my mission becomes clear: it is my duty to transform this goofy, horny jock into a sensitive, cultured young man. I am to be the Henry Higgins to his Eliza Doolittle.

When Kelly and Doug finish I ask them if they want to go into the city on Saturday to get twofers for *A Chorus Line*.

"What're twofers?" Doug asks.

The tutorial commences. "There's this booth in the middle of Times Square that sells half-price tickets to Broadway shows on the day of the show," I say. "Two fer one, get it? You have gone into the city before, right?"

"Oh, yeah," Doug says. "Last St. Patrick's Day I went in with the team and, man, we got shitfaced, it was comical. Boonschoft passed out on the train with his mouth open and we stuck his ticket to his tongue."

Charming. "But you've never been to a Broadway show?"

Doug strikes a military at-ease position to think. "I saw the Ice Capades at Madison Square Garden when I was a kid," he says.

"Doesn't count. So are we on for Saturday?"

"Sure."

Just then I hear a voice behind me say, "What're we doing Saturday?"

I turn, and there in front of me, or perhaps I should say below me, stands the diminutive and ubiquitous Nathan Nudelman, eager as always to insinuate himself into my plans with a determination that could only be described as viral.

Shit.

three

My dad only gave me one piece of advice when my mom left: "Kid, don't ever turn down a free meal." Consequently, I've mooched dinners off of my friends since the sixth grade. That being said, Al decided we should definitely eat together at least one night a week and we have done so every Wednesday at Mamma's, a pizzeria in downtown Wallingford. Since we have absolutely nothing in common beyond genetics and our sorry shared history, Al also decided we should make these "business dinners" so he could teach me and my sister about business and use the expense as a tax write-off.

I hate business. I'm an artist, not a businessman. I hate business and I hate Wednesday nights, and, as a result, I kind of hate my dad.

Al is the chief financial officer for Wastecom, one of New Jersey's many treatment storage disposal facilities, or TSDs, which are not to be confused with STDs, an entirely different kind of health hazard. "Y'know, there's a lot of job security in toxic waste," Al says.

Al.

I honestly don't know how I descended from this man. I take after my mother, which means not only am I a Free Spirit, but I, too, find it intolerable to be around Al Zanni. He's a nice enough guy, I suppose, in a crass New Jersey way, but there's no poetry in his soul. Al and I agree on exactly one thing: we both love Frank Sinatra. When you're from Hoboken it's practically a requirement. Forget Springsteen; as far as I'm concerned, Sinatra's the only native son of New Jersey who really counts.

I stand outside Mamma's waiting for Al. Big, Spielberg-y storm clouds blow in fast from the east, while the late-afternoon sun shines low in the west, lighting the trees from below and casting them in high relief against the lavender-gray sky, like you see in 1940s MGM Technicolor musicals. I put on my new sunglasses to heighten the effect. The glasses have a sort of pinkish tint to them that bathes everything I see in a rosy glow, and I'm pleased with myself for buying something that doesn't necessarily make me look good to the world (they are a little faggy, I guess) but which makes the world look good to me instead.

Al pulls up in his red Corvette convertible or, as I like to call it, his Midlife Crisis. He glances in the rearview mirror to check his hair, which looks like a toupee but isn't, then extracts his big, bearlike frame from the car and tosses the keys to the valet. Al's got a body like a linebacker gone to seed, which is exactly what he is, and which also explains why his runty, artistic son is a total mystery to him. Tonight he's got more cologne on than usual (if that's possible) and is wearing a short-sleeve silk shirt unbuttoned two, no wait, three buttons, exposing a pair of gold chains. With his golf slacks pulled up too high he looks like Elvis after he got fat.

My older sister, Karen, is with him on account of her losing her license for a DWI. She sits slumped in the passenger seat, looking miserable or stoned (or, in all likelihood, both), her too-skinny frame bent like a boomerang. I push aside her sheepdog bangs and squint at her pupils while Al gives the valet a lesson in how to properly drive his Midlife Crisis.

"You're high, aren't you?" I say to her.

"Can you think of a better way to get through this meal?" she mumbles.

"Faking your own death?"

"Nah, I've totally got the munchies."

The front door of Mamma's swings open and Paula leans out, dressed in her black-and-white waitress uniform. Or I should say her version of a black-and-white waitress uniform. She's doctored the whole thing up with lace so that she looks more like a French maid, albeit a well-fed one. "Hello, Zannis!" she chirps with the enthusiasm of a game-show host. "I've saved you a table in my section."

"Paula! How are ya'?" Al says, spreading his arms in that gesture that Italian men think is friendly but Italian women know just means they're gonna get pinched. He pats me on the cheek as he passes, his usual greeting.

"Hey, Mr. Z." Paula leans her cheek out for him to kiss, but Al grabs her face in his hairy hands and kisses her on the lips instead.

Ick.

Then he says the same thing he always says to her: "You look like you've lost some weight."

"Really?" Paula says, flashing a molar-grinding smile. "I could have sworn I had it when I came in here."

"No, you are definitely losing weight. Eddie, ain't she losin' weight?"

"Yeah, Pop, so are we while we stand here," I say. "Can we go in?"

"I tell you what," he says, the sun reflecting off his Rolex as he wags a sausage finger in her face, "you keep away from the cannoli and you'll be a regular Sophia Loren."

Paula thanks him, her molars ground to a fine powder by now, I'm sure.

Al puts his arm around her. "So, what are your plans for the fall?" he asks.

Karen sits down on the sidewalk.

"I'm going to Juilliard, Mr. Z, remember?" She's only told him like a gazillion times. I'm jealous as hell she's going before I do, but I take her getting in as a good omen. After all, we're practically the same person.

"Right, right," Al says, "but waddya gonna do to fall back on?"

I hate when people say that. It's like admitting defeat before you've even started.

"Remember," he says, *"connections*, that's what show business is all about, *connections."* He turns to me and Karen like he's said something worth noting. Just because everybody watches actors on television and in the movies, they think that automatically makes them experts on show business. It's really annoying.

"Can we go in now, Pop?" I say.

"Actually, tonight we're gonna eat in the restaurant." Mamma's has a fancy restaurant connected to the pizzeria which, much to Paula's consternation, only hires male waitstaff.

"What's the occasion?" Paula asks.

"I've got a little surprise," Al says.

Shit. The last time he said that we had to read his stock portfolio. Looks like I'm gonna have to fake food poisoning again.

"Well, *buon appetito*," Paula says and widens her big Disney eyes at me, the Internationally Recognized Signal for "Come talk to me as soon as you can and don't leave out a thing."

❊   ❊   ❊

It takes a moment to adjust to the light inside Mamma's Ristorante, or lack thereof. The owners obviously decided that whoever decorated it when it opened in 1956 did a fine job so why mess with a winning formula? It's also clear that their design scheme didn't extend much beyond making everything red — the banquettes, the lampshades, the walls, the ceiling. It's like they painted it with leftover spaghetti sauce.

We're seated, but not until Al shows off his entire vocabulary in Italian with the maître d', which consists of about nine words interspersed with a lot of nodding, backslapping, and fakey laughter about nothing whatsoever. I'm relieved when he orders a bottle of wine and asks for four glasses.

I'm about to ask who the fourth is when the answer walks in the door.

Now when they make the movie of my life, this'll be the moment when they go into slow motion and play Sinatra's recording of "The Lady Is a Tramp" or, better yet, maybe "Witchcraft."

She's probably about forty-five, but looks younger. It's hard to tell because she's got that tousled, just-been-fucked hairstyle that older movie stars wear when they want to hide the wrinkles or their plastic surgery scars. She glides across the room in a pair of leather pants that look like they've come from the Young Sluts Department at Fiorucci. There's no denying she's hot (in a tight-blouse-y, nipple-freak-out, Angie Dickinson–as–*Police Woman* kind of way), and Al jingles the change in his pocket as he walks over to her. Then he grabs her face in both of his hairy hands and proceeds to tongue her right there in the restaurant.

Double Ick.

The woman doesn't seem to mind, nor is she bothered by Al's meaty paw resting on her ass. Al's right about one thing: this is a surprise. The woman licks her lips and gives a shake to her tangled mane to get a better look at us. Her hair is so heavily frosted it appears to be six colors at once, like it's hedging its bets.

"Dagmar," Al says, "these are my kids, Karen and Edward. Kids, meet Dagmar."

"Hallo," she says, and holds out her hand to me, palm down, like I'm supposed to kiss it or something. I grip her hand awkwardly and am surprised to find that her skin is rougher than it looks.

"I didn't realize your children vould be zo goot-lookink," she coos in a German accent so thick it's practically dripping schnitzel with noodles. She smiles at me. "You take after your fahter."

I feel my face smile on its own accord. Dagmar's definitely got that Elke Sommer–Ursula Andress thing going on—you could easily imagine her cast as a Bond girl or as the busty blond nurse in a burlesque skit—so when she says you're goot-lookink, *vell*, you feel pretty goot-lookink.

Dagmar tickles Al under the chin and gives him that glassy-eyed adoring gaze that Nancy Reagan uses during Ronnie's speeches and that's when it hits me: they're in love. They fucking love each other. And from the way Al's groping her, I can tell they love fucking each other, too. How did this happen without my knowing about it?

We sit down. Neither Karen nor I bother to ask who this woman is or why she's here and, frankly, I don't care. For the first time since my mom left we've got a shred of refinement in our lives and I'm determined to enjoy it. Waiters slide in noiselessly and drop off appetizers despite the fact we haven't looked at menus. Clearly, Al had this whole thing planned out. Good for him. I think it's romantic.

"So you're, like, from Europe, right?" Karen says.

I'm glad to see that the drugs haven't dulled her finely tuned powers of observation.

Dagmar nods. "From Austria."

I respond with what I hope is a look of worldly recognition, despite the fact that the sum total of my experience with Austria consists of seeing *The Sound of Music* more times than I care to admit.

Karen descends on the antipasto like she's one of the cavemen in *Quest for Fire*. "You ever been to Amsterdam?" she asks.

"Of course," Dagmar says, her voice clipped with Teutonic precision.

"I hear you can buy drugs, like, really easy there."

Dagmar raises her eyebrows at Al, the Internationally Recognized Signal for "And now, back to you . . ."

"Uh, Karen here works in a pharmacy," Al says. "She's got a great interest in pharmaceuticals."

He means Karen would've graduated college if only they'd offered a degree in hallucinogenics.

"Oh, zo do I," Dagmar says. "I hef terrible allergies. And zo many drugs are not available here."

"You lemme know what they are," Karen says, a roasted red pepper hanging out of her mouth like a second tongue. "I can hook you up."

Noting the strength of her accent, I ask Dagmar how long she's been in this country and am surprised to discover it's been nearly twenty years. She explains that she tries to get back to Europe as often as she can. I don't blame her. I would, too.

"Dagmar here's a photographer," Al says. "I met her at a show she had over at that gallery, y'know, the one that's run by those two queers . . ."

Wait a minute. Al went to an art show? In a gallery? Owned by homosexuals? I've got to admit that this newfound sophistication impresses me and I immediately start envisioning the jet-setting life of adventure we'll all be embarking on together.

"I'd love to see your work," I say. To let Dagmar know that I'm a kindred spirit I lean over and pat her strangely rough hand. "I'm an actor," I whisper.

"I'm sure you're very goot," she says. Artists can always tell.

Al then begins to pontificate on the business side of art, a subject he knows nothing about, but a lack of information has never stopped him from forming an opinion. The veil of boredom descends.

Al cracks his hairy knuckles. "I keep tellin' these two, if they want to succeed in life, they're gonna have to understand business."

Oh, waiter, would you please pour a bucket of cold water on my head? Oops, never mind. Somebody already has.

"*Ach*, I am zo hopeless ven it comes to business," Dagmar says.

"That's what this one is always sayin'," Al says, pointing to me with a breadstick, "but I bet you've got a better head for figures than you realize. I'll show ya'."

"You *voult*?" she says, her eyes flashing. "I'd like tsat."

Finally, someone Al can share his bar graphs and pie charts with. It's like a reprieve from the governor.

Al leans over and whispers something in Dagmar's ear and she laughs, slapping him lightly with her napkin. Then—I'm not making this up—he actually growls at her.

Ick squared.

This is my cue to leave. I head toward the kitchen and some ass-hole at another table snaps his fingers in my face as I pass. "Can we have some more breadsticks here?" he says.

I don't know why, but every time I go out to eat I'm always mistaken for the waiter. In this case I suppose it's because I'm dressed like the Dr Pepper guy. You know the commercial: "I'm a Pepper, he's a Pepper, wouldn't you like to be a Pepper, too?" That's how I see myself: a Pied Piper figure (or perhaps I should say Pied Pepper figure) in an old suit vest and baggy chinos, elbows akimbo as I hitch kick my way down the streets of New York City, crowds of deliriously peppy Pepper people parading behind me. But the fact is I could be dressed like Daisy Duke and some idiot would still ask me what the specials were. I guess I just have a waiting look about me.

"I don't work here," I say.

I wander into the kitchen, waving hello to Dominick Ferretti, who is making lewd gestures with a zucchini. His parents must be so proud.

Over on the pizzeria side Paula is regaling her table with some elaborate pack of lies. She spies me and comes bounding across the room. Dominick's dad nearly drops a pizza as he follows the bouncing breasts.

She grabs me by both hands. "So?" she squeals. "Did you talk to Doug and Kelly?"

"Yeah, everything's set."

"Oh, *rapturous*," she says, jumping up and down. And the judge from Italy gives a 9.6 for that Boob Bounce.

"Listen, Sis," I say, "there's something . . ."

"Oh, Edward, just look at this. I wrote it out on my break." She reaches deep into her cleavage while Mr. Ferretti cranes his neck to see, the big perv. She pulls out a doily onto which she's scrawled the following:

> *A Plan for a Summer of Magic and Mischief*
> *by Paula Angela Amicadora*
>
> *Step 1) Have intimate poolside soirees full of witty conversation*
> *Step 2) Have delightful, madcap adventures*
> *Step 3) Lose virginity*
> *Step 4) Shop for shoes*

"Isn't it *splendid?*" she says. "This Saturday is the official beginning of what's surely going to be the very best summer of our lives. The *best.*"

"Yeah, about that," I say, staring at the floor, "uh . . . you don't mind if Natie comes along, too, do you?"

In the space of about four seconds Paula goes through all five of the Kübler-Ross stages of grief. "Oh, Edward, how *could* you?" she wails.

"He overheard me talking about it at play practice and just kind of wormed his way in. I don't know how he does it. He's like the KGB."

I'm sure when cavemen invented the wheel, there was a Nathan Nudelman there to invent a third wheel. Every high-school clique has one: someone too short or too tall, too skinny or too fat, too dumb or too smart, it doesn't matter, male or female, this is the friend who simply cannot, will not, get laid before graduation.

Natie's the too-short version, which means he usually gets the role of somebody's kid brother in the plays. He's got a mushy marshmallow face, the kind that aunts and grandmothers can't resist pinching, and little button eyes that always seem to have sleep schmeg in the corners. He'd look just like the Pillsbury Doughboy except he also has a huge Jewish Afro which, to add insult to injury, is carrot red. Back in elementary school his mother made the unfortunate decision of trying to square off his haircut so he wouldn't resemble a chrysanthemum, but it just ended up looking like he had a block of cheese sitting on his head, earning him the completely unshakable nickname of Cheesehead. The word has since entered the general vocabulary of Wallingford students as a synonym for "loser," as in the sentence, "Give me your lunch money, you cheesehead." Since he lives across the street from me, we've hung out together for forever, but I've got to admit he's kind of embarrassing to be around.

"*Well,*" Paula says, "you're going to have to explain to him that five is an entirely unsuitable number for a sophisticated evening in the city." She flicks her pad against my chest for emphasis. "You simply *have* to."

I agree, then use my dinner with the Austrian Amazon as an excuse to escape the inevitable lecture.

When I return, I discover Karen is alone at the table. She's building a house out of packets of sugar and Sweet'N Low with the obsessive concentration of the contentedly stoned. I grab a knife and tap her wineglass.

"Where'd they go?" I ask.

"Dunno," she mumbles. "Al left us some money and said you shouldn't come home for a coupla hours."

I pick up two crisp $100 bills off the table.

"Waddya think?" Karen says. "Is she gonna be our new mommy?"

I feel the sharp paper between my fingers. "I hope so," I say.

four

I can see Paula across the parking lot of the train station as I pull up, her hands on her wide nineteenth-century hips, not a good sign. She taps the face of her wristwatch in the gesture that punctual, responsible people reserve for us disorganized, late ones. But since she wears her wristwatch on her ankle, it's hard to take her seriously.

If all the world's a stage, then Paula certainly understands the importance of wearing the right costume. And she does so by integrating into her wardrobe elements that haven't been seen for centuries, like hoopskirts or mantillas or peplums. It makes a statement. Today she's wearing the dress she made out of her father's white oxford shirt; a flattering choice, given that he's about six foot two and I'd say three hundred pounds, so it achieves the desired effect of making her appear small by comparison. The look is completed with a black felt porkpie hat, a multicolored Guatemalan vest with tiny mirrors on it, and a pair of pumps, one red and one gold.

Paula.

The shoe thing is more than just fashion, it's a philosophy. "Pairs of shoes should be like pairs of people," Paula says. "They should complement one another, not match." In the interest of maintaining a graceful posture, however, Paula concedes that the shoes should be identical heights, but insists that buying two pairs in different colors and mixing them is cheating. No, the only way to properly "reunite" a shoe with its "sole mate" is to spend hours in thrift stores sifting through piles of rejected and neglected secondhand shoes. Paula always leaves the bins much neater than she finds them.

Kelly and I get out of the car. Kelly's wearing lace tights, a fuchsia miniskirt, and a pink cotton sweater worn off her left shoulder *Flashdance* style, balanced by a ponytail and a huge lace bow on the right side of her head. Normally she doesn't wear any makeup at all on her Ivory-girl skin, but today she's tarted herself up special just for the occasion.

"Does this outfit look all right?" she asks Paula. "Edward picked it out." (Okay, I admit it: I'm living vicariously through her. If guys could get away with wearing elf boots, I would.)

Paula gives Kelly a quick appraisal. "New Wave Barbie," she says. "It comments on both consumerism and trendiness."

"Is that good?" Kelly asks.

"You both look great," I say, putting my arms around them. I'm in my Willy Wonka outfit: purple velvet tailcoat with jeans and red high-tops. Simple, but elegantly sloppy.

Paula lifts a stray hair off my jacket. "You're certain Natie understood, right?"

"Yeah, I just explained to him that five was kind of an awkward number."

"*Absolutely*," she says. "It's not like this is *officially* a double date, though it is possible Doug might think so." She brushes at her skirt, which she made out of the ruffles from old tuxedo shirts. "I'm more concerned for Natie's feelings, really. We wouldn't want him to feel left out."

"That's nice," Kelly says.

Paula pops open a compact and checks her teeth for lipstick. "I'm concerned for Doug as well. For me this is just another evening in the city. In fact, I've scarcely given it a second thought . . ."

That's because she's shared thoughts three through thirty with me on the phone.

". . . but with Doug it's entirely a different matter. This could be a life-altering experience for him."

She's interrupted by the growl of a muffler and we look up to see Doug's old Chevy run a red light and tear into the parking lot, pulling into a space marked SHORT-TERM PARKING ONLY without so much as slowing down.

"Oh my God, does my hair look all right?" Paula asks.

I look at her curls. "New Age pre-Raphaelite. It comments on both . . ."

"Oh, shut up."

Doug leaps out of the car, his cowlick-y hair still wet from a shower, and sprints across the parking lot, unbuttoning his khakis as he jogs toward us and tucking in his wrinkled oxford. "Sorry I'm late," he shouts. "I had to pick up Nate."

Nate?

We turn in unison toward the car and see Natie lumbering out of the passenger seat, squinting at the sun like he's a groundhog on the second of February. Shielding his eyes, he smiles and waves to us as if there were nothing remotely strange about his being here.

Paula gives me a pop-eyed silent-movie look.

"Wow," Doug says, laughing at nothing in particular, "you guys look great. I'm sorry, I don't have anything cool to wear."

"Never fear," Paula says, flinging a meaty arm in the air for emphasis. "Madame Paula's House of Couture, she never closes." She shoots me one last dirty look and then narrows her eyes on Doug, a leopard going in for the kill. "Now let's see . . ."

She circles around him, humming "Whatever Lola wants, Lola gets" and supplying the percussion with her jangling bracelets and flamenco finger snaps. It's a bit much in the light of day, actually, but I figure since she's playing Miss Lynch in *Grease* she needs outlets for expression.

In one swift move she flings off her vest and snaps it like a matador before easing it over Doug's broad shoulders, then slides off her piano-key tie and lassos him around the neck, pulling him a little too close. Dragging him along as she does a few impromptu tango steps, she sashays over to the *Lost in Space* lunch box she uses as a purse, removes a button that says UNIQUELY MALADJUSTED, and pins it to his chest.

I've got to give her credit. He looks like one of us now.

"I was getting too hot with all that on, anyway," she breathes at him, and she unbuttons one, no, two, then (yikes!) three buttons on her shirt, flapping it to fan herself and, of course, give Doug a preview of her nineteenth-century hooters.

"What about me?" Natie asks.

"Yeah, here ya' go," Paula says, squashing her porkpie hat on his cheesehead.

She musses her curls in the manner of a 1950s Italian movie star and clears her throat as if she's about to make some kind of pronouncement when a champagne-colored Jaguar slides into the parking lot and pulls up next to us. We all turn to look at it.

When they make the movie of my life, this will definitely be a slow-motion moment.

I can't see her face as she steps out of the car, hidden as it is by a shiny black wall of hair, but I'm immediately struck by her endlessly long legs, slender and firm in a pair of ivory Capri pants, and her bony, almost boyish, torso braless under a silk camisole, the breasts small but alert. She flips her straight, silky hair just like a girl in a shampoo commercial and tilts her cocoa-brown face toward the sun, revealing cheekbones like shelves and a long, tapering nose, onto which she slides an enormous pair of Jackie O sunglasses.

"Who is *that*?" I whisper.

Doug devils me a grin. "That, Teen Angel, is my date," he says. "Nate here explained the thing about, y'know, five people being a funny number."

I don't dare look at Paula, and couldn't even if I wanted to. I can't stop staring at this . . . this *model* in front of me. I've seen her once or twice in the Workshop office but always assumed she was a grown-up.

"Who is she?" I hiss.

"Her name is Ziba," he says.

"Zebra?" I ask. Who the hell names their kid Zebra?

"No, Zeee-bah. She just moved here." He beams at her admiringly. "Is she hot or what?"

Even in a pair of gladiator sandals that lace up around the ankles, Ziba is still taller than the rest of us, I'd say close to six foot, and she has to lean way over to talk to her mother through the car window. I assume it's her mother because she, too, is beautiful and elegant and Ziba kisses her goodbye on both cheeks, European style. Her mother hands her an ivory silk scarf and a beaded clutch purse, then waves a manicured hand our way like she knows us (which she doesn't) as the Jag slowly slides away.

Doug tugs on his new vest and struts over to Ziba, smirking like a little boy who just got a pony for Christmas. Ziba takes her time wrapping the silk scarf around her head, crisscrossing the ends over the architecture of her neck and shoulders, the way you see in old Audrey Hepburn movies. She inclines her head so Doug can do the European two-cheek-kiss thing, which I must say he manages to pull off without looking too retarded. I make a mental note to practice this gesture until I can accomplish it with grace and ease. I glance up for the first time at Paula, whose left eye is twitching like she just drank something sour.

Ziba marches over, hips swinging like a runway model, and sticks her arm straight out to give each one of us a firm handshake as Doug introduces us, something I've never seen another teenager do.

"Well," Paula says, trying to look chipper, "we better go or we'll miss the train." I'm just about to feel sorry for her when she grabs her lunch box in one hand and Ziba in the other and says, "Now, I'm fascinated to know, what kind of name is Ziba? Let me guess. Is it Indian?"

"No, it's Persian," Ziba says, emphasis on the "purrrh."

"*Persia!*" Paula squeals, pulling Ziba toward the station. "You must tell me *all* about it."

Paula wasn't a National Merit scholar for nothing. Faced with insurmountable competition for Doug's attention, she solves the problem neatly by monopolizing Ziba's attention instead. I know her feelings are hurt, but she's too fair-minded to blame Ziba for it, and I can tell she can't help but admire someone who has the good sense to do the Audrey Hepburn scarf-on-the-head thing and carry a beaded clutch bag.

But if Paula's banter fills the train ride, Ziba's mere presence dominates it, and we all make minor adjustments to accommodate her. Natie rattles on about everything he's ever read in the *New York Times* about the Middle East, explaining to those of us who only read the Arts & Leisure section that Persia is the ancient name for modern-day Iran. He also guesses rightly that Ziba's family had to get out in 1979 when the Ayatollah came to power, although she doesn't volunteer why and we don't ask. Personally, I prefer to revel in the mystery where she's concerned so I just try to seem droll and blasé. Doug, on the other hand, tries to act all worldly and Continental because he's spent summers with his mother's family in Germany, like that's got anything to do with Persia.

Ziba doesn't say much, but sits with her long legs crossed, her head tilted at the most flattering angle, a closed-mouth Mona Lisa smile indicating that perhaps she finds us amusing, perhaps ridiculous, I can't tell. In the course of a one-hour train ride we do discover through various reluctant responses that, after fleeing Iran, Ziba lived outside of Paris, then outside of Washington, D.C., and now, of course, outside of Manhattan. "My parents think it's best to raise children outside of a city," she says in a voice that's deeper than Natie's. "They're wrong, of course." I nod in agreement, although I can't decide whether she's insulting us or not. "Ever since I arrived here I've tried to spend as much time in New York as possible, so naturally when Douglas mentioned this little excursion . . ."

There's something about her calling him Douglas that irks me, like she's poaching my Pygmalion project but, on the other hand, I can't help but feel grateful to meet a kindred spirit. Clearly I'm not the only one who feels this way. Compared with Ziba's understated elegance, Kelly and Paula both look like they're wrapped up as birthday gifts, and by the time we arrive in New York, Kelly's ponytail has migrated to the back of her head and she and Paula have discreetly discarded whatever bangles and bows they can.

As I watch Paula lead the way from Penn Station to Times Square I see that she's gained something, too: Ziba's gestures. It's as if she's inhaled her essence—the brisk runway-model walk, the provocative tilt of the head when speaking to you, the flip of the hair. She'll make a fine actress, Paula. We pick up tickets and try to get into Joe Allen's for dinner, but it's packed, so we have to settle for one of those New York delis where they act like they're doing you some big favor by overcharging you for a sandwich.

Paula and I have both seen A Chorus Line before—twice—but I'd go every weekend if I could. For you people out in Iowa who don't get any real culture, I guess I should explain that A Chorus Line is about these dancers who are auditioning for a Broadway show. The director asks them to talk about themselves so he can get to know them better and they do all these numbers about their childhoods and their ambitions and who they really are. They talk a lot about what it's like being a teenager and the stuff they say and do is exactly the kind of stuff that Paula and I say and do all the time. Our absolute favorite character is Bobby, the one who went down to busy intersections when he was a kid and directed traffic. Even better is the story he tells about breaking into people's houses—not to steal anything, just to rearrange their furniture.

That is so us.

But I relish every brilliant, inspired moment. This is who I'm determined to be—an actor/singer/dancer—no, I take that back, this is who I *am*. These people are my tribe, my destiny. I know it.

I can't wait for my life to begin.

Afterward, Doug, Natie, and I wait in the breezy open plaza of Shubert Alley while the girls pee. I ask Doug what he thought of the show.

"That was a great play, man," he says, his bright blue eyes gleaming. "I didn't know you could say 'fuck' in a play."

I make a mental note to teach Doug to only refer to dramas as plays. He probably calls original cast albums "soundtracks," too. I've got my work cut out for me.

"And I can't believe there was a song called 'Tits and Ass.' Man, that was comical, I was laughin'," he says.

I want to ask him if the show meant anything to him, if he could identify at all with the characters' anguish and frustrations, if he understood the sacrifices we artists make for our craft and our careers.

"Yeah, that was comical," I say.

Wuss.

The girls return from the bathroom, chatting among themselves. (What is it about peeing together that makes girls bond?) But as they get closer I see that Ziba and Paula are actually having an argument.

"All I said was that the characters were full of self-pity," Ziba says, her voice dark and low.

"*Wallowed*," Paula says. "You said they *wallowed* in self-pity." She turns to me. "Ziba said she found the show *masturbatory*."

"I thought it was pretty hot, too," Doug says.

Ziba lights a cigarette. "All art is masturbatory," she says baritonally.

There's a brief silence while we try to figure out what the hell she means.

"So, what do we do now?" Kelly asks.

"Why don't we get some beers?" Doug says. "There's this bar in Penn Station that served us on St. Patrick's Day."

Ziba and Paula both give him a look that makes it abundantly clear they have no interest in drinking beer under fluorescent lighting while transit employees make announcements like "Last cawll to Joisey City."

"I know a place in the Village that's exceedingly lax about checking ID," Ziba says.

"*Splendid*," Paula cries. "We love the Village, don't we, Edward?"

"What's it called?" I ask.

Ziba pauses to blow a smoke ring. "Something for the Boys," she says. "It's a gay piano bar."

"I didn't know a piano could be gay," Natie whispers to me.

"It's only attracted to other pianos," I explain.

Ziba ignores us by turning to Paula and Kelly. "The best part is that you don't have to be concerned that some cretin will hit on you." Kelly nods, being the kind of girl who cretins often hit on.

"Sure," Doug says, "that's okay for you. But what if someone hits on *us*?" He points to himself and me.

Ziba gives him one of those deadpan looks, like Cher does to Sonny after he's said something stupid. "Any man who's secure in his sexuality shouldn't feel threatened by the attention of another man," she drones. She fixes her dark gypsy eyes on him, daring him to contradict her.

"I'm cool," Doug says. "My uncle in Germany is gay."

Jesus, enough with the Germany thing already.

"He was on the Olympic gymnastics team," Doug adds, as if that explained it.

"*Smashing*," Paula says. "Edward, lead us not into Penn Station, but deliver us to the E train."

five

Since Natie's got less facial hair than Paula's cousin Crazy Linda, convincing even the most lenient of bars that he's of legal drinking age could prove challenging. He is, after all, the guy who still has to prove he's tall enough to go on the good rides. So we decide we have no choice but to pass him off as a girl. We huddle in front of a camera store called Toto Photo (WE'LL PRINT ANYTHING . . . SO LONG AS YOU LET US KEEP THE GOOD ONES), while Paula and Ziba both oversee the swapping of clothes between him and Kelly. It's quite astounding, really. Add some makeup, accessories, and Ziba's Audrey Hepburn scarf thing and voilà: a small, homely guy is magically transformed into an even homelier girl. Ziba hides a good part of Natie's baby face with her Jackie O sunglasses.

"I can't see a fucking thing," he mutters.

Just to be safe (or just because it's fun) we create new legal drinking age personas for the rest of us. Kelly and Ziba are to be a couple of seniors from the Yale women's track team; Paula and Natie, a pair of funky SoHo party girls out for a night on the town; and Doug and I are cast as a young, gay couple.

In love.

Poor Doug looks like he's about to have kittens, but I convince him he'll be safer going into the bar if he's already on the arm of another guy. What I don't tell him, of course, is that I've actually had a homosexual experience myself, having experimented last summer with a guy at the Bennington College summer theater program. I suppose that technically makes me bisexual, but I prefer to simply think of myself as open-minded. As an actor, you need to be receptive to all kinds of experiences.

We enter in pairs staggered a few minutes apart so as not to attract attention, and I find myself getting excited as we watch the others go in—there's something thrilling about acting in real life, even if it's just buying a bus ticket with an English accent or pretending you're retarded while waiting in line at the grocery store.

"You ready?" I ask Doug and, to my surprise, he responds by taking my hand.

It feels kind of weird. Even though I've fooled around with another guy, it wasn't his hand I held and, in a strange, Alice-Through-the-Looking-Glass kind of way, it feels almost, I don't know, comforting. I make a mental note to remember these feelings in case I ever play a homosexual.

We have to descend a small flight of steps below the street level to get in. According to the historic landmark plaque next to the door, Something for the Boys was originally a speakeasy during Prohibition, and I can't help but feel the thrill of the forbidden as we step into a place that once counted gangsters and their molls as its clientele.

It's a small subterranean cave of a room, bathed in a hazy magenta light that gives the Broadway musical posters on the wall an eerie, psychedelic look. The place is packed, but I immediately spy Ziba and Kelly lurking at a table in a dark corner. Doug looks nervous at the prospect of pushing through a crowd of a hundred men belting out the final chorus of "I Feel Pretty," but trouper that he is, he puts his arm around me and plunges in. I'm glad he's acting so cool, but I'm embarrassed at how soft and mushy my waist must feel to him. I really have got to get in shape this summer.

We arrive to find Kelly and Ziba sipping piña coladas through straws, which strikes me not only as elegant but sexy, too. "We made it!" I shout over the noise.

Ziba glances around like she's Mata fucking Hari. "Try not to be too conspicuous," she says, which seems entirely unnecessary, considering we're surrounded by men so flaming they're in danger of setting off the sprinkler system.

"Where are Paula and Natie?" I ask.

Kelly giggles into her piña colada. "Natie's been captured by a transvestite," she says. "Someone called Miss Demeanor grabbed him like a handbag and we haven't seen him since."

I look across the room and see a pair of Jackie O sunglasses peek out from behind the fleshy arm of someone who looks like a cross between Marilyn Monroe and a Teamster. A siren of a soprano starts to wail.

"*Summertiiiiiiiiime . . . and the livin' is easy . . .*"

I turn and there's Paula perched on top of the piano, practically fellating the microphone. So much for being inconspicuous. I venture off into the sea of bodies in search of beer. I'm halfway through the crowd when I find myself face-to-face with a skinny waiter holding a tray of drinks over his head.

"Oh, thank *God* you're here," he cries, handing me his tray. "Be a doll and deliver these to that table of horny Jesuits over there, will ya'?"

"I don't work . . ."

"Thanks, hon," he says. "I'm on as soon as this drag queen gets done singin' 'Summertime.'"

I look at the drinks in my hand and decide that the unexpected presence of alcohol paid for by the one holy, catholic, and apostolic church is surely a sign from God, so I bring the tray back to our table. None of us can tell what the horny Jesuits ordered, but it sure as hell ain't communion wine. We applaud loudly for Paula, who tries to do an encore, but is pushed aside (rather rudely, I think) by the skinny waiter, who performs "I Could Have Danced All Night." In Julie Andrews's key.

I watch Paula as she makes her way through the crowd, accepting compliments and working the room like she's the mayor of Gaytown. "Look," she cries, handing me a business card advertising something called *Les Femmes Magnifiques*. "A producer gave me his card, a *real* producer!" She points across the room at a roly-poly man chatting up Miss Demeanor. "It's a revue right here in the Village. It means *Magnificent Women*. Isn't that *enthralling*?"

After downing what we decide must be scotch and holy water I decide to do a number myself. I slither through the crowd as everyone belts out "Anything Goes," and squeeze in next to the pianist, a balding guy with a happy Humpty-Dumpty face.

"Greetings and salivations, cutie," he says. "Waddya wanna sing?"

"Do you know 'Corner of the Sky' from *Pippin*?"

He gives me a look like, "This is a gay piano bar. Of course I know 'Corner of the Sky' from *Pippin*," and segues into the introduction. I hop up on the lid and sit cross-legged, smiling in as puckish and beguiling a manner as I can, which, being puckish and beguiling by nature, is pretty easy. Within a few measures there's a perceptible change in the atmosphere. The crowd grows quieter and some of them smile knowingly at one another. They know talent when they see it, I'm sure.

> *Rivers belong where they can ramble.*
> *Eagles belong where they can fly.*
> *I've got to be where my spirit can run free,*
> *Got to find my corner of the sky.*

The crowd gives me a big hand and someone has the good sense to shout "Encore," so I graciously invite Paula up to sing our surefire showstopper, "Carried Away" from *On the Town*, which is something of a life philosophy for us. As far as we're concerned, more is more.

The number goes over even bigger, and since Kelly and Doug have pushed their way to the front it seems only natural to hand them the mics and insist they perform "Summer Nights." Doug looks embarrassed at first, but the guys in the crowd cheer him on, particularly when he starts doing Revolting Renée's pelvis-shaking choreography. No fewer than four men give him their phone numbers before the night is over.

I look at him and Kelly and feel a subversive sense of pride knowing that a high-school football player and a former cheerleader are performing for a roomful of ecstatic gay men. I look over at Paula, who's behaving as if she were Dolly Levi returned to Harmonia Gardens, then Ziba, chain-smoking foreign cigarettes in the corner and refusing to sing, and then Natie, who is in serious danger of losing his virginity in a way he never intended, and an almost evangelistic sense of purpose overtakes me. I realize that it is my duty to be the missionary for this Summer of Magic and Mischief; that I am to lead the Play People Parade like the Pied Piper or the Dr Pepper guy. I am to be my friends' Peter Pan, stealing them away to Neverland where you never grow up.

My objective clear, I leap onto the piano bench and encourage the crowd to sing along and soon the entire bar is swaying and singing together "Tell me more, tell me more." It's almost overwhelming to be at the center of all that energy and enthusiasm (I mean, just the sheer volume alone—do you have any idea just how loud a hundred gay men can be?), but I'm buoyed by the tide of goodwill that surges around me.

This is going to be the best summer of our lives.

six

The day after we go into the city I sit down and come up with a schedule. Missionary of Magic and Mischief or not, I have serious work to do.

First, there's my body. I've simply got to get it in shape this summer—not for vanity's sake, mind you; an actor's body is his instrument and mine is way out of tune. It's not so much that I'm overweight; it's that I'm both too skinny and too fat in all the wrong places. Soft. I read somewhere that if you get up just an hour earlier every day you can gain fifteen whole days a year, so I've resolved to rise each morning for a brisk jog (I sleep way too much, anyway) followed by some push-ups and sit-ups before going down to the Workshop to choreograph the kids' show which, no matter what Paula says, is indeed a real job because I'm being paid for it. (She's just jealous because I'm amassing a professional credit and she isn't.) Then after a light and healthy lunch I'll go over to Aunt Glo's and spend the afternoon poolside reading *The Complete Works of Shakespeare*, taking occasional breaks to swim laps and develop a swimmer's V-shaped torso.

I'm really quite amazed at how simple it is, once I've planned it out. There are nine weeks left in the summer, and thirty-seven Shakespeare plays, which averages out to about four plays a week, or roughly one every other day, which seems completely doable. In fact, if I can get through one a day I could even move on to some lighter reading—y'know, like Chekhov or Ibsen.

This summer is my big chance to improve myself and I'm determined to give up sugar, caffeine, alcohol, red meat, white flour, and fried foods, as well as finally learn to meditate and become the spiritually evolved person I know that I truly am inside. I am my mother's son, after all.

A week later I find myself feeling weak and craving a Whopper and fries, which probably means there's some essential oil in them that my body is accustomed to getting and needs. What's more, having just endured three hours watching Ingmar Bergman's *Fanny and Alexander* on Ziba's recommendation, we all could use some junk food to redress the balance.

"Why is it there's no Burger Queen?" Ziba asks as the six of us pull up to the drive-through. "There's a Burger King."

"Maybe he married the Dairy Queen," Natie says.

Paula pulls up to the window cautiously. Maneuvering Aunt Glo's Lincoln Continental, a vehicle so enormous we call it the Lincoln Continental Divide, is like trying to dock the *Queen Mary*. Paula requests six crowns with our order. "Everyone *has* to have a crown," she says, "you just *have* to," such a Paula thing to say, and she tells us we each need to decide which king we are.

There are so many to choose from. There's King Arthur, King Ludwig, and King Henry the Eighth. There's King Henry the Fourth, parts one and two. There's King Kong, King Size, and King Dom. There's the King of Kings, forever and ever. There's the King Family Singers. There's Stephen King. Plus there's no shortage of Edwards, Charleses, Georges, and all those Louies.

Natie impresses everybody by being able to name all the monarchs of England in order since William the Conqueror, which we're able to confirm because Paula always keeps a *World Almanac* handy in the glove compartment. She makes room for it by keeping the car's manual and registration in the trunk. "I'm much more likely to want to know what article two of the Constitution is than how to change a tire," she says. Aunt Glo doesn't drive much since her stroke, so Paula's been free to customize the car to her own peculiar needs, like making seat covers out of her old costumes from *Hello, Dolly!*

So we're driving around, bored as usual. There never seems to be enough to do when you're a teenager, and it's not just because we live in Wallingford. I've known kids from Manhattan who say the same thing, and they live in the greatest city in the world, for Chrissake. For lack of anything better to do, I suggest we take a ride over to Cramptown and look at the house I first lived in when we moved from Hoboken and didn't know any better.

Being a Cramptowner herself, Paula is very sensitive on the subject, and complains that all us "Wallies" are snobs, but as far as I'm concerned, being accused of snobbery just confirms that you have something to be snobby about. Anyway, we take a ride by the house because that's the kind of thing you do when you're bored on a hot summer night.

The house is a split-level ranch, not unlike Aunt Glo's, essentially a garage with a house attached to it, but it's what's in front that immediately gets our attention. There, in the middle of a bed of anemic-looking pansies, is possibly the ugliest lawn ornament I've ever set my eyes on. I mean, we're not talking some innocuous little lawn jockey here, no, but a hideous three-foot-tall green ceramic Buddha, his pudgy arms reaching up gleefully, his sloppy man breasts hanging over his huge distended belly, his toothless grin twisted into a horrendous and slightly disturbing spasm of joy.

I can't fucking believe it. There's a Buddha on my memories.

In a moment of blazing insight, I spontaneously leap from the car and start tucking and rolling my way across the lawn like I'm avoiding snipers. I can hear my friends' bewildered cries behind me, but that only invigorates me all the more as I zigzag across the lawn to the Buddha, and plop my Burger King crown on his head at a rakish angle.

I swear, it was like he was meant to wear it; it's almost like he's smiling because he knows he looks so snazzy. In that moment, the Manifesto for the Summer of Magic and Mischief is born.

We call it Creative Vandalism.

Our commitment is to bring a Bobby-in–*A Chorus Line* kind of flair and vitality to the sleepy New Jersey suburbs, but with Paula's proviso that we don't do any damage to personal property or engage in any illegal activity, such a Paula proviso to have.

So when they make the movie of my life, the summer of 1983 has to be one of those montage sequences filled with madcap adolescent high jinks, not the dumb shit you usually see in most movies like lip-synching into hairbrushes or squirting each other with the hose while washing a car. No, you'll see the cool Creative Vandalism stuff we *really* do, like putting department-store mannequins in compromising positions or hopping into the freezer section of the grocery store and pretending to be the cryogenically frozen Walt Disney.

We call it Disney on Ice.

You'll see us on those su-hum-mer nights as we tool around in the

Lincoln Continental Divide (Paula the designated driver, the rest of us the designated drunks) putting dishwashing liquid in the fountain downtown till it bubbles over, sending Paula's enormous bra up the school flagpole, drawing a hula hoop around the guy in the crosswalk sign, and, of course, visiting the Buddha.

Time after time, you'll see me tucking and rolling my way across the lawn to dress him up: first in Paula's communion veil, then in Doug's jockstrap, then in Aunt Glo's old flowered bathing cap; each time the Buddha blissfully, almost freakishly happy to be so arrayed. You'll see me and Doug dragging the Buddha to the front door and setting him up with a breakfast tray of orange juice, toast, and half a grapefruit balanced on top of his outstretched palms, ready to deliver Buddha room service. And you'll see us ringing the bell in the middle of the night so that the owners will find him lying on their doorstep, a Hawaiian lei around his neck and an empty bottle of Southern Comfort next to him, as if he'd passed out after a wild night at some swinging Buddha bar.

Meanwhile, Al and Dagmar are having a Summer of Magic and Mischief all their own. While having Dagmar spend the night is okay with me in theory, I have to say that in practice I find it pretty revolting. I'm sorry, but it's humiliating to have to cover your head with a pillow to block out the sounds of your own father making hot monkey love in the next room. Just the thought of Al climbing on top of Dagmar while she grabs his broad, hairy back makes me want to hurl. Al tries to justify their sleeping together by giving me one of those lame-ass father-son talks.

"Now you gotta understand, kid, that when it comes to sex, I'm completely monotonous."

Hey, he said it, not me.

Still, I'm thrilled to finally have someone in this house who understands me—a real artist. Frankly, I don't know what it is she sees in Al, but who cares? He's throwing money around like he's printing it and even takes me, Dagmar, and Kelly to see Sinatra at the Meadowlands. Box seats.

Seeing the Chairman of the Board in person is the closest thing Al and I have to a shared religious experience; and even with a toupee, a paunch, and a wobble in his vibrato as wide as the Lincoln Continental Divide, Frank still sounds like he's singing every song with a cocktail in his hand and a fedora slung rakishly over one eye.

Then, before I know it, it's closing night of *Grease*. I've got to say, for all my criticism of Revolting Renée, she's staged great curtain calls. Kelly and Doug make their entrance in Greased Lightning, just like in the movie, which gets a big hand and helps cover the fact that neither of them are really that good. Then, right as the cast takes a company bow, I swing in on a rope as Teen Angel, just like in the original Broadway version. (Okay, it was my idea to do it, but Revolting Renée had the good sense to take my suggestion.) I'm all in white, with a pair of wings I made myself and a gold halo that bobs over my head to great comic effect. As predicted, I'd stopped the show earlier with my one number, but the rope thing at the end slays 'em, just like when Peter Pan takes flight for the first time. To get that kind of rise out of an audience is a drug and I'm definitely an addict. What's more, I don't have to do any of Revolting Renée's strange semaphore choreography.

Al and Dagmar come to closing night (Al would never think to come to every performance like Aunt Glo does), and Dagmar tells me I'm "goot" in the offhand manner of a critic who's seen it all, which I take as a supreme compliment. Only the uninformed masses rave about how great you are; people who actually know what they're talking about say things like "You're good" or "I liked your work."

As I take Dagmar's strangely rough hand in mine and give her the European two-cheek-kiss thing I notice something different on her gnarled finger: a diamond roughly the size of a Volkswagen.

"Wow, what's that?" I say.

"Congratulate us," she says. "Your fahter and I are getting married."

seven

It's weird. It's definitely fucking weird. One morning I get up, put some drops in my eyes, pick up my sister, and drive over to Wallingford City Hall to watch my father get married. It's about as romantic as applying for a fishing license.

What's totally cool, though, is the minimalist elegance that Dagmar brings to our big, tasteless house. Everywhere we turn we're confronted with her stark black-and-white photos of eerily empty spaces: abandoned lots, dirty restrooms, and a whole series of unmade motel beds. I don't understand what I'm looking at, but as a fellow artist I respect her vision. In fact, I gladly cooperate when Dagmar asks me if I wouldn't mind moving into the guest room so she can use my room as her studio. Northern exposure is "zo important for tse verk."

She also tears out every bit of wall-to-wall carpeting. As a photographer, Dagmar has an almost pathological aversion to dust, but apparently she's also allergic to carpet mites, something I didn't even know existed until she shows me a brochure full of close-up photos that make the microscopic insects look like hideous giant reptiles. "Flakes of dead skin get caught in tse carpet," she says ominously, "and you can *neffer, neffer get tsem out.*"

I figure artists are allowed their eccentricities.

Dagmar arranges to have the floors redone while she and Al go on their honeymoon. "After all," she says to Al, "no one vill be here."

"I'll be here," I say.

"Oh, right," she says. "Vell, you can let in tse verkers."

I'm willing to overlook this little slight because I know that my time is limited in this house, with or without the Carpet Mites That Ate Detroit. In fact, one of the last things my mother said to me before she left was that I should try to get along with whomever my father married because eventually I'll leave and he'll need someone to be with him. Also, hardwood floors are going to look way more sophisticated than carpeting.

So I've got the place to myself for two whole weeks. (Well, me and "tse verkers.") I know you're thinking "Par-TAY!" but I'm determined to put my time alone to solitudinous good use. Sure, I may have allowed myself to get caught up in Paula's enthusiasm for the Summer of Magic and Mischief, but with Ziba off in the south of France with her manicured mother, Kelly on Cape Cod, and Natie at computer camp (such a cheesehead thing to do), I can finally get down to work and focus on *The Complete Works of Shakespeare*. With all these distractions I've only been able to read *A Midsummer Night's Dream* and half of *The Comedy of Errors*, plus watch the Elizabeth Taylor/Richard Burton *Taming of the Shrew* on the late show. But there's still a couple of weeks until school starts and I figure if I just skip the history plays (who really gives a shit about all those Richards and Henrys, anyway?) and read two a day I can still finish the other twenty-four before school starts.

Oh yeah, and get in shape.

Of course I have to help Paula with some last-minute college shopping (so many shoes, so little time) and to get in some quality bonding time before she goes off to Juilliard. We plan a final poolside soiree with Doug for her last night, as well as a farewell CV visit to the Buddha.

I show up with a birthday cake. Paula's got a thing for birthday cakes, believing that they're magical, imbued as they are with wishes. And since every day is somebody's birthday somewhere, there's no reason why you can't have birthday cake anytime you want. I consult the almanac I keep in my own glove compartment and have the bakery put "Happy Birthday, Coco" on the cake, in honor of Coco Chanel. The only problem is that Doug doesn't show up. I call his house and his strange foreign mother tells me he's gone out with "some of the guys from the team."

He's blown us off. I can't fucking believe it.

Paula and I sit in the dark swatting at mosquitoes as I light the candles on Coco's cake. This is the magic moment of birthday cakes, the moment that Paula and I love most. This is that time when they turn out the lights and everybody starts smiling at you and your mother comes through the door and the only light in the room is that fuzzy sort of glow from the flame on your birthday cake shining on your mother's face. And your mom is smiling that proud kind of "I'm your mom" smile and you're smiling that embarrassed kind of "this is my day" smile. And then you close your eyes and make a wish, any wish you want because it's *your day*. Then you blow out the candles and everyone claps and then, best of all, you get to eat cake.

With Paula's mother long dead and mine long gone, neither of us can get enough of that feeling.

Paula blows out the candles, not in her usual make-a-wish kind of way, but in a gimme-a-piece-of-that-goddamned-cake kind of way. "This was supposed to be my magic summer," she says softly.

"You are magic, Sis," I say. As if on cue, fireflies appear.

She drops the knife. "Well, if I'm so magic, how come I can't make someone love me?" Her eyes fill with tears.

I put my arm around her. "I love you."

"But as a friend," she sighs. "It's always 'as a friend.' Just once, can't I be something more to someone?"

Paula and I each eat two pieces of cake, agree to split a third, then figure we might as well finish the rest because there's no sense in letting it go to waste.

"Oh, I almost forgot!" Paula says. "I have a going-away present for you."

She's the one leaving, but she has a present for me. That's such a Paula thing to do. She rifles through her Mary Poppins carpetbag and pulls out a shirt box. "I made the wrapping paper myself," she says.

I take time to appreciate the hand-drawn images of nuns and Buddhas, then open the box slowly.

It's a priest's collar.

"Isn't it *splendid*?" Paula says, beaming. "I swiped one from Aunt Glo."

"Uh, thanks?"

"It's for buying beer, silly." Paula fastens the collar on me and I look at myself in her compact mirror. The combination of my long curls and the clerical collar makes me look like a hip young Jesuit and I immediately begin to construct a biography of a pot-smoking, guitar-playing rebel priest. Father Groovy.

We begin to run out of things to say, something that never happens to us, but the thought of starting a conversation so close to saying goodbye feels wrong somehow, like when you're sitting in an airport waiting to see someone off or when your mom leaves to find herself and you don't know when you'll ever see her again. Paula says we'll visit the Buddha over Thanksgiving but we both know it won't be the same; tomorrow she'll leave for Manhattan and her life will change and mine won't. I'm stuck in fucking Wallingford for a whole 'nother year.

"I should spend a little time with Aunt Glo before I leave," she says, even though I know for a fact Aunt Glo is fast asleep downstairs in front of *The Love Boat*. Paula walks me to the gate, then throws her arms around me tight, her soft, pillowy breasts mashed up against my chest. I feel like crying, but of course I can't, so I just hold on for a while and let her cry for both of us. Eventually I pat her on the back, the Internationally Recognized Signal that the hug is over, and we separate.

"This is *absurd*," she says, pressing her index fingers under her eyes to stop her mascara from running. "The city's only an hour away. You'll be in *all* the time." She straightens my priest's collar. "I'll see you very, very, very soon." She kisses the air in front of my face, then turns and walks back toward the house.

"Be splendid," I say, and she waves her tiny teardrop hand without turning around, just like Liza Minnelli does at the end of *Cabaret*.

Paula.

✹   ✹   ✹

The growl of MoM's diesel engine reflects my mood. How could Doug blow us off like that? How could he be so insensitive? Doesn't he realize how Paula feels? I stop where Wallingford Avenue dead-ends into Washington Street and try to decide which way to turn. It's too late to go over to Doug's house, but then again, why the hell should I be considerate? He certainly wasn't. Fuck it. I head toward the south side.

Wallingford is separated north and south by train tracks. For the most part there's not that much difference between the two parts of town, but neighborhoods like Doug's definitely contribute to the south side's wrong-side-of-the-tracks reputation—neighborhoods where the number of vee-hicles outnumber the occupants of a house because there's always an extra beater lying around for spare parts. Gone are Wallingford's usual stone walls and picket fences; here we're talking strictly chain-link.

The porch light flashes on when I ring the bell and I swat at moths as Doug's strange foreign mother opens the door. She has the same jagged features as Doug, but the sharp contours of her face curve at the ends, as if her bones were shaped like question marks. She rabbits back from the door and doesn't say anything to me, but calls for Doug.

"Who is it?" barks Doug's dad from the other room. Mrs. Grabowski scampers over to him and I lean in for a closer look. Mr. Grabowski sits in an easy chair, or perhaps I should say an uneasy chair, as his massive shoulders are so constrained by the frame. He grips the thick upholstered arms so tightly it looks like any minute he's going to tear them off and eat them.

"I said, who is it?" he grumbles, never turning his big square head from the television. All that's missing are the bolts on the sides of his neck.

"It's Teen Angel," Mrs. Grabowski hisses. "And he's wearing a priest's collar."

Oops. Forgot about that.

Doug clomps down the stairs in his boxers and T-shirt, looking surprised to see me. He steps outside.

"What's going on?" he says.

"Maybe I should ask you the same thing," I snap, sounding more like Bette Davis than I intended.

"What are you talking about, man?"

I roll my eyes. "Paula's final poolside soiree? The Buddha? Any of this ring a bell?" I hate how I'm acting, but I can't seem to stop myself.

"Oh, hey, I'm sorry, man, but some of the guys from the team stopped by and I, y'know, didn't think to call."

I don't say anything for a moment, but just stare at him while he scuffs his bare feet across the peeling porch. The buzz of cicadas fills the air.

"That's it?" I huff. "That's all you have to say? You disappoint Paula on her very last night before going off to college and that's the best you can come up with? 'Some of the guys from the team stopped by'?"

"I said I'm sorry, what else do you want me to do?"

I have no idea. A wave of nausea comes over me and I think for a moment maybe it's all the cake I ate, but then I suddenly feel itchy all over, like I'm going to burst out of my skin, like my body isn't large enough to contain the volcano surging inside me, and if I don't leave right now this very second I might spontaneously burst into flames or wet myself. I start to breathe heavy, like a woman going into labor; if only I could cry, I might feel better, but that is the very last thing I want Doug to see right now.

I stomp off the porch and run to MoM, but the door sticks and I kick it in frustration, then hide my face hoping somehow I'll blend in with the car. I feel Doug's hand on my shoulder.

"You okay, man?"

I'm so ashamed of how soft my body must be to his touch. "So this is how it's going to be?" I say. "It's okay for you to spend the summer with the Play People, but now that school's starting you're going to ditch us to hang out with Some of the Guys from the Team?"

"I didn't say that . . ."

My face is hot and I can't stop my chin from quivering. "Well, what was I supposed to think when you blew us off? Huh? Huh?" I cringe at how I must sound, but I can't stop. "It's like you really *are* Danny in *Grease* and I'm, I'm . . ."

Don't say it, Edward. Just shut up and get in the car.

". . . I'm Sandy and I'm not cool enough for you."

I can't believe I just said that. I'm not Sandy; I'm a goddamned idiot.

"I never said you weren't cool enough," Doug murmurs.

"Oh, you don't need to," I sneer. "I know everybody thinks we're freaks just because we dress weird and we sing show tunes in the halls. Okay, so we're freaks. We're the *Play People*. And if you're too embarrassed to be seen with us, then fuck you, 'cuz I think we're . . . we're . . ."

"*Splendid*," Doug says, taking me by the shoulders. "You're splendid."

His eyes are so blue, but with little flecks of white in them, like the world as seen from outer space.

"I'm sorry," he says. "I'm an asshole."

"No, you're not," I say. "They're your friends. I understand." I give him a punch in the arm in the way I think guys are supposed to.

He smiles. "Say, next time why don't you hang out with *us*?"

Hang out with Some of the Guys from the Team? You mean the guys who, in the fifth grade, set fire to my painstakingly accurate diorama of Heidi in the Swiss Alps? Then peed on it to put the fire out? Those guys? Is he *insane*?

"Yeah, sure," I say.

Wuss.

eight

Now, when they make the movie of my life, they need to make sure the big end-of-the-summer blowout at my house isn't the usual wilding you see in teen movies. I mean, I am way too smart to let the entire student body show up and destroy my house. Okay, sure, someone lights a couch on fire, and Some of the Guys from the Team (or SOTGFTT for short) play catch with a beanbag chair in the family room until it breaks and covers the floor with so many Styrofoam pellets it looks like a blanket of new-fallen snow, but there's more to it than that.

You see, now that we're all seniors, there are no upperclassmen to look up to, so there's no need to snub one another to get ahead socially. We're *it*. The party almost has the feeling of a summit meeting (granted, a very rowdy summit meeting) as we acquaint ourselves with people we've never even dared speak to.

People like Amber Wright, who arrives with a posse of Barbies, each swinging a six-pack like it's a purse. In an effort to affect a kind of Rat Pack coolness, I greet them at the door wearing a silk smoking jacket and sucking on one of those pipes that blows bubbles, but they just breeze past me like I'm lucky to be at my own party.

Then there are people like Thelonious "TeeJay" Jones, who is, to the best of my knowledge, the first black person ever to enter my house who wasn't there to clean it. TeeJay shows up with some of the black guys from the team (or SOTBGFTT for short) and I find myself completely overcompensating to make them feel welcome.

There are 1,500 students at Wallingford High School and less than one hundred of them are black. With the exception of athletes like Tee-Jay, they tend to keep to themselves, and a surprisingly large number of them seem to be related to one another. When they're not playing sports, they share space at the bottom of the social pyramid with other misunderstood minorities like the Audio/Visual Squad (Nathan Nudelman, President), the Latin Club (Nathan Nudelman, President), and the Chess Club (Nathan Nudelman, President). Also included are male athletes from non-team sports like swimming and track (as well as non-sport sports like golf and bowling), female athletes of all kinds, and, of course, the Marching Band, who everybody hates.

TeeJay enters with a case of beer in his huge cannonball arms.

"Yo, TeeJay, wha's happenin'?" I say, putting out my hand for five.

TeeJay gives me a look like I'm an idiot (which, of course, I am) and ignores my request, so I just make a fist with my outstretched hand to show my solidarity with Black Power. He shakes his head and groans like Lurch on *The Addams Family*. Y'know, I'm sure it sucks to be a discriminated-against minority, but it must be nice having people automatically think you're cool because of it. Not to mention well hung.

I turn the lights down low and go into the living room to put Sinatra's *Songs for Swingin' Lovers!* on the stereo. Normally no one lives in our living room. In fact, it's so stiff and formal my sister and I have always referred to it as the Museum of Furniture. But now it's full of life and I mingle like I'm Hugh Hefner at a sexy, swingin' do at the Playboy mansion.

It's not long before the place looks like Hieronymus Bosch's *Garden of Earthly Delights*. Every room with a door is being used by horny couples; I feel like I'm running a pay-by-the-hour motel. With even the bathrooms being used for carnal purposes, I have to go outside to pee.

I'm just starting to water a rhododendron when I notice Doug at my side. "Excuse me, sir, this bush is taken," I say.

"Yo, Ed, I've been looking for you." He unzips his Levis with one hand, reaches deep down inside and proceeds to pull out something that looks just like a penis, only bigger. I mean, it's like a cartoon version of a cock. "Man, you gotta do something about your girlfriend," he says.

"She can be a very nasty drunk," I say, trying not to stare. "I think it all comes from being such a doormat when she's sober."

Doug doesn't hold himself as he pees, but just stands there with his hands on his hips, like his penis could be trusted to urinate all by itself by virtue of its immense size. No wonder he acts so, well, cocky. "Nah, that's not it," he says. "I was doin' great with Ziba until Kelly showed up. Now I can't get 'em apart."

"What do you want me to do about it?" Don't stare. Don't stare.

"Go fool around with her, will ya'?" He glances down at himself. "The one-eyed milkman here needs to make a delivery."

Now it just so happens I'm starting to feel quite horny myself, so I go inside where the girls are curled up on the love seat in the furniture museum, bonding in that way that only girls who are equally pretty can. I grab Kelly by the hand in midsentence and motion with my head for Doug and Ziba to follow, leading us out of the kitchen and along the back of the house to the sliding glass door of Al's bedroom. I've locked the room from the inside so no one can fuck it up (I told you I was too smart to let anyone destroy my house), but I've left the slider open for just this reason.

The moon shines silver into the dark room and I pull Kelly to me, grinding my hips against her as I point Doug and Ziba toward a fainting couch over by the dressing room. Doug flashes me a devil's grin and I see him undo the top button of his jeans, presumably because they can't accommodate Russell the Love Muscle any longer.

I push Kelly's straight, silky hair aside to kiss her long, lean neck, inhaling the clean, Coppertone-y smell of her skin and exhaling lightly in her ear, which I know drives her crazy. I've missed her while she was gone. More important, I've missed this. She tilts her head, the Internationally Recognized Signal for "Kiss me, you fool," and I respond by tonguing her deeply and aggressively, the taste of beer mixing in both our mouths. She coils one sinewy leg around the back of my thigh and rubs up against me. I laugh knowingly into her mouth. She feels and tastes and smells so good I want to devour her whole. In one swift move I grab her other leg, hoist it around me, and carry her across the room. (It's nice to see those dance classes are good for something.) We hobble forward this way and fall hard onto the bed, laughing.

I prop myself up on my elbows and look at her face, the white of her eyes and teeth shining bright in the moonlight. She is so beautiful. I'm just reaching up to scoop her breasts in my hands when from across the room I hear Ziba shout, "No!"

Kelly and I both glance over in time to see Ziba give Doug a shove to the floor, where he lands with an unceremonious thud.

"What the fuck . . ." he says.

Ziba rises to her full Amazon height, flips her hair over her shoulder, and steps right over him. "Pig," she says, and walks out.

Yikes.

Kelly gives a little push to get me off of her. "I better see what's wrong," she says, then steps over Doug on her way out, too. "Excuse me."

I don't get it. Just yesterday over lunch Ziba was telling me how she stayed out all night in Saint-Tropez with a couple of guys in their twenties, but Doug unzips his pants and she totally freaks out. Then again . . .

I look at him crouched on the floor. "Fuck, fuck, fuck," he says, almost like he's in pain. I'm about to reach for him when he bounds up, punching the air. "She's such a fuckin' tease, man," he says. "I'm about ready to burst."

He looks down helplessly at his crotch, where the engorged head of his cock has pushed past the waistband of his jeans. It's the size of a doorknob. We both stare at it a moment, as if another person just entered the room. Time seems to stand still and I feel the pulse of my heartbeat radiate behind my ears. I look up at Doug's face and suddenly realize he's just inches away from me, his lips parted, the heat of his breath blowing lightly on my cheeks.

Please God, let him feel the same way I do.

nine

Doug licks his lips and swallows, his big Adam's apple bobbing in his neck.

"I need a drink," he says.

He pushes past me, adjusting his crotch as he goes through the sliding glass door.

I stand staring out into the yard. The moon is so bright it's casting shadows on the lawn. I don't quite know what to do, but every fiber of me says to follow him, so I step outside only to find myself face-to-face with Duncan O'Boyle, the captain of the football team. Duncan has a lean, ferret-y face and strawberry-blond hair that I envy because he wears it parted in the middle and feathered. I tried wearing my hair that way once but it's so thick I looked like Wile E. Coyote after he's had an anvil dropped on his head.

"We've got a little problem," he says. He explains to me how Kevin "Boonbrain" Boonschoft, a big St. Bernard of a guy and the cheesehead of the popular kids, tried to use his big brother's old ID to buy beer for them, but nearly got arrested when the guy at the liquor store revealed that he actually went to high school with Boonbrain's brother. Duncan focuses his beady amber eyes on me. "I hear you can score some beers for us," he says.

I've never liked Duncan O'Boyle. Once, in the fourth grade, he lured Natie onto the roof of his house with an invitation to go "hedgewalking" on top of the fifteen-foot laurel bush that surrounded his property. Natie went first.

He needed thirty stitches.

But just because I loathe and despise everything Duncan represents doesn't mean I don't want to impress him.

"Sure," I say, "just give me a sec."

I find Natie and tell him to look after things, then interrupt a fornicating couple in my room so I can change into Father Groovy's collar, adding a pair of round wire-rimmed glasses I wore when I played the tailor Motel Kamzoil in *Fiddler on the Roof*. I'm practicing a few Jesuit-y looks in the mirror when I hear the grind of the garage door opening. I dash outside and there is Duncan backing Al's Midlife Crisis down the driveway.

"What the hell are you doing?" I shout. "That's my dad's car."

Duncan grins at Roger Young, the team's quarterback, who's riding shotgun. "Oh, no," Duncan says, "this is no car, my friend. This is a penis on wheels."

"Well, it's my dad's penis, okay, so just stop right there." I tap on the side of the car and point to the backseat, which is already such a tight squeeze for Boonbrain that he appears to be wearing the car rather than sitting in it. "Look," I say, "there's no room for me, and you need me to buy the beer."

Duncan smiles. "We'll just take a little ride then, and come back and get ya'." He revs the engine and puts the car in first, but before he can take off I grab hold of the side and hop up on the trunk, shoving my legs next to Boonbrain's refrigerator-sized frame. I must look like the Catholic grand marshal of a St. Patrick's Day parade.

"Go Blue Devils!" Duncan screams, such a dumb jock thing to say, and he floors it.

Asshole.

Sociopath that he is, Duncan does everything he can to send me flying off the back, deliberately making sharp turns and sudden stops. It's not quite as malicious as it sounds—I guess for someone who engages in a sport that involves knocking the crap out of people, vehicular homicide is just good, clean fun. Luckily, all those dance classes really *have* been good for something, because I manage to keep my balance the entire way. Once we stop, however, I fumble the dismount as I attempt to hop out in the suave, easy manner of Magnum, P.I., and end up flat on my ass in the liquor store parking lot. Everyone laughs—not in a mean way, but in a way that shows they appreciate the irony of someone being capable of holding on to a sports car going seventy miles an hour down unimproved roads but failing to stay upright once it's safely parked.

Lightning shoots up my spine but I make faces at the guys like I'm only pretending to be in pain. I hobble into the liquor store, hoping that a limp will contribute to an overall image of maturity.

A big heavyset guy who looks like a Hell's Angel appears behind the counter. "Hey, Fawther," he says, "how can I help yuz?"

I say a silent prayer to St. Genesius, the patron saint of actors or, in this case, bold-faced liars, but the guy seems more focused on the clerical collar than the person wearing it. I lean across the counter like I don't want to be overheard. "Sister Paula from the Convent of the Bleeding Heart suggested I buy beer here," I say in a breathy, Father Mulcahy from *M*A*S*H* kind of voice. "Do you know what brand she normally gets?"

"Oh, sure, Fawther," Hell's Angel says with a conspiratorial nod. "We all know how Father Monty likes his beer." Father Monty is the old souse of a priest Paula invented as the reason why a nun would need to buy a case of cheap beer every weekend.

"I'm Father Roovy, by the way," I say. "Greg Roovy. I'm new."

"Nice to meetcha, Fawther. Where's Sister Paula tonight?"

"She's, uh, been transferred into Manhattan."

Hell's Angel gives me a look like someone just ran over his puppy. "She didn't even say goodbye," he says.

"It was very sudden," I explain. "That's why they brought me on to assist Father Monty—we're very shorthanded now."

Hell's Angel plops a couple of cases of beer on the counter. "Well, God bless her," he says.

"Yes, God bless her," I say as beatifically as I can.

He takes my money, but hesitates. "Y'know, Fawther," he says, "whenever Sister Paula came in, it was kind of like she brought the church with her, you know what I mean?"

"We're here to serve," I say. What the hell is going on?

Hell's Angel leans his elbows on the counter and says to me in a soft voice, "It's been kind of a tough week . . ."

Twenty minutes later I finally emerge from the liquor store. "What took you so long?" Duncan asks.

"Who knew I was going to have to hear confession?" I say.

(Later on when I ask Paula about it, she just says, "Now you be nice to poor Larry. His mother has been very sick and he's under a lot of stress right now." Such a Paula thing to say.)

My tailbone is really throbbing now and I'm in no mood for

fucking around, so I hold the beer ransom until Duncan agrees to get on the back and be the grand marshal. I just want to get my father's penis home in one piece.

Then I get behind the wheel.

I don't know what comes over me, but suddenly I'm worse than Duncan, tearing around corners, zigzagging up and down hilly backstreets, and probably ruining Al's alignment as I deliberately land in potholes. We approach the high school and, rather than go all the way around the block, I simply drive right up onto the playing fields and cut straight across, even rounding the bases a couple of times on the baseball diamond.

Duncan practically coughs up a lung from the dust.

Back at Oak Acres I take a shortcut across the lawn of our neighbor, Mr. Foster. Okay, I admit this is more Vandalism than Creative, but Mr. Foster's the kind of guy who gets up at six on a Saturday morning to vacuum his driveway. I figure he's got it coming to him.

SOTGFTT think it's fucking hysterical.

※　※　※

As a result, Duncan treats me with a begrudging respect for the rest of the night, although he and the others take every opportunity to mock Doug for being in a musical and liking to sing, calling him Florence Nightingale without realizing how stupid that makes them sound. I definitely sense Duncan is competing with me for Doug's attention because he keeps bringing up various "comical" things from their shared past that I don't know about and, frankly, aren't particularly comical. But then Doug will do something like know where the towels are kept in my kitchen or refer to us as "we," and Duncan will challenge me to a chugging contest or some such nonsense. Not that I mind; alcohol helps dull the throbbing pain in my tailbone. But it's like there's a little version of each of us on Doug's shoulders, a Teen Angel and a Blue Devil, both vying for his soul.

Doug stays over and as we clean up the house and talk trash about the guests I indulge in the fantasy that my suburban split-level ranch house is actually a converted SoHo loft that Doug and I live in together. I'm aching to tell him that I'm bisexual, that I'm destined for a life of sexual deviancy way more interesting than the buttoned-down future he can expect staying in Wallingford. I'm longing to whisk him away to

Neverland like I'm Peter Pan and he's one of the Darling children. What's more, I'm longing to reach for his peter and have him call me "darling."

But instead I just ask him if he'll drive me to the emergency room.

"I think I broke my ass," I say.

Wuss.

ten

There's this scene in *South Pacific* where Nellie, the hick army nurse, and Emile, the cultured Frenchman, sing a number called "Twin Soliloquies," but they never actually sing it together. In the original Broadway production, Mary Martin, who played Nellie, was afraid of being overpowered by Ezio Pinza, the Metropolitan Opera basso who played Emile, so they just traded verses back and forth, singing their thoughts. That's kind of how it is with me and Doug as we sit in the emergency room, except that occasionally we're interrupted by people with knife wounds and heart attacks.

There's something about sitting in a hospital late at night that makes you want to swap autobiographies. So I tell Doug all about how the 1960s and '70s hit my mom like a ton of wind chimes and made her have a Feminist Awakening, but how I completely understand because if I were married to Al and had to live in Wallingford the rest of my life, I'd get out as soon as I could, too. And I tell him how she rejected her Roman Catholic upbringing, threw off the yoke of bourgeois oppression, and became totally funky-woo-woo. Now, whenever I visit her, we always do cool New Age-y stuff together, like balance our chakras or make jewelry from hemp. She's in South America now, communing with the Incan spirits.

And Doug tells me about his creepy, square-headed father and how the happiest years of his dad's life were when he was stationed in Germany. But then his dad went to Vietnam and got weird and now he hates his life because he drives a Tastykake truck. And he says that sometimes his dad takes his frustration out on him, like the time he knocked over the breakfront and then chased Doug down the street, calling him a candy-assed pussy. "But then I got big enough to fight back," Doug says. "Now he just yells at the TV."

He goes on to tell me that his only reprieve from all that unrestrained testosterone was spending summers in Germany, visiting his mother's gay brother, the former Olympic gymnast.

That is, until he met me. (Sigh.)

Then he teaches me all kinds of dirty words in German, like *Schwanzlutscher* (cocksucker), *Arschlecker* (ass licker), and our favorite, *Hosenscheisser* (pants shitter).

Eventually the doctor shows up and informs me I have a "contusion" on my coccyx, which I guess is Latin for "you fell on your ass." Nothing's broken, but he gives me a three-week gym excuse and one of those foam doughnuts to sit on.

But I don't feel the pain in my ass (or, as Doug calls it, my *Arschschmerz*) because, like Nellie in *South Pacific*, I'm in love with a wonderful guy. I'm bromidic and bright as a moon-happy night pouring light on the dew, you might say.

Until Al and Dagmar come home.

I swear, they aren't in the house five minutes before they completely nail me for having a party, despite my putting the beanbag chair back together bean by bean and flipping the cushions on the smoking couch. Apparently the senior class of '84 scuffed Dagmar's new hardwood floors.

She goes ballistic. "Don't you know you cannot valk on tse floors vit *shoes*!" she screams.

Actually, I didn't. I always assumed that, being the indoor version of the ground, floors were meant to be trod upon, but apparently they do things differently in Austria. Al grounds me for a whole month, even though it's obvious he can't tell what's wrong with the goddamn floors, either.

School is great, though, a warm retreat from the frost that's occurring at home. With the exception of typing, a necessary evil Al insists I take even though I'm certain I'll never have any use for it as an actor, and gym, a necessary evil mandated by law, I've got a really good schedule.

AP history, for instance, is going to be way better now that Ms. Toquitz has taken over from Mr. Duke who, as the coach of the girl's track team, made the mistake last year of adding fucking as a track and field event.

And AP French looks good, too, not because Madame Schwartz is so *intéressante* (she's not) but because the unexpected arrival of Ziba in class is. I say unexpected because I know for a fact that Ziba's fluent in French and therefore is obviously scamming for an easy A. She spends the entire class that first day staring out the window, completely overdressed in a pair of pleated slacks and a silk blouse, answering questions distractedly and looking more like a woman awaiting an assignation with her lover in a café than some kid taking French in a suburban New Jersey high school.

After class she tells me she's never been particularly interested in school. "They don't teach anything I'm interested in, like fashion or cinema," she says as she strolls down the hall like it's the Champs-Élysées, "but this school is by far the worst." She waves a hand toward the hordes of students and says, "The people here are such snobs." She doesn't seem concerned that those snobs can hear her. "But I honestly don't understand what they've got to be so snobby about. Don't they realize they live in *New Jersey?*"

"I know," I say, feeling cool by association.

"I bet no one here has even heard of Fellini," she says.

I tell her you can't expect these uncultured philistines to appreciate the Renaissance masters.

Then there's AP English with Mr. Lucas.

Mr. Lucas.

I'm sure no one who's ever met Ted Lucas walked away not knowing how they felt about him. He's just the kind of person you can't help but have an opinion about. People on the anti-Lucas side find him patronizing and arrogant, cruel even. He hands back tests in descending grade order, will actually send people to the principal's office for being "absent mentally," and nearly got fired for throwing a book at a student, for which he was completely unrepentant. "Lucky for her it was just *The Metamorphosis* and not *Moby-Dick*," he said.

I think he's great.

Sometimes I'll deliberately say something trite and uninspired in a discussion just so he'll peer over his glasses at me and declare, "*Whell*, Mr. Zanni, *uh*bviously." But mostly I try to impress him. If Mr. Lucas starts tugging at his beard and staring off in space, that means you've said something to make him think. And if you can make someone as brilliant as Mr. Lucas think, *whell*, then *uh*bviously you're pretty smart yourself.

Best of all, he used to be an actor — a real, legitimate, classical theater actor who studied at the Royal Academy of Dramatic Art in London and performed Shakespeare and Molière and Chekhov all over the country. But then he had some kind of spinal cord injury and had to give up acting, which only adds to his quasi-tragic mystique. All manner of theories have circulated about the cause of his handicap, the most popular being that he was injured in Vietnam, which presumably explains why he's so moody. He walks using those crutches that wrap around your wrists, and more than once I've seen him swat through a crowd of kids like some giant praying mantis, shouting, "Out of my way, you juvenile delinquents. Can't you see there's a cripple coming through?"

As far as I'm concerned, Mr. Lucas is casting his pearls before swine. He got in a lot of trouble for his Viet Cong concept for our production of *The King and I*, even though it saved a lot of money on costumes, and no one understood why he had me play Tom in *The Glass Menagerie* as a dog on a leash when it's so frigging *uh*bvious. Frankly, I think Principal Farley just got upset with the scene where I peed on the carpet. The students don't really understand Mr. Lucas either, and are more impressed by the fact that he played the Tidy Bowl man on TV than anything else. Mr. Lucas says that just means his career was already in the toilet before he came here.

On the first day of school, he hands us a syllabus, just like they do in college classes. "Our theme this year," he says, pointing to an absurdly long list of titles, "is Rebels with a Cause. We'll begin with *Oedipus Rex*." He tosses copies of it at us without looking up, which may explain how he beaned that girl with *The Metamorphosis*.

"*Oedipus Rex*," he says in a voice so resonant it sounds as if his whole body were hollow. "A heartwarming little family story in which our hero kills his father, sleeps with his mother, and gouges his own eyes out. If it had been written last year, the school board would be burning it on the front lawn, but since it's two thousand years old, it's deemed acceptable for your impressionable little brainlets. I want a paper on whether Oedipus really has a tragic flaw or not by next Monday."

The class groans.

"Oh, quit complaining," he says. "At least you can walk unassisted."

✳   ✳   ✳

Back at home, the atmosphere grows increasingly Gothic. Now that she's got her claws into Al, Dagmar feels free to unleash the Beast

Within. The transformation is so swift and shocking, it's like a horror movie—*I Was a Middle-Aged Austrian Werewolf.* She informs my sister in no uncertain terms that she's not welcome to come home to do her laundry (I don't know why, it's not like Karen's asking *her* to do it) and tells me to stop having my friends call when I'm not there because it interrupts her from "tse verk." I try to explain to her that the only way my friends can tell if I'm home is if they call, but she just insists on telling me about the supposedly exemplary way things were done back when she was a girl. It seems like every conversation I have with this woman begins with the words, "Tse vay I vas raised . . ." followed by some example of how life was better growing up in Nazi-occupied Austria. Oh, and apparently everything I do is too loud, too, which is totally ironic coming from a woman who is so vocal during sex that even the Nudelmans across the street know when she's having an orgasm.

Meanwhile, Al's too pussy-whipped to notice or to care that he's married a raving lunatic.

Luckily I've got a lot of extracurricular stuff that keeps me out of the house (my classes in New York, for instance) plus my old standby for when I'm grounded: the faux babysitting job. Al still hasn't caught on that the only time I ever seem to look after the fictitious Thompson kids—Jason (nine), Kyra (six), and little Michael (just a year old)—is when I'm grounded. I've even snuck beer out of the house by wrapping a six-pack in "Happy Smurfday!" wrapping paper and pretending it was for one of the kids. I've actually developed a real fondness for the little tykes over the years, despite the fact that they don't exist.

Rehearsals for the fall play, *The Miracle Worker,* start but I don't have that much to do in it. I play the biggest male part, of course—Helen Keller's father—but it's still a supporting role. Mr. Lucas actually takes me aside and tells me he purposely chose something without a big male part because he wants me to focus all my attention on my Juilliard audition.

Kelly surprises everybody (me included) by landing the lead role of Annie Sullivan, which is a big stretch for her. She's nervous as hell about it, but I'm going to coach her. The first read-through is really ragged, but then again, it's hard to read through a play in which the principal character is blind, deaf, and dumb. I stay after and perform my audition monologues for the cast. *Amadeus* is solid, and for my classical I do "Bottom's Dream" from *Midsummer,* mostly because it's the only Shakespeare play I actually read this summer. It's funny and it goes well, but Mr. Lucas says he'll find me something else for better contrast.

Natie and I drop off Kelly, then rush home to change into dance clothes for rehearsals for *Anything Goes*, which Kelly and I are choreographing for the Wallingford Playhouse, the local community theater. "This must be what it feels like to be at Juilliard," I think as I drive, "dashing from rehearsal to rehearsal, full of artistic inspiration." I make a mental note to ask Paula about it; that is, if she ever gets the phone hooked up in that pit she's living in.

I park in front of the house because Dagmar has taken my spot in the garage with the Corvette Al bought her as a wedding present. In return, Dagmar bought them coordinated vanity plates—his says SEIN, hers IHR. It feels strange to come into my own house through the front door like I'm company, and every step I take in the entryway echoes because there's no carpet to absorb the sound. I pull off my shoes and slide across the floor like Tom Cruise in *Risky Business*, accidentally knocking a copy of *Forbes* out of Al's big, hairy hands as he rounds the corner.

"Where have ya' been?" Al says. "You missed dinner."

"What are you talking about?" I say as I go into the kitchen. "It's not Wednesday." I open the fridge to see what's available. Dagmar looks up from the stove where she's stirring what looks like hot cocoa in a saucepan.

"Don't make a mess," she says. "I just cleaned everytsing up."

Al glances at his Rolex. "You better hurry, kid," he says, "or we'll be late."

"For what?"

"Waddya mean, for what? For college night. I left the flyer on your bed the other day."

I sniff at a strange-looking casserole. "I went last year," I say. "There weren't any drama schools there."

"So?"

"So, I've already got the applications for Juilliard, NYU, and Boston University."

Al glances at Dagmar, who just keeps stirring the pot. "Well, maybe we should look at some other options," he mutters.

There's something about the way he doesn't make eye contact that gives me a tight feeling in my chest. "Like . . . what?" I say.

"I dunno," Al says. "That's why people go to college night, don't they, to find out?" He sticks his hands in his pockets and jingles his change.

I speak deliberately, like I'm a special-ed teacher and he's a mentally impaired student. "But I already know what I want to do," I say. "I have for years. That's why I've already chosen the best acting schools." I turn to leave the room. "Besides," I add, "I can't go tonight. I've got play practice."

"Well, you'll just have to miss it, then."

Miss it? What the hell is he talking about? "I can't miss it," I sputter. "I'm the *choreographer*. I'm in *charge* of the rehearsal."

"Well, I'm in charge of you and I say you're going to college night."

The words hit me like a slap in the face. My father's never talked to me like that before. He reaches for me to make up for it, but I flinch.

"Listen, Eddie," he says, "I know you've been having fun with all this drama stuff." He makes a vague gesture to indicate the airy-fairyness of it all. "But it's time you put all these fun and games behind you and started thinking about doing something serious."

The tops of my ears start to burn. "I *am* serious. I'm serious about becoming an actor." Dagmar grabs a whisk and begins whipping the cocoa vigorously. The clacking unnerves me and I feel my heart begin to beat faster.

"C'mon kid," Al says, chuckling, "you know what I mean. It's time you did something sensible. Y'know, like business."

"Business?" I say, spitting out the word like it doesn't taste good. "Where did you ever get the idea that I'd want to major in *business*? What do you think all those classes I've taken in the city have been about, all those plays I've done? Acting isn't just some little hobby for me. It's who I *am*."

"Quit being so dramatic," Al says.

I turn to Dagmar for support. "Dagmar, you're an artist, you understand, right? Explain it to him."

Dagmar doesn't look up from her cocoa, but just murmurs, "Vaht I understand is tsat you should do vaht your fahter says. You are, how do you say, a big fish in a small pond." She pours a cup for Al and brings it over to him like he's lord of the fucking manor.

"But that's why I need training," I say, "and Juilliard is the most prestigious school in the country for acting."

"Baloney," Al says, swatting the idea away with his hand. "I keep telling you acting's all about connections. Even I could do most of the crap you see on TV."

Dagmar slides on a pair of rubber gloves to wash the saucepan. "But I don't *want* to do the crap you see on TV," I say over the sound of rushing water. "I want to train to be a classical actor." It's infuriating that someone as uninformed as Al should be empowered to make decisions about my artistic future.

"I see," Al says. "And how much does it cost to train to be a classical actor?" He pronounces the words "classical actor" with the same contempt I used for the word "business."

"Tuition is $10,000 a year."

Al snorts. "So you expect me to throw away forty grand of my hard-earned money so you can go play in some fancy-pants drama school that will qualify you for exactly nothin'?"

Why is he pretending this is news to him? Going to acting school has been my plan all along. "But this is my dream," I say.

Al sighs like he's had enough of this nonsense. "Listen, kid, if you wanna pursue some wacky pie-in-the-sky notion, go ahead. Just don't expect me to foot the bill."

"But, but you and Mommy always said, 'Be whatever you want to be, as long as it makes you happy. You want to be a garbage man, be a garbage man, but be the best garbage man you can be.' Remember?"

"I never said that," Al says. "Maybe your crazy mother did, but not me."

This is a lie.

"But you were there," I cry. "I'm sure you were." My vision fogs and the whole room goes blurry. I grip the counter to stop myself from falling over. "How am I supposed to pay for college all by myself at this point?" I feel the walls closing in on me.

"Listen, I'm not payin' for acting school and that's that. If you wanna go to college, you've got to major in business or else forget about it."

Al's voice sounds far away to me, like I'm under water. This must be what it's like to drown. "If I have to major in business," I hear myself say, "I might as well shrivel up and die. Do you understand me? I will shrivel up and *die!*"

"Tsat is enough," Dagmar screams, tearing off her gloves and throwing them on the counter. "Your fahter, he owes you nutsing, you hear me? Nutsing! It is you who are indebted to him for all tse generosity he has shown you vile he puts up vit your foolishness!"

"Listen, honey . . ." Al says.

"No, I cannot stand it any longer." She marches over to me and wags a crooked finger in my face. "You and your sister are nutsing but spoiled sons of bitches . . ."

"Dagmar . . ."

". . . who don't appreciate anytsing tsis man has done for you, raising you all by himself after your crazy muhter abandoned you."

I feel my temperature skyrocket. "Don't you dare say anything about my mother!"

Dagmar's eyes go wild and her mouth curls up horribly. "Now I know vy she didn't *vant you!*" she howls.

I feel a wave of rage barrel up through me and I want to knock over the entire kitchen table the way they do in the movies or, better yet, smash a plate over her goddamned allergy-ridden head, but instead I just slam my hand down hard on the countertop.

It really, really hurts.

Dagmar leaps back like I've hit her and I turn and stomp out of the kitchen, my hand throbbing, my pulse racing, and anger surging through me so fast that I shake. I grab my shoes, throw open the front door, and slam it behind me as I go. Then I let out a scream that echoes around the neighborhood.

Across the street Natie steps out of his front door. "What's wrong?" he calls.

"JUST GET IN THE CAR!" I yell like we're refugees who need to flee before the border is closed. Natie scampers down his front lawn, jumps into MoM, and we tear off into the black night.

eleven

I'm so distracted and panicky at rehearsal I have to keep going out-side and walking around the block just to keep calm, asking myself over and over again, "What am I going to do? What am I going to do?" Thank God Kelly's there to run things. Afterward we go back to her house, which always makes me feel better.

Kelly lives in a cozy Tudor in Wallingford Heights set back on a large, woodsy lot. There's almost a fairy-tale quality to the house, like you'd expect a kindly woodcutter and his wife to live there, rather than a divorced, alcoholic therapist and her daughter.

As we step out of the car Kelly points to the sky. "Look," she says, "a harvest moon."

Natie and I turn and there, indeed, like an enormous pumpkin, hangs a bright orange moon. I stand behind Kelly and put my arms around her, the way you do in a musical when you sing a duet and you both need to face front. I reach up and cup her breasts in my hands. The night air is cool and I feel her nipples harden under her leotard.

It's a comforting feeling.

We open the front door, being careful to sidestep the two manic cats who guard the entryway, then toss our coats wherever we want to because it's that kind of house.

Kelly's mom is definitely not the type of person who worries about the disabling effects of dead skin in the carpet. "Hell," she says in her no-nonsense New England-y way, "I wouldn't be surprised if you found a dead *body* in my carpet." The house is about as tidy as most people's attics, which makes it a particularly hospitable hangout for sloppy teenagers. You can't sit down without having to move several unread is-sues of *The New Yorker*, some stray knitting needles, a couple of used wineglasses, and the occasional odd Christmas ornament, not to mention the TV clicker, which has the irritating habit of always being exactly where you want to sit but then mysteriously disappears the moment you want to change the channel. Every available horizontal surface—tables, chairs, windowsills, the piano bench, the piano, as well as every step leading both upstairs and to the basement—is utilized as a stacking space. It's as if the whole house were just one big, open closet. "A clean house is a sign of a misspent life," Kathleen says.

Everywhere you turn, the walls are covered with lopsided photos chronicling the lives of Kelly and her brother and sister, Brad and Bridget, both of whom are away at college. Kathleen so admires her children she wedges extra snapshots of them into the corners of the frames.

The whole house radiates with love.

Kathleen's standing at the kitchen counter when we come in, dipping celery sticks into cottage cheese and drinking a Bartles & Jaymes white wine spritzer. Her leotard and tights are damp, which means she's just finished working out to her Jane Fonda video, or "Pain with Jane" as she calls it. It also means she too has got that nipple freak-out thing going, which is kind of embarrassing to me considering she's my girlfriend's mother. But at forty-three years old, Kathleen still doesn't look substantially different from the old black-and-white wedding portrait that hangs on the living room wall, a photo she never tires of psychoanalyzing. "Note the demure *closed-mouth* smile," she'll say like she's a docent in a museum, "the hands folded discreetly over the lap, the enormous *white* dress. It's like I'm Miss Chastity Belt 1961."

Kathleen.

I share with her the wounds inflicted by the slings and arrows of my outrageous fortune and she listens intently, her brow knitted with therapeutic concentration. Occasionally she asks a question for clarification, but mostly she just nods her blond head and makes affirmative mm-hmm and uh-huh noises. I get more upset as I talk and she reaches across the kitchen table to grip my hand, her eyes all ripply with tears, like she's crying for me because, of course, I can't.

"What am I going to do?" I ask.

Kathleen swallows the remainder of her spritzer, then orders Kelly and Natie into the living room. She wants to talk to me alone. While they trudge bewildered out of the room, Kathleen pours us both a spritzer. "Here," she bleats in her brittle Katharine Hepburn-y way, "you look like you could use one." Some may question the mental-health wisdom of serving alcohol to minors but, as far as I'm concerned, Kathleen's my kind of therapist.

She sits back down at the table, the light from the stained-glass lamp casting shadows across her high patrician cheekbones, and she looks at me for a long time with what seem to be Kelly's eyes, or perhaps I should say Kelly's right eye, the one that favors blue. Finally, she says, "Edward, can I trust you?"

"Of course you can," I say.

"You can't tell this to anyone, especially Kelly. You understand?"

"I promise." One of the coolest things about Kathleen is how she treats kids like grown-ups.

"Do you know what Kelly's dad gave me for our twentieth anniversary?"

Of course I don't. I also don't know what this has got to do with my paying for acting school.

Kathleen doesn't wait for an answer. "He gave me a trip to the Caribbean," she says, "and a case of herpes."

I stare at her, not knowing how to react. It never occurred to me that middle-aged people got herpes, particularly those who are products of a Catholic education. She stares back at me, nodding her head, her lips pursed.

"And not the nice kind of herpes, either," she says, "but the kind you get for the rest of your goddamn life." She takes another swig of her Bartles & Jaymes. "I'm telling you this so you can understand a bit about what happens to men when they reach middle age." Kathleen then proceeds to expound her theory of male menopause. Kathleen's got a theory about everything. This one revolves around the idea that since men's bodies don't shut down the baby-making mechanism the way women's do, middle-aged men facing their mortality feel an increased biological need to propagate the species. As a result they start screwing around on their wives with younger, more fertile women.

"It's not like they want to have more children, although sometimes that happens, too," Kathleen explains, pouring herself another spritzer. "It's more that by choosing a new, younger wife, a man effectively has another child, but one he can sleep with, too."

"But Dagmar's not young," I say, "she's your age."

That didn't come out the way I wanted it to.

"Doesn't matter," Kathleen says, swirling her spritzer. "She's *like* a child, because she needs his support." Kathleen's never been one to let something as inconsequential as the facts get in the way of one of her theories.

"So what should I do?" I say. Okay, maybe I whine a little but I've got a right. I'd say Dagmar pulled the rug right out from underneath me, except she got rid of all the rugs.

Kathleen stands. "You've got to prove to him that you are a man yourself," she says. "The time for relating to him as a dependent child is over. Show him that you don't need his help, that you are perfectly capable of paying for college on your own."

"But I'm not perfectly capable of paying for college on my own."

Kathleen leans across the table and the light from the stained-glass lamp shines bright on her taut, freckled face. "Edward, don't ever let me hear you say that again, do you understand? You *are* perfectly capable of paying for college on your own and you will. You have to." She pulls up a chair and takes my hands in hers. "Listen, sweetie, I know it seems bleak and you feel betrayed and scared. But the only way out of a situation like this is through it." She strokes my face lightly with one finger. "So many things could happen between now and then, but what I know is this: you've got strengths you're not even aware of yet and you are going to be amazed at what you can do when this is all over. I believe in you; not just in your talent, but in you yourself. There is so much more to you than you even realize, I promise."

There are moments in your life when you see yourself through someone else's eyes, when your only hope of believing you're capable of doing something is because someone else believes it for you.

This is one of those moments.

"I've got to get out of these wet clothes," she says. "We'll talk again, okay?" She gets up to leave, but then turns and looks back at me. "Remember what I said, Edward. I'm on your side."

Kathleen.

❋   ❋   ❋

I put Kathleen's glass in the sink and am startled when a voice behind me says, "Jeez, herpes. Gross."

I turn around. "Natie, don't you have any respect for privacy?"

"Not particularly," he says, "and it's a good thing, too, 'cuz you're going to need my help."

Kelly comes back in and nuzzles against me. "You okay?" she asks.

"Don't distract him," Natie says. "We've got work to do. I've got it all outlined." He slides a piece of notebook paper across the kitchen table. "Take a look." It reads:

WAYS FOR EDWARD TO PAY FOR COLLEGE

1) WORK
2) SCHOLARSHIPS
3) THEFT
4) MURDER

"Murder?" I say. "This is a viable choice?"

"Don't get ahead of yourself. I'm just examining all your options." He puts on his glasses. "Let's start with number one: work."

Just hearing the word makes me tense up. "It doesn't seem right that someone as talented as me should actually have to work," I say.

"You work," Kelly says. "We're getting paid to choreograph *Anything Goes.*"

"That's right, we are."

"Terrific," says Natie, clicking his pen. "How much are you getting?"

"Five hundred dollars."

Natie writes down $500.

"No, no, no," I say, "that's for the two of us."

Natie scratches out $500 and writes $250. "Maybe I better use pencil," he says, pulling one from his pocket protector. He writes $250, his tongue sticking out as he does. "Okay, *Anything Goes*," he says. "That kills weeknights."

"And after school there's play practice," Kelly adds.

Natie scrunches his doughy face. "That doesn't leave a lot of time for a job."

"The shows are both over by Thanksgiving," I say. "I could get a holiday job."

"That's right," Kelly says, smiling. "You could wrap gifts or, like, hand out samples or something. You'd be good at that."

"Yeah, how much money could I earn doing that?"

"Well," Natie says, "let's say you get a retail job that you can keep the rest of the year at twenty hours a week . . ."

"Twenty hours? Do I really need to work that much?"

"How much does Juilliard cost?"

"Ten thousand dollars a year."

He shoots me a gimme-a-break look.

"Okay, I get your point," I say. "What does twenty hours a week add up to?"

"Twenty hours a week from December through June is, let's see, seven months or twenty-eight weeks. Twenty-eight times twenty hours a week is 560 hours, at minimum wage of $3.35 an hour equals $1,876."

"That's it?"

"Calm down, will ya? I'm not done yet," Natie says. "If you work full-time during vacations and all next summer, you could presumably earn another fifteen hundred bucks, which brings the total up to $3,376."

"Plus 250 from *Anything Goes*," Kelly says.

"Three thousand six hundred and twenty-six dollars. That's more than a third of the way there!" Natie looks up and smiles his lippy, no-tooth smile. He's got tiny little teeth like a row of Chiclets, which embarrasses him, so he's gotten in the habit of smiling the goofy way he does. He glances at his list. "Number two: scholarships."

My head droops. "Al earns too much for me to be eligible for scholarships."

"Don't be so negative," Natie says. "You're bound to get a couple of talent scholarships. Let's say $1,000 to be conservative. That's $4,626. Now we're almost halfway there. See how easy this is?"

"Assuming I don't spend any money between now and . . ."

"Number three: theft."

"You're not really suggesting I should steal, are you?"

Natie takes off his glasses and gazes upward like he's pondering the cosmic ramifications of theft. "Steal is such a cold, ugly word, don't you think?" he says. "Think of it as simply borrowing money that you don't intend to give back. Think embezzlement."

"Is that as bad as theft?" asks Kelly.

"It's better," Natie says, his button eyes bright. "That's when you steal from a company. It's a victimless crime. Or fraud. Oh, fraud is good."

"What kind of fraud could I do?" I say.

"Oh, I don't know, send bills to old people for stuff they haven't really bought . . ."

"That's not very nice," Kelly says.

"I'm just brainstorming," Natie snaps. "What about defrauding an institution, like a college or a university? When you consider how many of them fund research that supports Reagan's missile defense plan, fraud is really more an act of civil disobedience than an actual crime."

"I don't think Juilliard is researching missile defense."

"Good point. Let's stick with embezzlement. Does Al have any bank accounts you could siphon money out of without his knowing about it?"

"Are you kidding? Al knows where he keeps every nickel he's ever earned."

"There's just got to be another way for you to raise that kind of cash," Natie says. He gets up from the table and paces, tapping his forehead the way Winnie-the-Pooh does when he's trying to think. "Oh! What about blackmail? Blackmail's a great source of income."

There's something about the way he says it that makes me uncomfortable. The voice of experience, perhaps?

"Don't look at me that way," he says. "Just add it to the list."

Kelly takes his pencil and writes down the word "blackmail," dotting the "i" with a little smiley face.

"Blackmail is a perfectly fair exchange of money for services," Natie continues, "in this case Al's money for our silence. It's pure capitalism; criticizing it is practically un-American. Now think, Edward, you must know something juicy about your dad."

Aside from the way Al cheats in line at the bakery by pretending it's his number when no one else claims it? "No," I say.

"Well, maybe you could get your mom to tell you something," Natie says.

Kelly casts daggers at him and I can see he immediately understands he shouldn't have brought up my mother. Just the mention of her instantly makes me sad. Sure, Mom could probably tell me something, if I knew where to find her. I told her not to go to South America. I told her it's full of Nazis and drug lords and dictators but, no, she just had to climb Machu Picchu and get in touch with her past lives. I push my chair away from the table and go to the fridge.

"Murdering Al is starting to sound better and better," I mutter.

Kathleen returns, her freckled face scrubbed shiny, her blond hair dark with wetness.

"Then we better think about killing Dagmar, too," Natie says, "just in case he's changed his will."

Kathleen puts on a kettle for tea.

"It wouldn't be hard," I say. "I'm sure my sister could get us something from the pharmacy to poison them."

Natie scratches his frizzy head. "Then all we'd have to do is burn down your house to make it look like they got killed in a fire." I imagine Dagmar's fascistically finished floors buckling while her freaky photographs curl up on the walls and disintegrate. I smile as I think of her lifeless body melting away like the Wicked Witch of the West. But then I think about losing my father. Right now he's worth more to me dead than alive, but he is still my dad, after all.

I turn to Kathleen. "We're not really serious about murder," I say.

Kathleen reaches into the kitchen cabinet and pulls out a mug with the words LIFE IS SHORT. EAT DESSERT FIRST on it. "Oh, homicidal thoughts don't scare me," she says. "It's the suicidal ones I worry about." She smiles at me and I feel buoyed by her concern.

Maybe she's right. Maybe I am capable of doing things I haven't conceived of yet.

I turn to Natie. "Suppose I worked twice as hard," I say. "Suppose I work forty hours a week instead of twenty, or find a job that pays more, or start working right away. I might be able to sock away $10,000 all by myself, couldn't I?"

"It's possible," Natie says.

Kathleen reaches for a jar of honey.

"Then that is what I'm going to do," I say. "I'm going to join the working class."

Kelly squeezes my shoulder. "Good for you," she says.

"After all," I say, "how hard can a real job be?"

twelve

I rise the next morning feeling very I-did-it-my-way-ish and ready to lick this thing. The crisp early autumn air makes me feel focused and brittle, like the way you imagine preppies in New Hampshire must feel. Even the thought of going back to that necessary evil mandated by law, physical education, doesn't get me down. In fact, I'm actually looking forward to gym for the first time in my entire school career. You see, seniors at Wallingford High get first pick of the sports, so naturally they always choose the blow-off ones like archery or golf or badminton, sports no one is good at or, even if you are, who really cares?

So after changing into my appropriately irreverent gym outfit (tie-dyed T-shirt and flowered Bermudas — it's a statement about what a joke this class is), I head into the gymnasium looking for Ms. Burro, the phys ed teacher and my archnemesis.

Teresa Burro has movie-star looks. Unfortunately for her that movie star is Ernest Borgnine. Thus cheated by fate or genetics, this dump truck of a woman is obviously determined to make as many people miserable as possible. Her tragic flaw is that she's a stupid, ugly cow.

She's parked in the middle of the gym floor when I come out. "Glad to see you've finally joined us, Zanni," she sneers.

"I'm feeling better, thanks," I say. "So what are we doing, square dancing?"

This is a dig on my part. Burro and I haven't gotten along since the tenth grade, when I protested the exclusion of boys from square dancing on the grounds that it was discriminatory.

"Lemme see," she says, sticking her pen in her mouth as she consults her clipboard. I contemplate her hairy upper lip, dyed blond to no avail. It must suck to be ugly.

"You've got flag football, then basketball."

"What? What about archery or . . ."

"You missed the sign-up."

"But I had a medical excuse."

"Too bad. You shoulda signed up anyway."

I watch the other seniors pick up their bows and arrows, languidly squeaking their way across the gym floor in their sneakers, laughing and chatting in a congenial country-club way. Meanwhile, overzealous sophomores fight for the football and start whizzing it back and forth across the room.

"That's not fair," I cry.

"Tough," she says.

Evil. Evil. Evil. I'd drive across her lawn except she probably lives in a cave.

I trudge out onto the field and am mortified to discover that I am the lone senior in a group of pea-brained pituitary cases, the kind who actually like gym, probably because it is the only subject in which they excel. From across the field the other seniors stare at me like I'm some kind of reject who's been held back or has to ride to school on the short bus.

The day gets worse when I actually have to do the unthinkable and quit the school play. I've never quit a play in my life (why would I?), but Mr. Lucas completely understands my totally fucked-up situation. "The important thing, Edward," he says, "is that you get into Juilliard. I wouldn't be surprised if that didn't change your father's mind when the time comes." His voice is low and sincere and it makes me feel kind of shitty that my life sucks so bad he has to be nice about it. "Don't give a second thought to *The Miracle Worker*," he says. "It's completely actor-proof. You could cast Sylvester Stallone as Helen Keller and the audience would still cry their heads off." Seeing an opportunity to play a character who has actually been through puberty, Natie convinces Mr. Lucas to cast him in my role. Never mind that Natie is the same height as the girl playing his six-year-old daughter; in true Lucas style, it becomes part of the concept. "Mr. Nudelman's diminutive stature underscores the idea that the father is a petty, small-minded man," he says. I tell Natie to think of Al Zanni.

So once again I'm forced to break out the "F" encyclopedia and try to commit to memory football's seemingly arbitrary rules. Despite an ability to memorize pages of iambic pentameter, I still can't seem to understand what a "down" is, so I ask Doug to come over and give me a few pointers. The prospect of tossing a football around my yard feels very masculine and autumnal to me, and I even go out and buy a football jersey at a sporting goods store to get into character. What's more, I'm pleased to see that some of my dancing skills can be transferred to the language of sports.

"How am I doing?" I shout as I *jeté* through space to catch the ball.

"Looks more like fag football when you do it," he says.

I flinch reflexively at the sound of the other "f" word, but Doug just smiles his satyr's grin at me and I think perhaps all is well with the world. I charge toward him like I'm a fullback who just got the ball (See? Look how much I learned), and manage to knock him over. I straddle his waist and try to pin him down, but he's too strong for me and he flips me over and climbs on top of me, which is, of course, exactly what I'd hoped he'd do.

"Unsportsmanlike conduct," I yell. "Fifteen yards! Fifteen yards!" and Doug laughs. I love making him laugh.

We're interrupted by the sound of the back door banging open.

"Tsat is enough!" Dagmar yells. "I cannot verk vit such noise. Go avay! Go avay, boys!"

Dagmar's fetish for silence is working my last nerve. Claiming that music irritates her, she actually asked me to refrain from humming, whistling, or singing in my own home. She's like Julie Andrews's evil twin.

"We were just leaving, anyway," I say, then fake like I'm going to throw the ball at her. Bitch.

☀   ☀   ☀

I stop going into the city to take classes, but I do continue choreographing *Anything Goes* because Kelly and I are getting paid. Our usual method of working together is that I'm in charge of telling people where to go and Kelly is responsible for the actual steps. But I'm totally distracted, so Kelly practically takes over. I'm relieved to see she's good at it, much more inventive and commanding than I gave her credit for, and the cast really likes her. She's patient and understanding, even after somebody's tap shoe comes flying off during a number and nails her right in the gut. She'll do well in the dance program at Bennington.

Me, I've got other tasks to attend to.

My first job is as a parking valet at an expensive but tacky Mafia-run Italian restaurant in Cramptown. It's easy work plus I get tips and the opportunity to drive some really nice cars, which suits my self-image. But then I lock the keys in someone's Jaguar while the motor's running and the owner of the car insists I be fired on the spot. It seems to me that someone who could afford a Jaguar could also afford to be a little more generous of spirit.

I'm okay with losing that job anyway because I immediately get hired as a delivery driver for Petals Plus, a local florist. This is a terrific gig. First off, you get to be around flowers all day, and what's not to like about that? Secondly, when you're delivering flowers everyone is always really happy to see you unless, of course, you're delivering to a funeral. Or if you happen to back the delivery van into someone's BMW, which I do on my third and final day of work.

Kathleen says I'm subconsciously taking out my aggressions against my father by sabotaging luxury cars, but just to prove her wrong I purposely seek out another driving job delivering pizzas. Once again, this is a situation where everyone is always really happy to see you. I mean, it's not like anyone's ever going to say, "Shit! The pizza guy's here. Quick, turn out the lights and maybe he'll go away." And this time the accident is with a Honda Civic, so there goes Kathleen's theory.

Meanwhile, Mr. Lucas and I work on finding the perfect classical monologue for my audition. We try Mercutio's death scene from *Romeo and Juliet*, mostly as an exercise connecting with pain because Mr. Lucas says I'm too much of a clown. "No! No! No!" he bellows before I'm even finished. "Mercutio's suffering from a flesh wound, Mr. Zanni, not gastritis. Try it again, but this time use the sense memory of an actual wound you've had."

Having avoided any kind of physical activity that might cause a wound, I concentrate on the only injury I've ever had: Father Groovy's fall off the back of Al's Midlife Crisis. I stagger about, wincing as I grip my tailbone like Mercutio has been stabbed in the butt. I know I must look strange, but I try to compensate with a dramatic, Charlton Heston-y, talking-through-clenched-teeth kind of delivery.

"That's perfect," Mr. Lucas says when I finish. "Now if you just rang a bell you could play Quasimodo."

Exeunt Mercutio.

I'm actually bold enough to suggest one of Hamlet's soliloquies, "Oh that this too too solid flesh would melt" to be specific. Sure, it's the greatest role in the entire theatrical canon, but I am *so* like Hamlet; as far as I can see, he's just another sulky teenager with shitty parents. I mean, here's a speech where I really can connect with the pain by substituting Hamlet's mother with my evil stepmonster. I try it for Mr. Lucas one afternoon and must say I'm quite pleased with how my voice throbs when I say the last line about the breaking heart.

"Congratulations, Mr. Zanni," he says. "You've put the ham back in *Hamlet*."

Exeunt Hamlet.

Mr. Lucas suggests I try Edmund in *King Lear* because he, too, is enraged with his father. But rage seems to be all I can play these days and the whole soliloquy becomes too one-note. Mr. Lucas gives me all kinds of exercises to find the other colors ("Do it like you're waiting for a bus," "Do it like you've just discovered penicillin," that kind of thing), but frankly, the more I work at it, the worse it gets. I know I'm in trouble when I see him take off his glasses and rub his eyes. "That's enough, Edward," he says. "Your acting is hurting me."

Exeunt Edmund.

We're running out of time.

My next job is as a busboy at a steakhouse, although I prefer to think of myself more as a "waiter's assistant." But then I assist a plate of baby back ribs right onto some poor woman's lap and once again find myself looking for work. Honestly, people get so touchy about the tiniest mistakes. I mean, one little flesh wound to a Pekingese is all it takes to get fired as a dog groomer, even if you artfully arrange its hair so the scar doesn't show. And when I take a job delivering newspapers, the customers get frigging crazy just because a couple of times I deliver their morning papers in the evening. I'm sure if these people slept in once in a while, they wouldn't be so grouchy.

Sure, I'm bummed at losing all the jobs, but I view my ineptitude for the working world as a sure sign that I'm best suited for a life in the arts.

Meanwhile, back at the House of Floor Wax, Al and I can't seem to agree on anything anymore; the moment either of us brings up the subject of college it immediately escalates into yet another finger-wagging, door-slamming, yelling-at-the-top-of-our-lungs battle. I can hardly breathe when I'm in the house. I feel like Antigone: condemned by an unjust tyrant to be walled alive inside a tomb. With hardwood floors.

God, I miss my mother.

But it's thinking about Antigone that finally inspires me to find the right monologue: Haemon's speech to his father. I can't believe I haven't thought of it before. I am so like Haemon. We're both sensitive, misunderstood souls with petty despots for fathers. Here at last is a dramatic monologue where I can connect to the pain. It says everything I want to say to Al, and I practice it loudly around the house just to piss off Dagmar and maybe, just maybe, to get through to my father, who grows more distant, like someone on a faraway shore.

> *Father, you must not think that your word and no other must be so.*

(That's right, Al, you son of a bitch bastard.)

> *For if any man thinks that he alone is wise — that in what he says and what he does, he's above all else — that man is but an empty tomb.*

(Yeah, and you'll be sorry when I don't thank you in my Oscar speech.)

> *A wise man isn't ashamed to admit his ignorance and he understands that true power lies in being flexible, not rigid.*

(Hello-o?)

> *Have you seen after a winter storm how the trees that stand beside the torrential streams yield to it and save their branches, while the stiff and rigid perish, root and all? Or how a sailor who always keeps his sail taut and never slackens will only capsize his boat?*

(These are called metaphors, get it?)

> *Father, I may be young, but you must listen to reason. Please, I beg you to soften your heart and allow a change from your rage.*

(Please, please, please, please, please.)

Still, the misery that is phys ed continues to wear on me and I finally lose it during flag football when, after having made the simple error of tearing the flags off someone on my own team, I'm publicly berated by Darren O'Boyle, Duncan's younger brother and an obvious future wife-beater. Darren has the same nasty rodentlike features as his brother and you can tell in an instant that he's mean in that steal-your-lunch-box-on-the-playground-in-the-third-grade kind of way. For a month now he's been relishing the sadistic pleasure of being able to show how tough he is by humiliating an upperclassman. I'm sick of it. What's worse, soon we're going to switch to basketball, another game I cannot remotely begin to understand, and one in which we're submitted to the additional humiliation of having to play shirts and skins. I discuss the matter with Ziba over lunch at her favorite restaurant, La Provençal. So far, no one in the attendance office has noticed that she and I always leave school at the same time for faux doctor's appointments, during which we enjoy leisurely lunches in the Continental manner.

"Why don't you just take a hammer and break something?" she suggests, using her water glass as a finger bowl. "Something little you don't really need, like a finger or a toe."

"I don't know," I say. "I'm not sure I've got the guts."

"Oh, I'll do it for you, darling," she says like she's offering to feed my cat.

"You would?"

"But of course. You're an oasis for me in this cultural desert. You and Nathan are the only true gentlemen in this school. All the rest are hormonally imbalanced thugs whose idea of romance is to drag you into a dark room and hump you like a dog. Breaking your finger is the least I can do."

"Uh, thanks?"

"Don't mention it."

Rather than resort to self-mutilation I turn to Natie for advice, who, despite his more irritating qualities, can be as dependable as a Japanese car in these circumstances and twice as efficient. His solution is characteristically simple and insane.

"We'll just break into the school and change the sign-up sheets," he says.

"How do you plan on doing that?" I ask.

"It's easy. We'll cross your name off of basketball and add it to the list for one of the blow-off sports. You can tell Burro that one of your friends signed you up."

"No," I say. "I meant how do you plan on breaking into the school?"

Natie jingles his keys which, in an effort to uphold his reputation as a total cheesehead, he keeps on his belt. "Having keys to the school is just one of the privileges and responsibilities of running the stage crew."

Natie.

"So you see," he says, "it's not really breaking and entering; it's unlocking and entering which, as far as I know, is not a punishable offense."

"But even if I add my name to the list, do you really think Burro's going to buy that line about someone else signing me up?"

Natie scrunches his doughy little face. "Pleeeease," he says, "if she were that smart, do you think she'd be teaching *gym*?"

It may not be the best idea he's ever had, but it's worth a try.

thirteen

Now in case you ever decide to unlock and enter your local high school, let me tell you that it's not as easy as you'd think. You can't just open the front door and wander in. And for reasons I still don't understand, Natie's key only allows him access to the boiler room in the basement. It's like the setting of some slasher movie, all sweaty, mossy pipes, inexplicable banging noises, and that dingy caged area lit by a bare bulb where you expect the crazed serial killer will do in the unsuspecting night watchman. From there, you have to crawl up a flight of stairs on your hands and knees so you don't set off a motion detector. The deftness with which the normally unathletic Natie accomplishes this task leads me to believe he's done it before.

Once we're on the first floor we can move about freely, although we're still hyperconscious of getting caught. Doug's come along with us (it just wouldn't be a true CV Enterprise without him) and we wander the empty corridors together, the only sound coming from the squeaking of my sneakers across the linoleum floors. Why they call them sneakers I'll never know, because they don't seem very effective for sneaking. They should call them squeakers instead. To make matters worse, my left knee cracks every other step. "Jesus, Ed, you're like a friggin' one-man band," Doug says.

Everything looks different at night—the classrooms, the hallways, the offices—and it all appears more sinister and scary, like we're visiting an evil parallel universe. I'm aware of every echo, every shaft of light, every movement.

It's thrilling.

Natie accompanies me and Doug to the gym and leaves us there while he goes to the main office to intercept some detention slips and do a little forgery for his "clients." Apparently, he's been building up a little cottage industry among the rich, white-boy druggies who can afford to pay a handsome fee to have their school records cleaned up. "I'll meet you guys here at 0200 hours," he says. "And don't go wandering off. You don't know where all the alarms are."

Doug and I have to go into the girls' locker room to get to Burro's office and, as we pass through the door, it suddenly occurs to me—gym teachers go to work every day in a locker room. While admittedly there's a certain sexiness about it, overall it's got to suck, particularly for the men. Few things stink worse than teenage boys' feet.

The door to Ms. Burro's office is locked.

"Now what?" Doug asks.

"We've just gotta wait for Natie, I guess."

Doug ambles over to the lockers and tugs on the locks to see if any are open. "I've always wondered what the girls' locker room looked like," he says.

I glance around. "Not so different from the boys', is it?"

"Guess not," he says.

We wander through the shower room and out to the pool. The room is humid and smells of chlorine and mold. The only sound comes from the water lapping into the filters.

Doug Grouchos his eyebrows at me. "You up for a swim?" he asks.

The water is dark and scary looking and undoubtedly cold, but I'm not about to pass up an opportunity to see Doug naked. Normally I have to go to a lot of trouble to do just that—showing up early at his house so I might catch him stepping out of the shower, inviting myself to sleep over despite the fact that his father, the embittered Tastykake driver, totally gives me the creeps. Doug whips off his clothes the way little kids do, like he's eager to be liberated from them. But there's something almost graceful about the way he pulls his shirt off, reaching from the bottom instead of wiggling out from the neck the way I do, and I make a mental note to remove my shirt that way in the future. He strides past me, the muscles in his legs as attenuated as something you'd see in *Gray's Anatomy* and I feel ashamed that my body is so jiggly. He stands naked at the edge of the pool, spreads his cobra lats wide, and cracks his back before making a perfect javelin dive into the silver-black water. I descend the steps halfway and watch him flop about like a dolphin, his butt periodically popping above the surface of the water. He swims over to me.

"Aren't you coming in?"

I'm stuck in that stage between wanting to go in and being afraid to take the final plunge. So instead I stand there shivering like an idiot. "It's really cold," I say, my teeth chattering.

"Wuss," he says, then grabs me by the wrist and yanks me in. All I can hear is the plunging sound of water as it rushes past me and I feel quite lost for a moment. I swim for the surface and look around for Doug but I don't see him. I paddle to the center of the pool, unsure of what to do next. It's kind of creepy swimming in a dark pool at night, like any minute you expect to hear the theme from *Jaws*.

At that moment Doug grabs a hold of my foot and drags me under.

We sort of wrestle, each of us preventing the other from coming up for air. Doug's body is hard to the touch and, even as I struggle for breath, I find myself envying it. (How great must it be to go through life with that sense of firmness under you, like you have a solid foundation?) When we can't stand it any longer we rise to the surface.

"Very funny," I gasp.

Doug flashes me a lupine smile and I feel his legs brush up against mine as we tread water. He looks so handsome with his wet hair pushed off his face, like an old-time movie star. It's all I can do to stop myself from just leaning over and kissing him right on the lips.

"What's wrong?" he says.

"Nothing. Why?"

"You're looking at me funny."

"That's 'cuz you're funny-looking," I say and splash him. He pops up and dunks me and once again the water whooshes around my ears. I reach for his legs and find my head in his crotch and suddenly Doug is over my shoulder, his cock mashed against my neck, the muscles in the back of his thighs tensing in my hands. I have to push him off of me to get a breath, but as soon as I do, Doug whips around, thrusts his hand between my legs and gooses me.

I squeal, just like a little girl, the sound reverberating around the room. Doug backstrokes away from me.

"Hernia check," he says, winking.

This is what I imagine life with a male lover is like—rough and playful and grabby—and I revel in the sheer manliness of it all. I follow Doug down to the shallow end where we do handstands and have breath-holding contests until it's almost 0200 hours.

We don't have any towels so we sit on the pavement to air-dry.

Doug lies back, putting his hands behind his head and closing his eyes. I gaze at his lean and chiseled body, which reminds me of Jesus on the cross. (Is it just me, or is it strange that churches have statues that make our crucified Lord look like a triathlete?)

"Ed, can I ask you something?"

I turn and see that Doug has opened his eyes. Caught.

"Sure," I say.

"Promise you won't take it the wrong way."

" 'Course I won't."

I feel my heart skip a beat. Unfortunately, the blood rushes to my groin instead.

Doug sits up on his elbows. "Are you gay?"

fourteen

He's cool with it; he's totally, totally cool with it, and reminds me yet again of his homo-friendly credentials (the ubiquitous gay German gymnast uncle). In fact, he even seems to admire me for being bi, like it makes me some kind of adventuresome sexual outlaw. Slut Cassidy.

"But you gotta understand that I'm not like that," he says. "There's nothing wrong with it, of course, but I'm just really, really straight, you know what I mean?"

Methinks he doth protest too much. Now I just need to find a way to wear down his resistance without resorting to a blow to the head with a blunt instrument.

Natie can't get us into Burro's office, but he does offer to break my finger for me. I decline, and turn my attention back to the college issue.

Luckily, Mr. Lucas agrees to plead my case with Al. But just the thought of the two of them meeting (aka *When Worlds Collide*) gives me a pain in my chest like someone is gripping my heart and won't let go.

I want to assert my identity as an artist by wearing my lime-green harem pants and judo jacket, but Kathleen says I'll get further if I dress conservatively (or "normal" as she calls it), so I wear khakis and an Izod shirt, which I even tuck in, as well as one of those horrible preppy belts that looks like macramé. With my Hall and Oates haircut I look like a lesbian golfer.

Being unemployed at the moment (you make a couple of personal calls when you're supposed to be telemarketing and you're out of there), I slip in the back of the auditorium to watch the Act One run-through of *The Miracle Worker*. It's the first time I've seen any of the show since I quit, and the moment Kelly enters I totally forget my worries. Her performance as Annie Sullivan is an absolute revelation to me. First off, she's completely convincing, down to the character's Irish brogue and troubled eyesight and I often forget it's Kelly I'm watching, so swept away am I by her performance. I had no idea she could be so good. She's so real, so harrowing, it makes me want to cry (assuming I could do that kind of thing), partly because I'm so proud of her and partly because I want so desperately to be up there myself being real and harrowing.

When the lights come up at the end of the act, I see Doug leaning against the side wall by the door, his kinky hair wet and messy from a post-practice shower, his T-shirt damp in spots, like he dried off in a hurry to get over here. He tosses his gym bag and letterman jacket over his shoulder and saunters down the aisle, slapping his chest with one hand to applaud. Kelly pulls off the dark glasses she wears in the role to see who it is, then lights up with enthusiasm at the sight of him. He drops his gear on the floor, then hops onstage in one swift move and rushes over to give Kelly a hug, which lasts a little too long to be considered just friendly. They part, but still he grips her skinny forearms with his big monkey hands, nodding his head emphatically as he speaks, undoubtedly complimenting her on her performance. Kelly responds by looking down shyly, occasionally glancing up from under her bangs and making tentative "Do you really think so?" type gestures. I stand at the back of the auditorium watching them. They look so right together, these two, so lean and clean and L.L. Bean, that I almost don't want to interrupt them, but I'm so consumed by jealousy that I find myself dashing toward the stage to break them apart.

Just who I'm more jealous of I'm not sure.

I don't wait to reach the stage before calling out "Hey" and they both turn, looking surprised but happy to see me. Kelly holds her arms straight out in front of her as she advances toward me, the way you do when you're encouraging a baby to take its first steps. I slide into her arms and give her a longish kiss for Doug's benefit, then hold her face in my hands and stare into her mismatched eyes.

"You were great," I say, like my opinion should mean more than Doug's, which it does. "This is absolutely the best work you've ever done." Kelly smiles and squeezes me hard.

"I can really act, can't I?" she whispers in my ear.

I lift her up in the air, which I'm not really strong enough to do.

"Yes, yes, most definitely yes," I say, swinging her around. We part, but I don't let go of her hands. "I'd love to drive you home," I say, "but I've got this thing with Al and . . ."

"That's okay," Kelly says, "Doug'll take me." But she doesn't turn and ask him, which leads me to believe that this has become a regular arrangement in my absence.

From the auditorium Mr. Lucas bellows, "*Eggzellent* work, ladies and gentlemen, *eggzellent*." He peers over his glasses and shakes a crutch at Kelly. "Miss Corcoran, Miss Corcoran, Miss Corcoran," he says. "You are full of surprises. Today was your best day yet."

Kelly is so delighted she actually hops up and down in place.

"Now, all of you, out of here," he says. "Mr. Zanni and I have an appointment."

Doug gives me a thumbs-up, then gathers his gym bag and Kelly's knapsack. Kelly gives me a soft kiss on the cheek and whispers "Good luck" in my ear. A wave of sadness comes over me, a watching-my-mother-leave-for-the-last-time kind of feeling, and the tightness in my chest returns. Fuck Al for doing this to me.

As if on cue, the heavy auditorium doors bang open and Al saunters in wearing slacks and a Members Only jacket, stopping to say hello to Kelly in his usual repulsive fashion, grabbing her face in his hairy hands and kissing her on the lips. This breezy, "I've Got the World on a String" attitude of his just irritates the shit out of me. Someone who's deliberately ruining his son's life should at least have the decency to act a little more restrained. I look at him there, popping his gum and jingling his pocket change, and I wonder how it is I descended from anyone who would actually wear a Members Only jacket.

He strides in like he owns the place, cracks his hairy knuckles, and says to me, "Okay, kid, what's up?"

I introduce Al to Mr. Lucas, who puts on his best Sunday-school manners for the occasion. Al reaches out to shake hands, but Mr. Lucas's arms are in the wrist braces of his crutches, and as he struggles to free them up, he whacks Al right in the shin.

Things get worse from there.

Al plops his bulky frame down in the front row and spreads his arms across the backs of the seats, rubbing the upholstery like he's trying to decide whether to buy them. I pull over a chair for Mr. Lucas and then sit down on the cold floor next to him. He fixes his gaze on Al. "Mr. Zanni, I've asked you here this afternoon to give you my opinion, not only as Edward's drama teacher, but as a graduate of the Royal Academy of Dramatic Art in London and a former professional actor myself." Mr. Lucas emphasizes these credentials in a way that's meant to impress, but Al just unwraps another piece of gum, deposits the piece he's chewing in the wrapper, and pops the new piece in his mouth. He glances at his watch.

Mr. Lucas continues, undaunted. "Perhaps you're not aware of what great promise your son has. Edward stands an excellent chance of getting into Juilliard . . ."

"So what if he does?" Al says. It's disgusting that he'd treat someone as cultured as Mr. Lucas so rudely. He lives in the *city*, for Chrissake! I try to practice telekinesis on the gum in hopes of making it fly down Al's windpipe.

"Juilliard is the finest drama school in the country," Mr. Lucas says evenly. "Their seal of approval must be worth something."

"Probably," Al says, "but is it worth forty grand?"

"I'm not sure you can put a price tag on the value of education."

"Baloney," Al snorts, "of course you can. If I thought for a moment that Eddie here actually stood a chance of recouping this investment, I'd let him do it in a minute. But most actors never earn a dime and you wanna know why?" Al doesn't wait for Mr. Lucas to answer, but continues as if his misinformed opinion meant something. "Actors don't understand business and they don't want to, which is why most of 'em are losers. For Chrissakes, I could earn forty grand tomorrow as an actor if I wanted to, not because I know how to act but because I know how to make money. What Eddie needs is some business sense, not four years fartin' around in some drama school. He's dramatic enough as is."

"But I don't want to major in business!" I shout.

"See what I mean?" Al says.

Mr. Lucas glares hard at me, the Internationally Recognized Signal for "Shut the fuck up, you moron," then turns back to Al. "Mr. Zanni," he says, "perhaps there's a middle ground that could give you both what you want. Let's not forget that Edward has an excellent grade point average . . . in honors classes. It's not too late to consider a liberal arts school, even an Ivy League one. Edward would make an excellent English major, for instance."

"So he could do what—*teach*?" Al spits the word out so contemptuously I know the argument is over before it even starts. Frankly, I'm just as pissed. I don't want to be an English major at a liberal arts school.

I want to be an actor. Can't anyone understand that? Whose side is Mr. Lucas on, anyway?

Mr. Lucas takes off his glasses, pulls out a handkerchief from his coat pocket, and starts cleaning his lenses. "The value of a liberal arts education," he says in his teaching voice, "is not the specific knowledge one learns but that one actually learns to think for oneself. With those skills in place, Edward could excel in whatever field he chooses, be it business or the arts."

"Is that so?" Al says. "Lemme ask you something, Lucas. How much money did you earn last year?"

"I don't think that's any . . ."

"Never mind, that answers my question. You wanna know how much I earned last year?" Again, he doesn't wait for an answer. "A hundred and twenty grand," he says.

"That's impressive," Mr. Lucas murmurs.

"Yeah, I think so, too." Al rises and takes his keys out of his pocket. "So, with all due respect, why the hell should I listen to you?"

Mr. Lucas meditates on the question briefly; then in the plainest of voices says, "Because, with all due respect, I believe I understand your son better than you do."

Al looks at Mr. Lucas like he's a disease. "Yeah, I bet you do," he says.

fifteen

I replay the scene in my head as I drive over to Kelly's, marinating in my hatred of my father and banging my hands on MoM's steering wheel in frustration at Mr. Lucas's failure to broker the deal. Liberal arts college, my ass. What the fuck was he thinking? If I really am capable of getting into Juilliard, the best acting school in the country, then isn't that where I belong? You don't tell a champion javelin thrower to play Pick Up Sticks as some kind of fucking compromise for not going to the Olympics. Stupid goddamn crippled has-been. He's as powerless to help me as he is to walk across a room unassisted.

I'm busy ruminating on the pathetic existence of Ted Lucas when I run a stop sign. The sound of a blaring horn jolts me back to reality and I automatically wave my arms and scream apologies at the guy who has swerved to miss me. He shakes his fist, his face contorted in spasms of rage at the stupid spoiled kid behind the wheel of a Mercedes. I drive very slowly the rest of the way, both hands on the wheel, my breath fogging the windows.

I tap lightly on the front door because I know that today is one of the days Kathleen sees therapy clients (or as we call them, "cryents") in her office in the basement. On cryent days, you have to take off your shoes and tiptoe lightly around the house. Kelly and I call it the Anne Frank in the Secret Annex game. Kelly answers the door and I must look pretty shaken up because she reaches for me like she's Clara Barton and I'm a soldier wounded in battle. I lean my head on her shoulder and close my eyes and allow myself to be comforted. It feels so good in her arms, like I've docked in a safe harbor, and I grasp her to me tight as she rubs my back with smooth, liquid hands.

A floorboard creaks. I open my eyes and see Doug rising from the couch, his shirt untucked and his hair more cowlick-y than usual. He adjusts his crotch and I wonder whether Kelly's look of concern has more to do with being caught in the act than with thoughts for my well-being. But Doug doesn't seem to register any guilt or embarrassment; in fact he simply radiates this James Taylor-y you-just-call-out-my-name-and-I'll-be-there-yes-I-will kind of vibe as he slides across the hardwood floors in his socks, so maybe I'm imagining things. Silently he embraces both me and Kelly in a three-way hug, his long, muscular arms easily reaching around the two of us. It feels like the most natural thing in the world to lean my head on his shoulder and Kelly beams at the two of us like this is the sweetest display of male affection she's ever seen. The three of us just rock there together, me nuzzling Doug's neck, Doug nuzzling Kelly's, and Kelly nuzzling mine. I grip the two of them tighter to me. I feel so much love for them both right now, my best friend and my girlfriend, and I love the three of us together. Whatever bond the two of them have been developing in my absence only seems to bring us all closer.

I look at Kelly and she smiles at me shyly from under her bangs, the way Princess Diana does, and I just have to lean over and kiss her. She responds by opening her mouth and running her tongue along my teeth, which she knows drives me crazy. I open my eyes and see that Doug is breathing with his mouth open.

Kelly's and my lips part and we just stand there, clinging to one another, giggling very, very quietly. Doug and Kelly give each other a look, then turn, their eyes boring into me, and I know instantly they want my permission to kiss each other. All I can do is nod. Kelly inclines her head the opposite way to receive Doug's kiss and I feel myself stop breathing. Watching the two of them together is possibly the sexiest thing I've ever seen and if there were some way I could be a part of it, I would. Doug opens his eyes, winks, then scratches my ear like I'm some faithful dog needing attention. He gives us both a tug with his strong, hard arms, pulling us backward into the living room and onto the sofa. Kelly laughs and leans back, inviting us to both partake of her. Doug and I each slide a hand under her shirt, moving up her taut, flat belly to grasp a muffin-y breast in each palm.

"Fancy meeting you here," I whisper.

Doug reaches around to undo her bra and we both lean over to suck on her nipples, as hard and as tiny as the heads of pins. Arms get tangled as we try to unzip her jeans while she simultaneously tries to free us both of our pants and we all laugh some more. Doug doesn't bother waiting for any help and just stands up to pull his jeans and underwear to his knees.

You know those 1950s sci-fi movies where a nuclear reaction causes vegetables to grow to the size of crosstown buses? That's what Doug's erection is like. Kelly glances down and, I swear, does a double take, then grabs it firmly in her hand, like she better hold tight because there's no telling what this thing will do left to its own devices. She regards us both, like she's a housewife in the produce aisle trying to decide which zucchini to buy. Even hard, mine doesn't compare favorably; Doug's could easily feed a family of four, while I'm more of a snack by comparison. Damn Al and his lousy genetics. Yet another reason to hate him.

"Oh my God," Kelly says.

This is not exactly the warm, supportive affirmation I'm looking for, though I can't say I blame her. I prefer Doug's cock to mine, too. Still, it seems a rude thing to say, particularly since I kind of feel like this little ménage à trois is for my benefit.

"My mother!" she hisses.

For a fleeting Freudian second I try to figure out why two teenage boys' penises would make a girl think of her mother, but then I hear Kathleen climbing up the basement steps and I realize she'll be in the room in a matter of seconds. Each of us sets new Olympic records in speed dressing, then leaps to a different place on the large sectional sofa, grabbing the first thing we can so as to appear as if we were engaged in something, anything, other than group sex.

Kathleen rounds the corner looking tired and we all feign surprise at seeing her—y'know, "Oh, hiiiiyeee!"

"How did it go?" Kelly chirps, a little too enthusiastically. She folds her arms across her chest so her mother doesn't notice that she's not wearing a bra, which, at this moment, is stuffed between the cushions of the couch.

"Oh, these poor people," Kathleen says, leaning on the archway. "So much pain, so much pain." She heaves a sigh. "I need a drink."

She crosses through the living room then stops to look at me. "Since when have you taken up knitting, Edward?" she asks.

"It helps soothe the nerves," I say.

Kelly, Doug, and I don't talk about what happened, but there's an unspoken awareness now that we are some kind of threesome. Doug and I buy flowers for Kelly's opening in *The Miracle Worker* (well, actually, he steals them while I distract the clerk—part of my revenge on Petals Plus for firing me), and the two of us fawn all over her like she's Scarlett O'Hara and we're the Tarleton twins. I have to say I kind of like this two-buddies-vying-for-the-same-girl thing that we're playing out, so long as I'm the one who gets the girl in the end. Using Kelly as the bait to lure Doug's big fish is not something I'm necessarily proud of, but you work with what you've got.

Thanksgiving approaches and with it the annual homecoming game, which is supposed to be this big hairy deal because it's against our "arch rival," Battle Brook High. In anticipation of said event, we're all subjected to attending the school spirit assembly.

I fucking hate school spirit.

For some unfathomable reason, the Show Choir is required to perform. Show Choir is neither show nor choir and, as a result, I kind of hate it, too, particularly since Miss Tinker insists we perform our "Mary" medley, despite the fact it has absolutely nothing to do with school spirit. We begin with an a cappella arrangement of "Mary's a Grand Old Name," sung in six-part harmony, followed by the girls performing "How Do You Solve a Problem like Maria?" from *The Sound of Music*, sung in counterpoint to the boys doing "Maria" from *West Side Story*, which has the unfortunate effect of sounding like we just kissed a nun with a problem. We then make an utterly embarrassing segue into "Proud Mary," complete with watered-down Tina Turner–like choreography as interpreted by the rhythm impaired. We look about as hip as the Lawrence Welk singers. The audience doesn't even try to hide its disdain and they laugh all the way through our stirring rendition of the Schubert "Ave Maria."

High-school audiences are the worst.

Like Natie, Miss Tinker seems impervious to any humiliation and bravely chipmunks a toothy grin at us, exhorting us to "Smile! Smile!" despite the fact that we're in imminent danger of having something thrown at us. The woman is either highly deluded or highly medicated. Afterward, the Show Choir crawls back to its seats in the front row, no doubt wondering if there's any way we can get plastic surgery to render ourselves unrecognizable for the duration of the school year.

Principal Farley, the Dork of the Universe, takes the stage. "All right, settle down people, settle down," he says, and then adds insult to injury by insisting that the audience give us another round of applause. There are no boos this time, just the dispiriting drizzle of tepid clapping. I grab Kelly's hand and scooch down lower in my seat.

"Now we have something really special for you that I'm sure you'll find very enjoyable. Bringing the break-dancing craze to WHS for the first time . . ." (he pronounces "break dancing" like it's a foreign word he doesn't want to screw up) ". . . here are the Four Masters!"

The curtain opens to reveal about two dozen black guys. The audience roars, all coming to the same horrible, simultaneous conclusion: these guys can't count. It's a thoroughly chilling moment, far worse than anything the Show Choir had to endure. I see TeeJay, now decked out in a shiny warm-up jacket and pants, rush to the front of the stage and shout "That's the *Floor* Masters!" but he can hardly be heard over the laughter and the music.

I look at Kelly. She bites her lip and squeezes my hand harder. Like I said, high-school audiences are the worst.

Most of the Show Choir is respectful and attentive, sitting forward, heads tilted, like we're anthropologists observing the native dance of some visiting Zulu tribe. Sure it's condescending, but it beats the three sopranos who go running out in a panic when they realize that practically every black guy in the school is up there and they've left their purses backstage.

I can't wait to get out of this preppy prison.

＊　　＊　　＊

On Thanksgiving, Kelly and I decide to go to the big game. Now let me just say that I've never been to the big game; I've never wanted to go to the big game; in fact, I couldn't give two shits about the big game. But Doug's playing and Kelly wants to go and I'll be damned if I'm going to let those two have this shared bonding experience without me.

It's a crisp fall day with a sky as blue as the blood coursing through the veins of Wallingford's old guard. The air smells toasty with the scent of dry leaves and I'm determined to look as autumnal and football-y as I can for the occasion. So I put on a cable-knit fisherman's sweater and a down vest with a woolly hat instead of my usual Sinatra fedora. Since Kelly's a former cheerleader, I don't watch the game in the ironic, detached way I would with, say, Ziba or Natie. Sure, it's the usual snooze-fest—start, stop, start, stop—but I do enjoy the Battle Brook cheerleaders, a nearly all-black squad of girls whose booty-shaking choreography is worthy of *Soul Train.* They've got great cheers, too, like this one:

> *Pork chop, pork chop,*
> *Greazy, greazy,*
> *We'ze gonna beat you,*
> *Easy, easy.*
> *Corn bread, Jeri Curl,*
> *Bar-bee-cue,*
> *We'ze gonna beat the whoopy outta you!*

Beats "Ready to go, ready to fight" any day, as far as I'm concerned. I watch their high, hard asses flip and bump as they cheer and feel embarrassed for Amber Wright and the rest of the Wallingford rah-rahs, who seem about as hip as a squad of Girl Scouts by comparison. The crowd on the Wallingford side senses that we're being shown up and some drunk trust-fund types high up in the bleachers start chanting:

> *Hey, hey, that's okay,*
> *You'll all work for us someday.*

I see people snicker among themselves, clearly enjoying the joke, but not wanting to look like they do.

Kelly's really into the game and I feel like an asshole needing to have my girlfriend explain to me what's going on. A semester's worth of flag football has still not revealed the mysteries of this game to me, nor its appeal. Instead I content myself with making a mental note of Doug's nimble grace on the field and cataloguing every bit of body language that could be construed as evidence of repressed homosexual desires.

Afterward, Kelly and I wait by the field house for Doug. I don't know if this kind of stage-door-Johnny behavior is part of the postgame etiquette or not, and I feel weird and awkward standing there with nothing to do. TeeJay comes out and says hello to four black girls I've never seen before.

Okay, Edward, try not to sound like an asshole.

"Yo, TeeJay," I say. "Wha's happenin'?"

I'm an asshole. What is it about black people that makes me behave so stupidly?

"Yo, Edward, whassup?" he mumbles.

"Great game," I say.

"Yeah, too bad we lost."

Damnit. We don't encounter these problems in the theater. Even if the play sucks, no one admits it.

TeeJay introduces the girls he's with as his cousins from Battle Brook: Bonté, Shezadra, and one whose name I don't catch but I could swear sounded like Pneumonia. He looks over his shoulder at the fourth cousin, a short, cherub-y girl in a puffy down coat with a hood. "And this here's Margaret," he says.

Poor Margaret. Not only does it seem they ran out of interesting names by the time they'd gotten to her, but apparently all the glamorous genes had been used up, too. Black or white, every clique's got a cheesehead, I guess.

Doug emerges from the field house in his uniform, his spiky hair sticking up in different directions from having been under his helmet. Kelly and I wave and he trots over to us. Duncan and SOTGFTT stare at us like we're aliens.

Kelly gives Doug a squeeze as best she can around the shoulder pads, kisses him on the cheek, and says, "You did great!"

"Ya' think so?" Doug says. His eyes gleam at her like shiny marbles as she proceeds to enumerate all the good football-y things he did in the game, none of which I can repeat here because I have no goddamn idea what she's talking about. She goes on for a really long time, too, like she's Phyllis fucking George commentating on *Monday Night Football.*

Oh God. She's a leggy blonde who likes football and hand jobs. He's a muscular jock with a sensitive side and a huge dick.

I'm history.

sixteen

Despite Kelly and Doug's shared love of pigskin, it's me who's invited for Thanksgiving dinner and I make a point of holding Kelly's hand as we walk back to the car, leaves crunching under our feet, the crisp autumn air tight against our skin. I lean her up against MoM and we make out right there in the parking lot, stopping occasionally to wave hello to someone we know. She tastes so good and her body feels so right in my hands, like we were designed to fit together. In fact, this whole going-to-the-big-game-with-your-girlfriend thing feels so normal and all-American, the way being a teenager is supposed to feel, that for a moment I allow myself to imagine I'm some preppy guy with craggy Kennedyesque features and windswept hair. I grip Kelly tighter.

I don't want to let go of her or that feeling.

✳   ✳   ✳

It's warm inside the house and smells of good food cooking. Kelly and I go into the kitchen where Kathleen struggles with the pages of a recipe book with floury hands. There's an open bottle of Chardonnay on the counter next to her.

"Isn't it a little early for wine?" Kelly asks.

"It's just for cooking," Kathleen snaps. This is not an easy day for her. Neither of her other kids are coming home, what with Brad having gone to his girlfriend's parents and Bridget spending her junior year abroad. "Oh, sweetie," she says to me, "Paula Amicadora keeps calling." She hands me an electric bill with a phone number written on the back. While Kelly helps with dinner and acts as her mother's Chardon-nay sayer, I hunt for the phone amid the nuclear holocaust that is the living room. I've just found it underneath a copy of *When Bad Things Happen to Good People* when the Lincoln Continental Divide pulls up in front of the house.

I dash out into the yard in time to see Paula flounce out of the car while it's still practically moving, all bouncing hair and boobs.

"*Edward!*" she cries, her wide mouth in full curtain-up-light-the-lights mode. She's wearing a raspberry beret with a long ostrich feather coming out of it and a full-length coat made of crushed velvet the color of crushed frogs. She leaps across the lawn and practically picks me up as she hugs me. We part and she smacks me on the shoulder with a purse made of fake fur. "What the *fuck* is going on?" she says.

"What do you mean?"

"I called your house and Colonel Klink refused to tell me where you were—absolutely *refused*—so I tried here and Kelly's mom said you were at the football game—the fucking *football* game, of all things—so I knew at once that something had to be *terribly, terribly* wrong."

"I *was* at the fucking football game," I say, savoring the irony.

Paula gives me a stunned, horror-movie look. "Who the fuck are you and what have you done with Edward Zanni?" she says.

"What's with you and the word *fuck*?" I ask.

"Oh, it's a New York thing," she says, flipping her scarf over her shoulder, then adding conspiratorially, "and not only am I saying it, Edward—I'm *doing* it, too."

"No!" I scream.

"Yes!" she screams back, patty-caking her tiny hands together and jumping up and down.

I grab a hunk of flesh on her arm and lead her to the porch swing. "Tell me everything."

"Well," she says, "his name is Gino Marinelli. I know, he sounds like a macaroni dish, but he's this brilliant film student at NYU. We met when I auditioned for his film."

"You're going to be in a movie?" I ask.

"Actually, he hasn't decided yet, but who cares, I'm no longer a *virgin*! Isn't that *rapturous*? Me, the girl who always had to play the mother." Paula pulls out a compact to inspect her face. "Oh, and it's made such a difference in my craft, Edward, you wouldn't believe it. I did an improv where I reenacted losing my virginity and my professor gave me an A plus! An A *plus*!"

"You simulated sex in front of the whole class?"

"No silly, I did that one privately, you know, because it was so personal and revealing. Oh, Edward, you must, you absolutely *must* get into Juilliard. It is so . . . *profound*. And next year, oh my God, next year, you'll never guess who's coming to teach. C'mon, guess."

"Uh . . ."

"John Gielgud. Sir John fucking Gielgud. Can you believe it? Edward, are you all right? Do you have to throw up?"

"I'm okay," I say from between my knees.

"What's going on? C'mon, you're scaring me."

"Oh, Sis . . ."

I reach for her tiny teardrop hand and relate my whole sordid family drama. It feels good to talk to her, but strange that my life could change so drastically in such a short time. When I finish Paula stands up, pulls off her gloves, and says, "Well, there's only one thing for you to do."

"Patricide?"

"No," she says. "You've got to declare financial independence."

"Financial independence? What's that?"

"It means you emancipate yourself. I know some people who've done it. You've got to move out of Al's house and refuse to accept any money from him so he can't claim you as a dependent on his taxes. That way the school will only look at your finances instead of his and you'll be eligible for financial aid."

The storm clouds in my head start to clear. "I can really do that?" I ask.

"Absolutely."

"That's great!"

"Of course, you need to show three years of independent tax returns before they'll consider you."

"Three years? But I'll be almost twenty-one by then. I'll be ancient."

"True," Paula says, "but at least you'll be eligible for your senior year, which means we only have to figure out how to pay for the first three. Or you could get in, defer a year, make some money, and then have the last two years paid for. Oh, we'll figure something out. Don't worry."

"But what about Sir John fucking Gielgud?"

"Oh, *that*," Paula says. "I'm sure all the stuff they say about him being a brilliant teacher is just hype. I'll take lots of notes for you, I promise. The most important thing is that you look out for yourself. Why should Al get to keep you as a tax deduction when he refuses to support you? You've got to get out of that house by your eighteenth birthday, Edward, you've simply *got* to!"

"But that's just five weeks away," I say.

"Then I suggest you start packing."

❄   ❄   ❄

Kathleen's so Chardonnayed out by the time we finish dinner she staggers to bed, at which point Kelly begins tearing off my clothes like I'm a birthday present she can't wait to unwrap. I suspect her horniness has something to do with seeing Doug be all rugged on the field today, but I figure a make-out session is just the thing I need to get my mind off my worries. We go down to the basement.

Now, if you've been reading carefully you realize that going down to the basement means we're in Kathleen's office where she sees her cryents. But if you're thinking I'm unaware of the symbolic implications of making out on a psychotherapist's couch, well, then you'd be right. It doesn't even occur to me.

We stumble onto the couch, attached at the tongue, clothes flying. I grab Kelly's breasts like I'm holding on for dear life. She gasps.

"Sorry," I whisper.

"That's okay," she says, "I like it," and digs her fingernails into my back. You'd think by now I'd be used to Kelly's sexual appetite, but her girl-next-door looks always manage to throw me off. I give her a vigorous, tonsil-licking kiss and she reaches for my crotch and that's when I realize it.

I'm not hard.

This has never happened before; normally I go up like a flag in a park. I feel a slight flush of panic, but I tell myself it's a momentary lapse and grab Kelly's hand to suck on her fingers and buy myself some time, then start feeling her up so aggressively it's like I'm performing CPR.

Nothing. Nothing at all.

What the hell is wrong with me? Mission control to penis—are you there? Kelly grinds her hips against mine and I bump and hump to try to get something to happen, but nothing doing: my cock is simply not a member in good standing.

The thought of Kelly reaching into my pants expecting a hot dog and finding a cocktail wiener instead is just too excruciating, particularly after handling Doug's Polish sausage. So I do what any sensible person would do: I go down on her.

I've never done it before and figure my timing has got to be off because I'm just diving in when Kelly moans, "Oh yeah, talk to me."

Like I don't have enough on my mind, now I have to provide a simultaneous running commentary. I knew I shouldn't have bought her that subscription to *Cosmo*.

"What do you want me to . . ."

"Don't stop," she says, mashing my face into her crotch.

"I dnt thnk I cn tlk lk ths," I say into her pelvis. I sound just like the muffled teacher's voice in the Peanuts cartoons.

"Oh yeah, that's it," she purrs.

"I cnt brth."

She shivers and her pink skin turns to gooseflesh. I'm glad to see one of us is having a good time.

"Yu dnt ndrstnd."

"More," she says.

I have no idea what to talk about, never having conversed with a vagina before, so I say the first thing that pops into my head: *Listen, my children, and you shall hear/Of the midnight ride of Paul Revere.*

I'm not sure this is what Mrs. Sugden had in mind when she assigned it in the fourth grade, but I am here to tell you that Longfellow's poem and a supple tongue make an effective substitute if you do not have a long fellow of your own available. (So does "I am the very model of a modern major general," as it turns out.) More important, it keeps Kelly happy, and that's all I'm worried about. At one point she tries to curve her body around like maybe she should reciprocate, but I stop her by popping my head up and saying in my best sensitive, New Age-y, pro-feminist, Alan Alda–like way, "Let's just focus on you, okay?"

Kelly lies back, relieved to not have to bother, and stretches her arms out like she's a cat wanting her belly scratched, or in this case, wanting her cat scratched, I guess. I cup her firm butt in my hands as I reach deeper inside her with my tongue and start reciting all the various Shakespeare monologues I've memorized. She gasps and bucks her hips like she's trying to swallow me whole, which, frankly, would suit me just fine. I'm so freaked about not being hard there's nothing I'd like better than to peel back the secret layers of her and crawl inside, feeling my way along the dark, moist walls of her vagina until I've disappeared completely, leaving the world and my flaccid dick behind me. Then I could just curl up like a baby inside her womb, all quiet and warm and peaceful.

The good news is that my strategy works: for those of you who aspire to be cunning linguists, you should know that rapid iambic pentameter drives my girlfriend so wild that she almost boxes my ears in with her thighs when she comes.

The bad news is that now she wants to do it all the time.

seventeen

It only takes a few sessions for Kelly to grow suspicious of my "I only care about your orgasm, honey" attitude. I'm a seventeen-year-old guy; it's not natural to be so considerate. But no matter what I do, my cock is still as limp as a cooked carrot. It's freaking me out.

Things are no better on the job front. Desperate for any kind of work, I answer an ad for a chambermaid at a motel out on the highway. The manager, an old Asian lady, doesn't get it.

"Why you wanna be chambermaid?" she says. "You a boy."

"I just need a job and figured since I'm very clean . . ."

"But you a boy."

"Does that matter?"

"I don't want no trouble."

"I'm not making . . ."

"You a boy. Go get boy job. I don't want no trouble."

We continue in this vein until I realize that either I'm encountering some huge cultural divide or this woman is seriously insane.

My only option left is the mall. I can't believe it's come to this. I'm from Colonial Wallingford, for God's sake. We don't even shop at the mall.

I answer a help wanted ad for a fast-food place called Chicken Lickin'. I'm demoralized at the thought of working anywhere that sounds like an adorable Beatrix Potter character and I pray I don't have to wear a stupid hat. Chicken Lickin' is in the food court, an orange-and-yellow assault on humanity that Dante, were he alive today, would surely have included as one of his rings of Hell. Onion rings of Hell, to be precise. I wait in line behind two guys with combs in the back pockets of their Jordaches, confirming that this is indeed the Mall That

Time Forgot. The girl behind the counter has a blond frizzy perm with black roots—less of a hairdo and more of a hair don't—and wears black mascara on both upper and lower eyelashes for that my-boyfriend-beats-me look.

"Welcome to Chicken Lickin'. How can I help yuz?" she says without actually moving her lips.

Jordache Guy #1 leans his crotch against the counter and says, "Yeah, uh, are you the chick I get to lick?" He looks over his shoulder at Jordache Guy #2, who punches him in the arm and pants a voiceless laugh. Obviously National Merit scholars.

"That depends," Miss Hair Don't mumbles. "Are you the dick whose ass I kick?"

The Jordache guys don't know what to say, so they just get an order of Chicken Pickins, pay, and make a hasty exit. "Have a chick-a-licious day," Miss Hair Don't says in a tone that's usually reserved for phrases like "Come near me and I'll break both of your fucking legs."

I step up to the counter and announce I'm here about the job. Miss Hair Don't responds with the same level of unbridled enthusiasm.

"So?" she says.

I fill out an application full of lies and hand it back to her. I tell her I really need a job and that I'm available for any shift outside of school hours.

"That's good," she says, " 'cuz, here at Chicken Lickin' we do things the Chicken Lickin' way. We don't work around no one's schedule. We pay more than minimum wage, y'know, so we expect more of yuz."

Minimum wage is $3.25 per hour. Chicken Lickin' pays $3.35 per hour. I'm not at the job more than a day before I start calibrating what I think constitutes ten cents an hour more of effort. What's worse is that I continually get shifts with a girl too stupid to realize that this job sucks. We call her Nice Shirt, because she always has some cheery compliment for every single person with an IQ low enough to want to actually eat at Chicken Lickin'. "Ooh, where'd you get your earrings?" she'll coo, or "I like your pants," or her signature line: "Nice shirt!" Customers love her.

She makes the rest of us look bad.

I entertain myself by imagining Nice Shirt in other social situations where her chipper demeanor might be less appreciated, like a funeral ("Nice casket!"), or the hospital ("Cool catheter!"), or a prison ("Love your jumpsuit, where'd ya' get it?"). Sometimes I just fantasize about drowning the silly bitch in the deep fryer.

I feel like Pip in *Great Expectations*, working at a job I loathe and am certain I'm too good for. Like Pip, I too have great expectations, or as Sinatra would say, high hopes, although it's hard to keep them in mind when your job requires you to say things like "Would you care for one of our chick-a-riffic side dishes?" At least I don't run into anyone I know except TeeJay, who works weekends at Meister Burger. Occasionally we'll nod a brief but solemn hello to one another across the food court, like we're in prison and don't want the warden to notice us communicating. His boss, a sweaty lump of a guy with a comb-over, is always standing over him at the grill, carping about something.

To add to the endless cycle of misery that is my life, I continue to endure playing basketball in gym. As with football, I have no idea how to play this ridiculous game, nor do I care to learn. It all seems like a lot of gratuitous running back and forth to me, which is exactly what I do, in the hopes that I'll appear to be playing the game when in actuality I am avoiding it. As expected, Ms. Burro makes us play shirts and skins, which is particularly demoralizing because I haven't taken a dance class all fall and now have the added pressure of trying to scamper about without letting any accumulated fat jiggle unbecomingly.

It's exhausting.

Once again, not only am I the worst player but I am also the oldest and, once again, I have to contend with Darren O'Boyle, the evil sophomore, who looks like he's going to have an aneurysm every time I make a little mistake like pass the ball to someone on the other team. (How do mean kids get so mean? Are their parents mean, too? Say what you want about Al and Barbara Zanni, at least they didn't raise mean kids.) Smashing my finger with a hammer is starting to sound more attractive.

As if that weren't bad enough, I'm growing increasingly panicked about my Juilliard audition. Even the thought of performing my monologues for Mr. Lucas in drama class makes me constipated. I don't know what the hell's wrong with me. Usually I can't wait to get onstage. I ask Ziba to follow on book in case I need prompting.

I come out onstage and face the big black giant that is the audience. "I am Edward Zanni . . ." I say. (Mr. Lucas told me to say "I am" instead of "My name is" because it sounds more confident and assertive.) "And this is Haemon's monologue from Sophocles' *Antigone*."

So far so good. I close my eyes to collect myself, then look up to begin.

I can't remember a fucking thing.

"I'm sorry, can I start again?" I say.

"NO!" Mr. Lucas bellows, his voice echoing in the darkness like the voice of God. "Pretend this is the real audition."

"I'm sorry. I guess I'm a little nervous," I say.

"Keep going."

What the fuck is happening? I know this monologue cold. I must've recited it into Kelly's vagina a gazillion times. I close my eyes again to collect myself. The first line is "Father, you must not think that your word and no other must be so." Got it. I look up.

"Father, you must not think that your word and no other must be so. For if any man thinks that he alone is wise . . ."

Oh, God.

"Line?" I say.

"That in what he says and what he does . . ." Ziba says.

"That in what he says and what he does . . . uh . . ."

This can't be happening to me.

"Line?"

"That man is but an empty tomb . . ."

"That in what he says and what he does he's above all else — that man is but an empty tomb . . ."

"A wise man," Ziba says.

"I know it, don't tell me," I say. "A wise man . . . A wise man . . ."

". . . isn't ashamed . . ."

". . . isn't ashamed to admit his ignorance and he understands that true power lies in being . . ." I stop. "I'm sorry, I can't seem to do it," I say. My entire body is soaked in flop sweat. I see Kelly and Natie in the front row, looking pained.

"Of course you can," Mr. Lucas says. "You're doing fine. Don't worry."

Oh shit. If Mr. Lucas is being nice, then I must really suck.

"Just give me a second," I say. Okay, Edward, concentrate. Concentrate. Concentrate.

"I have no idea what comes next," I say.

"Ziba, please read the rest of the passage to Edward."

Ziba reads:

"Have you seen after a winter storm how the trees that stand beside the torrential streams yield to it and save their branches, while the stiff and rigid perish, root and all? Or how a sailor who always keeps his sail taut and never slackens will only capsize his boat?

"Father, I may be young, but you must listen to reason. Please, I beg you to soften your heart and allow a change from your rage."

"Maybe you ought to be auditioning for Juilliard instead of me," I say, trying to laugh.

"Just finish," Mr. Lucas says.

I clear my throat and crack my neck. "Okay," I say, "Have you ever seen after a winter storm how a sailor keeps his sail taut . . . and, oh, that's not right . . ."

"Keep going!" Mr. Lucas bellows.

"And his root stiff and rigid," I yell back.

The class laughs and my face starts to burn.

I'm going to work at Chicken Lickin' for the rest of my life.

Afterward, Ziba suggests that she, Kelly, Natie, and I go to the movies, y'know, to take my mind off my troubles (which, as far as I'm concerned, is really just another way of saying I sucked). So we go see *Yentl*.

Now I'm going to assume that anyone reading this story has a working knowledge of the Barbra Streisand oeuvre, but just in case you don't, I'll fill you in. *Yentl* is about a young Jewish girl in Eastern Europe at the turn of the century who disguises herself as a boy so she can go to yeshiva and study. There she falls in love with another student who, of course, doesn't realize she's a girl. It's like *Tootsie on the Roof*.

As I sit in the darkened theater I realize that I am *so* like Yentl: we're both prevented from going to the school of our dreams, we both break into song in public places, and we're both so in love with our best friend it's almost physically painful.

It's true. Despite my erection problems with Kelly, one look at Doug and I'm harder than calculus.

I don't share this insight, of course, but instead listen to Ziba as she analyzes the film on the way back to the car. Ziba takes "the cinema" very seriously, which you can tell because she always makes us sit through the credits and she compares everything to the works of Kurosawa. "The direction was surprisingly polished," she announces, "and the cinematography was astounding, but I still think it would have served the story better if the whole thing had been in Yiddish with subtitles."

This from the Muslim girl.

"I think Barbra Streisand should have actually had sex with Amy Irving," Kelly says.

We all stop.

"What are you looking at?" she asks.

Even though she agreed to a three-way and asked me to talk dirty into her vagina, I'm still surprised when Kelly says things like this.

"Interesting," Ziba says, as she chews over the notion. "But how would she get around not having a penis?"

Kelly thinks for a moment. "She could go down on her."

I don't like where this conversation is heading, so I change the subject. "Anyone notice how Yentl wore the same glasses as Father Groovy?" I say.

"Yeah," Natie says. "Maybe you oughta go live in a yeshiva."

"I don't think they let in Catholics."

"Okay, a monastery."

Suddenly Kelly throws her arm in front of me, the way you do when you want to stop someone from stepping into traffic. "That's it," she says.

"What?"

"You could live at my house."

"What are you talking about? Your mom would never go for that."

"She would if she thought you were gay."

"But I'm not," I say, my voice rising higher than I intended.

" 'Course not, silly," Kelly says. "You'd just pretend to be—y'know, like Yentl pretends to be a boy."

Natie nods his head like he's impressed. "Y'know, that's not a bad idea."

Kelly's eyes brighten with excitement. "It'll be great!" she says. "I'll tell my mom we broke up and of course she'll want to psychoanalyze me, so I'll go on about how you broke my heart but I understand because you're gay, but still I'm not sure I can ever trust men again, blah, blah, blah . . ."

Natie and Ziba continue this train wreck of thought with her, cheerfully hypothesizing about the various ways that Kelly could have discovered my latent homosexuality. While they entertain themselves with the presumably hilarious notion that Doug and I are secret lovers, Kelly leans over and whispers in my ear. "The best part," she says, "is now we can be together any time we want."

As they say in the yeshiva: Oy vey.

eighteen

I don't go home after I drop everyone off, but instead drive around try-ing to sort out Kelly's idea. If I tell Kathleen I'm gay, I'd kind of be telling her the truth, but I'd actually be lying to Kelly, because she thinks I'm totally straight. On the other hand, if Kelly and I are fooling around, then I'd definitely be lying to Kathleen. Then again, how much of a threat can I be to her daughter if I don't have an erection? The whole thing makes my head hurt.

On top of everything else, thoughts of Doug keep knocking at the door of my subconscious. I know he's way too Timberland boots and flannel shirt-y to ever feel about me the way I feel about him, but the forbidden, star-crossed-lovers thing is partly what makes him so ap-pealing. I see us as a modern Romeo and Juliet or, in this case, Romeo and Julius. I imagine us growing up and getting married (to women, I mean) but still carrying on annual clandestine trysts in the manner of *Same Time, Next Year.* I see us renting a cabin with our unsuspecting wives, then stealing away to the woods where we'll fuck like the rugged, outdoorsy men we truly are.

I can't stand it any longer. Just thinking about him is torture, but an almost exquisite kind, like the transcendental agony you see in the paintings of martyred saints. I must be losing my mind.

I drive over to his house.

It's too late to ring the bell, so I prowl along the creaking front porch and peek in the window. Someone is sitting in Mr. Grabowski's uneasy chair watching scrambled porn on cable, but I can't tell who it is from behind. I'm almost sure that it's Doug from the tufts of kinky hair rising above the back of the chair, but I don't want to risk it being his creepy dad, either. Finally, the figure rises and stretches and I see from the boxers and football jersey that it is indeed Doug. I tap on the window. Cupping his eyes with his hands, he leans against the glass to see who it is, then indicates he'll let me in the front door.

"What's up?" he whispers.

"We need to talk," I say, pushing past him.

The room feels suffocatingly small for the enormous thing I'm about to say and I pace the dingy carpet like a caged animal. Doug looks concerned.

"What's wrong, man?" he says.

"I don't know how to say this, except to just come out with it."

"What did you do, kill somebody?"

"I'm serious."

"Okay," he says, "then just say it."

I'm certain my lungs have collapsed and that there's no possible way I can draw enough air to speak, but there must be because I hear myself blurt out, "I'm in love with you." Just like that, as if the words fell out of my mouth and landed on the floor.

Then it's like I can't shut up. "I'm sorry, I had to tell you; I couldn't keep it inside me anymore. I am totally, head over heels in love with you. I think about you a thousand times a day, and even more at night. I don't know what to do anymore. It takes every bit of discipline I have not to leap across a room and grab you whenever I see you."

Which is exactly what I want to do right now. I want to grab him and kiss him forever, but I don't dare. I'm guessing Doug's more likely to let me blow him before he'd ever submit to something as intimate as a kiss.

Doug doesn't say a word, but his icicle eyes begin to melt. I'm not sure he even realizes it because his face remains expressionless as the tears stream down his cheeks, like water trickling out of a rock at a river base. I can't even begin to understand what this reaction means.

"I'm so sorry," he whispers. "I just . . . can't."

✳   ✳   ✳

I drive around the dark, sleepy streets of Wallingford feeling deflated and spent. I'm such an idiot. I had this great, intense friendship with lots of touchy-feely, homoerotic action and then, like Frank says, "I go and spoil it all by saying something stupid like I love you." Doug will probably never talk to me again. What's more, I've got nowhere to live, I can't remember the words to Haemon's fucking monologue, my father doesn't care about me, my stepmother hates me, my mother has probably been kidnapped by South American guerrillas, and I've eaten so many baskets of Chicken Pickins that my pants don't fit. Then, to top it all off, I've got to play basketball with a bunch of sophomores out of *Lord of the Flies*. Something's got to give.

It's time for the hammer.

I drag myself into our dark kitchen and open the junk drawer to hunt for a hammer to break my finger, but instead of the usual assortment of paper clips, twist ties, and rubber bands, I'm surprised to see my sister's face staring back at me, tanned and airbrushed, blissfully unaware that she's inside a junk drawer instead of on the wall where she belongs. I pull out Karen's picture and there I am underneath, looking smiley and carefree in my skinny tie. I spin around to look at the wall where our school portraits have hung for the last ten years and see that we've been replaced by one of Dagmar's photographs, a still life of a bowl of fruit.

Now maybe, just maybe, if she'd replaced us with something of equal sentimental value like, say, her ancestral Austrian home or a portrait of her precious Nazi collaborationist father, then *maybe* I wouldn't get so upset. But to be replaced by a goddamn bowl of fruit—that does it.

I snap. Like a rigid root in winter.

Al saunters into the kitchen in nothing but his bikini briefs, looking like the first guy in the evolution of man to walk on two legs.

"You want to explain this to me?" I say, pointing to the photograph.

"Like it?" Al says, scratching his hairy belly and opening the fridge. "Dagmar won some prize for it last weekend."

"Well, lah dee fucking dah," I say.

Al glances over his shoulder. "Hey, watch your fucking language."

"You just don't get it, do you?" I say, my voice rising. I grab our pictures out of the junk drawer. "Don't you see what she's trying to do? She's stuck us in the *junk drawer*. Your own kids. Doesn't that mean anything to you?"

"Don't be so sensitive," Al says.

There are certain phrases I can't abide hearing, and "Don't be so sensitive" ranks right up there with "Could you please keep it down?" and "No personal calls allowed." I feel a surge of rage course through me. "How can you support her career as an artist and not mine?"

"What I do with my money is my own goddamned business," Al

says, slamming the refrigerator door. "I could spend it all on bubble gum and blow jobs if I wanted."

"You got that half right," I mutter.

Al waves a hairy finger in my face. "You watch your mouth, you little shit. That's my wife you're talking about, and I'll have you know that woman does more for me than you or your lazy-ass sister ever have. All these years I've raised you by myself and I've gotten nothin' but grief in return."

"I see. All those straight A's I've gotten, and the awards, and the leads in the plays, that's been grief to you, huh?"

"I'm talkin' about respect. And obedience. And maybe some appreciation once in a while. You think I can't see how you sneer at me, Mr. Honor Roll, like I'm too dumb to notice? You and your sister treat me like I'm a fuckin' bank machine. Well, finally somebody comes along who thinks about me for a change. Somebody who cooks and cleans for me and cares for me and loves me; so, yeah, you're damn right, I'm gonna support her."

"So you're saying if I could fuck you, you'd support me, too?"

"Why, you sick little . . ."

"Well, here you go, watch me," I say, then I point to my mouth and enunciate in my best actor's elocution: *Fuck . . . you!*

It feels really good to finally say it.

From behind me I hear a growl like the mouth of Hell opening and I turn just in time to duck a wineglass being thrown in my direction.

"Asshole!" Dagmar screams, except, being foreign, she gets it all wrong, putting the accent on the last syllable. "Azz*hull*! Get out, you fuckink azz*huuull*!"

She lunges for me, claws bared, and Al has to hold her back. "You ungrateful azz*hull*, you . . . you . . ." she struggles for the word, ". . . *Schwanzlutscher.*"

Now, thanks to Doug, I happen to know she just called me a cocksucker, which gives me the satisfying opportunity of leaning my face right into hers and saying, "Well, it takes one to know one, you evil bitch."

Dagmar's eyes go wide and she flails like a mad dog, huffing and sputtering, undoubtedly enraged because, as a non-native speaker of English, she's not able to think of a good comeback. I brush past her into the entryway, a little more like Bette Davis than I intended.

"Call me when she's dead," I say, then slam the front door behind me.

I lean against the door to catch my breath, the sharp cold air piercing my skin. From inside, I can still hear Dagmar screaming like a crazed harpy.

"Azz*huuuull.*"

I start to run, trying to put as much distance between me and the House of Floor Wax as I can.

nineteen

I run all the way to Kelly's, banging on the door like a madman until Kathleen answers. I'm soaked with sweat and the frozen air in my lungs burns me from the inside out. I collapse in Kathleen's arms, hyperventilating and feeling like I'm going to throw up. Kelly appears at the top of the stairs. "Get a blanket," Kathleen says, "quick."

"Why do they hate me so much," I gasp. "Why?" I feel like I'm drowning and I grip onto her like she's a lifeline. "I just want to go to college, I just want to be an actor, I just want . . ."

"I know, dear. Ssh. Everything's going to be all right." I sink slowly onto the floor and Kathleen goes right with me, wrapping me in a wool blanket.

"I don't get it," I say. "There are so many kids who are so fucking ordinary and their parents love them. And I do so much and . . ."

"Ssh," she says, "just rest." She tells Kelly to get something warm for me to change into.

"He'll be sorry," I say. "He'll be sorry when I'm famous and don't thank him when I accept my Oscar. He'll be sorry when he realizes his kids hate him. I'll show him . . ."

Kathleen doesn't say anything, but just holds me tight, humming and rubbing my back the same way my mother did when she sang me to sleep.

> *I'm a lonely little petunia in an onion patch,*
> *And all I do is cry all day . . .*

Kelly returns. Out of the corner of my ear I hear Kathleen whisper, "What the hell is that?"

"It's all I could find," Kelly whispers back.

"Edward, sweetie," Kathleen says, "you need to get out of these wet clothes and into this." I open my eyes and look down to see that she's handed me a tartan flannel nightgown. It's got a white ruffle at the collar. For the first time in what feels like forever, I laugh. We all do.

"If your father could see you now," Kathleen says.

I go to change while Kathleen cracks open a bottle of wine and pours us each a big glassful. "Merry fucking Christmas," she says.

"And a happy fucking New Year," I reply, clinking glasses.

Then the three of us get completely bombed, even though it's a school night. Kelly is particularly affected and decides, for reasons known only to her, to put on the *Evita* album and perform the entire thing for us, after which she crawls into the corner behind the tree and says, "Hi, everybody, I'm the talking Christmas tree. Merry fucking Christmas," before passing out.

Kathleen and I sit in the dark watching the blinking lights. "What am I gonna do?" I ask.

She swirls her wine in her glass. "You'll live here with us, of course."

"So Kelly told you . . ."

Kathleen laughs. "About you being gay? Oh, sweetheart, I figured it out on my own."

While I'm glad to see Kelly's plan worked, a little incredulity on Kathleen's part would have been nice.

"Do you honestly think I'd let you live here if I thought you were screwing around with my daughter?"

I must look tense again because Kathleen reaches over and rubs my back. "Stop worrying," she says. "Just for tonight, okay? You can worry again tomorrow, I promise." She exhales and so do I and I begin to feel warm and safe again. "Now why don't you go put that star on top of the tree where it belongs?"

On what must be the worst night of my life, I don't think I've ever been so happy.

※　※　※

Part of the deal with declaring financial independence is that you can't accept more than $700 of support a year from your parents, which means I have to pretty much give up everything: no money, no insurance, no car, nothing. Leaving MoM behind is the hardest. Natie and I actually consider parking his parents' car at the bottom of a hill and releasing the parking brake on mine so it totals both and Al has to pay for a new one for the Nudelmans. But in the end, I do like my mother did and just walk out, taking only my books and my clothes and a couple of records from Al's Sinatra collection. I do score a little extra cash by placing an ad in the *Thrifties* and selling my bedroom furniture. (Another Natie idea.) When Al discovers it's gone he says to me, "That wasn't your furniture to sell. I own that furniture."

"No," I say, "Marvin Nelson of Camptown, New Jersey, owns that furniture." Possession is nine-tenths of the law.

Al shakes his head. "How much did you get for it?"

"Five hundred bucks," I say.

"That much?" he says. "Marvin got took." We both smile and laugh a little. Naturally Al's against me moving out, calling it "selfish." He can't even bring himself to refer to Kathleen's house except by its address, as if I were simply moving into one of his investment properties. But my decision to leave has actually eased the tension a little and occasionally we even have a quasi-friendly moment, like this one at Marvin's expense. Dagmar, on the other hand, seems to have radar that goes off anytime Al and I are remotely civil to one another, and she stalks in, rubbing lotion on her rough, calloused hands.

"Tsis room looks zo much bigger vitsout all tsat crap in it," she says.

Bitch.

Paula comes home, full of vigor and enthusiasm from her first idyllic semester at Juilliard, which naturally irritates the shit out of me. She's prepared to pick up right where the Creative Vandals left off, visiting the Buddha and rearranging someone's Nativity scene so it's the Adoration of the Lawn Jockey, but my heart's just not in it. Last summer seems like a lifetime ago, and I feel old and jaded and bitter. Most of the time I can barely stand being inside my own skin. I can't sleep. I can't concentrate. The only thing I can seem to do is eat, so when Aunt Glo offers me Christmas cookies I figure, what's the diff?

Aunt Glo asks us to sing for her, so Paula and I harmonize on a few Christmas carols while Aunt Glo rolls out dough and cries. The sound of Paula's velvety voice makes me want to cry myself (that is, assuming I could). I look at her wide mouth parted in a blissful smile, her fleshy throat smooth and relaxed as the sound flows out of her like water. She's so open, so uncomplicated, so free.

I'd like to strangle her sometimes.

Afterward, Paula asks me to do my audition monologues.

"I thought I'd start with my contemporary one," I say.

"Oh, no, no, no" Paula says, "begin with the classical. That's what they're really interested in. It's all about classical training. We're even taking fencing." She leaps up to demonstrate various "en garde" and "touché" type moves. "Isn't it *splendid*?"

Paula and Aunt Glo take their seats while I psych myself up for Haemon's monologue.

"Okay, Edward, nice and easy," I tell myself. "You can do it. Just relax. Relax. Relax, goddamnit!"

I'm so freaked I might forget my lines that I speak v-e-r-y s-l-o-w-l-y like Haemon's got a learning disability. Paula squints as she watches me, as if I were far away. When I'm finished, she says, "You wouldn't have anything else, would you?"

"Well, there is Mercutio's death scene," I say.

"Oh, that sounds *grand*," Paula says. "Don't you think so, Aunt Glo?"

"Oh yeah, I love a good death scene. Didja see *Terms of Endearment*? That Debbie Winger, she sure died good in that."

I perform Mercutio's death scene and this time Paula tries to keep a placid expression on her face, but she can't help but wince and twitch from time to time. I stop in the middle.

"You hate it," I say. "I can tell."

"I don't hate it," she says. "Besides, you shouldn't be focusing on how I react, you should be focusing on the scene."

"What's wrong with it?"

"Well . . . you just seem, I don't know, disconnected from the pain."

"Jesus Christ—excuse me, Aunt Glo—what is so great about pain?"

Paula picks an imaginary thread off of her long woolly skirt. "I don't suppose you have anything else, do you?"

"There's always 'Bottom's Dream,' but . . ."

"Oh, yes, do 'Bottom's Dream,' absolutely," she says. "Don't you think so, Aunt Glo?"

"Dreams are nice," Aunt Glo says. "I had a dream once that Liberace unclogged my drains."

"See?" Paula says. She smiles her curtain-up-light-the-lights smile to encourage me.

So I do "Bottom's Dream," followed by my contemporary monologue from *Amadeus*. Paula and Aunt Glo laugh in all the right places. "Definitely these two," Paula says. "Trust me."

"But they're so much alike. Shouldn't I do something that shows off my range?"

"Not if you don't have a ra . . . not everyone is suited for dramatic scenes, Edward. Don't worry, it'll be fine."

Fine? It can't just be fine. It has to be kick-ass amazing. I've sacrificed everything for this: I've moved out of my house, I've given up my car, I've gone to work at Chicken Lickin', for Chrissake.

"And don't be concerned if they don't ask for a second monologue," Paula says. "That doesn't necessarily mean they didn't like you."

Yes it does. Everyone knows that.

I'm doomed.

twenty

Kathleen and Kelly go to "Nana's house" on the Cape for a huge Kennedy-style Christmas, leaving me with two neurotic cats and a station wagon so old we call it the Wagon Ho. I don't want to feel like some pathetic Dickensian orphan at someone else's family holiday, so naturally I turn to Natie.

"What do Jews do on Christmas?" I ask him.

"Go to the movies and eat Chinese food," he says. "Ya' can't beat it."

On Christmas Day we see *Terms of Endearment*. Aunt Glo is right: that Debbie Winger does die good. I sit in the theater, wincing, trying to connect with her pain, searching for that reservoir of emotion in myself.

"You all right?" Natie whispers.

"I'm fine," I say through gritted teeth.

"Chinese food gives me gas, too," he says.

The Thursday after Christmas I take the train into the city with Paula because my audition's at ten o'clock the next morning. I've chosen a bulky black turtleneck to wear because (A) black is slimming and (B) I can wear it untucked so no one can see that my jeans are too tight. I wear a pair of black Keds with it, and my long thrift-store overcoat. Paula thinks it's a good look for me. "Very Serious Young Actor," she says. "You'll be *splendid*, I'm sure!" She squeezes my arm to give me encouragement, but the more she tries to boost me up, the more convinced I am that I must suck. Otherwise, why would I need a boost?

Paula lives in Hell's Kitchen, though the neighborhood looks more like Hell's Bathroom to me. It's like Beirut, except colder. A couple of hookers shivering in miniskirts and fake furs stand outside her building and Paula cheerfully greets them both.

The taller one leans in to kiss her. "Thank you, child, for that Shalimar you left me," she says.

"And the penicillin," says the other. "Girl, you're a godsend."

"Well, Merry Christmas to you both," Paula says, beaming. "This is my friend Edward." I reach out to shake the hookers' hands and notice that the taller one is a guy. His (her? okay, her) big mascaraed eyes bore into me.

"I'm Anita," she says, "Anita Mandalay. Now where you been hidin', sweet thang?"

"Uh . . . New Jersey?" I say.

"Well, you better watch out, I might just stuff you in my stockin'." Anita throws her head back and laughs, revealing a mouth full of gold fillings. And herpes sores, no doubt.

"Nice meeting you," I say. We go inside. The whole place smells like sweaty feet. Paula calls it rent controlled, which is an optimistic way of saying it's a welfare hotel.

"Isn't this place fucking *wild*?" Paula says. "The people are so *real*. Next door to me there's an unwed teen mother whose boyfriend is a drug dealer. And across the hall are Pakistanis who set up rugs outside my door and pray to Mecca."

"Which way is Mecca from here?"

"Down the hall and past the bathroom," she says.

"You share a bathroom?"

"You get used to it. Oh, Edward, living here has done *so* much for my acting."

"Sure, if you ever play a Muslim drug dealer."

"Don't be so provincial. Ooh, look at the time," she says, glancing at her ankle. "We've got to meet Gino downtown in half an hour and he hates it when I'm late. Do you need to use the bathroom before we go?"

I peek at the room with the rusty plumbing, the cracked tile, and the peeling paint. I'd rather get toxic shock.

"I can wait," I say.

Paula and I take the subway down to the Village to have dinner with her boyfriend, the pasta-monikered Gino Marinelli. We arrive at a Greek diner fifteen minutes early, then wait forty-five minutes for Gino to arrive.

"There he is!" Paula squeals finally. I look across the room but don't see anybody who could possibly be a Gino Marinelli.

"Where?" I ask, but Paula has already leaped up and bounded across the restaurant to grab what appears to be a pile of hair with a person attached. With a name like Gino Marinelli I've been expecting a dumpy meatball of a guy, but this Gino looks like a bass player for a heavy metal band. He's got long, skinny legs shrink-wrapped in the tightest of stone-washed jeans and wears a leather jacket with shoulder pads the size of a linebacker's. I can't see his face, partly because of all the hair, but also because he gives Paula a long, sloppy tongue kiss without actually touching her lips, the way you'd imagine Mick Jagger would kiss Gene Simmons. He grabs her big, soft butt with both hands and dry humps her right there until she finally extricates herself and points to me. She takes him by the hand and leads him across the restaurant while he struts behind her.

"Edward, this is Gino. Gino, Edward."

I reach out to shake his hand and he does that thing where we're supposed to knock fists, whatever the hell that's about. He slides into the booth and appraises me from under his bangs.

"I'm so *thrilled* you two are finally meeting!" Paula crows.

Gino narrows his eyes at me and I can tell immediately he doesn't feel the same way.

I paste a grin on my face and try to keep it there. "Paula tells me you're a film student at NYU."

"Gino's going to be a brilliant filmmaker," Paula says. He shoots her a sideways glance and she flushes. "I mean, he *is* a brilliant filmmaker. Tell Edward all about your student film, honey."

Gino flips open his lighter and stares at it as he flicks it on and off. "Nah, you tell him," he says, leaning back in the booth. His voice is barely audible, like it's too lazy to bother coming up out of his throat.

"Well, it's about this woman—that's me—who loses her shirt and wanders all over New York half naked looking for it. Eventually she gets bludgeoned to death in front of the Stock Exchange. There's going to be a lot of blood—it's very Scorsese."

"You're going to go topless?" I say.

"Yes, but it's very artistic," Paula says. "She loses her shirt, get it? It's a metaphor for the plight of the neglected urban poor."

"Plus she had the biggest jugs of anyone who auditioned," Gino says.

"Isn't he *funny*?" Paula squeals and covers his face with kisses, what little of his face that shows, that is. How he can possibly see through a camera lens with all that hair, I'll never know.

He shrugs her off and says, "I gotta take a leak," as he skulks away. Paula leans across the table. "So what do you think of him?" she says, flapping her tiny hands in excitement.

What do I think of him? He's horrible. He's all wrong, wrong, wrong. Give him a bath and a haircut before he takes all your money and dumps you for somebody else. He's a disgusting low-life pig and you could do so much better.

"He's great!" I say.

Wuss.

Gino comes back and orders a plate of mashed potatoes and gravy. I learn through various reluctant monosyllabic responses that he lives in Brooklyn with his parents and that he has an uncle who knows Robert De Niro, but otherwise it's Paula who works to keep the conversation afloat. Gino's only interested in one thing, or perhaps I should say two things. He leans in and whispers to her.

"Not tonight," Paula giggles. "I've got company."

Gino sticks his tongue in her ear and I see him reach his hand into her lap. Paula closes her eyes and gives a little moan. I tear my paper napkin into tiny pieces and try to pretend I don't know he's fingering her right in front of me.

He leans across the table and smiles at me for the first time. Suddenly, it's like he plugged in the sun and I can begin to understand what Paula might see in him. "Hey, Ed," he says, "you can entertain yourself for an hour or two, can't ya'?"

"Sure," I say.

"Make it three," Paula whimpers.

They leave me with the check. I finish Gino's mashed potatoes and trudge out into the cold, damp streets of Greenwich Village. I figure maybe I'll catch a movie, but I'm too nervous to sit still. So I roam around, squinting at brownstones and trying to imagine the Greenwich Village of Henry James's time when I see a sign in a window that says WE'LL PRINT ANYTHING . . . SO LONG AS YOU LET US KEEP THE GOOD ONES, and I realize I'm standing in front of Toto Photo, the place where we transformed Natie from a small, homely guy into an even homelier girl.

I must be near Something for the Boys.

I round the corner and stand across the street trying to decide whether to go in. What's the big deal, right? It's not like I haven't been before. But going into a gay bar with a group of friends from high school is very different from going in alone. Anything could happen by myself. Any*one* could happen.

What the hell am I waiting for?

The place is only half full, and a number of guys look up when I come in the door. No one's performing, but a small group of men cluster around the piano singing "I'm Just a Girl Who Can't Say No." It's really warm and I take off my big thrift-store overcoat. I try to affect a mature demeanor as I order a beer at the bar and then hover on the outskirts of the piano. Across the ceiling they've strung rows and rows of tiny white lights, giving the effect of a starry night sky. The guys around the piano keep pointing at one another as they sing, changing the lyric to "*You're* just a girl who can't say no," and laughing. They seem completely at home and normal. Well, as normal as a group of grown men who want to play Ado Annie can seem. They finish and the pianist notices me. It's the same guy from last summer, the one with the happy Humpty-Dumpty face. He gives me a knowing smirk and launches into the introduction to "Corner of the Sky."

The music draws me to him like a magnet. "That's amazing," I say as he vamps. "How did you remember that?"

"Oh, honey, I'm lousy with names, but I never forget a theme song. Are you gonna sing or what?"

I take the microphone and sing "Corner of the Sky" to the small but attentive audience. They all smile and beam at me and I feel very adorable. I work the winsome-youth thing a bit, like when I sing for the Wallingford Ladies Musical Society, and the reaction is pretty much the same, except the ladies don't flirt. Well, not as much.

When I'm done, the pianist reaches over and gives me a little pat on my butt. "How old are you anyway, Corner of the Sky?"

"Old enough," I say. "How old are you?"

"Too old, darlin', too old," he says, and he begins playing "Time to Start Livin'" from *Pippin*.

The whole crowd is too old, really, like at least thirty, but as I huddle around the piano in this little cave of a bar, I feel as if I'm being initiated into some kind of secret brotherhood, like the Masons, except everyone knows the entire score of *Follies*. Including the songs that were cut.

An advertising executive with a fake tan and a Duran Duran haircut starts buying me tequila chasers to go with my beers, and it's not long before I'm feeling warm and happy and attractive. His name is Dwayne but he pronounces it D. Wayne, which makes me kind of hate him. I'm willing to overlook it, however, because he pays for our drinks with a huge wad of cash held together by a money clip in the shape of a dollar sign.

I get a little melancholy as we sing "Losing My Mind," thinking of Doug:

> *I want you so,*
> *It's like I'm losing my mind.*

D. Wayne massages my neck, his long, thin fingers probing my skin. I don't really find him attractive—his face is the color and texture of a paper bag—but I don't care. After months of scheming and strategizing how to get into Doug's pants, to be touched by a man—to be wanted by a man—makes me feel complete.

Eventually all those beers and tequila want out, so I stagger to the bathroom. There are two, one marked "Men," the other "Gentlemen," and I hesitate, trying to decide which I feel like being.

I choose "Men."

I've just unzipped my pants when D. Wayne saunters in and steps up to the urinal next to me. He glances down at my dick and smiles a better-to-eat-you-with-my-dear smile, then pulls out his, giving a little tug on it as he does. I kind of hate him, but I still glance down to see what he's got and am relieved to see his is roughly the same size as mine.

He doesn't pee.

Fuck Doug. Why do I torture myself with wanting him when here in Manhattan there are rich men in bathrooms wagging their penises at me? As I'm standing there I begin to construct a new life for myself—Edward Zanni, kept boy. I see myself the favored male companion of some wealthy real estate tycoon, living in a penthouse apartment that has a big terrace with plants in clay pots.

I can't pee now, of course, particularly since D. Wayne reaches over and takes me in his hand. His long fingers are cold and I flinch. "Don't worry, sweet stuff," he says. "Daddy won't hurt you."

Ick.

He pushes me up against the side of a stall and does this thing where he licks along my throat. His tongue is long and lizard-y, like his fingers. He rubs his hands over my chest and I feel ashamed I'm not in better shape. O, that this too too solid flesh would melt. "Relax," he says, and grinds his crotch against mine.

I'm not hard.

Shit.

I close my eyes and grip the cold metal handle on top of the urinal. Come on, cock, what's wrong with you? Rise and shine. Stand up and be counted. D. Wayne jabs his stiffy against my softy like he's trying to beat it into obeying. I sense his impatience.

"I'm sorry," I say, stuffing myself into my pants. "I can't." I push past him and dash out the door.

I lean against the wall outside the bathroom, trying to compose myself. What the hell is wrong with me? Old guys get impotent, not seventeen-year-olds. I was beginning to think not getting it up with Kelly meant I really was homosexual instead of bisexual, but if you can't get it up with men, either, then what does that make you? A can't-grow-sexual. A floppy-dough-sexual. An I-don't-know-sexual. I close my eyes and take a deep breath. D. Wayne brushes by me and I can almost feel the cold breeze as he passes.

I wish I'd never come in here. I go to the bar and order a whiskey, down it and order another, just like tortured drunks do in the movies. Okay, I admit it, I've always wanted to do that. The whiskey tastes like turpentine, but I feel a warm glow spread across my cheeks and neck and I lay my head down and try to forget who I am.

Then from the other side of the room a song pierces my consciousness like a beacon in the fog. I recognize the tune, but can't quite place it, and I flip through the catalogue of music-theater trivia in my brain to figure it out. The voice is familiar, too—a full, rich, professional-sounding baritone, someone I've heard on a Broadway cast album, maybe? The song surges and builds and pushes on my brain until suddenly I recognize it.

> What's wrong with wanting more?
> If you can fly then soar,
> With all there is, why settle for
> Just a piece of sky?

It's the finale of *Yentl*, from the scene where Barbra stands on the bow of a ship (just like she does when she sings "Don't Rain on My Parade" in *Funny Girl*, by the way) and heads for a new life in America.

It's a sign. I know it. It's a message meant just for me and I shove myself away from the bar and weave across the room, drawn by the beckoning sound, determined to see the messenger sent to inspire and fulfill me. The singer holds the last sustained note for what seems like an eternity and just as he finishes I push my way to the front, the crowd around me applauding like mad, and right then he turns and looks straight at me.

"Edward?" he says.

"Mr. Lucas?"

twenty-one

Mr. Lucas's apartment looks just like him: neat, compact, bookish. The kitchen is no bigger than a phone booth, but there's a little terrace that looks out on a quiet courtyard. The room is boiling from the steam heat and Mr. Lucas takes off his sweater. It's the first time I've ever seen him in anything but a sports jacket and I'm surprised at how muscular his torso is, particularly for a guy who must be forty. The sleeves of his polo shirt are tight on his thick, veiny arms, undoubtedly made strong from years of dragging his legs around. He traipses into the bathroom.

I've never thought of Mr. Lucas sexually before, but as I watch him I find myself wondering if his spinal cord injury prevents him from having sex. I flop onto the couch and spread my legs in what I hope is a seductive pose while I pretend to call Paula and claim to get no answer. You'd think that someone having erection problems would give it a rest, but hope springs eternal, I guess. Mr. Lucas returns with a glass of water and some aspirin. "Might as well get a head start on tomorrow," he says, pivoting gracefully on one crutch.

I must say he's handling the whole running-into-a-student-in-a-gay-bar thing rather well. Then again, it's not like I can tell anybody; otherwise I'd have to admit that I was there in the first place. So Mr. Lucas and I are now linked in our shared secret. We're both part of the brotherhood.

"Izzit okay if I crash here?" I say.

He gives me a withering Mr. Lucas look over his glasses. "Apparently you already have," he says, tossing me a blanket.

"Thanks." I really want to take off my sweater, but I don't want him to see that I can't close the top button of my jeans. "Can I open a window?" I say.

"This place is either too hot or too cold," he says. "And the pipes clang all night, too, just like Marley's ghost."

Fuck it. I'm burning up. I get out of my jeans first, then peel off my sweater.

"It's a good thing I came along," Mr. Lucas says, looking the other way. "You can't be too careful nowadays. I assume you've heard about AIDS?"

This isn't the sexy, precoital conversation I was hoping for. "Yeah, I've heard," I mumble.

Mr. Lucas touches me on the arm. "It's serious, Edward. Gay men are getting sick all over this city." He moves his hand away and shudders. "It's scary."

All the more reason to have sex with someone I can trust, I think.

"Well, you better get some sleep," he says. "You've got a big day tomorrow."

"You sure gotta lotta books," I say, stalling for time. I scan the meticulously alphabetized shelves, leaning on them so I don't fall over. There are a lot of authors I've heard of—Brecht, Shakespeare, Whitman, Woolf—but there are just as many I don't know—Isherwood, Lorca, Maupin.

Mr. Lucas smiles at his books like they're old friends. "What are you reading these days?" he says. "For fun, I mean."

Fun. I haven't thought about fun since Dagmar moved in, let alone reading. "Nothin'," I say.

Mr. Lucas frowns. "What's the last book you read that wasn't assigned to you?"

I have to think about that one. "*Catcher in the Rye*," I say finally. "I got pissed 'cuz all the other classes got to read it 'cept us."

"You don't have to assign *The Catcher in the Rye* to get teenagers to read it," Mr. Lucas says. He leans on the arm of an easy chair. "What did you think of it?"

"Salinger's an asshole."

Mr. Lucas laughs, something he doesn't often do.

"Don't hold back," he says. "What do you really think?"

"I mean, here's this guy, Holden Caulfield, that every teenager can, like, completely identify with, and what happens to him in the end? He goes nuts. Thazz not very encouraging."

"I'm not sure it's supposed to be."

"If you ask me, Holden's in a homosexual panic."

Mr. Lucas strokes his beard. "Is that so?"

I pull a copy of Salinger from the shelf where it sits next to a volume of poems by Sappho, whoever he is. "It's in the part where he's sleeping at his English teacher's apartment." I move next to Mr. Lucas and hand him the open page, leaning over his shoulder. "You see, right here, after his teacher makes a pass at him, Holden says: 'That kind of stuff's happened to me about twenty times since I was a kid.' Twenty times! I'm sorry, but I've got just two words for Holden Caulfield: Ho Mo."

Mr. Lucas hands me back the book, but I remain where I am, my crotch close to his face. "If you ask me," I say softly, "I think Holden would have been a lot happier if he'd slept with his teacher."

Mr. Lucas clears his throat and rises, placing his hand on my arm to steady himself. He takes off his glasses. His eyes are soft and pretty, like a deer's. "I don't think you're right, Edward," he says. "I think sleeping with his teacher would've screwed up Holden even worse." He pats me on the shoulder and takes a step away. I grab him by the arm.

"Even if Holden really wanted it?" I say. Just kiss me. Please, please, one kiss.

Mr. Lucas sighs. "I know you won't understand this, Edward, but a student places an enormous amount of trust in a teacher, more than the student realizes, and more than any teacher even wants. But no matter how tempting the offer . . ." he smiles at me ". . . the teacher just . . . can't." He touches my face lightly and I sink into the chair.

Can't. Why is it always can't?

Mr. Lucas hobbles over to the bookcase and scans the shelf. "I'm going to tell you something important, Edward, and I want you to listen closely."

"Will there be a test later?"

"I'm serious."

I sit up.

He pulls a book down from the shelf. "After I had my accident, I thought my life was over. I was bedridden for a year and in muscular therapy for a very long time after that. I wasn't sure I'd ever walk again. My acting career was over, and as far as my love life was concerned— well, I had suddenly become invisible. I'll be honest with you, I wasn't entirely certain I wanted to go on. But what I did have was books. Some mornings I'd wake up and the pain would be so great I wanted to end it all, but then I'd think, 'No, Ted, you can't kill yourself today. You're right in the middle of a really good book.' I know it sounds crazy, but I'm one of those people who, once they start a story, has to find out how it ends, even if I don't like it. So I kept reading, just to stay alive. In fact, I'd read two or three books at the same time, so I wouldn't finish one without being in the middle of another—anything to stop me from falling into the big, gaping void. You see, books fill the empty spaces. If I'm waiting for a bus, or am eating alone, I can always rely on a book to keep me company. Sometimes I think I like them even more than people. People will let you down in life. They'll disappoint you and hurt you and betray you. But not books. They're better than life. Even before I got hurt I relied on them. Back in the early seventies, there was this ridiculous ritual where you could signal to other gay men what you were into by what color bandana you had in your back pocket or by the way you wore your keys on your belt. I refused to take part in it, of course, but it did give me the idea to always carry a book with me. I'm sure it sounds ludicrous and terribly theatrical to think of me standing in a bar with a copy of Ginsberg poems, but it was my way of telling the world what I was into, that I was a reader. And believe it or not, it worked. It attracted other readers to me, men of substance and sensitivity. It didn't always get me laid, but it led to some very interesting conversations. So don't ever let me hear you say you're not in the middle of reading a book. It might save your life someday."

He tosses the book he's holding at me in his usual offhand way. "Start with this."

I look at the title. A Boy's Own Story by Edmund White.

"I think you'll like it better than The Catcher in the Rye," he says.

"Thanks," I say. I suppose he's got a point. If I can't be well hung, I can at least be well-read.

Mr. Lucas turns off the light in the living room.

"Hey, Mr. Lucas, can I ask you somethin'?"

"Yes, you may," he says.

"How did you, y'know, get injured?"

His face is silhouetted and I can't tell how he feels about my asking, but he sighs and leans against the door frame. "I was at a cast party for a production of Henry the Fourth, Part One. I had too much to drink and I fell down a flight of stairs."

I'm not sure what I was expecting to hear, but that certainly wasn't it.

"I'm sorry," I say.

He flips off the light in the hallway, plunging us into complete darkness.

"Not as sorry as I am," he says.

❋   ❋   ❋

The rattling of Marley's ghost wakes me, and I stagger into the bathroom, hunched over like a question mark, trying to figure out how I was able to turn my skin inside out while I was sleeping. Every part of me aches: my back, my head, even my hair. I flip on the bathroom light and squint to see myself in the mirror. Mother of God, I look like Sylvester Stallone at the end of *Rocky*. I turn on the faucet, but no, no, water loud, water bad. Not only am I totally hungover, but I'm also wide awake. And hungry. Great. The digital clock says it's 5:45 A.M. I don't want to wake Mr. Lucas. As a matter of fact, I don't even want to see Mr. Lucas. Not after the way I acted last night. I creep back into the living room and put my Serious Young Actor clothes back on. They smell of stale smoke, as does my skin. I let myself out, forgetting to take my copy of *A Boy's Own Story*.

The fog is so thick I can't see the other side of Washington Square Park. The sky is turning from black to gray and I stop to remember this melancholy moment for my acting. I huddle on a bench in my big thrift-store overcoat and my painful hair, watching my breath make clouds and thinking Holden Caulfield-y thoughts, like how come you never see any baby pigeons? This is what those people on black-and-white French postcards must feel like. I find myself craving a cup of coffee and a cigarette despite the fact that I neither drink coffee nor smoke.

I wander back to the diner where we ate last night and sit in the same booth. I figure maybe a little food will make me feel better, but when I get there I can only eat part of a muffin. I look at my ankle to see what time it is: 6:45. Three and a half hours until my audition. Maybe if I just put my head down for a few minutes. If I could just lie down on this banquette and rest for a while, I'm sure I'll be fine. I just need to sleep for a couple of minutes.

twenty-two

Shit. Shit. Shit. Shit. Shit. What the hell kind of diner lets you sleep in their booth for three goddamn hours?

I dash through the tangle of Greenwich Village streets, certain that they've been rearranged just to piss me off and make me late. The entire city, no, the entire *universe* is conspiring with Al to keep me from becoming an actor. Where the hell is the goddamn subway, or a bus or a cab? My kingdom for a cab!

There's not one part of me that's not sweating. My eyelids, my knuckles, the tops of my feet—every bit of me is wet. I finally find the subway, but from the top of the stairs I can hear a train coming. Like a nightmare, the stairwell seems to telescope in length. I'll never make it.

"HOLD THAT TRAIN!" I scream like a madman as I dash down into the depths. I thrust a sweaty, crumpled bill under the Plexiglas to the woman in the booth and see a young Hispanic guy on the train lean against the door to hold it open. I leap through the turnstile and into the car.

I bend over to catch my breath. "Thank you so much," I pant at him. "I've got to be at Lincoln Center in five minutes."

He shakes his head. "Then you need the northbound train, man. This here's the southbound."

SHIIIIIIIT!

I throw my Sinatra hat on the floor and yank on my painful hair, while I grit my teeth and growl (yes, actually growl) in frustration. A tiny old lady with one of those little two-wheel shopping carts New Yorkers use reaches into her purse and quickly tosses a dollar in my hat, like she's afraid I'll bite her. I want to scream, "I'm not homeless, you stupid bitch," but then I realize I kind of am and, what's more, I suppose I could use the dollar. Her kindness calms me for a moment and I kneel down to pick it up. I smile weakly at her and say, "I'll put this toward college."

"Or medication," she says, frowning.

I switch trains and start the long ride uptown to Lincoln Center. At this point, there's no way I can be on time. I'm doomed. They're going to think I'm a complete fuckup. My hair is greasy and matted, I haven't shaved, I smell of sweat and stale smoke. My only chance of being accepted is if Juilliard wants actors who look like strung-out junkies.

I get lost at Lincoln Center (Why, why, why didn't I plan this ahead of time?) and go dashing around the complex looking for the right entrance, my overcoat flailing behind me in the wind. I finally find it and go banging through the double doors into the lobby of the theater building. The clock on the wall says 10:30.

Fuck. Fuck. Fuck. Fuck. Fuck.

I see Paula across the lobby. She bounds across the room, waving her arms. "My *God*, what the fuck happened to you last night? I was *petrified*. I thought for sure . . ."

I push past her and head straight to the check-in table, where a woman gives me a look like I'm some street person who wandered in by mistake. "I'm Edward Zanni," I gasp.

She glances down at her list. "You missed your time."

"I know . . ."

"You'll have to wait until we can fit you in."

"That's fine," I say. "I'm really, really sorry, I . . ."

"Fill out this card and sit down over there," she says, waving to a group of young actors mumbling their monologues to themselves like patients in an insane asylum.

Paula puts her arm around me and leads me away. "You're going to be *fine*," she says, opening up her purse. "Let me put some drops in your eyes." She's just squirted Visine at me when I hear the woman behind the desk shout "Edward Zanni!"

I stumble across the room, half blind like Oedipus.

"We've had another no-show," she says. "You're next."

"But I haven't even filled out my . . ."

"Go down that hallway and the monitor will let you know when they're ready for you." Dazed, my overcoat hanging halfway off my shoulder, I sleepwalk down the hall. This can't be happening. I see a bored-looking student with a clipboard.

"You Walter Mancus?" he says.

"Actually, I'm . . ."

He thrusts the door open. "You're on."

I can't fucking believe it. After all my hard work, after sacrificing everything, it comes to this. I stagger into a low-ceilinged room with acoustic tile and fluorescent lights. I'd expected a darkened theater; instead I'm facing a firing squad just a few feet away. Sitting in front are a middle-aged man with a magnificent mass of hair that swoops across his head like a crashing wave, an older tweedy-looking guy with a walnut face, and, in the middle, tall and erect as a dowager empress, a woman who appears to have been carved from stone. I don't know who the others are, but I'm certain that the woman is Marian Seldes, the grande dame of the American theater and the Juilliard Drama Division.

"Walter Mancus?" she asks.

"No, I'm Edward Zanni," I hear myself say in a phlegmy voice. The room is frigid—the heat's probably been off during vacation—and my sweat feels cold and clammy against my skin.

Marian Seldes scowls and shuffles her papers like she's annoyed at me for not being Walter Mancus. The man with the wave of hair folds his arms and sighs. The tweedy old guy smiles a kindly shopkeeper smile and says, "And what have you prepared for us today, Walter?"

"I'm not, uh . . . you see . . ."

The wave man rolls his eyes. "Your monologue? What is it?" he says impatiently.

I flinch and hear myself say, "Haemon from *Antigone*."

Why did I say that? I'm supposed to do "Bottom's Dream." Take it back. Take it back, Edward, before it's too late.

The wave man gives me a look like, "Well, what are you waiting for?" and I hear myself say, "Father, you must not think that your word and no other must be so. For if any man thinks that he alone is wise . . ."

But I can't remember the next fucking line.

In an instant my face is blazing hot and my crotch gets sweaty. My feet begin to itch and burn so badly I want to bite them off and smack them against my head. Stupid. Stupid. Stupid. Marian Seldes is still shuffling through her papers, the wave man is staring out the window, and the tweedy man just blinks at me through his thick glasses. Think of something, Edward, anything, anything.

". . . for if any man thinks he alone is wise," I say swallowing hard, "then that man is totally fucked up."

Marian Seldes and the wave man both look up.

"Yeah," I say, "that man is totally fucked in the head. 'Cuz you might think because you're my father you can just roll right over me and tell me what to do, but I am here to tell you, old man, that I am fed up to HERE with taking your shit."

I feel snot drip out of my nose and I make a horrible hocking noise as I suck it back in. "I'm sick of you judging me, I'm sick of you lording your money over me, I'm sick of . . . sick of . . ."

I feel a churning inside my stomach, like a volcano about to explode and there is absolutely nothing I can do to stop it. I think I'm going to throw up. Or have a heart attack. Or shit my pants.

"I'm sick of not being good enough for you," I howl. "Why can't you . . . why can't you . . . oh, *God* . . ." I shove my fists against my eyes, trying to push the feelings back inside of me, trying to get a grip on myself and remember something from the goddamned monologue. This isn't acting. This is a nervous breakdown. *Promising Young Actor Goes Mental at Audition, Film at Eleven.*

"Why can't you just love me the way I am? Why can't you accept me the way I am?" I scream. My vision clouds over. Everything goes blurry and the room begins to spin. My face crumbles into tiny pieces and I begin to choke on my phlegm. I can't stand being inside myself and I start beating my head with my fists as if it were a punching bag. "I hate you, don't you see? I hate you for what you've done to me, I hate you for how you've made me feel. I hate, hate, haaaaaaaate you, you goddamned fucking asswipe shit-for-brains pussy-whipped toad!"

I stop and cover my face with my hands to stop myself from falling over. My hair hurts again. My kneecaps are going to pop off. And someone please, please tell me that I didn't just say "goddamned fucking asswipe shit-for-brains pussy-whipped toad" at my Juilliard audition. I look up and see the entire panel staring at me, their mouths open and their heads tilted, like I'm some kind of abstract painting they're trying to figure out.

"Which translation of *Antigone* is that, exactly?" Marian Seldes asks.

Say anything, Edward. Any name. Say Ted Lucas. Say Doug Grabowski. Just say something, Edward, and save your goddamned life.

"I dunno," I say.

Marian Seldes turns to each of the men next to her. "Well," she says, "I think we've seen all we need to see. Thank you."

That's it. They're not going to ask to see a second monologue. Why would they? I wouldn't be surprised if they got security to escort me out. My only consolation is perhaps they'll think I was Walter Mancus and they'll never know who I was. I don't say a word, but just turn, my overcoat dragging on the ground, and stagger out of the room. It's over. I've failed. I'm going to live in New Jersey and work at Chicken Lickin' the rest of my life.

I limp zombielike across the lobby of the theater building, where I see Paula waiting for me. I push past her, bang out the double doors, and in full view of her, the people at the desk, and all the other actors, proceed to throw up all over Lincoln Center.

✲ ✲ ✲

I spend the whole next week in bed. I don't have any particular ailment, just a sort of generalized frailty, like the consumptive heroine of a nineteenth-century novel. I sleep most of the day, and Kelly and Kathleen kind of tiptoe around me like I'm the cryent they're trying not to disturb. I can tell from the worried looks on their faces that I must be in bad shape. The only plus is that I have an excuse not to fool around with Kelly. There's no way I could handle the pressure.

Paula leaves a number of messages, as does Natie, who finally admits, somewhat apologetically, that he's been accepted to Georgetown early decision. I don't call anyone back but instead spend my few waking hours watching children's television. Mr. Rogers likes me just the way I am.

I rally a bit on my birthday, even though there's still no word from my mom. You'd think she'd at least have sent a card. I try to comfort myself with the thought that maybe she mailed it to Al's house and Dagmar threw it away out of spite, but no matter how I look at the situation, there's no denying that my life sucks. But still, it's my day and I'm determined to wring some joy out of it. The fifth of January always has a bleak, dead-Christmas-tree-by-the-curb kind of atmosphere, not to mention the whole this-is-for-Christmas-*and*-your-birthday thing, but I like the symmetry of being one age for practically the entire year. That way, the year takes on the character of that age, instead of being split awkwardly like if you were born in May or October. It's simpler. The year I was ten: 1976. The year I was fourteen: 1980. The year I'm eighteen, a legal adult at last: 1984.

It's Independence Day.

The morning of my birthday I arise shortly before the crack of noon, and as I stumble out of bed I catch sight of myself in the mirror. What I see surprises me. I haven't shaved in over a week and, since I've inherited Al's lycanthropic genes, I find I've practically grown a full beard.

I'm not sure if it looks any good, but I like it. It makes me feel like a man, even though I'm wearing Kelly's sister's tartan flannel nightgown.

I open my bedroom door to find an envelope lying on the floor. On the outside it says, "For all the years we've missed having you in our home. Love from Kathleen and Kelly." I open it and see that it's a birthday card for a one-year-old:

> *You're 1 today! Harooh! Hooray!*
> *'Cause on the day that you are 1,*
> *We want to say, "We love you, son!"*

Son. I've been adopted. A few steps away lies another card, this one for a two-year-old, followed by a card "For a big boy who's 3," and, at the top of the stairs, another one that says, "Wow! You're 4!," and so on through the years and down the stairs and into the kitchen until finally there's a card for an eighteen-year-old on the table. Next to it is a present: Uta Hagen's *Respect for Acting.* I'm going to assume they bought it because it's the best book on acting as opposed to being some kind of comment on my failed audition.

I hope.

The doorbell rings, making the cats scatter. I wander into the entryway, open the front door, and there he is in front of me, wearing a party hat and holding a balloon.

The Buddha.

For the first time in 1984 I laugh out loud.

"Happy Birthday," a voice says, and I turn to see Doug leaning against the house, a Cheshire cat smile on his lips.

I immediately feel my spirits lift. It may not be a love offering, but it's at least a peace offering, and it means Doug's ready to be friends again. We move the Buddha to a place of honor in the garden and then go out to lunch.

✳   ✳   ✳

They keep the interior of Mamma's as dark during the day as they do at night; in some ways it seems even darker because of the bright winter light outside. The large overstuffed banquettes provide a good hiding place for guys with Mob connections and truant high-school students. Doug and I both order chicken scaloppine.

"Youz kids want anything to drink?" the waiter asks, emphasis on the kids. No wine for us, I guess. Maybe once the beard grows all the way in.

"I'll have a Coke," Doug says.

I click my tongue. "Actually, we'll both have 7Ups."

"Why?" Doug asks. "I don't even like 7Up."

"Because you only drink Coke or Pepsi with meat and pork," I explain quietly, trying not to embarrass him in front of the waiter. "With chicken or fish you drink 7Up or Sprite."

He still has a lot to learn.

Doug's just starting to fill me in on what's been happening at school when he stops cold and says, "Don't turn around."

Now it's a funny thing about people telling you not to turn around, because that's precisely the first thing you do when they say it. It's almost an invitation, really, as if they were tempting you to turn into a pillar of salt. So, naturally, like a stupe, I turn and who do I see coming through the door? My evil stepmonster.

Happy fucking birthday.

She's got another member of the master race with her, a blond Valkyrie just like herself, and they stride purposefully toward the back of the restaurant and the booth next to ours. Feeling panicked, I do the very first thing that comes into my mind: I hide.

Now I realize that sliding underneath a table in a restaurant is somewhat of an *I Love Lucy* response to a crisis, but once I'm down on the floor I can't very well reappear without giving some thought as to how I'm going to accomplish it. So while I sit pondering my colossal stupidity, Doug drops his fork and leans over to talk with me.

"Stay where you are," he hisses. "They're talking in German."

While on the surface his statement may appear to make no sense whatsoever, I immediately understand that what he means is that he's going to eavesdrop and that my reappearance would spoil his cover. This gives me a certain satisfaction in my decision—like, "Oh, that's why I'm lurking underneath this table"—and I settle in, resigning myself to spending my birthday lunch on the slightly sticky floor of an Italian restaurant.

I'm down there a long time but Doug is thoughtful enough to pass food my way, as if I were the family dog begging for table scraps. To add to my humiliation, I find myself exactly eye level with Doug's crotch which, while pleasant enough viewing, is also torturously enticing. It's a full hour and several leg cramps later when I'm finally allowed to emerge.

"So, what did she say?" I ask Doug as I limp out of the restaurant.

"Now you gotta remember," he says, "I'm not a German scholar . . ."

"Yeah, yeah, yeah, just tell me."

"Well, as far as I could make out, not only did Dagmar marry your dad for his money—but she's stealing from him, too."

"What? Are you sure?"

"She told her friend that she's been funneling money into an account Al doesn't know about. In fact, she said Al's made it easy for her because he's always teaching her about his finances by taking her out for—I think I got this right—'business dinners.'"

I'm just about to respond when someone mistakes me for a waiter and asks for more salad dressing, despite the fact I'm wearing an old admiral's jacket and leg warmers.

"Not my table," I say.

When I get home, I forget all about this new development. There, on the floor with the mail, sits a letter. From Juilliard.

It's a thin envelope.

Everyone knows what a thin envelope means. Rejection. Colleges don't send big packets with maps of the campus and stuff when they're rejecting you. I don't know why I'm so disappointed; it's not like I'm surprised. I guess I just wasn't expecting it to come so soon. Happy fucking birthday squared.

I consider tossing it out unread (Why bother, right?), but I figure I might as well get it over with. I open the envelope.

```
January 2, 1984

The Juilliard School
Drama Division
60 Lincoln Center Plaza
New York, NY 10023
```

```
Edward Zanni
1020 Stonewall Drive
Wallingford, NJ 07090
```

Dear Edward,

Let me be the first to congratulate you on your acceptance to the Juilliard School's Drama Division, Group XVI.

Oh. My. God.

The Drama Division prides itself on being the finest training ground for the best young actors in America. We sincerely hope you will make Juilliard your school of choice.

This has got to be a mistake. Right now poor Walter Mancus is opening a rejection letter and thinking, "But I did such a great job."

twenty-three

I grab the telephone and punch in Paula's number. After about ten rings I hear a groggy, distracted voice that has to be Gino trying to speak through his wall of hair. Either that or it's the transvestite hooker from down the hall.

"Is Paula there?" I ask.

"She's . . . uh . . . busy," he says.

"Gino, this is Edward. Listen, I've got to talk with her."

I hear Paula's muffled voice say, "Who is it?" to which Gino replies, "Ouch, baby, watch the teeth." The phone drops and there's some shuffling in the background.

"Hello?"

"It's me," I shout. "I'm in, I'm in, I'm in!"

"I *knew* it!" Paula crows. "Congratulations!"

"ARE THEY OUT OF THEIR FUCKING MINDS?" I shout.

"What are you talking about?"

"Sis, I vomited on their school."

"It's an arts school. They're used to eccentric behavior."

"But I sucked."

"That's not what I heard," Paula says.

"What?"

"If you'd answered my calls you would have known. I asked my improv professor about you, you know, the one who gave me an A plus when I reenacted losing my virginity?"

I hear Gino shout "Hey!" in the background.

"Gino, don't be such a fucking Neanderthal," she says to him.

"Is he an old guy or a middle-aged guy?" I ask.

"He's a middle-aged guy with beautiful hair and a bored expression."

"He didn't hate me?"

"No, he always looks like that. He's not bored, he's deep. Anyway, he said that in all his years of teaching he's never seen an audition like yours."

That's for sure.

"He said you were like a raw exposed nerve, a gaping open wound."

"And that's good?" I say.

"Are you kidding? That's what every actor dreams of. I knew you had it in you, I just *knew* it. I'm so happy for . . . oh dear . . . cut it out, will ya', I'm on the . . . just . . ."

I hear more shuffling bodies.

"Listen, I've got to go," Paula says, giggling. "Something's . . . uh . . . come up. But know that I love . . ."

And she's gone.

I return to school revived and invigorated. Finally my baggy life seems to fit. I am one of the Best Young Actors in America. I am a raw exposed nerve. I am a gaping open wound. And I am not going to let that Austrian bitch stop me.

The whole school seems to know the good news and even people who never talk to me, like Amber Wright, offer congratulations. I can't stop smiling. My life is bathed in a rosy glow, like an MGM Technicolor musical.

For four periods.

In a stunning display of colossal stupidity, I have, once again, missed the sign-up for the cushy sports in gym. Ms. Burro initials my absentee note (presumably because she can't spell her own name) and then spreads her mouth into what, on people with lips, would be called a smile. "Looks like a whole semester of basketball and softball for you, Zanni," she says, and then actually tosses her head back and fires off a round of laughter, like she's the evil matron in a women's prison movie.

When I'm famous, she's going to be the first person I remember to forget.

I'm one of the Best Young Actors in America, goddamnit, I should be studying fencing or ballet, not dashing aimlessly about on the floor of a high-school gymnasium. I've endured this needless torture for forty minutes a day, four times a week for eleven fucking years. Excluding vacations, that's 144 gym classes a year, which comes to a lifetime total of

1,584; multiply that by forty minutes a class and it comes to 1,056 hours of nonstop harassment, or forty-four days of round-the-clock terror. POWs have died from less.

I won't take another minute of it.

I have got to get a medical excuse, but the only doctor I know well enough to ask is Kelly's father and I don't think he's unscrupulous enough to do it. If he were, Kelly wouldn't be taking gym. On the other hand, *I'm* certainly unscrupulous enough to fake an injury and clearly have the acting skills to pull it off. In fact, I can't believe I haven't thought of it before. Using sense memory, I can re-create the pain I felt when I fell off the back of Al's Midlife Crisis. How hard could that be?

In the interest of creating verisimilitude, I decide to stage a fall; and where better to do it than right in front of Burro? First, I make sure I'm on the opposing team from Darren O'Boyle, even though it means I've got to play skins. Realizing that actually participating in the game might arouse suspicion, I hang about on the periphery a little more lazily than usual, not even bothering to go through the motions of trying to appear busy.

My lethargy doesn't escape Commandant Burro's notice. "Hey, Zanni," she yells, "get it in gear."

I cup my hand to my ear, the Internationally Recognized Signal for "I can't hear you, you stupid cow."

"C'mon, Zanni, move your butt."

That's all I need. In one swift, graceless move I place myself between the basketball hoop and the Evil Sophomore from Hell and flap my arms like some great, goony bird about to take flight. I feel as if my whole life has been a preparation for this moment. I narrow my eyes and think, "Come and get me, you mouth breather."

Darren brushes past me, his sweaty arm barely grazing mine, and in an instant I throw myself in the air and land with an echoing thud, which I accomplish by slamming the floor with my hands like those fakey pro wrestlers on TV. Burro blows her whistle.

"I didn't touch him!" Darren shouts.

Ms. Burro jogs over and kneels next to me. "You okay, Zanni?"

Subtlety is the key here, not my strong suit, but crucial to making the scene believable. I look up and flash a quick, embarrassed smile, the kind where your upper lip disappears. "I'm fine, really, I'm fine," I say.

I stand up and wince, then bend over and exhale a couple of times,

Lamaze-style, shutting my eyes tight to see if I can force out some tears. I am a raw exposed nerve.

Ms. Burro looks worried, hopefully more about her job than me. "Why don't you sit down?" she says.

I rub my tailbone. "I don't think that's a good idea," I say through clenched teeth. I am a gaping open wound.

"Hey," she yells at Darren, who's dribbling the ball in circles while he waits, "why don't you cool off and take Edward here down to the nurse?"

"I didn't do nothin'," he says.

"GO!"

Darren spikes the ball on the ground in frustration and heads for the door. I limp across the gym, my sneakers squeaking as the game resumes behind me, presumably now at a human pace. Darren struts ahead of me, his shiny, straight hair bouncing as he walks. I wish I had hair that bounced.

"Sorry," he mumbles as he holds the door open.

I wince again, just to rub it in.

❊   ❊   ❊

I bring Natie with me to Dr. Corcoran's office, which is downtown in a brick building designed to look like Independence Hall. "What good is getting a gym excuse for just three weeks?" Natie asks.

"That's where Nathan Nudelman, Ace Forger, comes in," I say. "You're going to add a two before the three and turn it into a twenty-three week gym excuse, which is exactly how many weeks there are left in the school year."

"Who the hell ever heard of a twenty-three week excuse?" he says. "Don't you think Burro's gonna find that kind of strange?"

I remind Natie that if Ms. Burro were that smart, she wouldn't be teaching gym.

I take a moment outside the office door to prepare, then turn to Natie and say, "Now try to look real concerned about me but don't call too much attention to yourself, okay?" Natie nods, then holds the door open as I shuffle in. I make my way slowly to the counter and wait for the nurse to look up, but she's busy color coding files.

"I'm here to see Dr. Corcoran," I say finally.

"Sign in and take a seat," she says, still not looking up.

I turn to sign in, but Natie stops me. "You take it easy, pal," he says, oozing sincerity. "I've done it for you."

"You're the best," I say, oozing back, but since the nurse isn't watching, our performance is wasted. Pearls before swine.

We sit flipping through out-of-date issues of golf magazines for a long time. A couple of other people come in, some looking pretty banged up, which makes me feel kind of guilty for wasting Dr. Corcoran's time. Nurse Ratched treats them with the same comforting level of warmth and compassion she showed us. Finally, at what seems to me to be a completely arbitrary moment, she picks up the sign-in sheet and calls out the next name on it.

"Craven Morehead?" she says. "Craven Morehead?" She looks around the room, but no one responds. "You there, with the magazine in front of your face," she says to Natie, "are you Craven Morehead?"

Natie looks up, all Bambi eyes. "I beg your pardon?" he says.

"Are you Craven Morehead?"

"No, ma'am," he answers. Then, under his breath, he whispers, "At least not from you."

"Then who is Craven Morehead?" she asks, annoyed at the inefficiency. She stands up and leans over the counter to see if there's someone she's missed. "Is there anyone here who's Craven Morehead?"

Natie puts the magazine in front of his face again.

The nurse finally calls my name, but only after asking for Phil McCracken and Mike Hunt. ("Mike Hunt? Has anyone seen Mike Hunt?")

Nurse Ratched leads me to the little room, checks my vitals indifferently, then tells me to strip down to my underwear and wait. I don't know why doctors make you do this. It's like they want to strip your dignity as well as your clothes. The room is cold and is painted that comforting shade of institutional gray favored by medical offices and prisons. After I read a brochure on osteoporosis and wait about a millennium, Dr. Corcoran finally strides in, all toothpaste-commercial teeth and out-of-season tan, his ashy blond hair graying at the temples like a newscaster's.

"Edward!" he says, shaking my hand with an intensity usually reserved for arm wrestling. "How ya' doin', son?"

I'm not your son, you herpes-infected cheating bastard.

"Fine," I say.

Wuss.

"Good," he says without really looking at me. "Now let's see . . ." He gives a quick glance at my chart and then tosses it aside. Pushing open his lab coat, he places a fist on each side of his slender waist, like he's a superhero about to save Gotham from evil: Orthopedic Man to the rescue. "So, what seems to be the problem?" he says.

One of the Best Young Actors in America begins his performance. I explain how I fell last summer and got a contusion on my coccyx (I figure that using the fancy medical term will lend credibility) and how I fell today and hurt it again.

Dr. Corcoran chuckles. "Playing a little too rough, eh?"

I chuckle back and give him a knowing sort of shrug, as if to say, "Yeah, what are we overenthusiastic athletic types to do?" Dr. Corcoran was like some big lacrosse player in college, or maybe it was rugby, I don't know. One of those preppy sports.

"Well, let's just take a few X-rays and see how bad it is, shall we?"

I'm prepared for this. "Sure," I say, "it's just that . . ." I bite my lip and look down.

Dr. Corcoran cocks his head, radiating doctorly concern. "What is it, son?"

I sigh, giving him the most David Copperfield-y look I dare. "I had to give up my health insurance because I'm declaring financial independence," I say, my chin quivering ever so slightly. "Do you think . . . well, maybe we could just hold off doing the X-rays . . . for a little while?"

Dr. Corcoran frowns. "I'm not so sure about that, Edward . . ."

"The pain is *exactly* like it was last time," I say. "I'm sure if I could just get out of gym for a week or two it'll heal up fine. And if it doesn't, I'll be certain to come back and get them, I promise."

Dr. Corcoran puts his hand to his dimpled chin and considers the idea. For a moment I worry that he'll offer to do the X-rays for free, but I remind myself that Kathleen has complained time and again what a cheap bastard he is.

"Okeydokey . . ." he says.

Whew.

". . . let me just give you a little digital exam to make sure nothing's broken."

Digital exam? Dear God, I hope he's talking about computers.

"Pull down your boxers and lie back, Edward. This'll just take a minute."

Danger, danger, Will Robinson. There's an unidentified object about to enter Uranus.

Dr. Corcoran yanks out the end of the table and hands me a worthless airline-sized pillow to prop under me. I shimmy my underwear down and lean back. The air is cold on my crotch and I feel my balls retract into me, as if they were saying, "Let's get the hell away from this."

I hear the sinister snap of a rubber glove. Sweet Jesus, there has got to be an easier way to get out of gym.

Like a surfer catching a wave, Dr. Corcoran hops onto one of those wheeled doctor's stools and rolls over to me. I raise my head and look at him between my legs, my naked self reflected in his glasses. He peers at me with what seem to be Kelly's eyes, or perhaps I should say Kelly's left eye, the one that favors brown. It's easy to see why Kathleen fell in love with him, the snake, which is really not the kind of thing I want to be thinking about during a rectal examination.

Then Dr. Corcoran says the thing that doctors always say right before they do something painful to you.

"Now just relax."

I feel the cold tip of his gloved finger against my butt.

"This might sting a little."

Ow. Ow. Ow. Ow. Broomstick. Butter churn. Red-hot poker.

"Easy, son," he says, "I haven't done anything yet."

Oh.

"Just close your eyes," he says, "and think about . . . the Grand Canyon. Or a beauuutiful flower opening up to the sun."

I exhale and try to think big, open thoughts, but I wince as I feel his finger enter me.

"Relaaaaax," he murmurs.

I grip the sides of the table, take another deep breath and exhale while he prods and pokes at me like he's stuffing a turkey. Then he presses his finger downward, sending a shock wave through me. I start to feel light-headed and that's when I realize it.

I'm getting hard.

I can't fucking believe this. The first erection I've had in six weeks and it happens while I'm getting a rectal exam from my girlfriend's father. I try thinking of dead babies or baseball scores, but I don't know anything about baseball except that the players look really sexy in those tight pants and . . . okay, that's it. Captain Standish is at full attention.

I look up at Dr. Corcoran. "Sorry," I say.

He smiles his Pepsodent smile. "It's okay," he says, "it happens." Then he glances down and, using his free hand, pulls aside his lab coat.

There's a bulge in his pants. I'm going to be in therapy forever.

twenty-four

I arrive home bowlegged and unsure of what's freaking me out more: the fact that I got a woody during a rectal exam or that my girlfriend's father asked me if I'd like to have coffee sometime.

Ick squared.

Anyway, I have my gym excuse. Now I just want to take a shower and wash away this whole ordeal. I open the front door and immediately notice something's amiss. For starters, the only light in the room comes from the flickering glow of candles. Sinatra's on the stereo, crooning "I've Got You Under My Skin," the 1956 Capitol session with the amazing elephant-in-heat trombone solo, and sprawled on the couch in a silver lace teddy, giving me a shy, come-hither stare, is Kelly.

"What took you so long?" she coos, tilting her head in that way that pretty girls do. "We've got the place to ourselves."

Uh-oh.

She stands and turns around to give me a look. The lace teddy stretches tight across the smooth landscape of her ass. She looks just like a model in the Victoria's Secret catalogue. Too bad I've got a secret or two of my own.

She undulates toward me, then wraps her arms around my neck and rubs up against me like a kitten. She tilts her head, the Internationally Recognized Signal for "Kiss me, you fool."

Luckily I knock a picture off the wall with my head as I back up.

"Sorry," I say. "You surprised me." I bend down to pick up the photo. It's a shot of Dr. Corcoran, Kathleen, and the three kids at Nana's house on the Cape. I look up at Kelly and she smiles at me with both rows of teeth. She tousles my hair.

"You're silly," she says. "You want a drink?"

I can't think of anything I'd like more, unless she's also got a Valium, too.

"Go sit down," she says. "I'll get you a spritzer."

I shuffle over to the couch. I must remember this feeling for my acting in case I ever play someone who got fingered by his girlfriend's father.

I flop down on the sofa and take off my shoes. Kelly has cleaned up the usual debris and I can see the coffee table for the first time, which is a different color than I remembered. More important, though, I can see what's on top of the coffee table.

Condoms. I'm in Hell.

Kelly returns, slipping onto my lap as she hands me a Bartles & Jaymes. I take a long swig, like I'm a ventriloquist and she's my dummy. God knows, my hand'll be up inside her in a matter of minutes. Just like her dad's was . . . oh, try to think of something else, Edward.

Kelly nuzzles my neck.

"Listen," I say, shifting my weight, "I'm all funky. I, uh, need a shower."

"Okay," Kelly says, "why don't I take one with you?"

"NO," I say, much louder than I intended.

Kelly pulls away like she's been slapped. "What's wrong?"

I pitch forward, hiding my face in my hands. "I . . . I just can't do this. I'm sorry."

"Can't do what?"

Can't get an erection, except with your father. Can't handle the pressure of knowing that at any moment your mother could walk in on us and throw me out in the street. Can't handle the fact that I'm still head over heels in lust with Doug.

"Edward, what *is* it?" she says.

I swallow hard. "I don't think . . . we should be together," I say.

"What? You want to move out?"

"No, no, no," I say. Jesus, where would I go? "No, I mean, I don't think we can *be* together."

Kelly's mismatched eyes go wide. "You're breaking up with me?"

"It's not you, it's me."

She crosses her arms to cover up her lingerie-clad body and her eyes turn to watercolors. "But why?" she cries.

"I . . . I can't really say." I am a raw exposed nerve. I am a gaping open wound. "I am so sorry." I reach for Kelly's shoulder, but she pulls away.

"Y'know, Edward," she says, her voice quivering, "for one of the Best Young Actors in America, you sure have shitty timing." Then she turns and runs up the stairs.

I suck.

※　　※　　※

Since Kelly can't kick me out of the house without telling Kathleen how we lied to her, she kicks me out of the locker we share at school instead, offering it to Ziba, a definite improvement when you consider that Ziba doesn't keep anything in her locker except a pack of cigarettes and a bottle of Perrier.

I feel like a total heel about the whole thing, but at least I can focus all my attention on finding a way to pay for Juilliard. Natie and I arrange another brainstorming session, this time at his house. He even buys the beer, having created for himself a very credible-looking fake ID on the computer. ("Waddya think I do all day on that thing? Play Pong?") He still looks like someone's baby brother, but he addresses the issue by getting very indignant with Larry the liquor store guy, yelling, "What's wrong with you? Haven't you ever seen a dwarf before?"

Chez Nudelman is a virtual replica of Casa Zanni, except in reverse, and I've often thought of it as something of a parallel universe. There's even a topsy-turvy quality to the place, what with Fran Nudelman's penchant for carpeting the walls and wallpapering the ceilings. The family is the reverse image of mine, too: Fran is so absorbed by her parental duties that Natie calls her "Smother" behind her back; Stan's medical research job is so arcane that I can't even tell you what it is he does; and Natie's brother Evan got into Yale early decision when he was just sixteen. They are, essentially, a happy family, in their scream-at-each-other-from-the-other-end-of-the-house kind of way and I've always felt at home around them. Jews are a lot like Italians, except smarter.

"Okay, let's take a look at the minutes from our last meeting," Natie says, pulling a sheet of paper out of his briefcase, such a Nudelman thing to have. It's dated September 22, and says *Ways for Edward to Pay for College* at the top. "The first item on our list was getting a job. Edward, could you give us an updated financial report?"

I'm not sure who "us" is, but I figure let him have his chairman of the board fantasy. "There's . . . uh . . . $816, no, $916," I say, adding in the hundred bucks Dr. Corcoran gave me.

Yeah, I know that makes me a whore. So what?

"That's it?" Natie says.

"Yup."

He sighs. "All right, $10,000 minus $916 leaves . . . let's see . . . $9,084 to go."

"Oh God, I'll never make it."

"Get your head off the table, people eat there," he says. "Let's look at number two: scholarships. Any progress there?"

It's not like I haven't tried, but apparently Al isn't the only one who thinks becoming an actor is a waste of money. It seems to me scholarship committees are way too concerned about who's poor rather than who's talented. "I won't be eligible for financial aid for three whole years," I say. "By then I'll be ancient."

"You're right," Natie says, "but don't panic. We have other options. Number three: theft."

I've never seriously considered the idea, but that was before I got into Juilliard, before John fucking Gielgud decided to teach for one year only, before I discovered that my life-long aversion to work was well-founded.

I tug on my beard like Mr. Lucas does. "What would I have to do?" I ask.

Natie smiles his lippy, no-tooth smile. "I was hoping you'd ask." He reaches into his briefcase to pull out another document. "I worked on this in typing when I should have been doing 'The quick brown fox jumps over the lazy dog.' Take a look. It's simple, but inspired."

I study the page carefully. "Couldn't we go to jail for this?" I ask.

"Actually, just you. I've made sure there's no way to connect me to the crime."

"That's a relief," I say.

The doorbell rings and Natie scurries to get it. "Don't worry so much," he shouts. "With good behavior you'd be out in three years. At least then you'll be eligible for financial aid."

Yeah, assuming Juilliard accepts convicted felons.

From the hallway I hear a voice gravel, "Hello, darling," which means either Tallulah Bankhead has risen from the dead or Ziba's here.

I get up to see her and she greets me by thrusting a brownie wrapped in a napkin at me. "Congratulations," she monotones, "you've received a Brownie Award."

"A Brownie Award?"

"You've heard of the Emmys and the Tonys. Well these are the Brownies. We're giving them as rewards for meritorious behavior."

"Who's we?"

"Oh, Kelly," she says, failing to sound nonchalant, "and Doug."

I glance over her shoulder and see the Wagon Ho blowing smoke at the curb.

"Read the napkin," Ziba says.

The napkin reads, "For saying goddamned fucking asswipe shit-for-brains pussy-whipped toad and still getting into Juilliard." Natie earns a Brownie Point, too, for having lowered the movable stage last week while the Wallingford Symphony was performing at the high school. Right in the middle of *Eine Kleine Nachtmusik* the entire front section of the orchestra slowly disappeared, like an ocean liner sinking into the sea. Natie's napkin reads, "For the most moving performance by a stagehand."

"Listen, darlings, I've got to fly," Ziba says, giving us both the European two-cheek-kiss thing. "We've still got to deliver the Ralph Waldo Emerson 'society whips me with its displeasure' award for non-conformity."

"Who to?" I ask.

"That sophomore girl who shaved her head."

"You don't mean the one who's got leukemia, do you?"

"Oh, is that why?" Ziba says, frowning. "Well," she says, flipping her scarf over her shoulder, "it's still a marvelous look for her." Then she pivots like a runway model and strides back to the car. I can't help but notice that the windows are fogged up.

I have no one to blame but myself, but the thought of Kelly and Doug together really pisses me off.

"So waddya say?" Natie asks, licking chocolate off his fingers.

"About what?"

"Reagan's economic policy. My proposal, stupe!"

I lean my head against the front door. "I don't know, Natie, I'm not sure I want to risk going to prison."

"Just think what it'll do for your acting if you do," he says. "Besides, do you really want to work at Chicken Lickin' for the next three years of your life?"

I tear off a piece of brownie and chew on the prospect of working in the Mall That Time Forgot while everyone I know goes off to college.

"I'm in," I say.

twenty-five

While Natie makes the necessary preparations I convince Ziba to try out for Mixed Choir (or the Mixed-Up Choir, as we like to call it) so she can come with us to Washington, D.C., for the big choral competition in March. I tag along to her audition for moral support.

"What would you like to sing, dear?" asks the perpetually cheerful Miss Tinker, as she pulls out a stack of Broadway vocal selections.

"I'm going to sing *Je ne regrette rien*," Ziba says, as if she were announcing it in a nightclub.

"Oh, dear," Miss Tinker says, "I'm afraid I don't have the music for that one."

"That's all right. I don't need it," Ziba says and then, leaning against the piano and tilting her head up like she's Marlene Dietrich searching for her key light, she begins to make a sound that can only be described as a braying cow with a head cold.

"N-*o-o-o-o-o-o-o-o-o-on rien de rien* . . ."

Miss Tinker valiantly tries to maintain her Romper Room–lady smile for encouragement, but she obviously doesn't know what to make of this strange girl. I must say, though, that what Ziba lacks in vocal talent she sure makes up for in commitment. It's a very dogmatic interpretation, kind of how you'd imagine Mussolini would sing.

"That was very . . . original," Miss Tinker says when Ziba finishes, "though I'm not sure you're really old enough to sing about regret, dear."

"That's what you think," Ziba mutters.

Miss Tinker tells her that unfortunately there's no room in the soprano or alto sections, but Ziba informs her she'd much rather sing with the boys anyway. Unorthodox as it may be, even Miss Tinker has to admit that we could always use tenors.

＊　＊　＊

Natie keeps a watchful eye across the street to see when Al and Dagmar go out together. The first step in his supposedly simple plan requires us breaking and entering into my old house to get at Al's financial records. Of course, it's actually unlocking and entering, which, as we've discussed before, isn't a crime, as far as we know.

When Natie finally calls I'm alone at Kathleen's without a car; Kelly's been taking the Wagon Ho even though she hates to drive, just to spite me. I go out to the garage to see if I can find a bicycle.

Now it's a funny thing about people with old money. They seem to take pride in having old stuff, even if that stuff is old crap. So, unlike the garages at my house or Natie's, which are spacious, well-lit, two-car deals, Kathleen's garage is more like an abandoned garden shed where you'd expect to find a key hidden under a flower pot in an Agatha Christie mystery. No one even parks in it. After struggling to open the antique door and then bumping my head on a kayak hanging from the ceiling, I scrounge around in the dark until I find a creaky old bike that looks like it was last used when Miss Gulch tried to bring Toto to the sheriff. It's a humiliating mode of transport, but it's all I've got. I make my way slowly on the icy streets, almost getting run off the road by a couple of assholes in a TransAm who roll down their window to mock me for riding a bike that has a wicker basket with plastic appliqué daisies on it.

I arrive at Natie's both sweaty and freezing. I ring the bell and hear Fran scream, "SOMEONE'S AT THE DOOR!"

Natie answers it. He's dressed in black pants, black turtleneck, and a black woolly cap. He looks less like a burglar than a big charcoal briquette. "Jeez, what took you so long?" he says.

"You know, if you actually bothered to get your license you could have picked me up," I gasp.

Natie shrugs. "Some of us are meant to drive, others are meant to be driven." He glances at Miss Gulch's bike. "Hide that thing behind the hedge, will ya'? You're lowering the property values."

Then he turns and shouts, "HEY MA, EDWARD AND I ARE GOING TO BREAK INTO HIS HOUSE NOW."

"WHAAAAAAAAAAAAAAT?" Fran screams from the other room.

This is why I couldn't have lived here.

"WE'RE GOING TO EMBEZZLE SOME MONEY FROM HIS DAD TO PAY FOR EDWARD'S COLLEGE," Natie shouts.

From another part of the house I hear Stan Nudelman shout, "WHAT ARE YOU BOYS UP TO?"

"THEY'RE GOING TO BREAK INTO EDWARD'S HOUSE TO EMBEZZLE MONEY FROM AL TO PAY FOR EDWARD'S COLLEGE," Fran shouts.

Stan laughs. "YOU KIDS," he says.

As far as Fran and Stan Nudelman are concerned Natie can do no wrong, which is why he possesses so much self-confidence despite the fact that he's a total cheesehead. Over time Natie has discovered that rather than lie to his parents about his various nefarious schemes, he might as well tell the truth because they refuse to believe he's capable of doing such things anyway. Which is how we find ourselves slinking across the street to Al's house with Fran and Stan's blessing.

✵   ✵   ✵

It's only been a month since I left, but the house feels foreign and strange to me, as if I've never lived in it at all, which, of course, is exactly what Dagmar wanted. Natie and I creep down the hallway to Al's study, our feet echoing on the carpetless floors. I suppose the creeping isn't really necessary, but it just seems like the thing to do. We skulk into Al's office and Natie holds the flashlight while I open the drawers of the desk, hunting for checkbooks. There are files marked "Insurance," "Investments," "Receipts," and "Taxes," among others, but the actual bankbooks are nowhere to be found. I start to wish I had paid more attention during those boring-ass business dinners.

"I thought you said you knew where all this stuff was kept," Natie whispers.

"I thought I did," I whisper back.

"Well, it's not there now," he hisses.

"Why are we whispering? Nobody's here."

"Right," says Natie. "Okay, let's think. If you were Al, what would you do?"

What would I do if I were Al? Get a better haircut, for starters. C'mon, Edward, think, think. I try to imagine I've been cast in the role of my father and it's my job to figure out his motivation, but I can't even conceive of how my father thinks. If I were Al, I'd want to be, well, more like me: an artist, not a businessman. Now if it were Dagmar's checkbook, that would be a different story . . .

That's when I remember my evil stepmonster's secret bank

account. "C'mon," I say, and lead Natie back down the hall and into Dagmar's studio.

The walls are lined with contact sheets and works in progress—photos of toxic waste sites, canneries, and a Dumpster behind a Dairy Queen—and I find myself thinking how strange it is that such a compulsively neat woman would photograph such filthy places. Mixed in are some exceedingly silly fashion shots of Dagmar from her days as a model.

"What are we doing in here?" Natie asks, peering at a picture of a dead squirrel.

"You remember the account that Doug said Dagmar was using to siphon off Al's money?"

"Yeah."

"Well, if this were your room, and you didn't want Al to find something, where would you hide it?"

Natie doesn't even need to think about it. "The closet inside the closet!" he says.

"That's using your Nudelman."

Back when Natie and I were kids we sawed a hole inside my closet so we'd have a secret place to hide things like firecrackers and matches. (Natie used to be something of a pyro, although they never proved a thing when that gazebo in the park burned down.) As I got older I used it to stash porn and the occasional bag of weed.

We push a table out of the way and slide open the closet door. There, hidden behind some rolls of background paper, we see the jagged hole we created ten years ago. I reach in, convinced as always that I'm going to get bitten by a rat, but instead feel something shaped exactly like a bankbook. I pull it out and wave it in the air, nearly knocking over a light stand in the process.

"*Wunderbar!*" I cry.

Natie grabs the book, flips it open to the ledger, and points his flashlight. "There's $12,320 in this account," he says. "Jeez, Al really is a shit-for-brains pussy-whipped toad."

John fucking Gielgud, here I come.

I hold the flashlight while Natie carefully removes a check from the back of the book, explaining to me that this way Dagmar won't notice the check is missing until after it's too late. "And it's not like she can go tell Al about it because she stole it from him in the first place. It's the perfect crime."

We both jump up and down and do a little happy dance. "I just need a signature I can forge and we're done," he says. "Where do you suppose she keeps her canceled checks?"

I grin. "We don't need canceled checks," I say. I wave the flashlight around the room at Dagmar's photos. Each one is signed "D. Teufel" in huge letters, like she wanted to be certain everyone knew who did them.

Natie's button eyes brighten. "Jeez, this is almost too easy," he says. He does a few practice drafts while I relax on the floor. I lie back, gazing at a still life of moldy bread. For the first time in months I feel completely, totally at peace. I've bought myself a year, a whole year! Natie writes a check for $10,500: ten grand for Juilliard, five hundred for his commission. He leaves the rest in the account in case Dagmar writes a check.

"Now all we need to do is launder the money and we're done," Natie says.

"Okay, explain to me what money laundering is again."

"Jeez, Edward, didn't Al teach you anything at those business dinners?"

He's about to explain when we hear the rumble of the garage door. "Shit, they're home!"

We frantically put the closet back together, knocking our heads together like we're Laurel and Hardy, then make a mad dash down the hall for the front door. But right as we reach the entryway the back door opens. Adrenaline soaring, I grab Natie by the scruff of the neck and pull us both behind the sofa in the furniture museum. My heart is beating so hard it feels like it's banging on my chest to get out, but I feel reasonably safe. No one ever goes in the Museum of Furniture.

I hear the click of Dagmar's spiky heels on the kitchen linoleum, followed by the sound of Al's keys as they slide across the counter. "I still don't understand what I did wrong this time," Al says.

"Vell, if you don't know, I'm certainly not goink to tell you."

"That makes no sense. How am I supposed to find out, then?"

"Oh, you know already."

"No, I don't. I really don't."

"LIAAAAR!" Dagmar screams.

I feel Natie flinch next to me. The yelling at the Nudelman's doesn't sound anything like this.

"You play tsese games to torment me!"

Al groans. "I don't know what the fuck you're talking about," he says. "All's I said was 'Did you have a good time tonight?' and you've been screaming at me ever since."

"Goot time? Goot time? I'll show you a goot time."

For a split second I worry that this little scene might be some kind of sick prelude to a noisy, angry fuck when I hear the unmistakable sound of glassware being thrown.

"What're ya' tryin' to do, kill me?" Al yells.

"No, it is you who are tryink to kill me," she screams. "How can I create ven I am subject to your rules, your restrictions, your chudgments? I am suffocatink here! Suffocatink!"

I know how she feels.

Dagmar starts to wheeze and I hear her grab her asthma inhaler and suck in.

"You all right?" Al asks.

"Stay avay from me," she croaks. I hear the swoop of the keys as they're lifted off the counter, then the clicking of Dagmar's heels on the linoleum.

"Where are you going now?" Al asks.

"Avay from you!" she bellows, then slams the door.

"Crazy bitch," Al mutters.

From the garage we hear Dagmar's voice echo, "I heard tsat, azz*huuuull.*"

It's quiet for a long time and I wonder what Al's doing, but I don't dare move. Finally there's the sound of crunching glass as he walks out of the kitchen and around the corner to the entry of the furniture museum. I peek between the couch and the end table and see him standing there, rocking back and forth on his heels and jingling the change in his pockets absentmindedly. He looks old to me. His shoulders sag and he sighs as he slouches over to the liquor cabinet. He pours himself a drink, straight, downs it and then pours another. Can't say I blame him. I knew Dagmar was a monster, but I hadn't realized it had come to this. Al flicks on the stereo and pulls a record off the shelf.

It's Frank, of course. "That's Life." A good choice.

Al roams the room aimlessly, listlessly picking up various pieces of bric-a-brac and putting them down as he sings along. He begins softly at first, but as the music builds, his voice grows stronger and louder and I hear for the first time what my father's singing voice sounds like. He sounds just like me, actually, or I guess I should say I sound just like him. I had no idea. It's a warm and croony sound, and has a real vibrato. I always assumed that I got my talent from my mother, who is the creative one, so it's a real shock to realize I inherited my voice from my dad. Al gives a full Vegas-style performance, and it's really so good I almost want to applaud at the end. But when the song's over, he turns off the stereo and, shoulders sagging again, trudges out of the furniture museum and down the hallway to his bedroom.

I almost feel sorry for the guy.

❋   ❋   ❋

The next day after school Natie and I go to the Wallingford Public Library to do research. We have to walk there because Kelly's off in the Wagon Ho with Doug, no doubt losing her virginity, and by the time we've arrived the place is full of students pretending to work. We wander around looking for a table until we see Ziba by herself in the corner with her Jackie O sunglasses on, as if she were hiding from the paparazzi. A shaft of sunlight falls across her table from a tall library window and as we get closer I can see all the particles of dust floating in the sunbeam. Is that really what the air we breathe looks like? Disgusting. Ziba is concentrating very hard on three open volumes of encyclopedias spread out in front of her.

We put our backpacks down on the table. "Whatcha doin', Zeeb?" Natie asks.

She doesn't look up. "Trying to decide which of these articles to plagiarize for American history."

"It's best to take a little from each," Natie says. The voice of experience.

Ziba takes off her glasses and rubs her eyes. "It's useless. There's no way Ms. Toquitz is going to believe I could write anything so dull." She slams a book closed in frustration. "Persian culture dates back to 3,000 BC," she says. "As far as I'm concerned, something that happened two hundred years ago isn't history, it's gossip." She gathers her hair in a bun and sticks a pencil in it to hold it in place. "What are you boys up to?"

I look at Natie. I'm not sure it's necessarily a good idea to tell anyone we're looking to find the name of someone our age who died as a baby so we can steal his identity.

"We're looking to find the name of someone our age who died as a baby so we can steal his identity," Natie says.

"Oh," Ziba says like she hears it every day, "need help?" This is what I love most about Ziba: she is completely unshockable. She treats identity theft as if it were a cool elective she couldn't get into because of a scheduling conflict.

The whole reason we're stealing an identity is so we can launder the money we're draining from Dagmar's account. I just wanted to make the check out to cash, but Natie told me we'd have to cash it at Dagmar's bank and such a large amount would immediately raise questions. By opening a bank account under an assumed identity we can deposit the check into a new account and withdraw it as cash without Dagmar being able to trace it back to us.

Now in case you've never stolen an identity, here's how it works: you comb the obituaries of your local paper from around the time of your birth and find the name of someone who died in infancy. Then you get a resourceful but unscrupulous friend like Nathan Nudelman to find out the Social Security number for you and forge a new birth certificate.

Do I have great friends or what?

Unfortunately, as the three of us sift through the microfiche of back issues of *The Towne Crier* we discover that infants don't die very often in Wallingford. After three hours of thoroughly depressing reading all we've come up with are three Vietnamese orphans and two Thalido-mide babies. Despite being one of the Best Young Actors in America, I think I'm going to have a hard time convincing a bank teller that I am either Asian or three feet tall with flippers instead of arms. While Natie and I argue over the possible use of makeup and prosthetics I notice Ziba lean back from her microfiche machine and wipe a tear from her eye.

I've never seen Ziba cry before and I rush over like I'm the little Dutch boy who has to plug up the hole in the dike. I kneel down next to her and look at a microfiche of a page from *The Towne Crier* dated June 11, 1968.

> (Battle Brook) Four-year-old LaChance Jones was killed Tues-day afternoon while playing in her front yard, the innocent vic-tim of a bullet intended for her uncle, Leon Madison, 28, a convicted felon and suspected drug dealer. The identity of the two gunmen hasn't been determined, but Mr. Madison has been held for questioning. The girl's mother, Alicia Jones, 25, was shot in the side as she tried to shield her daughter from the

spray of bullets. She is reported to be in stable condition and
is expected to recover.

"Expected to recover," Ziba says, shaking her head. "You don't ever
recover from something like that." Her voice is heavy, like it's got the
weight of the world in it.

We all have our personal sadnesses: my mom left, Paula's died,
Doug's dad smacked him around, but none of us lost a whole country,
a whole way of life. Ziba's family was in the south of France on holiday
when the Shah was overthrown, and they suddenly found themselves
exiled with whatever belongings they had brought on vacation with
them. Their money was in Swiss bank accounts, but they lost everything else, not just a house and cars and furniture, but the things they
could never replace, like family photos or, even more important, family
itself. I can't help but feel that her sorrow runs deeper than the rest
of ours.

Next to the article is a picture of a little black girl, her hair in two
poofy buns on the side of her head like Minnie Mouse. It's one of those
Sears shots with a fake autumnal background. Her mouth is wide open
like she's laughing and she grips a small pumpkin in her pudgy arms.

"That's horrible," I say.

"Yeah," Natie adds from behind me, "if it had been a little boy we
could have used his name."

Ziba and I both turn to scowl at him.

"Don't look at me that way," he says. "I didn't shoot her. I'm just
saying it's too bad Edward couldn't pretend to be a twenty-year-old
black woman, that's all."

I suppose he's right in his completely cheesehead way. Except for
the occasional unguarded moment when certain Diana Ross manner-
isms creep in, I don't think I'd make a very convincing black woman.
"So much for LaChance," I say.

"It's pronounced *LaShaaahnce*," Ziba says, lingering on the vowel
in the French manner.

"How do you know?"

"I just do," she says. She turns to look at the screen again. "I feel . . .
I don't know . . . an almost mystical connection to this little girl." She
runs her long, tapered fingers across the screen, like she's trying to reach
inside. "LaChance," she repeats to herself. "It's almost like a poem."
She swivels around in her chair to look at me and Natie. "Why is it

white people in this country never give their children such lovely names?"

The setting sun shines across Ziba's high cheekbones and her deep-set eyes, casting nearly half of her taut, cocoa face into shadow. In that light and with her hair up on her head she almost looks like Lena Horne ready to sing some sultry number in an MGM Technicolor musical.

"Why are you two looking at me like that?" she asks.

twenty-six

Despite Ziba claiming her "performing days are over," like she's Garbo in retirement, she agrees to take a chance on LaChance. I don't know how Natie goes about getting LaChance's Social Security number and forging her birth certificate and I don't ask. All I know is that he doesn't show up at school for three whole days. I'm beginning to worry, so I call his house.

"Helloooooo?" says a voice trilling up an octave. It's Fran. For reasons known only to her, she always tries to sound British when she answers the phone.

"Hi, Mrs. Nudelman, it's Edward. Is Natie there?"

Fran puts the phone down, but not far enough. "STAN, DO YOU KNOW WHERE NATHAN IS?" she screams.

"HE SAID SOMETHING ABOUT NEEDING TO FAKE SOME LEGAL DOCUMENTS."

Fran laughs, a rattling noise like a fork stuck in the garbage disposal. "THAT KID," she says, then suddenly she's Julie Andrews again. "Edwaaaard? Are you still theeeere?"

"I heard," I say. "Just tell him I called, all right?"

※　※　※

Two days later I still haven't heard from him. What's worse, Ziba stops showing up at school, too. I appreciate them working so hard on my case, but since I'm the one who could go to jail for fraud, it'd be nice if I knew what was being done on my behalf. I've just gotten home from school and am compulsively making my way through an entire lasagna when there's a loud knock at the front door. The cats scurry, knocking over a basket that contains, inexplicably, sheet music and mittens. As I lean over to move the basket out of the way a slip of paper comes shooting through the mail slot and lands at my feet.

It's a bank deposit for $10,500 into the account of LaChance Jones.

I yank the door open and there's Ziba, her angular body leaning nonchalantly against the door frame as she nibbles on a brownie. She raises it like she's giving a toast.

"I gave it to myself for Best Performance by an Identity Thief," she says.

She's dressed as a nun.

I'm about to ask her why when Natie pops out from behind her.

"Congratulations," he says and hands me some slips of paper.

"What are these?"

"Receipts. If you can't reimburse me today, I can wait until tomorrow. Say, you got anything to drink? I've got a bad taste in my mouth."

He's also dressed as a nun.

"I'm all out of communion wine, Sister," I say. "How about some holy water?"

"The outfits were my idea," Ziba says, following Natie into the kitchen, "but we had to have them altered. Whoever made these for *The Sound of Music* had no sense of style." She sits down. "You wouldn't have any Perrier, would you?"

"How about a Mountain Dew?"

"Perfect."

"Me, too," says Natie.

"So what's with the costumes?"

"Well," he says, "it turns out that you have to show proof of address to open a bank account—a phone bill or an electric bill or something. So we thought to ourselves, 'Who would have a legitimate reason not to have bills?' and we came up with nuns. Ooh, look, lasagna, cool." He goes to the silverware drawer to get a fork.

"So now what?" I ask as I admire the fake driver's license Natie made for Ziba/LaChance. "Can we write a check to Juilliard?"

"Not yet," Natie says, shoveling in a forkful of lasagna. "We've still got to find a way of getting the money to them without it being traced."

"How about a money order?" I ask.

"Nope," Natie says as he chews. "There's a $500 limit. We've got to get a cashier's check." He coughs and starts to choke on his food.

Ziba gives him a whack on the back and continues for him. "The problem with a cashier's check is that the bank keeps a record of it." She looks down at Natie. "Good God, Nathan, are you all right?"

Natie nods and takes a sip of Mountain Dew.

"Why don't we just withdraw it as cash?" I ask.

Natie rolls his watery eyes. "We can't very well pay Juilliard in cash," he gurgles. "It'll arouse too much suspicion."

"Okay," I say, "why don't we withdraw the funds as cash and then go to another bank and write a cashier's check there?"

"We could," Natie says as he takes another bite, "but it's so . . ."

Simple? Logical? Easy?

"Uninspired," Ziba says.

Natie nods. "Exactly. Let's face it, when Dagmar realizes that ten grand is missing . . ."

"Ten thousand five hundred," I say.

"When she realizes all that dough is missing, she's bound to go sniffing around. You're going to need a sound alibi about where you got that money from."

"I could say I earned it."

Natie and Ziba cast gimme-a-break looks at me.

"Okay, I could say it was a scholarship."

"That's right," Ziba says. "We could create a scholarship ourselves and then award it to Edward."

Natie smiles his lippy, no-tooth smile. "I like how you think," he says.

✳   ✳   ✳

We open up a jug of wine (Kathleen goes through so many she'll never notice) and set about designing a fake scholarship. Natie has the idea that we actually donate the money to Juilliard with the stipulation that it can only be used for a scholarship so narrow in focus only I could be eligible for it. That way the money goes through Juilliard and will appear to have no connection to me at all. I think it's risky, but we come up with a scholarship from the Catholic Vigilance Society of Hoboken, New Jersey (Father G. Roovy, Executive Director) for "a promising young Italian-American actor from Hoboken." After a few glasses of wine, it starts to sound pretty good to me.

"How will they know you're from Hoboken?" Ziba asks.

"My place of birth is on the application," I say.

"But what if another actor was also born there? Then what?"

I give her a withering Mr. Lucas–like stare. "You've obviously never been to Hoboken," I say.

Just in case, Natie says he'll get the list of all the actors who've been accepted at Juilliard and run background checks on them.

"You can do that?" I ask.

"What do you think we do in the Computer Club, play Pac-Man?"

He scares me sometimes.

※　※　※

Along with fraud, forgery, and embezzlement, creating a 501(c)3 non-profit organization counts as yet another thing I never thought I'd do in my life. Hell, I had a hard enough time just figuring out my W-2 from Chicken Lickin'. Luckily for us, the IRS allows personal gifts of up to $10,000, so we don't have to worry about being audited and thus adding federal crimes to my ever-expanding dossier.

The first order of business is getting a post office box for the Catholic Vigilance Society (the CV initial was Ziba's characteristically droll contribution), which requires a trip into Hoboken, something I typically avoid. Kelly lets me borrow the Wagon Ho (now that she's officially dating Doug she's been feeling a little more charitable toward me) and Father Groovy makes a painfully easy trip to the post office; after all, who's going to question the motives of a priest? But I have to provide an address to open the box (which is ridiculous because if you had an address, why would you need a post office box), so I use the Convent of the Bleeding Heart. Then I make a side trip to visit the house I was born in.

I have a hard time finding it, there's so much new development going on. Hoboken is quickly becoming the yuppie commute of choice into the city because the rents are still affordable. As a result, new condos and renovations are happening all over. After stopping to ask directions several times (people are always so nice to priests), I find the little two-story box I lived in until I was six. I guess it shouldn't matter, but it makes me happy to see the house has been well taken care of. It's been painted butter yellow with black shutters and a bright red door. There's a new hedge around the property and the tree in the tiny front yard has gotten so tall it now shades the house. Al once put up a swing in that tree but Karen and I played so hard on it, it fell and she broke her collarbone. My mother got so hysterical that by the time the paramedics arrived she had to be sedated and strapped down in the back of the ambulance while Karen rode to the hospital in front with the driver.

Good times.

*　　*　　*

Once we have a post office box, we need to go to the career center at the high school to learn how to write a proper business letter. Who would've guessed an actor would have to know all these things? I hate to admit it, but I'm glad that Al forced me to take typing. Here's our letter:

> February 3, 1984
>
> The Catholic Vigilance
>   Society of Hoboken
> P.O. Box 216
> Hoboken, NJ 07030
>
> The Juilliard School
> Office of Financial Aid
> 60 Lincoln Center Plaza
> New York, NY 10023
>
> To Whom It May Concern:
>
> On behalf of an anonymous donor to the Catholic Vigilance Society of Hoboken, I am pleased to enclose this $10,000 check to the Juilliard School's Drama Division with the express purpose that it pay the first year's tuition of a promising Italian-American actor born in Hoboken, New Jersey.
>
> Our donor, a native son of Hoboken, understands from firsthand experience the challenges facing performing artists and hopes that this first donation will help in the development of a talented individual from his cherished birthplace.
>
> Respectfully,
> I am,
> *Father G. Roovy*
> President

The Sinatra implication is my idea. It helps lend some credibility (Frank's generosity is legendary), not to mention some swagger and swing.

My freshman year thus secured, I decide it's okay to be in the spring musical. We're doing *Godspell* and I'm perfect for the role of Jesus, despite the fact that I'm committing several felonies. So I quit my job at Chicken Lickin'.

Goodance riddance, I say.

It's bad enough having to wear a paper hat to work, even though I coped the best I could by tilting mine at a stylish and slightly ironic angle, but then, to my complete mortification, my boss decided my hair was too long and I needed a hairnet, too. (Like Miss Black Roots and Dried-Out Perm is in any position to be giving tonsorial advice.) Between the little military-style hat and the hairnet I looked like one of the Andrews Sisters about to launch into "Boogie Woogie Bugle Boy." And not the pretty one in the middle either, but the tall, gawky one; you know, Maxene or LaVerne, I can never remember which is which.

Besides, it was Jesus himself who said, "Consider the lilies of the field, how they grow; they neither toil nor spin," so I figure why the hell should I? Hard work may pay off in the long run, but the benefits of laziness are immediate.

❊   ❊   ❊

The first day of rehearsal is awkward. Mr. Lucas has asked Kelly to choreograph the show ("*Whell*, you certainly don't expect me to do it," he says) and, believe it or not, it's going to be harder to avoid each other at play practice than at home.

I slip in backstage and watch from the wings. Mr. Lucas and Kelly are chatting with Ziba, who is stage-managing, and Doug, who's essentially playing opposite me in the dual roles of John the Baptist and Judas. I stand there frozen, uncertain what to do and feeling like a cheesehead for being uncertain. From behind me I hear a voice say, "This is bullshit."

I turn around and see Natie, his face screwed up like kneaded dough. He grabs me by the arm and says, "C'mon, let's get this thing settled once and for all."

"Cut it out," I say, but he pushes me hard enough that I stumble forward and drop my books on the stage. Everyone turns to see what happened and I feel even more stupid. I pick up the books, silently cursing

Natie, and shuffle over to Kelly. Everyone else tries to look as if they're not watching me, except Mr. Lucas, who seems to regard this little daytime drama as vastly amusing.

"Excuse me, Mr. Lucas," Natie says, "but we need a minute to take care of something."

Mr. Lucas regards us over his glasses, and mutters, "*Uh*bviously."

"Okay, listen," Natie says to me and Kelly, "if you two don't want to talk at home that's fine with the rest of us, but enough already with it here at school, okay? We've got a show to do and you're just gonna suck all the fun right out of it. Kelly . . ."

Kelly turns, her mismatched eyes moist. She bites her lip.

". . . we all know Edward did a shitty thing to you, but he's really, really sorry. He's been under a lot of pressure right now so you need to cut him some slack."

She looks like she's about to say something, but Natie turns directly to me. "Edward, you had your chance with Kelly and you blew it, so stop acting like such a freak show around her and Doug."

Doug snorts. Natie thrusts a pudgy finger at him.

"Listen, buddy, for Edward's supposedly best friend you haven't done shit to help him pay for college, so shape up, okay? And Ziba . . ."

"Yes, Nathan?"

"Nice outfit."

"Thank you."

"You're welcome. Oh, and listen, cut the ice-queen routine, okay? Doug's totally over you." He appraises us like he's a drill sergeant and we're the sorriest bunch of recruits he's ever seen. "I'm working my ass off here trying to raise Edward's tuition and I need everybody to work together. Now on the count of three, we'll have a big group hug and all start acting like friends again, all right? One . . . two . . . three!"

Natie.

* * *

A week later two priests (Fathers Groovy and Grabowski) and three nuns (Sister Ziba, Sister Kelly, and Sister Nudelman) pile into a station wagon headed for Hoboken. I'm not sure the disguises are necessary, but we've come to think of them as the official uniforms of CV Enterprises and a sign of our mutual solidarity. We go together like ramma lamma lamb of God.

I like dressing as a priest. Not only does it put me in a spiritual frame of mind but lots of people apologize to you for not going to Mass more often and you get to forgive them. It's nice.

First stop is LaChance's bank in Cramptown where, just for fun, Ziba withdraws the ten grand in $100 bills. That's *one hundred* $100 bills. No one but Ziba has ever seen that kind of cash before and we all take turns counting it, everyone making the same joke of pretending to steal it for themselves. We're all so excited none of us seems capable of having a normal conversation so we sing songs from *Godspell* for the rest of the trip. (I know it's totally queer, but that's how we are.)

We all go into the bank in Hoboken for safety reasons although, realistically, who but the most hardened of criminals would dare mug a group of nuns and priests? What's more, Hoboken has a long and distinguished history of Mob connections, so the sight of a priest with $10,000 in cash doesn't seem to faze the teller at all. Everyone gathers around as I write the words "Juilliard School" on the cashier's check.

"Praise Jesus," says Sister Nudelman.

I put the check in the envelope with the letter from the Catholic Vigilance Society and lick it shut, getting a tiny paper cut as I do.

We're almost done.

The only thing left is getting the check to Juilliard. There was some debate about how to handle this step, but we eventually decided that delivering by hand was the safest way to be certain it got there.

We stop and have lunch first where, despite being dressed as a priest, I'm still mistaken for a waiter. We're coming out of the restaurant, laughing and joking, when I hear a familiar voice call my name. I turn and there, standing on the sidewalk in a hat with a veil, is Aunt Glo.

"Oh, baby doll," she cries, her pudgy little body flopping into my arms. "I prayed to St. Christopher to help me find the way, and here you are to help me. Thank you." She crosses herself.

"What are you doing here?" I ask, trying to look as if there was nothing unusual about my standing on the streets of Hoboken dressed as a priest.

"Oh, Eddie, it was terrible." She pulls a tissue out of her purse to wipe her nose and sees everyone else for the first time. "Waddya know, it's the LBs!" she says. "Don't you all look nice."

"We're doing research," Natie says, "for *Godspell*."

Aunt Glo seems to neither understand nor care. "So, this morning I got up and decided it was such a beautiful day I'd come into Hoboken for my Angelo's funeral."

"Angelo's dead?"

"Of course not," she says, crossing herself. "God forbid. He was saying a funeral Mass. Oh, my Angelo does such a beautiful job with funerals. You kids should come sometime, they're practically like musicals. And there's always food after. Anyway, what was I talking about?"

I'm never quite sure how to answer that question. In fact, I've always been tempted to throw out an entirely different topic ("Greyhound racing! Margaret Thatcher! The famine in Ethiopia!") just to see if she starts talking about it.

"The funeral today . . ." I say.

"Right," she says, patting her neck with a tissue. "Paula's too busy having premarital sex with her long-haired boyfriend to drive me anyplace, so I say to myself, I say, 'Gloria, take the train.' So I do. Well, nothin' looks the same anymore in this damn—excuse my language, Father—city. So here I am wandering the streets like a crazy person when, thank you, Jesus, Mary, Joseph, and all the saints in Heaven, I find you."

"What time is the funeral?" I ask.

"Oh, I missed it already. I just wanna go home. You kids didn't drive, didja?"

"Well, actually . . ."

"Oh, Eddie, do an old lady a favor and take me home, will ya'? I'll pay ya' in cannolis. I just made a fresh batch."

"But . . ."

"Great. Where's the car?"

I bug my eyes out at Natie, the Internationally Recognized Signal for "What the fuck are we supposed to do with this crazy old lady?"

"Listen, Mrs. D'Angelo . . ." Natie says.

"Please, Sister, Aunt Glo," she says. "Everybody calls me Aunt Glo."

"We need to make a stop in the city. Is it okay with you if we swing past Juilliard?"

"You kidding?" she says. "I can finally give my fornicating niece a piece of my mind."

I'm thinking Aunt Glo needs to hold on to whatever pieces she has left. We put her in the Wagon Ho.

I pull Natie aside and whisper, "What are you *thinking*?"

"Don't you see, she's the perfect cover," he says. "It's like hiding in plain sight. Who's going to suspect anything of a priest and a sweet old lady?"

"I'm not so sure that's a good idea."

"Trust me," he says. "You walk in, you drop off the check, you leave. What could possibly go wrong?"

twenty-seven

As Aunt Glo and I approach the double doors of the theater building, my mind travels back to the day I said "goddamned fucking asswipe shit-for-brains pussy-whipped toad" in front of Marian Seldes. I find it ironic that on the day I was supposed to be acting, I couldn't help but be myself. Now on a day when I should just be myself, I'm acting. Going into Juilliard is a risk, of course, but between the beard and the glasses I think I look sufficiently different from the sweaty, crazed lunatic who auditioned here. What's more, experience has proven that most people tend to focus on the clerical collar rather than the person wearing it. That's just how it is with priests, even the phony ones.

I hold the door open for Aunt Glo and a gaggle of noisy students passes by. I'm a little concerned we'll run into Paula, but since she's the one who swiped the priest's collar to begin with, she's hardly in a position to question it.

The school is pretty small, being so exclusive and all, and everyone seems to want to help a bewildered-looking priest and an old lady find their way. I open the door of the financial aid office for Aunt Glo, then walk up to the counter. A black woman with cornrows is seated in front of a computer monitor while a gray-haired white woman looks over her shoulder. Gray Hair looks momentarily surprised (I'm guessing it's not every day that the clergy walks into the financial aid office of Juilliard), then smiles.

"What can I do for you, Father?" she asks. Everyone's always so nice to priests.

I look down, in part to affect Father Groovy's humble demeanor, but also to avoid letting her get a good look at me. "Would you be certain that the head of financial aid gets this? It's very important," I say in Father Groovy's gentle, breathless voice.

"Certainly." Gray Hair turns to Cornrows. "It's for you," she says, handing her the envelope.

I love New York. You'd never see anybody with cornrows in charge of anything in New Jersey. The woman rises with difficulty, revealing that she's very, very pregnant, and ambles over to the counter. "Hello, I'm Laurel Watkins," she says in a deep professional way. "How can I help you?"

How can you help me? You can take this letter and pretend you've never seen me, that's how.

"We wish to donate money for a scholarship," I say to my shoes.

She smiles. "Won't you come into my office?"

I glance at Aunt Glo briefly to see what she's making of all this, but she's just grinning like she's enjoying the opportunity to meet new people. She doesn't get out much.

We go in. I swear, if Natie had a neck, I'd wring it.

Laurel Watkins points to a couple of chairs for us to sit in. "Would you care for some coffee, Father . . . ?"

"Roovy," I say, "Greg Roovy. No, thank you."

"And you . . . ?" she asks, looking at Aunt Glo.

"No, thanks," Aunt Glo says. "It's a long ride back and I've got a bladder the size of a fava bean. Up and down all night, I am."

Laurel Watkins looks bewildered, not an unusual response to Aunt Glo, then says, "I'm sorry, I didn't catch your name."

"Gloria D'Angelo," she says, extending a pudgy hand, "mother of a priest. I'm also the aunt of a stu . . ."

"On second thought I think I will have that cup of coffee," I say.

"Certainly," Laurel Watkins says, not looking happy about trying to get up again. "Black or with cream and sugar?"

"Yes," I say.

She frowns, hoists herself up, and slowly shambles out of the room. As soon as she's gone I grab Aunt Glo's fleshy little palms. "Please, please, please just play along, will you?" I whisper. "I'll explain later."

"Of course, Eddie, whatever you say," she says in a hushed tone, or at least Aunt Glo's idea of a hushed tone. She takes a hanky out of her purse. "Here, lemme wipe that sweat off your nose."

Laurel Watkins returns with a small tray containing a cup of coffee, cream, and sugar, none of which I touch because, of course, I hate coffee. "Ms. Watkins, we won't take up too much of your time," I say. "Everything you need to know is in the letter."

She sits down at her desk, puts on her glasses, and opens the envelope. "Oh, my," she says, "this is indeed a surprise. Thank you. I don't know what to say."

"Oh, you don't need to thank us, dear," Aunt Glo says. "We're but the messengers . . ."

"That's right," I say, "the actual donor wishes to remain anonymous."

"Of course," Laurel Watkins says. "That's not unusual." She pulls a manila file folder out of her desk drawer and puts our letter into it.

I continue. "The only thing that matters to our donor and to the Catholic Vigilance Society is that the money be used for a promising young Italian-American actor from Hoboken, New Jersey."

"Yes, I understand that," she says, removing her glasses. "But I hope you realize, Father Roovy, that it could be some time before an actor fulfilling that criteria is accepted here."

I give a beatific, crinkle-eyed smile. "Of course, of course," I say, "but our donor feels especially strong about helping someone from his hometown."

Aunt Glo leans forward and adds, "He's a big supporter of the Catholic Vigilante Society."

"Vigilance," I say, "Catholic Vigilance Society." I turn to Laurel Watkins. "Well, if there aren't any more questions we have some very sick people we need to visit."

"Certainly," Laurel Watkins says, "and please tell your donor how grateful we are for his generous gift."

"I will."

"It was a pleasure meeting you, Mrs. D'Angelo," she says. Damnit. Of course Laurel Watkins is the kind of person who remembers names. And Aunt Glo is the kind of person who isn't easy to forget.

"Likewise," says Aunt Glo, smiling. "Now, c'mon, baby doll," she says to me, "I gotta make peeps."

✳   ✳   ✳

"She seemed nice," Aunt Glo says as we step out into the bright winter sun. It's windy on the plaza and a sharp breeze cuts into us. "Now do ya' mind tellin' me what the hell is goin' on?"

Over by the fountain a nun sits on a priest's lap while nearby two other nuns nonchalantly smoke a cigarette and eat a hot dog. I lead Aunt Glo to a bench out of the wind. I can't even look her in the face. "Listen," I say, "it's probably better if you don't know. It's kind of bad."

She puts her hand on my knee. "Are you in some kind of trouble, baby doll?"

"No . . ." I say. "Well, possibly . . . if I get caught." Where do I start? How do I even begin to explain this whole cheesehead scheme?

I tell her everything, putting particular emphasis on the fact that Dagmar stole the money first, and avoiding words like embezzlement, fraud, forgery, or money laundering. To passersby it must look like a priest is hearing an impromptu confession from an older parishioner, but in reality it's the other way around. "Do you think I'm a bad person?" I ask when I'm finished.

"Oh, baby doll, that's for God to decide, not me."

I guess the mother of a priest is bound to give you an answer like that.

"Are you going to tell on me?"

Aunt Glo straightens my collar. "Who am I going to tell? Your father? That man oughta be ashamed of himself, not supporting a talented boy like you." She sighs and shakes her head. "With Italians, you're not considered a man until you can beat up your father. It's stupid, but there you have it. I thank the blessed Virgin my Benny is dead, God rest his soul, so my precious Angelo didn't have to go through something like this. He's just like you, my Angelo, sensitive." She takes my face in her pudgy hands. "But you listen to me. Two wrongs don't make a right—never have, never will. Eventually you're gonna hafta make your peace with God."

I nod. "But in the meantime, do you think He'd mind if I went to Juilliard?"

Aunt Glo squeezes both my cheeks. "All's I know, baby doll, is that when you're onstage singing, you're a pure expression of God's grace. And I can't believe that God doesn't want that, no matter what."

I hug her for a really long time and she rubs my back just like my mother used to.

"How am I ever going to make this up to you?" I say.

She takes my hand in hers. "I'll think of somethin'," she says.

* * *

A week later I get a phone call from Paula. "You'll *never* fucking believe it!" she shouts over the street noise. "Just listen to what's on Page Six of the *New York Post*.

"Ol' Blue Eyes is at it again. Sources at the Juilliard School of Drama say that the Chairman of the Board himself is the anonymous donor for a full-tuition scholarship. Sinatra didn't have any comments on the report, but the crooner is well known for his generosity. The only question remains, 'Why the secrecy, Frank?'

"I called the financial aid office and they said it's for a promising young Italian-American actor who, get this, was born in *Hoboken*! Isn't that fucking *amazing*? It's like it was made for you!"

I give a convincing performance of fucking amazement. I am, after all, one of the Best Young Actors in America.

"You've got to call them right now," she says. "Oh, Edward, didn't I say something like this would happen? I knew it, I just *knew* it. Let me give you the number . . ."

I know the number (by heart, as a matter of fact) but I pretend to write it down, then do a little happy dance around the living room before calling.

"Hi, my name is Edward Zanni," I say, trying to sound as much like myself as I can. "I'm an incoming freshman in the acting program and I'd like to inquire about the Sinatra scholarship mentioned in today's *Post*."

"The origin of the scholarship is a completely unsubstantiated rumor," says the voice on the other end of the line, which I recognize as being the gray-haired woman behind the counter. "The *Post* never should have run that item."

"Oh," I say, sounding disappointed. "I was just interested because I was born in Hoboken and . . ."

"Could you hold for a moment please?"

I'm on hold for just a couple of seconds when a deep voice comes on, saying, "This is Laurel Watkins. How can I help you?"

twenty-eight

Of course Laurel Watkins doesn't come right out and say the scholarship is mine (she needs to confirm this, that, and the other thing, blah, blah, blah), but it's obvious Natie's scheme is going to work. I mean, what could go wrong?

Unshackled at last from the tyranny of Al Zanni, I feel ready for some magic and mischief in my life and the Mixed-Up Choir's trip to Washington, D.C., provides the perfect opportunity. When they make the movie of my life, this trip will definitely have to be another of those montage sequences filled with madcap adolescent high jinks; y'know, like blackmailing the son of a U.S. senator.

Maybe I'd better explain that one.

First you'll see us rehearsing the "Hallelujah Chorus" in preparation for the big choir competition held every year in D.C. There's Miss Tinker trying to be all serious classical-music conductor-y, alternately closing her eyes in great reverence, waving her arms with ecclesiastical vigor, and otherwise looking like Sally Field battling multiple personality disorder in *Sybil*.

Then there's Kelly with the sopranos, her pink skin shiny, her eyes alive and bright—how she loves to sing—her lips curled to form the perfect pear-shaped tones Miss Tinker desires.

Cut to Doug directly across the room in the baritone section, his dimples deep and long as he smiles his satyr's grin, the veins in his neck pulsing as he belts out his part—how he loves to sing—his eyes riveted on Kelly's perfect pear-shaped mouth.

Cut to the tenors, where Ziba stands a head taller than most of the guys and two heads taller than Natie, her creamy cocoa face tilted slightly upward like a statue of an Egyptian goddess, her expression totally blasé as if she were singing "Hand me my lighter, darling" instead of "For the lord God omnipotent reigneth."

Close-up on Natie, his doughy face spread in a cheerful grin as he changes the words to "For the lord God *impotent* reigneth."

Then there I am, thinking there's nothing funny about impotency.

Then you'll see us in the Nudelman's kitchen busily making marijuana brownies, giggling like Keebler elves gone bad, and planning our mission to get stoned at every monument in our nation's capital.

And there we are: eating brownies at the Lincoln Memorial, at the Jefferson Memorial, at the Washington Monument—the music of the "Hallelujah Chorus" growing higher and higher as we do, too.

Then we're at the White House, where square-jawed young-Republican types hand out buttons that say JUST SAY NO and Ziba pulls a lipstick out of her purse to change hers to JUST SAY NO NUKES. One of the Secret Service guys seems to think it's funny so we give him the Brownie Award for Coolest Federal Employee.

Next you'll see Natie in our hotel bathroom, setting up the bar with the assurance of a professional as he mixes powdered lemonade with grain alcohol because grain alcohol has neither smell nor taste, and as such can't be detected by the chaperones.

Cut to the members of the Mixed-Up Choir lined up for the privilege of shelling out three bucks a pop for this swill. Demand is so great that when we run out of grain alcohol, Natie simply fills up the empty bottles in the tub, then sits back and watches everybody get bombed on tap water and powdered lemonade mix.

Then you'll see us the next day in competition, wearing our blue choir blazers, the boys with our striped ties in the school colors, the girls in blouses with Peter Pan collars, all of us looking alert and awake through sheer adrenaline as we belt out, "And He shall reign forever and eh-heh-ver," except Natie, of course, who sings, "And pee shall rain . . ." Sure, it's unprofessional to perform while you're high, but once you've learned the tenor part in the "Hallelujah Chorus" you know it for life. It's just that kind of song.

We lose the competition anyway. Stoned or not, we don't stand a chance against a clapping, swaying, call-and-response gospel choir from Newark. We shuffle dejectedly onto the bus, the chaperones applauding us in that rah-rah, way-to-go way grown-ups do when they want to buck up your esteem even when everybody knows for a fact that you sucked. Ziba, who treats all mandatory activities like they're optional, slips away to meet up with an old boyfriend, the aforementioned U.S. senator's son. Kelly and Doug retreat to her room and put up the DO NOT DISTURB sign while the rest of us descend on the hotel pool, where Natie and I oversee the altos in a synchronized swimming routine.

When they make the movie of my life, the montage will end with the final notes of the "Hallelujah Chorus": *Halleeeeee-luuuuu-jaaaah!*

Afterward, Natie and I do a little exploring, taking in the view of the city from the hotel roof and swiping a name tag we find in the hotel laundry that says HI, MY NAME IS JESÚS. When we get back, I'm surprised to find Doug waiting for us.

"We need to talk," he says.

"Sure."

He glances at Natie. "Alone."

"I'm not going anywhere," Natie says. "Ziba said she'd bring Jordan Craig back here to meet me."

Jordan Craig is the son of Senator Jordan Craig Sr., the dishonorable gentleman from one of the square states, I can't remember which. Senator Craig is well known for his support of Reagan's missile defense policy and for sleeping with women who are not his wife. Since it's Natie's fondest wish to either become a politician or to own one someday, he's very excited at the prospect of meeting Jordan Jr., who is a student at Georgetown.

I offer to show Doug the roof, which you get to by climbing a ladder and opening one of those porthole-type doors. We walk to the edge and look over because that's what people do when they're on the roofs of buildings. In the distance, the Washington Monument juts skyward.

"So what did you want to talk about?" I ask.

"Can you keep a secret?"

"Not particularly."

He frowns. "I'm serious, man. You can't tell anyone."

"Okay, okay. What is it?"

He hoists himself up on the ledge and dangles his legs over the side. He sighs. "We can't do it," he says.

"Can't do what? Who are you talking about?"

"Me and Kelly. We can't do it."

"You mean you haven't . . ."

"We've tried. But I get it in like halfway and she's all, 'Take it out, take it out, it hurts, it hurts.'" Doug slams his hands on the ledge. "It's not fair, man! Every chick I've been with takes one look at the cock-asaurus and they, like, totally freak out."

Maybe it's me, but I find it impossible to muster any sympathy for someone who complains that their penis is too big.

Doug looks down at his crotch, frowning like he's angry at it. "No one's even been able to suck it without totally gagging," he whines. "I swear, if I don't at least get a blow job soon, I'm gonna fuckin' explode."

Cue the "Hallelujah Chorus."

Of course Doug is reluctant, but eventually I wear down his resistance by telling him he doesn't have to touch me and if he just closes his eyes then, well, a mouth's a mouth, right? I even go so far as to sing a little of Aldonza the whore's song from *Man of La Mancha*:

"One pair of arms is like another . . ."

I admit it's a bit much, but I'm determined to work any angle I can. To be honest, the thought of going down on Doug without any recip-rocation makes me feel kind of sleazy and desperate, but that's not nec-essarily a bad thing. Besides, what are friends for?

After much discussion of the merits of only a guy knowing what feels good to another guy, I finally find myself on my knees ready to be of service. I reach for the button on Doug's jeans. He stops me.

"Let me do it," he says.

He unzips his pants and pulls his boxers down to his thighs and there in front of me is Ol' Faithful, ready to blow. I glance upward to make sure Doug has his eyes closed, then move my hands up his firm, taut legs in as gentle and feminine a manner as I can, the hair on his thighs going all static-y as I do. I lean in, open my mouth, and am about to lick the love lollipop for the very first time when I hear a voice be-hind me.

"Edward?"

Fuck. Fuck. Fuck. Fuck. Fuck.

Doug lunges away from me, yanking his pants back up, while I wheel around to see who has interrupted us and, in all likelihood, ru-ined my life forever.

From across the roof I can just see his little cheesehead peeking out from the porthole like Kilroy.

"You guys gotta come right away," Natie says.

We were about to, goddamnit.

twenty-nine

As we dash down the hallway, we see Ziba pacing outside our room, wiggling her fingers like she wished she had a cigarette in them.

"He won't leave," she says.

"Who?" asks Doug.

I open the door and there on the bed, watching some sports thing on TV, is Jordan Craig Jr.

One glance at the bloated, bleary-eyed slab in front of us immediately confirms to me that the senator's son is just another frat boy majoring in beer bongs and gang bangs. Natie must be really disappointed. In a voice that sounds just like belching, Jordan says, "Who the fuck are you?"

"These are my friends," Ziba answers, "Doug and Edward."

"This is our room," Doug says, taking a step forward.

Jordan stands, his buzz cut seeming to graze the ceiling, and grabs Ziba with one of his big, meaty hands like a bear swatting a salmon out of a stream. "Why don't you pussies get the fuck out of here before I kick the shit out of you?" he snarls, then reaches his paws around Ziba, pinning her arms against her sides. "C'mon, baby, gimme a kiss," he gurgles. It's all very *Perils of Pauline*.

Doug lunges forward, but I intervene to stop things from escalating into a fight. "Listen," I say to Jordan's brick wall of a back, "a chaperone's going to be coming around to do bed check any minute, so why don't you just say good night and . . ."

Jordan whips around and backhands me across the face, just like that, sending me flying into a bureau. I've never been hit before, managing to have survived elementary school and junior high with only the psychological scars of verbal abuse, but I'm here to tell you that, at least in the short term, the physical kind hurts way more. I sink down onto the floor, the knobs of the bureau digging into my back as I do. Ziba reaches for me, but Jordan shoves her to the floor, then turns and actually head-butts Doug.

I thought they only did that in professional wrestling.

Doug lunges for Jordan, body-checking him in the gut. But the senator's son raises his knee and clocks Doug right in the chin. Doug winces and stumbles backward onto the floor, his mouth bleeding.

Pleased with himself, Jordan turns around and laughs as if to say, "That was fun, now what should we do?" then lets out a big, hearty "Hah!" as he pounces onto the bed. He grunts and is just about to leap on top of Ziba when we hear Natie call out from the bathroom.

"Break time!" he chirps. From around the corner Natie waddles in, a tray of plastic cups in his pudgy hands. "Who wants a cocktail?" he says, as if there were nothing unusual about the son of a senator smacking around three of his best friends.

"What's that?" Jordan grumbles, his rheumy eyes trying to focus.

"Grain alcohol," Natie says. He speaks slow and loud, like he's talking to an elderly deaf relative. "Try it, it's good."

Jordan bounces off the bed and swipes at a cup, making the others on the tray wiggle and spill a little. Behind him, Ziba slides slowly across the wall.

Jordan sucks down the lemonade in one long, revolting gulp, his Adam's apple bobbing. Ziba reaches for the first heavy object she can find on the desk, which is a table lamp. She motions to Doug, who's slumped on the floor, to pull the cord out of the socket.

Jordan exhales a satisfied "Ahhh," grinning stupidly at his accomplishment. "I'm the chugging champ of my frat," he says, wiping his mouth with his sleeve.

Senator Craig must be so proud.

"Have another," Natie says.

Ziba grips the lamp in one hand.

"These are good," Jordan says. "You can't even taste the grain alcohol."

Ziba tries to lift the lamp, but it doesn't budge. It's fucking bolted to the desk. Goddamn hotels. She looks around for something else.

Natie hands Jordan another lemonade. "Y'know," Jordan says, trying to focus, "you're okay for a little fuck."

"Thanks."

"Watch this." Jordan tilts his head back and chugs the next glass down whole, punctuated by a noisy "glug" at the end.

Then, as if the air had been let out of him, he crumples in a heap. "That one didn't go down so good," he says, then belches, then belches again. By the third belch there's no question what's coming next. He starts spewing right there, before he can even make it to the bathroom door. We all back away from him, partly to clear a path, and partly because that's just what you do when somebody starts to hurl in front of you.

None of us moves while we listen to him puke his guts out in the bathroom. It's one of those horribly endless barfing sessions, the kind where the moment you think it's over, it starts up again. Finally we hear him moan, followed by a long silence.

"And the Swedish judge gives a 9.5 for that projectile vomit," Natie whispers. The four of us tiptoe to the bathroom and peek in to see the senator's son lying on the floor like a beached walrus. A beached walrus lying in his own puke. We turn on the fan and shut the door.

"What the hell was in there?" I hiss.

"Rubbing alcohol," Natie says. "I use it to clean my skin."

"Natie! You might've killed him."

"What was I supposed to do? Stand by and let him rape Ziba?"

None of us say anything, because we all know he's right. Ziba leans over and kisses him, not her usual European two-cheek thing, but a soft, gentle peck on the lips. "Thank you," she whispers.

Natie's face turns the color of his hair.

There's a knock at the door. "Bed check!" a voice yells.

Now adrenaline is a funny thing. You'd be amazed how quickly you can get vomit out of a rug if you're motivated. I spray the air with Right Guard and open the door.

"Hey, guys!"

It's Chuck Mailer, the band teacher who plays piano for the chorus. We call him Chuckles behind his back because he's always trying to be palsy-walsy with the students when in fact he's a total cheesehead. The band kids love him.

He winks at Ziba. "Now listen here, young lady, just because you sing tenor doesn't mean you get to stay in the boys' room. Ha-ha-ha-ha-ha." Chuckles says everything like it's a punch line, whether it's funny or not. Usually, it's not.

Ziba slips past him. "I was just leaving," she says.

Chuckles gives her a quick little shoulder rub the way male teachers sometimes do to female students. "Now you go straight home," he says, "ha-ha-ha-ha-ha."

"Good one, Mr. Mailer," Ziba monotones. "Good night, boys." She blows us a kiss and slides out the door.

Chuckles claps his hands together. "Okay," he says, "everything A-Number-One-Super-Duper here?"

"Just duper," I say.

"Ha-ha-ha-ha-ha. Say, what's that smell?"

You wouldn't mean the vomit of a U.S. senator's son, would you?

"What smell?" says Natie.

Chuckles sniffs again. "It's kind of like . . . air freshener."

Thank you, Lord.

"Cleanliness is next to Godliness," I say. "Ha-ha-ha-ha-ha."

"Ha-ha-ha-ha-ha," says Chuckles.

"Ha-ha-ha-ha-ha," say Natie and Doug.

"It's nice to see you boys so calm and quiet," Chuckles says. "Some of the baritones are getting pretty wild tonight. I shouldn't tell you this, but there was a water-balloon fight that got a little out of hand."

"Really?" I say, looking suitably shocked. "We don't have the energy for that kind of thing." I make a big show of stifling a yawn.

"Well, then, I'll let you boys get to sleep. Say, mind if I use your bathroom?"

"No!" we all scream.

Chuckles flinches. "Why not?"

"It's broken," I say.

"It stinks," says Doug at the same time.

Chuckles looks bewildered.

"Edward took this totally toxic dump," Natie says, "and it . . . uh . . . broke the toilet. That's why we sprayed the air freshener."

"Really?" Chuckles says. He puts a hand on my shoulder to show his tender concern. "You all right there, Eddie boy?"

I don't appreciate having been cast in the role of the smelly dumper but, trouper that I am, I go with it. "Onion rings," I say, rubbing my belly. "I like them, but they don't like me."

✳   ✳   ✳

As soon as Chuckles is gone we open the bathroom door to check on Jordan, who is dead to the world though not, mercifully, actually dead.

"Do you think we should clean him up?" I ask.

"Let him sleep in his own puke," Doug says, rubbing his jaw. "Serves the fucker right."

"The whole room's going to reek by morning," says Natie. "We better hose him down."

We wet some towels in the tub and mop up the mess while Jordan lies there, completely unaware of all the activity around him. "We should do something to him," Doug says as he lifts up Jordan's shoulders so I can pull off his puke-covered Izod. "Once, when Boonbrain passed out, some of the guys from the team put him in a rowboat in the middle of Echo Lake without the oars. Man, it was comical." Doug looks down at his own shirt, which now has the senator's son's vomit on it. "Aw, gross," he says, tearing it off and throwing it in the tub.

Natie walks out of the bathroom.

"Where the hell are you going, Nudelman?" Doug says. "We could use some help here." Jordan's khakis are also packed with puke.

"We're going to have to take his pants off, too," I say.

"Lucky you," Doug whispers.

"Bite me."

"You wish."

He's right.

I undo Jordan's pants and then we each take a leg to pull them off. Even his boxers are soaked.

"He's all yours," Doug says, patting Jordan's thigh like he was a used car.

I bend down and shimmy them off, taking note of Jordan's nasty-looking prick, which is all wrinkly and uncut, like a wonton. I've just pulled off his shorts when I'm blinded by a flash of light.

"What the hell are you doing?" I say, blinking to get my vision back.

"Paying for your sophomore year," Natie says.

"What are you talking about?"

He wiggles the camera in his little hand. "Two words," he says. "Black mail."

"You cheesehead," Doug says. "You can't blackmail a guy like this with a picture of him passed out naked. He probably passes out naked all the time."

"I know that," Natie says, "but we *can* blackmail him with pictures of him naked and having sex with another guy."

Doug and I both frown.

"Well, don't look at me," Doug says. "Edward's the bisexual one."

"Doug!"

"Oops. Sorry."

"He's just joking," I say.

Natie gives me a who-do-you-think-you're-kidding look. "I suppose you were just helping him tie his shoes up there on the roof."

Shit.

"This is fucked up, man," Doug says.

"Calm down," Natie says. "I helped steal ten grand and I didn't say anything about that now, did I?"

He's got a point.

"So why don't you just get over yourself and drop your goddamn pants."

"Me?" Doug shouts. "Why me?"

"Because yours'll photograph better."

Again he's got a point.

"Man, I don't know . . ."

Natie throws his hands in the air. "Jeez Louise, am I the only one around here who cares how Edward's going to pay for college?"

"Of course not," Doug says.

"So then shut up already and get naked."

Doug exhales, then undoes the button on his jeans. I make a mental note to try this approach myself next time. The phone rings. I reluctantly go into the bedroom to get it.

"Hello?"

"Edward, darling . . ."

Either Lauren Bacall knows what room I'm in or it's Ziba.

"I'm so sorry I couldn't help you boys. Is it dreadful over there?"

"Nah, we've got everything under control." I see Doug's underwear fling into the hallway.

"I can't believe Jordan was such a beast," Ziba says. "He used to be such a gentleman."

"Okay," Larry Flynt Jr. says from the bathroom, "now straddle his shoulder so it looks like he's about to give you a blow job. Great, say *cheesehead*."

"It's that wretched fraternity," Ziba says. "I should have known."

"Just take the damn picture, will ya'?" Doug says.

"Is everything all right there?" Ziba asks. "I hear yelling."

"Back up," Natie says. "Your cock is blocking his face."

"We're watching scrambled porn," I say.

"You boys only think of one thing."

As Natie instructs Doug to rest his balls on Jordan's forehead I assure Ziba that, no, we don't mind having the would-be rapist son of a U.S. senator passed out in our bathroom and listen, I gotta go, okay, bye-bye. After I hang up, I trot back to see what I've been missing. I peek over Natie's shoulder and see Doug lying on the floor next to Jordan, whose open, drooling mouth makes him appear as if he's in spasms of rectal ecstasy.

"That one alone may cover a year's tuition," Natie says.

We step around Jordan as best we can while we brush our teeth, although it's a little weird trying to take a piss when there's someone lying between your feet. But by the time I climb into bed I've almost come to think of Jordan affectionately, like he's our big St. Bernard asleep on the bathroom floor.

❉　❉　❉

I'm awoken by the sound of the fan in the bathroom. I look up and see the light from under the door, then glance at the digital clock. It's 3:22. Doug is still fast asleep next to me, but Natie's awake, his Afro flattened on one side from where he's been sleeping. His head looks like the top of the Citicorp building.

"He's awake," Natie hisses.

The two of us listen in silence while Jordan attempts to set the Olympic record for endurance peeing. The longer it takes, the more nervous I get. Will he fall back asleep? Will he try to beat us up again? Will he mistake one of us for Ziba and rape us? I'm just about to wake up Doug when the stream of pee slows, first to a trickle, then finally to a drip . . . drap . . . drop. Jordan moans and staggers out of the bathroom, his water-heater frame silhouetted by the bathroom light. I lie completely still, the way you're supposed to when you come upon a grizzly bear in the woods, and listen to Jordan release a long, cheek-flapping fart. He stumbles toward the empty space on Natie's bed, lunges face-first onto the pillow, and in an instant is snoring like a buzz saw. He rolls onto his side and thrusts a lumpy arm around Natie.

"What I go through for you," Natie mutters.

thirty

A long, vertical line of light slicing between the curtains tells me it's morning, but otherwise the room is as dark as a cave. I roll over to go back to sleep (as is my custom) but the thought of a violent would-be rapist son of a senator in the other bed smashes into my consciousness and I sit up to see what's happened to him.

Jordan is sprawled across the entire bed, nude, unconscious, and completely unaware that Natie and Doug are fastening his wrists to the bedposts with their choir neckties. I get up and we pack our bags as silently as we can, sneaking out like thieves in the night, albeit ones who make sure to hang the MAID, PLEASE CLEAN THIS ROOM thingy on the doorknob when we go.

Serves him right.

We spend an uneventful day at the Smithsonian (I mean, try topping blackmail), followed by an even more uneventful bus ride home. Kathleen picks us up and, as we round the bend into Wallingford Heights, I notice immediately that something about the front yard doesn't look right. I scan the curved path of stepping stones to the front door, trying to figure it out—yes, something is definitely missing, but what is it? I'm heaving my duffle bag out of the back of the Wagon Ho when it dawns on me.

"Where's the Buddha?" I ask.

Kathleen bites her lip. "Oh, sweetie, I hate to tell you," she says, "but he got stolen."

"Stolen?"

Kathleen nods. "I'm sorry."

I turn to Kelly and we both bust up laughing. "What kind of fiend would do such a thing?" I say. "I mean, besides us?"

I don't know much about Buddhism, but I'm guessing that this is what's meant by karmic justice. It almost makes me feel as if there's a divine order to this random universe.

✳   ✳   ✳

The next morning I skip school so I can get Jordan's blackmail pictures developed. It's a testament to just how corrupt I've become that I can embark on such an errand so matter-of-factly, as if I were off to do some shopping or banking which, I suppose, in a way I am. Figuring that the Wallingford Fotomat might not want to develop pictures of naked men simulating sex, I go to the only place I know of that might: Toto Photo, the camera store in the Village near Something for the Boys.

I drop off the film with the clerk (a gay guy, good-looking in that well-groomed gay kind of way, but with a shiny, overmoisturized face) then roam around the neighborhood for an hour while I wait. I wander into a shop called Dionysus—okay that's not entirely accurate: I make a point of crossing the street to go into a shop called Dionysus. They have a window display of blow-up sex dolls wearing leather and whipping each other; I figure that just because I'm cutting school doesn't mean I shouldn't get an education.

Dionysus is clean and well lit, cheerful almost, which seems odd for a store selling studded leather harnesses and barbed-wire corsets at ten o'clock in the morning. The girl behind the counter wears a mohawk, black lipstick, and a Catholic schoolgirl's uniform. She doesn't even look up when I come in, engrossed as she is reading a magazine called *Sister Fister*. The place is full of various kinds of leather paraphernalia, including all sorts of metal chains, clips, and straps, most of which I can't figure out how you'd actually use. I admire a few dildos, some the size of baseball bats and one in the shape of Jesus crucified on the cross, but I get sucked into the gravitational pull of the magazines at the back of the store, particularly by a section marked CHICKS WITH DICKS. The magazines are sealed in clear plastic, but it's obvious from the covers that the description is entirely accurate. I honestly had no idea people like this existed. I flip through the stacks of various "she-male" publications and come upon one called *The Bust of Both Worlds*, featuring someone named Jenny Talia. It's as if someone had grafted Kelly and Doug together into one person. The only thing that could make Jenny more perfect would be if, after sex, she turned into a pepperoni pizza.

I buy the magazine.

✳   ✳   ✳

Back at Toto Photo the clerk greets me by fanning his shiny face with an envelope as if what's inside has made him glisten instead of the industrial moisturizer he must use.

"Are these of you?" he says, addressing my crotch.

I shake my head, not like he's looking anyway. "They're of my friend," I mumble. It's sort of humiliating to constantly stand in the shadow of your best friend's dick, as it were. "How much do I owe you?" I ask.

He hands me the envelope. "Don't worry about it. Just be sure to tell your friend he's welcome here anytime."

As someone who's not above borrowing his friend's penis for blackmail photos, I certainly don't mind using it to get them for free either, but this guy's uncontained lust for Doug makes me feel sort of inadequate. "Thanks," I say, addressing my Keds.

Monsieur Moisturizer leans over the counter. "And tell him to take some shots of your hot ass next time, okay?" he says, smiling a said-the-spider-to-the-fly kind of smile.

Now it's my turn to fan my face.

He tilts his head in that way that pretty girls and gay guys do. "You don't even know how cute you are, do ya', kid?"

I don't know how to answer a question like that. I guess I don't. I've always thought I was okay-looking, but there's nothing like unrequited love to make you feel like a real bowzer. The clerk reaches his hand toward me and lifts my chin up to look at him.

"Oh honey, believe me," he murmurs, "if I didn't have to work right now I'd throw you over my shoulder, carry you back to my place, and bang you like a screen door till Tuesday."

Strange as it may sound, that's about the nicest thing anyone's ever said to me. I turn to leave, pleased in the knowledge that he's watching my hot ass as I go.

I can still make it to English after I get back to Wallingford. It's not that I'm particularly motivated academically; I just want to get the pictures to Natie as soon as possible.

Mr. Lucas is assigning another in-class writing exercise to practice for the AP exam. *"Nineteen eighty-four,"* he declaims in a debating team voice. "Has Orwell's vision come to pass? Are we oppressed by sinister forces? Or is it more like Aldous Huxley's *Brave New World,* in which we're seduced by irrelevant pleasures? I want a five-paragraph essay on the subject—thesis, three body paragraphs, and a conclusion." Around the room there's the sound of notebooks flipping open, along with the clicks of three-ring binders as some students loan paper to people who don't show up prepared, like me. I scooch my desk closer to Natie's and, reaching into the pocket of my judo jacket, discreetly pull out pictures.

"Wow," Natie whispers as he gazes at a shot of Doug dangling over Jordan's head like a pendulum. "How do you suppose he stands up without tipping over?" He flips through the rest, making favorable comments on his talent as a pornographer. "I'll write Jordan's letter tonight and send these babies off tomorrow," he says. "Stick with me and you won't even need Al's money."

"What are you going to say?"

"Oh, you know, the usual, give us $10,000 or we'll send these to your dad and the Republican National Committee, that kind of thing."

"Do you really think we could get $10,000 for these?"

Natie snorts. "Hell, if Doug were still a minor we could've gotten twice that."

From over my shoulder I hear Mr. Lucas clear his throat. How a man on crutches could manage to sneak up on us is beyond me.

"Illustrations won't be necessary, gentlemen," he says.

❋　　❋　　❋

I'm pretty fried from the weekend in D.C., so I'm ready to crash by the time Friday rolls around. Kelly, Kathleen, and I hang out at home because Kelly's brother, Brad, is due to arrive that night for spring break. We watch *Victor/Victoria* for like the gazillionth time on HBO. Julie Andrews is about as convincing as a man as Barbra Streisand is in *Yentl,* but we don't care; we've practically got the whole thing memorized, not just the songs, but the dialogue, too. Brad shows up before the movie's over, which is a shame because I like the scene where Lesley Ann Warren does the number in her panties and you can almost see her pubes.

Brad was already at Notre Dame when Kelly and I first started going out, so I've only met him a couple of times. But now that I'm part of the family, so to speak, he greets me like we're old buddies, giving me one of those one-armed hugs that guys do to show affection without appearing queer.

Brad Corcoran looks just like his dad. In fact, if you look at the photo albums of Kathleen and Jack back when they were in college (which Kelly and I did on one particularly icy Saturday night last winter), you'd swear it was Brad and not Dr. Corcoran whooping it up at all those corny-looking socials thrown by Delta Ramma Lamma Ding Dong. The lean sprinter's build, the toothpaste-commercial smile, the craggy sun-kissed features—it's all there.

It makes me uncomfortable.

Brad's brought his girlfriend with him, a boxy-looking preppy girl in a headband named Kit. She's one of those hearty field-hockey types who everyone describes as having a lot of personality, which really means she talks too much. Wallingford is full of them—bossy, beefy women who, for some unknown reason, often seem to be the wife of choice for slender patrician men; y'know, like Barbara Bush.

It's an awkward reunion. Kit laughs too much at nothing in particular and Brad makes demeaning inquiries into Kelly's "little dancing thing," as if her future college major and life ambition were some trifling whim on her part. Kathleen seems glad to see her son, but I can tell she feels disconnected from all the hardy-har-har tales of dear old Delta Ramma Lamma Ding Dong. Kathleen, Kelly, and I have, in our own little functional dysfunctional way, formed a new family during the last few months, one that seems to have more in common with the two neurotic cats than with these two rambunctious preps. Luckily, Brad and the Headband are eager to meet up with some friends for drinks, leaving Kathleen, Kelly, and me to our HBO and an early night.

※　※　※

It's like dark o'clock when I'm stirred out of a coma by the sound of someone banging around. At first, I think it must be Brad coming in late but, as I pry open my eyes, I realize Brad's actually risen early and is on the floor with his feet locked under the spare bed, doing sit-ups.

He is obviously mentally ill.

I squint so I can admire his flat, lean belly and rippling colt's legs without it appearing as if that's what I'm actually doing, but as he comes up for his final sit-up he glances over and catches my eye.

Oops.

"Sorry to wake you," he whispers. He smiles at me with both sets of teeth, the way Kelly does.

"S'all right," I gurgle. "I had to get up anyway."

This is, of course, an outright lie, but one that forces me to make good on it, so I flop down the hallway to the bathroom to take a leak. When I come back, I nearly knock Brad in the head with the door because he's doing push-ups on the narrow strip of floor in front of the beds. He springs up, his body unfolding like a pocketknife, and stands too close to me, massaging the spot where his chest meets his shoulder, the muscles quivering under his skin. His eyes are as green as an Irish meadow.

"You wanna take a jog?" he asks.

A jog? At this hour? I'd rather stick pins in my eyes.

Brad bends over to stretch and his shorts ride up the backs of his thighs.

"Sure," I say.

Wuss.

I grab the first clothes I can find in the pile on the floor—in this case my Keds, a pair of Bermuda shorts, and an old *Chorus Line* T-shirt that's so worn-out most of the dancers are missing limbs. Compared to Brad in his spiffy Notre Dame Track and Field outfit I look like a homeless person.

We tiptoe out of the house, stretch for an inadequately short time on the Buddha-less front lawn, and then take off into the dim morning light. Brad is annoyingly articulate for this hour, but since I'm hyperventilating after only two blocks, I'm grateful he is monopolizing the conversation, even if it means listening to more stories about all the "righteous" times he's had at Notre Dame. I just don't have the energy to tell him that "righteous" is a word better suited to black civil rights activists in the 1960s than Reagan-loving frat boys of the 1980s. He goes on and on about his interviews for various soul-killing jobs on Wall Street, but finally gets my attention when he pulls off his T-shirt, leaving me to concentrate on the dappled rising sun shining on his back like flecks of gold. Even the freckles on his shoulders seem to glow with good health.

But if you think there's anything pleasurable in admiring the trim muscular form of the brother of your ex-girlfriend and the son of a man who fingered you until you got a stiffy, you'd be mistaken. With each step on the pavement, lurid, unwelcome thoughts of Dr. Corcoran pound in my brain and I'm helpless to stop them.

"Y'know, 'Dward," Brad says (being a true prep, he's already invented a nickname for me), "you really oughta come up to the lake with us sometime. There's some truly righteous fishing to be had."

"Really?" I huff. "That sounds great . . ." (Your father got me hard. Your father got me hard. Your father got me hard.)

"You sail, then?"

"Oh, yeah," I lie, "I'm a born sailor . . ." (Your father got me hard. Your father got me hard. Your father got me hard.)

I run six goddamn miles, despite suffering from what I'm sure is a collapsed lung. What's more, Brad's got that competitive Kennedy-brothers-playing-touch-football-on-the-lawn-at-Hyannisport thing going on, so somehow we manage to do it in just under forty-five minutes. My skin is so red and wet by the time we get back I look like Carrie on her prom night.

Kit's up now, and she scolds Brad for not waking her to go jogging, blah, blah, blah. She hands him a Bloody Mary, which is the first sensible thing either of them have done since they got here. I collapse on the couch.

"You hungry?" she asks in her too-loud voice. "I'm making blueberry pancakes."

I shake my head and Brad tells me I can have the first shower while he eats breakfast. I trudge upstairs, noting that neither Kathleen nor Kelly have stirred yet, which is just one of the many reasons I love them both.

I'm resting my head on the tile when I hear the shower curtain swoosh open, giving me a Janet-Leigh-in-*Psycho* kind of scare.

"Yo, 'Dward. What's takin' so long?" Brad yells. "Ya' jerkin' the gherkin?" He swats me on the ass with the back of his hand and laughs like this is the height of wit, when in fact it's kind of true. I shut the curtain and try to conjugate French verbs to make my cock go down.

"There's no need to be shy around me," Brad says. "I live in a frat house. I see dudes naked all the time."

This visual doesn't help at all. *J'aime, tu aimes, il aime* . . .

"Besides," he says, "you've got nothin' to be embarrassed about. A beefy Italian guy like you, all you have to do is work out a little and, whammo, you've got muscles."

"Really?" I say.

"Sure," he says, pushing open the curtain again. "If you'd like, I'll show you a thing or two."

He better not mean that to be as sexy as it sounds, though it's difficult to tell because he's standing there completely naked.

"If you don't hurry, I'm gonna have to come in there with you."

Like father, like son, I guess. I turn the water to cold.

thirty-one

The next week is like boot camp. Every morning, Brad and I rise at the ass crack of dawn and do our lung-collapsing regimen of jogging and calisthenics, most of which seem to involve touching each other in a Greco-Roman wrestling kind of way. It's torture, not just because my muscles are so spasmed that I twitch all day like someone with Parkinson's, but because the homoerotic subtext of Brad's every statement drives me insane. (He actually feels up my pecs at one point and says, "Yo, 'Dward, if you were a chick, I swear I'd fuck ya'.") A little homoerotic subtext goes a long way, though. All Brad has to do is smile his Irish eyes at me and I find myself doing those push-ups where you clap in between. I even promise him and the Headband I'll come out to Notre Dame for some "righteous keggers."

❈ ❈ ❈

On Saturday, Father Groovy takes the train into Hoboken to check our post office box. There's a brochure for the summer series at Lincoln Center (guess we're on the mailing list), but no word from Jordan yet. Then I head into the city, stopping in the men's room at Penn Station to remove Father Groovy's collar and spectacles.

Paula's standing in front of the theater as I come running up, her tiny teardrop hands knotting and unknotting a purple scarf that matches her left shoe. I call to her from across the street and she waves the scarf at me in the grand manner of someone departing on a luxury liner. I dart through traffic to get to her.

"Sorry I'm late," I gasp.

"Don't worry about it, scruffy," she says, taking my face in her

hands and giving my beard a scratch. "You're here now and we're together and that's all that really matters in the end, isn't it?"

I love Paula, too, but I'm used to getting a little lecture on punctu-
ality first. She blinks her Disney eyes at me and I notice the thin blue
vein that courses under the white-white skin of her forehead. "Are you
okay?" I ask. There's something about her curtain-up-light-the-lights
smile that seems forced.

She gives my shoulder a squeeze and pulls a thread off of my herringbone sports jacket, or perhaps I should say Father Groovy's herringbone sports jacket. "I just wanted you to know that no matter what
happens," she says, "I'll always be here for you."

What the hell is going on?

❅ ❅ ❅

The show is Neil Simon's new play, *Brighton Beach Memoirs*, which is
something of a departure from his usual urban comedies. It's an auto-
biographical coming-of-age story—like there aren't enough of those already. But I suppose every writer has to write about his childhood at
some point, and at least Neil Simon has the good sense to make his
funny. That being said, I fail to see what the big deal is about the kid
who plays the lead.

"I ask you," I say to Paula as we leave the theater, "what does this
Matthew Broderick have that I don't have?"

"Besides an agent and the lead in a hit Broadway show?" Paula says.
"Nothing."

"Exactly! I mean, I could have done that part. And I would've been
a lot funnier and less, y'know, *real*."

"Absolutely," Paula says.

"Do you want to wait at the stage door and get his autograph?"

"Of course."

There's a big crowd in the alley filled with the usual loser wanna-
bes with no lives as opposed to serious thespians like us who want to
learn more about our craft. We get in line behind a couple of blue-
haired matinee ladies reminiscing about Brighton Beach and the Depression. As Paula pulls a compact out of a purse she's made from a
Smurf plush toy I ask her how Gino's doing.

"Oh, we broke up," she says, fluffing her curls.

"You're kidding. I'm so sorry."

"No you're not. He was a creep."

"You're right. What the hell were you thinking?"

Paula snaps her compact closed and puts it away. "He wanted me, Edward," she says. "Not because I'm witty and talented and smart, but quite simply because I have a big rack." She looks down and grabs her boobs in her hands like she's weighing them. "No one in high school ever wanted this body," she says. "*No one!* They wanted skinny girls like Kelly and Ziba. Frankly, this fascination with girls who are built like little boys smacks of suppressed homosexual desires, but that's another story. The point is, Gino may have had the brains of a calamari but he sure liked having something to grab onto when he fucked." She demonstrates by grasping her meaty butt in her hands. "And he wanted to do it all the time. Every day, just fuck, fuck, fuck, fuck, fuck, fuck, fuck."

The blue hairs scowl at her. Paula ignores them.

"And for a while it was simply *splendid*," she says. "But then he bought me a vibrator and I began to realize what I was missing."

"He didn't care about your orgasm, did he?" I say.

"Worse," she says, holding up her pinky at me. "Also like a calamari."

This is definitely the wrong thing to say to someone who's insecure about his equipment. "Let me ask you something," I say. "Does size really matter?"

"Depends," Paula says. "In my case, well . . . do you see these big, childbearing hips?"

I nod.

"I've got just two words for you: big vagina."

The two blue hairs in front of us turn around, disgusted, and bustle out of the alleyway. As they pass, one of them mutters, "Slut."

Paula's Disney eyes go wide. "Did you hear what she called me?"

"A slut," I say.

"Yes," she says, clapping her fleshy little hands together. "Isn't that *splendid*?"

✳   ✳   ✳

The crowd begins to thin, more out of boredom than because of Paula's dirty talk. Various actors from the show come through the door, but no Matthew. Eventually it's just the two of us standing there. "He's probably waiting for the all clear," Paula says.

"Do you think he might invite us into his dressing room?" I ask.

"Maybe."

It's happened before. Paula and I met Angela Lansbury that way when we saw *Sweeney Todd*. And the same with Geraldine Page in *Agnes of God*. The really great theater stars are gracious like that.

"Maybe we could impress him so much with our serious-actor questions he might go out for a bite with us between shows and we could become friends with him and I could get a job as his understudy."

"You'd be *perfect!*" Paula says. "Then you'd have a job and you wouldn't have to worry about . . ."

"Worry about what?"

"Nothing. Isn't this alley *divine*? I just love stage-door alleys."

"No, really, what's up with you? You've been acting funny all day."

"Listen," she says, "why don't we go get a drink? We can talk about it there."

"Talk about what?"

"Nothing, really. Come on, Joe Allen's is just a couple of blocks . . ."

"No, tell me now."

"It'd be better . . ."

"Sis!"

"You didn't get the Sinatra scholarship."

She blurts it out so fast I'm not sure I heard her right. "What did you say?" I ask.

"You didn't get the Sinatra scholarship. They gave it to some relative of his—Anthony Something, from Hoboken. Oh, Edward, I'm just *anguished* for you."

The walls of the alley start to close in around me. I get dizzy and actually have to lean against the stage door to keep from falling over.

Paula rubs her little teardrop hand on my back. "People are saying he wasn't even accepted before the scholarship was donated . . ."

This can't be happening to me.

". . . but that they changed their minds when they realized they might get more money in the future."

Ten thousand dollars gone.

"The whole thing is a travesty," she says, "an absolute *travesty*."

Her voice sounds far away to me, like I'm underwater.

"Don't worry, Edward, you'll find another way to pay for school. I know you will." She embraces me, but I just stand there, rigid.

The door opens, shoving us both aside, and out steps Matthew Broderick, wearing a baseball cap and a leather jacket.

"Oh, sorry," he says as he passes. "I didn't know you were there."

thirty-two

Like Superman, I jump into the phone booth at the Wallingford train station as soon as I get back and dial Natie's number.

Stan answers. "The Nudelman rrrresidence," he says, trilling the "r." Like Fran, he, too, becomes inexplicably British when he answers the phone.

"Hey, Mr. Nudelman, it's Edward. Is Natie there?" I pull back the receiver in anticipation of the usual shoutfest, but to my surprise he speaks like a normal person.

"Nathan went out for a little while," he says. "Something about getting a real steal on computer equipment."

I don't know and I don't ask.

"Will he be back soon?" I ask. The booth feels stifling and claustrophobic to me, so I stretch the cord as far as I can and step out onto the pavement to gulp the humid spring air.

"He's gotta eat sometime. Are you okay, Eddie?"

I don't know why, but his asking how I am both comforts and panics me at the same time. No, nothing is okay, nothing at all, and I can't possibly tell him why.

I want my mommy.

"Will you just tell him to wait for me when he gets back?"

"Sure thing," he says. "Say, bet you're pretty excited about Juilliard, huh?"

I can't even answer him.

❃ ❃ ❃

Naturally it starts to rain, and not the cool, restorative sort of rain either, but the oppressively muggy New Jersey kind. Father Groovy's herringbone sports jacket starts giving me the itch, so I strip it off and carry it like it's some dead gray animal, switching arms every block or so as it grows heavier with wetness. Finally I quicken my pace to a jog, hoping that'll somehow make me less wet, all the while trying to work out in my mind what just happened. I can only guess that Frank Sinatra must have read the item in the *New York Post* and called Juilliard to inquire about it. In true Hoboken never-turn-down-a-freebie style, Frank probably mentioned he had a relative who qualified, and in true fund-raising suck-up-to-potential-donors style, Laurel Watkins made it happen.

Courtesy of my ten grand. It's a shame Natie won't live to see adulthood, but it's obvious I'm going to have to kill him.

By the time I get to the Nudelmans' I'm completely soaked. I lean on the doorbell and hear Fran scream, "FOR GOD'S SAKE, SOMEONE GET THE DOOR!"

I step out of my muddy Keds, partly out of politeness, but mostly because my feet itch like crazy and I can't wait to scratch them. I feel like I'm about to burst out of my skin.

Natie answers.

"Jeez," he says, looking me up and down, "what have you been doing—gathering two of every animal?"

"Frank Sinatra stole my money."

"WHAT THE FUCK . . ."

From the other end of the house Fran screams, "NATHAN, ARE YOU ALL RIGHT?"

"JUST A LITTLE TOURETTE'S, MA," he hollers back.

"You don't have Tourette's," I say, rubbing my bare feet on the mat to relieve the itch.

"They don't know that," he says. "Why do ya' think they don't pay attention to anything I say?"

He really does scare me sometimes.

I drop my wet coat on the linoleum floor and lean against the carpeted wall to catch my breath.

"Let me get you a towel or something," Natie says. "Fran just had that wall steam cleaned." He scampers down the hallway, hitching up his sagging pants as he goes.

I bend over and rest my hands on my knees. The swirling patterns in the linoleum look like those meteorological maps you see on the news and it makes me dizzy. I close my eyes.

Natie returns with a robe that has Palm Beach Hilton stitched on the breast pocket, then leads me into the laundry room, where I stick my clothes in the dryer. I tell him the whole horrible story, putting special emphasis on how the scholarship was his idea. Natie doesn't look at me while I talk, but concentrates on tearing sheets of Bounce into tiny little pieces.

"Okay," he says when I finish, "the first thing we need to do is eat something. Come on, I got rugallah in the kitchen."

"I'm not hungry," I say.

Natie blinks his little button eyes. "Jeez, you must be upset."

I slam my hand on the washer, which echoes like a tin drum. "Natie, last month I had $10,000 in *cash* in my hands and now I've got nothing because I listened to your cheesehead scheme."

"Don't be such a baby," he says, Pooh-bearing over to the cookie tin. "You wouldn't have had that $10,000 in the first place if it hadn't been for me." He opens the tin. "You sure you don't want some rugallah? It's good."

I shake my head.

"This is just a momentary setback," he says, chewing. "Think of it as the price of doing business. We've got Jordan as a backup, don't we?"

There's something about having blackmail as the backup to your failed money-laundering scheme that doesn't sit right with me.

Natie gives me a pat on the back. "You're just tired," he says. "Let me take you home." He grabs a set of keys off a hook by the door.

"You don't drive," I say.

"I've got a license, don't I?"

"Yeah, but it's fake."

"Only you and I know that," he says, shaking the keys.

❈   ❈   ❈

The house is dark and quiet when I get home and I feel depression envelop me like a wet blanket. Ten fucking grand. I bend down to say hello to the cats when I hear a groggy voice call out my name from the living room. I stand up and go to the entryway and see a figure huddled in the elbow of the sectional couch. She's cleared a warren for herself among all the usual debris and sits with her knees pulled up to her chest, her blond head resting on them, shining like a light.

"Kathleen?"

"Kathleen's not here right now," she mumbles into her knees. "Would you like to leave a message?"

Two wine bottles sit on the coffee table—one empty, another well on its way. "Yeah," I say, "tell her I'm worried about her." I pick up the bottles and move them to the piano where I put them on top of the score of *Godspell* so they won't leave rings.

"You're sweet," Kathleen says, and makes room for me on the couch by shoving aside a transistor radio, a roll of paper towels, and two phone books. She pats the spot, the Internationally Recognized Signal for "Sit here on this stained, crumb-infested piece of furniture," then regards me with moist, fermented eyes.

"Do you think I'm an alcoholic?" she says.

I nod.

Kathleen sighs. "Yeah, me, too. I suppose that means I should get some help, what with being a mental-health professional and all." She blinks, like she's not sure she's seeing right. "Why are you wearing a bathrobe from the Palm Beach Hilton?"

I pull the robe across my legs to make sure I'm not hanging out. "Fashion statement," I say.

Kathleen rests a slender hand on my wrist. "You know," she says, apropos of nothing, "Brad really liked you."

I guessed that from the way he ground his crotch against my ass when he cracked my back.

"I wish I could say I felt the same about him," Kathleen says, tracing figure eights on the sofa cushion. "Don't get me wrong. I love my son. But just between you and me, I can't say I like him very much."

That seems to me a remarkable thing to say about your own child. Kathleen blinks back a tear. "He's turned out just like his father."

If she only knew.

She gets up and takes the bottle of wine off the piano. "I shouldn't be surprised," she says. "Everyone's always said that Brad's just like Jack and Bridget's just like me."

"What about Kelly?" I say.

Kathleen looks at the bottle and puts it back down again. "Kelly," she says. "Who knows what Kelly is like? She's got so many secrets. Just when I think I understand her, she surprises me again. She's like those Russian dolls; you know, the kind where one is inside of another." Kathleen staggers along the wall of family photos, peering at them like she's never seen them before. "Kelly is my great hope for this family." She points to my senior portrait, which I rescued from the junk drawer. "You and Kelly. Neither of you are willing to do what people expect of you." She smiles. "I admire that."

It feels weird to have a grown-up admire you.

Kathleen turns and appraises her wedding portrait, Miss Chastity Belt 1961. "Look at me," she says. "I didn't have a fucking clue. I dropped out of college my junior year to get married and I got pregnant with Bradley on my honeymoon. I told both of my girls that when it came to having sex, stick with oral. No one ever got knocked up giving a blow job."

Words to live by.

She stumbles back over the couch and rests on the arm. "You know I love you kids; there's not a thing I wouldn't do for any of you: lie, cheat, steal—kill if I had to. But I've got to say I understand how your mother felt. Of course, I don't approve of her leaving you and your sister, but you just can't imagine what it was like for us back then. Here we were in the suburbs, driving the kids to Little League and making brownies for the Brownies, and suddenly there were all these books and magazines telling us we should be self-actualized and liberated and free. But we had noses to wipe and diapers to change. It was like we had missed the parade."

"But you stuck around," I say.

She smiles and tousles my hair. "I wouldn't have missed it for the world. But if I had a chance to do it all over again, I'm not sure I would have had my kids when I did. I don't know. It doesn't really matter now anyway." She brushes the hair out of my eyes and looks at me. "What I'm trying to say is this, sweetie: don't let twenty years of your life go by before you join the parade."

I reach for her and she puts her arms around me. Her touch isn't anything like her daughter's, or her husband's, or her son's for that matter. It's a mother's touch, warm and comforting, and I lay my head on her lap as we sit silently in the dark together, both enjoying our dozy, miserable happiness together.

❋   ❋   ❋

We're both startled by a banging on the front door. The cats scurry, making scratching noises on the floors as they go. "I'll get it," I say.

I open the door and there, like a blast of hot air in my face, is my evil stepmonster.

"Azz*huuuuuuuuuuull!*" she screams.

I shut the door.

"Who was that?" Kathleen calls from the other room.

"Jehovah's Witness," I say.

Dagmar bangs again. I pull the curtain aside in the little window next to the door. She looks distorted through the beveled glass, like her face is all banged up.

If only.

"What do you want?" I yell.

"I know it vas you!" she screams. "*You* did tsis! *You* did tsis!" She shoves what looks like a bank statement against the glass.

"Go away. I don't know what you're talking about."

"OPEN TSIS DOOR!" she bellows, and pounds again.

From the living room I hear Kathleen mutter, "Oh, for Chrissake." She gets up and weaves her way into the entryway, where she opens the front door. "Now listen," Kathleen barks, "in this house crazy people belong in the basement, not on the front porch."

Dagmar takes a step back and shakes her head, her tangled curls writhing like Medusa's. "He stole money out of my account," she says, handing the bank statement to Kathleen.

Kathleen glances at the statement, then turns to look at me, her face just inches from mine. "Sweetie, is this true?"

I may be one of the Best Young Actors in America, but I'm not sure I've got it in me to lie to Kathleen anymore. About anything. I take a deep breath and look her right in the eye.

"I don't have her money," I say.

Hey, it's true.

"There must be some mistake," Kathleen says to Dagmar. "Maybe Al withdrew it and forgot to . . ."

"No!" Dagmar barks. "He doesn't . . . it is not possible." Dagmar snatches back the statement. "First tsing Monday mornink I vill be calling tse Financial Aid office at Juilliart," she says, sounding like the gestapo in a World War Two movie.

I feel my stomach drop to my knees.

"And maybe tsey can tell me who tsis LaChance Jones is."

Evil. Evil. Evil.

"I don't care how much time it takes," Dagmar says, shaking a bent twig of a finger at me, "I vill not give up until I see you in jail, you azz-*huuuull.*"

And your little dog, too.

"Well, thanks for stopping by," Kathleen says, starting to close the door. "It was horrible meeting you."

Dagmar turns on her spiky heels, clicking and muttering to herself as she goes.

Kathleen shuts the door and leans against it. "She must be great in bed," she says. "There's no other explanation."

❉   ❉   ❉

I consider calling Natie for advice but, frankly, I've kind of had it with his suggestions. Nor do I want to talk to Kathleen, even though she's very sympathetic. I just want to go to bed for a really, really long time and forget I was ever born. I pass out into a dreamless sleep until about three o'clock in the morning when I sit bolt upright in bed to discover that, while I was sleeping, I've taken every bit of bedding—the blanket, the sheets, even the mattress pad—and tossed them across the room. I lie awake, the sound of my heartbeat pounding in my ears as I envision the step-by-step process of being tried, convicted, and sent to prison where I'll have the words "Raoul's Bitch" tattooed on my ass. Eventually I'll be killed in prison and God will consign my eternal soul to the fiery pits of Hell where I'll burn forever because I'm a very, very bad person. Like Hamlet says, "My offense is rank. It smells to heaven." Suffocating under the tyranny of my mind, I finally get up around five o'clock and do the only thing I can to escape, which is take an absurdly long jog.

❉   ❉   ❉

All day long at school I watch the clock, praying that Laurel Watkins has either gotten another job or has suffered a blow to the head rendering her incapable of remembering Edward Zanni, Gloria D'Angelo, or the Catholic Vigilance Society, but then I remember that Laurel Watkins is pregnant, so instead I try to telepathically induce her labor so she's not in the office when Dagmar calls.

The announcement comes over the loudspeaker while Mr. Lucas is discussing the hollow, decadent lives of the idle rich in *The Great Gatsby*. "Would Edward Zanni please report to the main office right away? Edward Zanni, to the main office right away."

The class makes that "oooh" sound students make when someone is called to the office, completely unaware that the next time they see me it will be on the evening news in an orange prison jumpsuit. I feel strangely calm actually, almost relieved that all the lies and deceit are finally over. Loyal to the end, Natie comes with me, not to admit anything, mind you, but for moral support. ("Why should both of us take the rap?" he says. "I can be much more helpful to you on the outside.") We go into the office together.

There is not, as I expected, a pair of armed police officers waiting for me, but just the usual clacking of typewriters and people going about their business. One of the secretaries motions for me to come behind the counter. "Edward, there's a lady on the phone who says it's urgent that she speak to you."

A lady? I grab the receiver.

"Hello?"

"Oh, thank *God*," the voice on the other end of the line says.

"Paula?"

"Listen," she says, "you've got to get down to the Camptown police station *right away*."

"Why? What's wrong?"

"Aunt Glo's been arrested."

thirty-three

Kelly's not in her eighth-period class and I curse myself for being the person who taught her how to cut school undetected. We need a car, and fast. Natie and I intrude on four different science classrooms before we finally find Doug, who looks relieved to have any excuse to get out of Mr. Nelson's treacherously dull chemistry class. The three of us run all the way to Doug's house to get his old Chevy. Or perhaps I should say Doug and I run all the way to his house to get his old Chevy, then double back to pick up Natie, who's lagging behind like the Poky Little Puppy. I'm not convinced, however, that Doug's tin can of a car is actually capable of getting us there, but it's the best we have, so I caress what's left of the dashboard as we drive, trying to coerce the old girl to make it just a little bit farther, baby, just a little bit farther.

Since I flat-out told Laurel Watkins on the phone that I was eligible for the scholarship, you'd think she and Dagmar would have put two and two together and come after me instead of Aunt Glo. What's more, I'm amazed at the swift arm of justice. I don't remember Aunt Glo actually mentioning to Laurel Watkins where she lived, so I'm not sure how they found her so fast. But then again, never having committed fraud before, I'm not real familiar with the protocol.

After getting lost a couple of times (just because I'm a criminal doesn't mean I know where the Cramptown police station is), we finally locate the building, a nondescript brick box. We dash through the doors and explain to a skeptical-looking receptionist why we're here. She points to a couple of those cup-shaped plastic chairs that are supposed to be comfortable but aren't and tells us to take a seat. Natie and Doug flip through old *Reader's Digests* while I pace the well-scuffed floor, wishing that I smoked instead of masturbated as a nervous habit, so I'd have something to do. Believe it or not, I'm more worried for Aunt Glo than for myself. She must be terrified.

The receptionist buzzes us in and an officer leads us down a long hallway to an open area containing a lot of cluttered desks, bad overhead lighting, and, in the center of it all, Aunt Glo. There she sits on a high stool, chatting and laughing with Cramptown's finest and otherwise looking like she's having a marvelous time. It's like that scene you see in old movies when little Timmy or Bobby disappears and everyone is frantic with worry until they go down to the police station and find him sitting on the chief's desk, happily licking an ice-cream cone, an oversized policeman's hat on his head. Aunt Glo sees us and flaps a pudgy hand from across the room.

"The LBs!" she screeches like she's throwing a party and she's so glad we could make it. "And Maya Angelou!"

I turn around to see if indeed the esteemed poet is standing behind me (at this point I'd believe anything), but instead I find myself face-to-face with a dark, bearded priest who looks alarmingly like Father Groovy. For a split second I fear that this poor guy has been picked out of some kind of clerical line-up, when I realize that Aunt Glo must have said, "My Angelo."

If I ever wonder what I'll look like in fifteen or twenty years I need only stop in at the Church of the Holy Redeemer in Hoboken, New Jersey, and see how Father Angelo D'Angelo is doing. We've been introduced a couple of times over the years, but it's only after having seen myself dressed as Father Groovy that I realize how close the resemblance is. Sure, there's some gray in his curly hair, and he is, believe it or not, more athletic-looking (who knew priests worked out?), but otherwise we could be, pardon the pun, cut from the same cloth. I find him, in an unsettling way, attractive.

He doesn't seem particularly happy to see me, however, and he rushes over to his mother.

"Ma, you all right?" he says.

Aunt Glo calls him Maya Angelou again and gives him a hug that could easily be mistaken for a chiropractic adjustment. This is when I notice Paula who, rather than taking center stage the way she normally does, hovers off to the side. Perhaps it's because she's wearing nothing but a leotard, a corset, and a long muslin rehearsal skirt. She looks like a Victorian whore brought in on charges of soliciting in the wrong century. I walk over to her and she frowns. "Right now two sisters are sitting in a rehearsal hall wondering why the third took off for Moscow without them," she mutters.

Aunt Glo tries to give up her seat to Angelo ("You look tired, baby doll") then makes introductions all around. I'm impressed she can remember the cops' names (Officer Atkinson, Officer Barker, Officer Salazar) until I realize she's reading their badges. "You kids hungry?" she says to us. "You wanna doughnut? I'm sure these nice policemen wouldn't mind."

Aunt Glo.

Paula kneels next to her, giving seven men an unimpeded view of her nineteenth-century cleavage, not like it was hard to miss before. "What's going on?" she asks.

"You!" Aunt Glo sniffs. "If you weren't off having premarital sex with your long-haired boyfriend, you'd know!"

"You're having premarital sex?" Angelo asks.

"We broke up," Paula says, as if that answers the question.

I wiggle my pinky at Doug to explain.

Paula turns to Aunt Glo again. "What's that got to do with you being arrested?"

"Well," Aunt Glo says, "since you left, it hasn't been easy, y'know, trying to find people to drive me . . ."

Paula's eyes immediately fill with tears. "I told you I'd help you whenever you needed," she says, taking her aunt's tiny hand in hers.

"I don't like to be a bother," Aunt Glo says as she pulls a tissue out of her purse. "Today I woke up feeling pretty good, so I said to myself, I said, 'Gloria, it wouldn't hurt anybody if you drove the Lincoln over to the A&P to pick up a little veal chop . . .' "

Angelo looks dismayed. "Ma, you didn't . . ."

". . . and before ya' knew it I got cops swoopin' down on me, sayin' I gotta come into the police station."

"Her taillight was out," says Officer Atkinson. "And when I asked her for her registration all we could find in the glove compartment was the 1983 *World Almanac*."

Oops.

"You brought her in for driving without her registration?" Angelo asks.

"No," says a voice behind us. We turn around and the cops make room for a tall man wearing a shirt and tie and the air of someone in charge. "I'm Detective Bose," he says, shaking Father Angelo's hand.

He's got a 1950s buzz cut, a caterpillar mustache, and a very *Dragnet*-y manner about him. "Your mother was detained because her vehicle was identified as the same one used to perform a number of acts of vandalism last summer."

"Vandalism?"

The detective looks at his clipboard. "Vandalism involving a certain ceramic Buddha."

You can almost hear the *Dragnet* music: *Dum-de-dum-dum-duu-uum!*

I can't fucking believe it. In the last eight months we've engaged in underage drinking, reckless driving, illegal drug use (on federal property), unlocking and entering, blackmail, fraud, forgery, and embezzlement, and we're getting nailed for grand theft Buddha.

Detective Bose places a large box on a desk. "We collected evidence all last summer," he says, then proceeds, without the slightest trace of irony, to pull out Paula's communion veil, Doug's jockstrap, Aunt Glo's flowered bathing cap, an empty bottle of Southern Comfort, a breakfast tray, and a Hawaiian lei, each one catalogued and sealed in a clear plastic bag.

"I was wondering what happened to that bathing cap," Aunt Glo says.

Detective Bose continues: "We almost had an ID on the car last summer, but then the crimes tapered off and became more random throughout the fall until, of course, said Buddha disappeared entirely." He makes it sound like the Buddha had been murdered. "So when some of our officers saw a vehicle fitting the description today, naturally we had to bring Mrs. D'Angelo in for questioning."

I clear my throat. "It's my fault, sir," I say.

Detective Bose turns and looks at me. "Did you take it, son?"

"Well, not exactly, but I'm the one who had it and I should have brought it back and I'm really, really, really sorry."

"You're only sorry because you got caught," Detective Bose says.

"Oh, detective, have a heart," Aunt Glo says. "It was just a stupid prank. Even Maya Angelou had a little incident with a statue of St. Francis when he was a kid . . ."

"Ma . . ."

Detective Bose taps his clipboard. "It's all right," he says. "The owner of the Buddha has already told me that she won't press charges, so long as her property is returned to her."

All eyes turn to me.

"You're not going to believe this . . ." I say.

✳   ✳   ✳

I'm right. He doesn't. I call Kathleen so she can confirm that the Buddha was indeed stolen, but her machine picks up, which must mean she's seeing cryents. Aunt Glo asks Detective Bose to give us a chance to prove our story and, with a little coercion from Father Angelo, he agrees, telling us we have four hours to come up with the Buddha.

Angelo takes Aunt Glo home while Natie, Doug, and I pile into the Lincoln Continental Divide with Paula, who lectures us all the way to Kathleen's about our foolishness and how we violated the basic tenets of Creative Vandalism. Good thing she doesn't know about the blackmail, fraud, forgery, and embezzlement.

The Wagon Ho is in the driveway, which must mean Kelly is home. I tell Paula, Natie, and Doug to wait in the car while I slip into the house, opening the front door as quietly as I can so the cats don't freak out. As I pad around the first floor in my socks I can hear the muted monologue of the cryent in the basement, a sad song with the volume turned down. Kelly's nowhere to be found, so I tiptoe up the stairs to see if she knows Kathleen's schedule.

The therapeutic murmur actually seems to get louder as I ascend the stairs and for a moment I think there must be some vent I don't know about when I realize that the noise is actually coming from Kelly's bedroom. I follow the sound down the hallway to her door, which is slightly ajar. I stop to listen and hear a groan. Figuring Kelly went home sick, I open the door a crack to see if she's okay.

She's not alone.

Kelly sits up in bed and yanks the sheets to cover her naked torso. "Shut the door! Shut the door!" she screams.

I do as I'm told.

"No, you cheesehead, with you on the other side."

Out of the corner of my eye I see that the source of the moaning is under the sheets with her, between her legs, to be precise. But in her panic Kelly's rammed her knees together, trapping the poor guy, who makes low-voiced grunting sounds like he's being suffocated. "Get out, goddamnit, get out!" Kelly yells.

I assume she means me and not him, so I yank hard on the antique doorknob and dislodge the door with a huge clunk. I dash out and slam the door behind me, mortified yet dying to know who the hell is trapped between Kelly's legs.

From the inside of the room I hear Kelly say, "You stay here something something something . . ."

A deep voice answers, "That's stupid. At this point something something . . ."

The voice sounds familiar, but I can't quite place it.

"Don't call me stupid," Kelly says.

"I'm not," the voice answers, "it's just that something something something . . ."

I hear Kelly's footsteps, so I fly down the stairs to get away. As I round the corner who do I see standing in the entryway but Kathleen.

"What the hell are you kids doing," she says, "practicing for the rodeo?"

"KATHLEEN!" I scream like I'm Fran Nudelman. "I'M SO SORRY TO BOTHER YOU!" It's an automatic teen impulse: no matter what your friends are doing, you cover for them and ask questions later.

"Edward are you all right? What's gotten into you?"

"I'm . . . uh . . . uh . . ."

An idiot, apparently. I can't think of a thing to say.

"Uh . . ."

Kathleen glances up the stairs behind me and says, "Do you two have any idea what's wrong with him?"

You *two*? Who are you *two*? I whirl around and there, on the landing next to Kelly, stands the person who, just moments ago, was being suffocated between her legs.

thirty-four

It's Ziba.

Somehow I'm able to babble the tale of the Buddha to Kathleen, all the while trying to rethink my entire perception of Kelly's and Ziba's sexual orientations. "It's really simple," I say to Kathleen. "If you could just come down to the police station and explain to them that the Buddha got stolen, everything should be fine."

Kathleen looks down at the floor and bites her lip.

"What?" I say. "What is it?"

"You're not going to believe this . . ."

✳   ✳   ✳

She gave it away. To one of her cryents. I can't believe my shitty luck. The gods must be punishing me for my evil ways. "I'm sorry I lied to you, sweetie," Kathleen says, "but this woman has had such a hard life and she actually admired it one day, and, well, frankly, it really was such an eyesore . . ."

"Where is it now?" I ask.

"At her house in Battle Brook. Listen, I'll just call her and let her know you need to come get it. She'll understand."

"Are you sure?"

"If not, that's what therapy is for," she says and goes to hunt for the phone. I turn to Kelly and Ziba and give them a wide-eyed, open-mouthed look, the Internationally Recognized Signal for "Since when are you two muff divers?"

In a dead-on impersonation of Ziba, Kelly gives a shampoo-commercial flip to her hair, and murmurs, "Edward darling, don't look so shocked. You're not the only one around here who's bisexual." Then laughing her machine-gun laugh, she turns and smiles at Ziba with both rows of teeth.

Holy Lesbos, Batman!

I'm about to get the whole story when Kathleen returns. "She's not answering," she says, "but she should be home by the time you get there. I'll get you the address."

❋   ❋   ❋

Of course we get lost, driving past row after row of bail-bond places, check-cashing stores, and taverns advertising topless dancers. The shops all have those metal gates that pull down to protect them from burglary, and every bus shelter and traffic meridian is covered with gang graffiti. Suffice it to say, none of us are too happy to be in Battle Brook so close to sundown.

Kathleen's cryent lives on a treeless street where houses aching to be painted hover near cracked and crooked sidewalks, as if they were afraid to move too far away from the light of the streetlamps. But the house is easy to find owing to the fact that there's a Buddha on the tiny front lawn. Paula makes me and Doug go alone while she, Natie, and the happy couple wait in the car. I open the gate on the hip-height chain-link fence around the property, noting the BEWARE OF DOG sign, and go to the front door. The doorbell doesn't seem to work, so I knock, then leap out of my skin when the dog to beware of starts howling on the other side of the door. No one answers.

"What time is it?" Doug asks.

I check my ankle. "Seven-thirty."

"We've got to be back in Camptown in half an hour. We're going to have to take it."

I hesitate, wondering if perhaps this Buddha has been stolen enough, but I've got to admit he's right. I open the gate and we lift the Buddha together. Paula flounces out of the car.

"What do you think you're doing?" she says.

"We've got no choice. We've got to take him now."

She glances around. "But what if someone sees?"

"It doesn't belong to her anyway," Doug says. "Now, c'mon, open the trunk."

"I don't want anything to do with this."

"Fine," I say. "I'll take full responsibility. Just give me the damn keys."

We load the Buddha into the trunk and I get behind the wheel to drive, with Paula sitting between me and Doug in the front so she can criticize. We've just turned onto the main drag when I see red lights flashing in my rearview mirror. Everyone starts talking at once.

"Someone must've called the cops."

"I told you this would happen."

"Pull over, pull over."

"Shut up, just be cool."

"Isn't there some law you can't be arrested for the same crime twice?"

I become hyper-aware of my driving, as if pulling over properly will somehow earn me extra credit with the cop. I take a long inhale through my nose and try to relax my hands and feet the way my mother showed me to when she was in her Yoga phase.

I look in the side-view mirror and see the cop get out of the squad car. He's youngish with an unintelligent look about him, like a basset hound. I roll down my window.

"Hello, officer," I say, assuming an expression that I hope is interpreted as serious yet innocent.

"Evening, sir."

I'm always embarrassed when people older than me call me sir.

He shines the flashlight in the car. "Are you aware that one of your taillights is out?"

I can feel everyone in the Lincoln Continental Divide exhale with relief.

"Is that so?" I say, giggling a little. "Oh my, how do you like that?"

"I'm going to have to give you a ticket for that."

"Of course you do," I say. "Absolutely. Yessiree. Go right ahead."

"May I see your license and registration, please?"

"Certainly," I say. I reach into my back pocket and pull out my wallet. "Here it is," I say, handing it through the window.

"And the registration?"

I turn to Paula, who gulps audibly.

"It's in the trunk," I say.

"In the trunk? What's it doing in the trunk?"

I tell him the truth. "We needed room for the almanac." I'm aware how dumb this sounds.

"Would you step out of the car, sir?"

I get out. He flashes the flashlight in my face, presumably to see if I'm wasted. Even though I am sober, I try to look even more so.

"Would you please walk slowly to the back of the car and open the trunk for me?" The cop follows me to the back of the car and stands next to me as I put the key in. I lift the lid, and the cop jumps back, drawing his gun.

"Don't shoot, don't shoot," I scream.

"What the hell is that?" he yells.

"It's a Buddha."

The cop takes a closer look. The Buddha smiles back at him, like he's thoroughly enjoying this latest adventure. The cop puts his hands on his hips and shakes his head.

"Why the fuck do you have a Buddha in your trunk?" he says.

"Uh . . ."

From the front of the car I hear Paula shout, "We're Buddhists."

"Get your head back in the car," the cop yells.

She ducks back in.

"That's right," I say, "and . . . uh . . . carrying a Buddha in your trunk is . . . a sign of good luck. It's like the Buddhist version of a St. Christopher medal."

The cop takes the registration, and goes back to his squad car to make a report while I stand next to the car feeling conspicuous and stupid. "A 1972 Lincoln Continental blah blah blah, registration number blah blah blah, Buddha in the trunk . . . that's right, a Buddha in the trunk . . ."

It's not long before a second squad car shows up. A pair of cops get out of that one and all three advance toward me.

That can't be good.

"This statue is reported stolen," the first cop says. "I need you to place your hands on the back of the car."

I can't fucking believe this.

He pats me down, then handcuffs me. That's right, handcuffs me.

The second cop walks over to the driver's side window and points his flashlight inside. "Okay, one at a time, each of you step out of the car. You first . . ."

You know when you're driving along the highway and you see a cop forcing people to abandon their car and you think, "Hmm, must be a drug bust"?

Yeah, well think again.

It's just like on TV. The cop recites our Miranda rights, then holds our heads as he puts us in the back of the squad car, the girls in one, the guys in the other. Natie nearly gets us pistol-whipped when he tries to explain, so we just keep our mouths shut as we're driven to the county jail.

The county jail. Cue the banjo music from *Deliverance*.

There we're fingerprinted, made to empty the contents of our pockets, and sent off to his and hers cells. Cells. With bars. That lock.

I nearly shit my pants.

Everything in the cell is made of concrete: the walls, the floors, the bench, the guy standing guard. The only other thing is a lone toilet stationed in the middle of the room. Now there's a metaphor for the state of my life if ever there was one.

There's a guy asleep on the concrete bench. He's got a hollowed-out skull of a face and broomstick arms lined with track marks. "Alas poor Yorick, I knew him Horatio," Natie whispers.

"This isn't funny," I hiss. I turn and gaze at our new roommate. Natie's right. With his bald head and paper-thin skin, he does look like the skull from *Hamlet*. From five feet away I can see the thick vein at his temple pulsing. Without warning, Alas Poor Yorick opens his eyes. I jump back and grab Doug for protection. But the guy doesn't seem to see anything.

"Is he blind?" I ask.

"Nah, I think he's sleeping with his eyes open," Doug whispers.

"Ca-*ree*-py," Natie says under his breath.

Alas Poor Yorick's vacant, rheumy gaze is way too *Night of the Living Dead* for comfort and the three of us back away as far as we can get, plunking ourselves down on the concrete bench at the other side of the cell.

Doug buries his face in his hands. "My old man is going to kill me," he says.

"Not if this guy does it first," Natie whispers.

I can't believe it's come to this. I grew up in a house with a circular driveway, for Chrissake. How did I end up in jail with Skeletor? Finally, to our relief, Alas Poor Yorick shuts his horrible yellow eyes and rolls over, his shirt riding up to reveal bruises on his back.

"It's always nice to get out and meet new people, isn't it?" Natie says.

I use my one phone call to contact the Camptown Police Department but, what with getting confirmations from both Kathleen and her cryent, it takes over an hour and a half to get us released, which is sufficient time for me to envision my entire future working in the prison laundry and fending off knife attacks from scary guys in hairnets.

✳   ✳   ✳

The girls are standing in the parking lot next to the Lincoln Continental Divide when we get out. "Are you all okay?" I ask.

Ziba flicks her cigarette on the ground and rubs it out with her foot. "We learned all about prostitution from these two hookers," she says, like it's yet another tedious high-school class she had to sit through.

"And venereal diseases," Kelly adds.

"It was absolutely *fascinating*," Paula says. "I hope I can remember it all for my acting."

Paula.

"You guys were lucky," Natie says. "We watched a heroin addict choke on his own vomit." He frowns at me like it's my fault.

"C'mon," Doug says, giving Natie a shove into the car, "we've got a Buddha to deliver."

✳   ✳   ✳

The house is dark and for a moment I wonder whether it's too late to be doing this, but there's a light coming from the kitchen. "You guys stay here," Doug says. "I'm the one who stole it."

"But I kept it," I say.

"*We* kept it," Kelly adds. "It's my house, too." She opens her door to get out.

"She's right," Paula says. "We got into this together, we should get out of it together."

Natie clears his throat. "Don't you think at least one of us should wait with the car?" he says. "This isn't the nicest neighborhood, y'know."

"All of us," Ziba says, and she shoves him out the door.

The seven of us (including the Buddha) go around the side of the house to the kitchen door. We knock.

A middle-aged woman with a dried-out perm and split ends peeks through the curtain, then unlocks the door. Sneering at us like we're the most contemptible bunch of fiends ever, she shouts, "Ma, they're here." We all take extra care to wipe our feet, partly out of politeness and partly to stall, then slouch our way into the kitchen. You'd think that after everything I've been through I wouldn't shock easily, but what I see truly takes my breath away.

Buddhas. Everywhere.

I mean, everywhere. There's a Buddha cookie jar, a Buddha egg timer, and Buddha oven mitts; a Buddha lamp, a Buddha clock, a Buddha salt, and a Buddha pepper; here a Buddha, there a Buddha, everywhere a Buddha Buddha, all of them laughing deliriously in spasms of joy, taunting us with their lopsided grins.

Now when they cast the role of the Buddha woman in the movie of my life, they'll need to find the smallest, oldest, most arthritic-looking grandmother type you've ever seen. Better yet, imagine for yourself the absolute last person on earth you'd ever want to harm and then cast her.

The Buddha woman reaches for her walker so she can stand.

Jesus, Mary, and Joseph, the woman needs a walker. I'm going to burn in Hell for eternity.

I have no idea what to say. I consider introducing myself, but it feels weird and somehow wrong. Everything feels weird and wrong. "We brought your Buddha back," I hear myself say. "We're so . . ."

Thoughtless? Selfish? Evil?

". . . sorry."

The Buddha woman regards us through her trifocals and I can tell that forgiveness is not forthcoming. "I certainly hope you are," she says in a chipped teacup of a voice. (Lord almighty, even her voice is frail.) "You kids have no idea the hell, excuse my language, you've put me through. I can't for the life of me understand why you chose to pick on me, ringing my bell in the dead of night, scaring me that way and making me move my statue back time and again."

I try to imagine this parchment-y looking woman, barely bigger than the Buddha itself, trying to lug a fifty-pound ceramic statue back into her garden. Did I mention I'm going to burn in Hell for eternity?

"And then to steal it from me, like it's a big joke. My dead husband gave me that statue, you know."

Oh God, and it was probably the last thing he did before expiring from a sudden heart attack, leaving her without life insurance and only her Buddha collection to give her solace in her lonely remaining years.

O, what a rogue and peasant slave am I.

You know how on *The Flintstones* when Wilma is scolding Fred and the more ashamed he feels, the tinier he gets? I feel about as small as the Buddha air freshener above the sink.

"I don't know how we can make this up to you," I say.

"You can't," she says. "Just put it back in the garden where it belongs and don't ever bother me again."

I must remember this shame for my acting.

Edward.

thirty-five

Once the trauma of being arrested, jailed, and completely humiliated passes, I'm able to finally get my head around the other mind-altering event in our lives: Ziba and Kelly.

There are more things in heaven and earth, Horatio, than are dreamt of in your philosophy.

In retrospect, I suppose there were some clues, like how Ziba could be so worldly and yet act like such a prude; and as for Kelly, well . . . still waters, I guess. Doug drops some completely unsubtle hints about wanting to be with the two of them at once, but Ziba makes it abundantly clear that she's had enough of men. ("And no, you can't watch either," she adds.) I try to take advantage of Doug's pent-up sexual frustration, but he's not buying the whole Aldonza the whore one-pair-of-arms-is-like-another thing.

"I'm sorry, man, you know I love you, but you just don't do it for me," he says, almost as if he were apologizing for not being more of a sexual deviant. "I swear, if you were a chick I'd be with you in a heartbeat, but I just can't get past you being hairy and having muscles and stuff."

At least he said I had muscles.

What's worse, though, is that now I find myself wanting Kelly more than ever. And I hate myself for it because I know it's just some knee-jerk reaction to her being unavailable, but the fact is I can't stop thinking about her. Living in the same house has become a whole new kind of torture.

So here I am—no girlfriend, no boyfriend, no father, no mother, no money, no job, and no future. The only thing I do have is a psychotic Austrian trailing me like a hired assassin. I give up.

I call off Jordan Craig's blackmail.

One night in the county jail was all I needed to realize I'm way too big of a wuss to consider white-collar crime as a viable career option. I wish I could say that sending Jordan the negatives makes me feel better (that is, after I pry them out of Natie's pudgy, clenched fists), but as far as I can see, an unwillingness to blackmail still ranks fairly low as a standard for ethics and morality.

Still, shame clings to me like a bad smell and the only peace I get is from taking insanely long runs, which become increasingly more compulsive the closer we get to the opening of *Godspell*.

Godspell.

I know it's going to make me sound like one of those glassy-eyed Young Life kids (you know the type—the ones who always quote scripture in the yearbook and whose major social activity is the church lock-in, a scary brainwashing ritual where they play volleyball in the church gym all night until they're too exhausted to be reasonable and then accept Jesus as their personal savior just so they can go to sleep), but the fact is, right now Jesus is my only salvation.

Playing Jesus, I mean.

I've begun fasting on Fridays—okay, mostly because I have to take off my shirt in the baptism scene and I don't want to look jiggly—and I have actually read all four Gospels for research and even tried to do some of the Zen meditations my mother taught me, even though I have the attention span of a mosquito on cocaine. Everyone thinks I'm acting totally freaky ("You were more fun when you drank, man," Doug says), but it makes me feel, I don't know, purer in a way.

Which is not to say that my version of Jesus is a wimp. I hate it when Christ is played all profound and dull, like he's addicted to morphine instead of inspired by God. Personally, I see Jesus more as a Pharisee-ass-kicking Christian superhero. Mr. Lucas agrees. Being a Mr. Lucas production, this *Godspell* promises to be unlike any ever seen before. The usual cast of Jesus and the disciples is backed by a chorus of fifty, which gives the whole thing a much more spectacular *Jesus Christ Superstar* kind of feeling.

You see, *Godspell* was written in 1971, so it's usually done in this hippie-dippy, flower-child kind of way, with the cast dressed as clowns and acting out the parables all wild and funny, but Mr. Lucas thought the whole thing was a little too *Hair: The American Tribal Love Rock Musical* for his taste so he's set it in a high school in the 1980s, which is particularly good for the weaker cast members because they won't have to stretch as much as actors. Our version is very *Fast Times at Ridgemont High*; there's still a lot of running around and being nutty, but it's our kind of nutty, with Mohawks and Moonwalks, and imitations of ET and Boy George and Ronald Reagan. No matter how crazy the show gets, though, Mr. Lucas makes sure that Jesus doesn't get lost in the mayhem.

I swear, it's the only thing that's keeping me in school. I mean, otherwise, what's the point? Since I'm legally emancipated I can write my own notes, so I pretty much come and go as I please; Mr. Lucas calls it the OAP—the Optional Attendance Plan. Pissing off the secretaries in the attendance office is one of the few pleasures I have left. Here are a couple of my faves:

> *To Whom It May Concern,*
> *Please excuse my absence. Or don't. Like I care.*
> *Edward*

> *To Whom It May Concern,*
> *Please excuse Edward's tardiness. He was mentally ill this morning.*
> *Love and kisses,*
> *The people who live in Edward's head*

> *To Whom It May Not Concern,*
> *Please allow me to leave early today. I'm bored and I'd like to get home in time for Match Game.*
> *Later,*
> *E.Z.*

On Easter Sunday, Kathleen, Kelly, and I go with Paula and Aunt Glo to Mass at Father Angelo's parish in Hoboken. Kathleen hasn't been to church since her parish priest refused to serve her communion because she got divorced, so Kelly and I get to enjoy watching Kathleen defiantly commit a minor heresy by allowing the Holy Host in her formerly married mouth. Aunt Glo is right about Angelo's version of the Mass; it is like a musical. There are two choirs, a small orchestra, and a soloist who was Betty Buckley's understudy in *Cats*. Angelo even sings

("Such a voice Maya Angelou has," Aunt Glo says); it's all we can do to stop ourselves from applauding his rendition of the Holy Eucharist.

Afterward we go back to Aunt Glo's where lots of short, loud people eat and shout conversations at one another from opposite sides of the room. It makes me miss all the Zanni relatives in Hoboken, but it's not like I'd be seeing them anyway; Dagmar's cut Al off from all of them, too. Kathleen seems a little too Wallingford Tennis Club at first, but once she's gotten some wine in her she surprises everyone by knowing all the words to "Volare." Paula and I harmonize on "Ave Maria" like we did at her cousin Crazy Linda's wedding, and every male D'Angelo cousin between the ages of fourteen and forty asks if I'm dating Kelly and, if I'm not, could I maybe hook him up?

If they only knew.

Kathleen gets a little too happy, however, and staggers off to bed as soon as we get home. I've just changed into the tartan flannel nightgown when I see Kelly standing in the doorway, her face scrubbed Ivory Girl clean and her hair pulled back in a ponytail. She wears an oversized Wallingford High football jersey that Doug gave her.

"I hate when she gets like that," Kelly says.

I pat the place next to me on the bed. She climbs on, pulling the jersey over her knees like a tent.

"She's just unhappy," I say.

"I know." We sit in silence while Kelly traces patterns on the quilt with her slender fingers. She shivers.

"You want to get under the covers?" I ask. She looks at me through her bangs and nods.

I pull the blanket aside and we climb in. The bed is too small for two and I have to put my arm around her shoulder, but just in a snuggly, slumber-party way. "Your feet are freezing," I say. "What are you, a corpse?"

"Sorry," she says, "let me just warm them." She rubs her frigid feet against my calves.

"Cut it out, icicle girl," I say, fidgeting. "You're killing me."

She laughs and nestles her head in the crook of my neck. It feels nice, but I'm not reading anything into it.

"You mind if I just lie here for a while?" she says.

"Stay as long as you'd like."

Please God. I've got nothing. Let me just have this.

"Shall I turn off the light?"

I can hear her swallow. "Sure," she says quietly.

I inhale and get a whiff of Kelly's shampoo. Herbal Essence. I've missed that smell. She rests her arm across my stomach.

"You're getting skinny," she says.

"Really?" Thank you, Jesus. Literally.

"Yeah, right here," she says, poking at my side.

"That tickles," I say. I don't know why the reaction to being tickled is always to announce it, because inevitably it only inspires the tickler to tickle you some more.

"C'mon . . . stop . . . really . . . ," I say, "your mother will hear . . ." This stops her. "Nah, she's passed out," I continue, and start tickling Kelly back.

"No fair, no fair, no fair," she says, trying not to laugh too loudly.

Kelly rolls over on my thigh and I stop tickling her. A strand of hair has gotten loose from her ponytail and I reach up to brush it out of her mouth. She looks so beautiful and, well, I'm sorry, I can't help myself— I just have to kiss her. Her mouth tastes minty and fresh and alive. I pull her to me, like I want to inhale her entire being as she gently grinds against me and . . .

Happy Easter! Jesus ain't the only one to rise today.

I worry for a moment that I won't stay hard, but a little dry humping convinces me that I am once again a member in good standing. In fact, all I want to do is get as close to Kelly as I possibly can.

"Do you want to?" I ask.

"You mean . . . ?"

"Yeah."

"Yeah," she whispers. "But first you have to . . ."

"Put on a condom, I know."

"Well yeah, duh," she says, "but first you have to take off my sister's nightgown."

We make love: slowly, gently, quietly. Climbing inside her feels like slipping into a warm, soothing bath. Or a dream.

You couldn't ask for a better first time.

✻　　✻　　✻

I lie with my head on her breast for a long time afterward, listening to her heartbeat. "Thank you," I murmur.

"You're welcome."

I lean over and make butterfly kisses on her belly with my eye-lashes.

"Still think you're bisexual?" she asks.

I prop myself up on my elbows. "Do you?"

"I asked you first."

We look at each other a moment and then both of us bust up laughing.

"Hell, yeah," we both say.

"Nothing personal," Kelly says, "but I think maybe only a girl can, like, really know what feels good to another girl, you know what I mean? Oh, not that it didn't feel good when you went down on me, even if you were doing it to avoid sex."

I sit up. "You knew?"

Kelly rolls her mismatched eyes. "I'm a therapist's daughter," she says. "How dumb do you think I am?"

"And you didn't mind?"

"What? That you, like, practically gave yourself lockjaw trying to satisfy me? That's a lot more than I can say for Doug, I tell you that."

"Really?"

Kelly gives a feline stretch. "Please," she says. "He thinks all he needs to do is fuck gently and carry a big stick."

This girl never ceases to surprise me. I take a good, long look at her. "Have you always been this cool and I just never noticed?"

Her eyes cloud and she nods. "Actually, yes," she whispers.

"I'm sorry."

"Thanks." She lowers her head and does that coy Princess Di thing that pretty girls do. "I know how you can make it up to me, though."

"Oh, yeah?"

She gives a little push on my head. "Why don't you finish what you started?"

I'd answer, but it's rude to talk with your mouth full.

✳   ✳   ✳

You know that scene in *Gone With the Wind* when Scarlett wakes up humming and singing to herself the morning after Rhett carried her up the stairs and gave her the banging of her life? That's how I feel the next day. Just the thought of the night before gets me hard, often at very in-opportune moments, like while practicing to play our Lord and Savior Jesus Christ. Kelly and I agree not to mention it to anybody, least of all

Ziba. Given my new sense of ethics, I'm not crazy about the idea of sneaking around behind Ziba's back, or Kathleen's, for that matter, but hey, I'm only human. And eighteen.

We have a harder time staying quiet during the Anne Frank in the Secret Annex game. Over the course of the next couple of weeks we progress from making love to making hot monkey love, complete with little high-pitched chimpanzee noises and that totally sexy thing when you call out each other's names while you're doing it. I think having someone acknowledge by name that you and you alone are the reason for their pleasure is such an immense turn-on, unless of course you have an unsexy name like Agnes or Wendell. It must be tough getting aroused when your partner shouts, "Oh, yeah, do me, Wendell!"

I'm concerned, of course, that we're too vigorous and noisy, but I'm like a kid with a new toy and getting Kelly to reach orgasm through intercourse alone becomes something of a personal mission to me. ("Look Ma, no hands!") So we're going at it pretty hot and heavy one afternoon, me running lines in my head to keep from coming (Blessed are the peacemakers, for they shall . . .) when suddenly Kelly's eyes go wide.

"Are you there? Are you there?" I pant. "Please tell me you're there."

"Do you hear that?" she says.

"Hear what?" (Blessed are the peacemakers, for . . .)

"That sound, downstairs."

I stop and listen.

Footsteps. Coming up the goddamn stairs.

Kelly and I leap out of bed and do that hopping-around dance that people do when they're trying to hunt for their clothes and get into them at the same time, all the while saying, "Shit, shit, shit!" Kelly's managed to find her shirt and I've got my pants to my knees when there's a tap at the door which, because we are obviously destined to be punished, swings wide open. I turn, and there she is, her eyes and mouth wide open like a flounder.

Ziba.

She looks at me, my boxers bobbing in front of me like a circus tent, then at Kelly, who's trying to appear nonchalant with her shirt on inside out and, I swear, it's like a water main bursts inside her. Tears erupt from Ziba's eyes and her face seems to crumble into pieces. It's kind of a distressing sight, to be honest. She spins around and pounds down the stairs, slamming the front door as she goes. Kelly jumps into her jeans and takes off after her without even putting on her shoes.

Who needs Juilliard when I've got all this drama right here?

I throw on the rest of my clothes and am just wiping some lipstick off my neck when, from downstairs, I hear a scream.

I fly down the steps and, as I whip around the corner, I see a very panicked psychotherapist frantically waving a knitting needle at a very large black man. "Who the fuck are you?" Kathleen screams.

The man backs away from her. "It's cool, it's cool," he shouts as he raises his hands to show he's unarmed. He glances over his shoulder. "Edward, tell her you know me!"

"I know him, I know him!" I say. "We go to school together. It's okay."

Kathleen drops the knitting needle.

"Kathleen, this is TeeJay."

"I came here with Ziba," TeeJay says. "Honest."

Kathleen exhales and leans against the wall. "I'm sorry," she says. "I heard a big crash and when I came upstairs and saw you, I . . ."

A worried-sounding cryent calls up from the basement, saying, "Is everything okay?"

"Everything's fine," Kathleen says. "Just the cats again." She runs her fingers through her hair and then hardens her eyes at me. "Edward. Sweetheart. I work very hard to make these people in the basement sane. Could you please try not to do anything that will make them crazy again?"

"Sure. Sorry."

"Thank you." Kathleen nods to TeeJay and then disappears down the stairs. He and I stand there, gaping at one another.

"Can we go outside and talk?" he asks. His voice is low and woody, like how you'd imagine an oak tree would sound if it could speak.

"Sure," I say. We go out on the front porch.

"So, what can I do for you?" I say. "I mean, you're welcome here anytime, of course, but it's not like . . . well . . ." Why am I always such an idiot in front of black people?

TeeJay folds his huge cannonball arms across his chest and stares at me. "A couple of days ago this guy showed up at our door," he says, "saying he worked for Frank Sinatra."

"Frank Sinatra? *The* Frank Sinatra?"

"He said he was looking for information on LaChance Jones."

My stomach does a backflip. "LaChance Jones? Who's LaChance Jones?" I say.

TeeJay burns a pair of holes in me with his eyes. "She was my sister."

Oh. My. God. I'm going to roast in Hell forever.

"This guy asked if we knew anything about someone opening a bank account in my sister's name. My mama got so upset she just ran out of the room crying."

Flames licking at my feet.

"He asked me if I knew who this was," TeeJay says, and hands me a piece of paper. It's a photocopy of the fake driver's license Natie made for Ziba/LaChance. The bank must have xeroxed it when she opened the account.

Devils piercing my skin with their blazing-hot tridents.

"What did you say?" I ask, trying not to wet my pants.

"I told him no," he says.

"What?"

TeeJay folds his arms again, the muscles in his biceps bunching. "I had no idea if this guy was who he said he was. But I knew Ziba was cool, so I figured I better talk to her first. She told me everything."

Shit. "I'm so sorry," I say. "I didn't mean to . . ."

TeeJay takes a couple of steps closer to me. "Didn't mean to what?"

"Didn't mean to cause you any harm." I stagger backward, knocking into the porch swing.

"Come here," he says.

Oh God.

"I said come here!"

I take a step forward. "Listen, I'm not good at this kind of thing, so can you just make it quick so we can get this over with?"

TeeJay unfolds his arms.

thirty-six

TeeJay grabs me roughly by the shoulders and I brace myself to get knocked into next week. But then he takes me in his huge arms and gives me the most bone-crunching, back-cracking, oxygen-depleting *hug*.

"Thanks, man," he whispers as he squeezes me.

"Fr wht?" I say into his chest. What the hell is going on?

TeeJay lets go of me and rests his enormous hands on my shoulders. "That guy who works for Frank Sinatra, he hung around for a while and asked me what I was doing and was I gonna go to college or what. And I told him straight I didn't have enough money 'cuz my mama and my little brother depend on my paycheck. Then this afternoon, this showed up. Special delivery." He hands me a letter.

```
May 1, 1984

Harvey Nelson
Financial Aid Office
Rutgers University
620 George Street
New Brunswick, NJ 08901

Mr. Thelonious Jones
319 First Street
Wallingford, NJ 07090

Dear Mr. Jones,

I am writing this letter to confirm that
Rutgers University has received an
```

anonymous donation on your behalf for
the express purpose of paying the
entire cost of your tuition (including
books and fees), as well as room and
board for four years of undergraduate
education.

We look forward to your joining the
freshman class this fall. Enclosed
please find the necessary forms for
class registration as well as room
assignment.

Congratulations.

Sincerely,
Harvey Nelson
Director of Financial Aid

That's so like Frank. He swipes my ten grand with one hand and gives away forty with the other.

"Don't thank me," I say, as I hand the letter back to TeeJay. "Thank Frank Sinatra."

"Yeah, but if it wasn't for your fucked-up plan, this never would have happened."

"I can't take all the credit," I say. "Natie thought most of it up."

"Who?"

"Cheesehead."

"Oh, yeah, I know that kid."

I plop onto the porch swing and rest my face in my hands.

TeeJay sits next to me. "You okay, man?"

"Yeah, I'm just tired."

" 'Cause if you need anything, you just let me know."

"Not beating the crap out of me was enough."

"I'm serious," TeeJay says. "You need some money? I've got plenty saved."

"Oh God, no, please, no. But thank you. Go buy your mother something nice."

"You got it," he says and rises to leave.

I look up at him. "So what are you going to study?"

"Pre-law. I'm going to be a lawyer."

"Good. I may need one."

❊ ❊ ❊

The doorbell at Ziba's house is one of those old-fashioned kind that twist like a key, and I always ring it more than is necessary because I like turning it. The house is a gingerbread Victorian, complete with a turret where Ziba lives like an exiled princess in a fairy tale. Kelly answers the door. She mouths "Hi" to me, or "Hiyee" to be exact, and stares down at the ground like she's either embarrassed or has suddenly developed an extreme interest in Oriental rugs.

"Figured you could use a ride home," I say.

"Thanks," she says, almost inaudibly.

"Where's Ziba?" I whisper. I don't know why I'm whispering, but it feels like the thing to do.

Kelly glances over her shoulder. "Upstairs," she says, then looks at me in the eye for the first time, which I take as an invitation to grab her in my arms and kiss her, movie-star style. Kelly complies for the briefest moment, then stops me by pressing her palms against my shoulders. She backs away, wiping her mouth with the back of her hand. "We can't stay long," she says. "Ziba's parents will be home soon."

Ziba's parents are a strange pair, so stiff and formal in their foreignness that all of us, Ziba included, spend as little time as possible in their house. There's something about the place—with its hardwood floors, its paintings with those little art lights above them, and its bookcases lined with titles in multiple languages—that makes one feel as if one should be discussing literature or art while sipping a fine vintage wine and using the word "one" as the subject of the sentence. You can tell that sophisticated people live here because all their photographs are in black-and-white.

Kelly and I climb to the third floor, then up the little winding staircase that leads to the turret. Ziba's room is so spare that you'd think it was a nun's cell were it not for the framed eight-by-ten glossies of Greta Garbo, Marlene Dietrich, and Lauren Bacall. It's a tiny round space the color of a brown egg with just a single bed, a nightstand, and a small chest of drawers. Ziba actually has a whole other room on the third floor just to keep her many clothes and shoes.

"You decent?" Kelly calls as we reach the top of the stairs.

"Come on in."

Ziba is standing in the middle of the room in a satin robe, a large bath towel over her head. She rubs with both hands to dry her hair, then flips the towel off and shakes.

I gasp.

"Well, what do you think?" she asks.

"It's so . . . short," I say. Ziba has chopped off her long wall of hair so that nothing remains but the shortest of spikes, like an unmowed lawn. With her enormous eyes and beaky nose she almost resembles a baby bird, a very chic baby bird, mind you, but a baby bird nonetheless.

"I think it's kind of punk," Kelly says.

"It's kind of necessary, is what it is," Ziba replies, dropping onto the bed and flipping her head as if she still had long hair, "just in case the Mob comes looking for LaChance."

"Those are just rumors about Frank," I say.

"I still don't understand how he traced the money to you," Kelly says. "We withdrew it as cash."

"Never underestimate the power of Sinatra," I say. "After Laurel Watkins told him about the Catholic Vigilance Society, he probably used some Hoboken connections to investigate the post office box, which must have led him to the Convent of the Bleeding Heart and LaChance Jones." I look over at Ziba with her butchered hair. "Oh, Zeeb," I moan, "I'm so sorry I got you into this mess."

Ziba flicks the notion away like it was a piece of dust. "Edward darling, don't be so dramatic. My whole life there have been people who've wanted me and my family dead. Your evil stepmonster and the Mafia will just have to get in line behind the Ayatollah Khomeini." Her eyes shift to Kelly. "No, if I wanted to be angry with you, I have a much better reason."

Kelly blushes.

"Yeah, sorry about that, too," I say.

"Oh, I can't blame you," Ziba says. "Look at her." She traces Kelly's jawline with a long, tapering finger. "She's irresistible." Kelly pats the space on the bed next to her for Ziba to sit down and gives her a longish kiss.

It's really hot.

"That being said," Ziba says, licking her lips, "I've never played well with others and I don't intend to start now. I know it must sound terribly *bourgeois* and frankly, I'm a little disappointed in myself for acting so . . . *traditional*," she says it like it's the worst thing imaginable, "but that's the way I feel."

I look at the two of them sitting on the narrow bed together, so impossibly gorgeous and perfect, like sunshine and darkness, and I see that Kelly has made her decision already. If I were being mature about it, I'd say she made the right one: as much as I care for her and am loving the sex, I don't think I could show her the kind of devotion that Ziba just did. If I weren't being mature about it, I'd do everything I possibly could to undermine their happiness so I could continue to get laid. But I don't.

When they make the movie of my life, this would be the moment when I graciously leave the two of them together, like I'm Humphrey Bogart telling Ingrid Bergman she has to get on the plane at the end of *Casablanca*. In the next scene you'd see me driving home alone in the Wagon Ho while Frank sings "In the Wee Small Hours of the Morning" on the soundtrack, generating sympathy for my luckless, loveless state, but in real life that's not what happens. In actual fact, while I may be luckless and loveless, I still have to drive Kelly home where we will continue to live together platonically, except now I'm the one who wants to have sex all the time and she's the one avoiding it.

Turnabout is a bitch.

thirty-seven

Opening night of *Godspell* Mr. Lucas lets me lead the entire cast in a guided meditation as a warm-up. I know it's a little too funky woo-woo for a public high school, and some of the kids snicker and giggle, but I think it's important that we get in the right frame of mind for the show. I talk them through a visualization my mother taught me, nothing radical, mind you, just imagining your body filling with white light and exhaling out all negativity. It calms me, too, but also makes me kind of sad, which is usually what happens when I slow down enough to realize how I'm feeling. Everywhere I turn, parents of kids who do practically nothing in the show are bounding about, bringing them flowers and making a big woofy deal over them. It would never occur to Al to do anything beyond show up, which is more than I can say for my mom, who I can only assume is lying dead somewhere in a mass grave. That happens in South America; you know, people just disappear. I know. I saw *Missing*.

I go into the bathroom in Mr. Lucas's office to check my makeup one last time and to get away from all the hoopla. What I see in the mirror surprises me. Originally, Mr. Lucas and I had thought I would keep the beard for a more biblical look, but since his concept for the production is so modern, he asked me to shave it off. I'm pleased to see that all that running seems to have made a difference. My eyes look big in my face and my cheekbones and jaw are sharp and lean. I've also grown an inch, for which Kathleen takes complete credit. "I raised another son," she says.

There's a knock on the door and, as if on cue, there is Kathleen with a bouquet in her hand.

"Am I interrupting the artist at work?"

She's brought stargazer lilies. My favorite. A wave of emotion crashes inside me and I throw my arms around her, almost knocking her over.

"You okay, sweetie?"

I lean my head on her shoulder. "You've done so much for me," I croak. "I don't know how I can ever repay you."

Kathleen pulls away so she can look me in the eye. "You can't," she says. "And you shouldn't." She reaches up to play with a stray curl on my forehead. "Just remember that when you get to be my age and someone younger than you needs help, pass it on. Okay?"

I nod. "I got makeup on your shoulder," I say.

She glances down at the blot on her shirt. "I'll treasure it forever. Someday that smudge will be worth a lot of money."

Kathleen.

The auditorium is packed. Even from behind the curtain you can hear the buzz of excitement. Since Doug's in the show lots of the popular kids who wouldn't normally come to the plays have shown up. I get a couple of wolf whistles when I strip off my shirt for the baptism scene, which, considering I'm playing Jesus, isn't really appropriate, but I appreciate the compliment. Natie gets all the biggest laughs, particularly when he recites the beatitudes in a Donald Duck voice. And Doug does surprisingly well in the dual roles of John the Baptist and Judas. We have a big duet together that Kelly's choreographed with a lot of complicated hat-and-cane stuff. The number goes over real big.

Yes, it's all for the best . . .

During intermission, Mr. Lucas gathers the cast together, tells us how well he thinks it's going, and reminds us to concentrate. "They're a great audience," he says, "but they're a tad rowdy, and will be even more so after the marching band sells them all that candy. So you must remember that when Judas betrays Jesus with a kiss, it is essential that you set the tone for the audience. Remember, that kiss is the confirmation that your savior is being condemned to death. If you take it seriously, so will they." He glances at me and Doug. "We hope," he mutters. It's just a quick peck, but this is high school, after all.

Mr. Lucas's concept for the second act is supercool. Instead of our funky 1980s clothes, we come back dressed in yuppie power suits; the idea being that we're grown now and Jesus is almost like a political candidate. The Pharisees come on wearing hollowed-out televisions on their heads and talk in Southern accents like they're televangelists. Mr. Lucas wants people to understand that even if Jesus were to come back today, he'd still be rejected and crucified.

I wouldn't be surprised if he lost his job over this one.

The second act goes really well, but the closer we get to the betrayal scene, the more nervous I become. I can sense the tension onstage, but then I wonder if maybe it's just me. That's the funny thing about tension. When you're tense how can you tell if anyone else feels that way, too? Maybe they just seem tense because you're tense. Anyway, the door at the back of the auditorium clangs open and everyone in the audience turns to watch Doug as Judas walk down the aisle to the edge of the stage.

I look deep in his eyes, the world as seen from outer space. "Friend, do quickly what you have to do," I say.

A spotlight follows him as he climbs the stairs to the stage. He crosses to me, stops, and turns to the audience as if to signal the Roman police. I turn, too, and stand ready for him to kiss me on the cheek.

Then, in one totally shocking, totally unexpected, totally *welcome* move, Doug grabs my face in his hands and kisses me right smack on the lips. Everyone gasps: the chorus, the audience, and, undoubtedly, Doug's father, the embittered Tastykake driver. No one laughs or says a thing, it's just so startlingly radical. I mean, here in Colonial Wallingford.

Time seems to stand still as I savor the feel of Doug's thin, soft lips on mine. I don't know if this was Mr. Lucas's idea or some strange whim of Doug's and, you know what, I don't care. I've dreamed of a kiss like this countless times before I drifted off to sleep, but never, ever, ever did I dare believe it could actually happen, and certainly not in front of the entire school. It's not like he uses his tongue or anything, but his mouth is open and, for just a second, I inhale as he exhales, as if he were breathing the very life into me. I'm telling you, if Judas's kiss was anything like this one, then Jesus died happy.

Our lips part. The show must go on, and pretty fucking quickly if we want to avoid totally freaking out everyone. As directed, I step up to a podium and speak to the audience as if I were addressing a rally. But just as I begin, a tall figure in the fifth row stands up and says, "Excuse me, Jesus . . ."

I lean forward to search the blackness for the voice. The figure raises a pistol and fires a shot that echoes all over the auditorium.

The place goes nuts. People scream. I smash the blood pack under my shirt and collapse on the floor as the figure (Boonbrain) dashes out the nearest exit. A couple of audience members actually run after him like it's real. The stage goes to red and the electric guitars start to wail.

It's fucking brilliant.

There's no time for the audience to recover. Onstage it's chaos: fifty teenagers keen and scream, choristers dressed as cops, paramedics, and reporters dash on trying to restore order, but only complicating things. And in the middle of it all is me, lying in a pool of blood. This, this, this is what being an actor is about. To be able to elicit such a strong reaction from hundreds of people at once — that power is awesome and irresistible and humbling. If you want to think I'm needy because I love applause, go ahead. But I know that the reason I perform is for moments like these, moments when you connect with an audience and take them somewhere, whether it's scary or funny or sad, it doesn't matter. That's what makes it worthwhile.

The cast surrounds me as I gasp my final lines.

"Oh God, I'm dying . . ."

All around me disciples cry real tears, even Natie who, much to my surprise, heaves huge soul-rattling sobs. But I can't help but feel so very, very happy as I indulge in the sheer sensual pleasure of pretending.

To die, to sleep; To sleep: perchance to dream.

Natie gently closes my eyelids for me. Some of the disciples can hardly sing, they're so choked up, but me, I feel nothing. No, nothing's not the right word. It's more like nothing*ness*, and a sense of calm washes over me like warm water. As the disciples carry me to the back of the auditorium, I have no worries. There is no Al, no Dagmar, no Juilliard. I don't even have to carry my own weight. The disciples sing the final notes of "Prepare Ye" from the lobby, then gently lay me down on the cool linoleum floor. I don't want to move. Ever. Slowly I open my eyes like I'm awakening from a dream and listen for the applause.

Silence.

We're not prepared for this. Shows end, people applaud, that's how it works. "What do we do?" someone whispers.

"Wait," I say.

Then, all at once, it starts. I'm not talking that phony-baloney thing you see in the movies where a few people start slowly and eventually everyone joins in. No, this applause starts like a clap of thunder. I've never heard anything like it. It's as if the sky opened up. The music begins and we run down the aisle to the stage and the audience goes wild, leaping to their feet in a real, honest-to-God standing ovation. Not the kind where a couple of idiots get up in front because they're the type of assholes who always give standing ovations, and then the people behind them have to get up because they can't see or because they want to stretch their legs or duck out early to beat the traffic. No, this time the audience rises as a body, as if they were carried on a gigantic wave. It's pandemonium. We sing the final reprise of "Day by Day" and I feel so exhilarated I could leap out of my skin.

On my cue, we take a company bow, once, twice, three times. The applause is still going strong and I allow us to stand there, basking in the goodwill of people rewarding us for a job well done. I gesture to the band, which takes a bow, then walk into the wings where Kelly and Mr. Lucas are standing. Mr. Lucas gestures to Ziba at the stage-manager's desk to join them, and I lead the three onto the stage. The applause rises to acknowledge them. Mr. Lucas is always subdued and humble about this part, but his eyes shine with pride. I think he'd rather not come out onstage at all, but he knows we'll insist on it. We take one final bow together, then back up to make room for the curtain. We turn to one another the way a cast does after the curtain closes. We're mature enough not to cheer (it's so unprofessional), but Mr. Lucas stops us in our tracks by shouting, "Nobody move." We stand listening to the sound of applause coming down like so much rain and he gestures with his crutch to the wings. "Curtain!" he says.

The curtain opens again and the audience is still there, clapping rhythmically now while we take a final bow. I don't care what I have to do—I'll clean toilets or dig ditches—but there is no way I'm going to give up a lifetime of this. No way.

✳   ✳   ✳

The curtain closes and I turn to Natie, whose face is as red and puffy as his hair. I clasp my arms around him and he leans his little cheesehead against my chest.

"It was just so real," he whispers.

I pat him on the back. "Yeah, I know," I say.

Then everyone converges on me at once like they want a piece of me: people I know, people I don't know, Mr. Lucas, Kathleen, Kelly, Ziba, Fran and Stan Nudelman, Aunt Glo. Everywhere I turn there are hugs and congratulations but these aren't the usual *way to goes* and *you were greats*. No, something different happened tonight, something that affected everyone in a profound and meaningful way, something bigger than me and the show and all of us.

The jocks and cheerleaders—people like Duncan O'Boyle and Amber Wright—gather around Doug and I get just a glimpse of him across the crowded stage. He winks at me and I feel my face smile.

Mrs. Foster, the wife of my old lawn-obsessed neighbor, appears out of nowhere, grabs me by my elbows, and says, "Edward, I just wanted to tell you that when I was your age I wanted to major in drama, too, and my parents wouldn't let me." Her eyes fill with tears. "I've regretted it ever since," she says.

We've never spoken before.

She steps away, suddenly providing me an unobstructed view across the stage. And then I see him, jingling the change in his pockets and glancing around like a caged animal.

Al.

He nods his head at me several times, smiling a tense, tight-lipped smile as he leaves Dagmar behind him and crosses the stage. I meet him halfway.

Silence.

"Good job, kid," he says finally, and gives me a little pat on the shoulder.

"Thanks, Pop."

More silence.

"Looks like you lost some weight."

"Yeah," I say.

"They feedin' you enough?"

"Yeah."

"Okay," he says, as if that settled something. He glances over his shoulder at Dagmar. "Guess I better be going," he says.

I nod.

"You take care of yourself."

"I am," I say, but it comes out sounding angrier than I intended, and I immediately regret it.

Al rubs his hands together and slowly turns away. "Good . . . good," he says.

Suddenly, from behind, a pair of huge arms wraps around my waist and lifts me in the air, and I know instantly it must be my new best friend, TeeJay. "You were amazing, man!" he crows. "I'm coming back tomorrow." He puts me down and gives me that handshake where you knock fists. I glance over to catch sight of Al and Dagmar but they're gone already.

"You remember my cousins, right?" TeeJay says. I turn and say hello to Bonté, Shezadra, and the one whose name sounds like Pneumonia. Standing behind them is the little dumpy one, Margaret, who chews on the drawstring of her hooded sweatshirt. They all smile and say hello, but a little reverentially, like my having played Jesus automatically entitles me to respect.

"Na-*tay*!" TeeJay shouts, and gives him five. "Man, you're *funny*. When you did that Donald Duck voice I thought Margaret here was gonna pee her pants."

"Shut up," Margaret says, giving him a limp slap on the arm. She smiles shyly at Natie.

"Come on," TeeJay says, "do it again."

Natie blushes. "You don't really want to hear it, do you?"

The girls insist. Natie starts reciting the beatitudes in the Donald Duck voice and the girls hold on to each other as they laugh. A small crowd gathers for the encore and I feel TeeJay's large hand on my shoulder.

"Can we talk a minute?" he says. We walk into the wings and huddle at the stage manager's desk.

"I hate to tell you this on your big night," he says, "but I figured I better let you know right away."

I feel my heart leap into my throat.

"Some crazy foreign lady came to talk with my mom today."

thirty-eight

Dagmar knows just about everything she needs to know. She knows that the very same day someone pretending to be LaChance Jones withdrew $10,000 in cash from her account, the Catholic Vigilance Society donated $10,000 to Juilliard for a scholarship for which I was eligible but did not receive. As worried as I am for myself, I'm even more concerned for Ziba, whose photocopied picture is now in Dagmar's gnarled hands. What's more, now that she's traced LaChance back to TeeJay's mother, Dagmar is just one step away from the awesome (and possibly Mafia-related) power that is Frank Sinatra. Forget jail time. I'm going to sleep with the fishes.

So you'll understand why I don't feel much like going to the prom. It's hard to muster enthusiasm for adolescent rites of passage when you're facing the prospect of a painful, lingering death. Kelly suggests we throw our own anti-prom party instead.

I'm not really up for anything, to be honest. I always feel a certain letdown after a show, but this is the worst one ever, even though I win the Brownie Award for Most Messianic. I just hadn't realized how empty my life would feel without *Godspell*; it's like I've left Technicolor Oz and gone back to black-and-white Kansas. (Frankly, I've never understood why Dorothy didn't stay in Oz, anyway. Why leave a land of talking trees and dancing scarecrows to go back to doing farm chores in the dust bowl?) What's more, the grim reality of having to find another job sets in. All around me, people are preparing to go away to school. I'll join a conversation and a hush will come over the group, and I'll know immediately they were talking about college and don't want to make me feel bad. I feel like I'm some kind of untouchable, like I've been lumped in with all the burnouts and wastoids in the smoking section who aren't going anywhere with their lives either. I imagine my friends coming home for the holidays, full of excitement and new ideas and erudite collegiate banter that I can't relate to or possibly understand, until eventually they begin to avoid me altogether, the One Who Stayed Behind, the loser who tries to relive his high-school glories but eventually ends up a sad, bloated alcoholic hanging around New Jersey bars and picking fights.

Reluctantly I agree to go with the gang to Something for the Boys.

On the way we stop at Dionysus where Ziba dashes any hope I had of getting back in Kelly's pants by buying a strap-on dildo. My only consolation is that they choose one that's about the same size as me instead of Doug.

We stop at the door of Something for the Boys and Ziba pulls a long, silk scarf out of her beaded clutch purse.

"What's going on?" I say.

"It's a surprise," she says, tying the scarf around my eyes. Natie and Doug each take an elbow and lead me into the club, where a group of men are singing a stirring rendition of "Climb Ev'ry Mountain." I feel stupid and self-conscious, like everyone must be looking at me. We stop.

"Stay right there," Doug says, and I feel someone untie the blindfold. I blink for a second to adjust to the hazy purple light and then see Paula in front of me, giggling with delight. She's holding a birthday cake that says "Happy Birthday, Salvador."

"Salvador?" I say.

"Dali. He's eighty today. Quick, make a wish before the candles go out."

I stop for a moment to take a mental photograph of my best friends, the fuzzy glow from the candles shining on their smiling faces: Ziba, with her spiky hair and dark eyes, beaming her Mona Lisa smile; Kelly, tilting her head in that way that pretty girls do; Paula, her mouth spread wide in full curtain-up-light-the-lights mode; Doug, deep-dimpling his satyr's grin; and Natie, the light surrounding his little cheesehead like a halo.

They all look so beautiful to me, like angels in an Italian fresco. I close my eyes to make a wish. You'd think that I'd wish for Juilliard to come through somehow, but you'd be wrong. I don't even want to think about Juilliard at this point. No, what I wish for is to feel normal again, to feel as carefree and happy as I did last summer, to feel the magic and the mischief and the laughter. I want all the uncertainty and weirdness of these past months to be over, no matter how it turns out. It's not like I want to be stupid and naïve again; I just want to be happy. And safe.

Most important, I want my friends to be happy and safe, too.

I blow out the candles and everybody claps, including the guys at the piano. The pianist with the Humpty-Dumpty face strikes up "Happy Birthday" and everybody in the place sings along. I can't very well tell them to stop, so I just stand there, embarrassed and grinning stupidly while the wave of sound washes over me. I feel something wet on my neck and when I reach up to brush it away I realize that I'm crying, not a pushed-out, constipated kind of crying, but an easy, steady flow, like a light rain.

It's transcendental.

Paula's done up extra special for the occasion. She's wearing combat boots (one brown, one black, of course), a large skirt made out of tulle, and a bustier which pushes up her enormous boobs like a shelf. There's no mistaking her for a drag queen this time.

"You look like that chick from MTV," Doug says, "you know, the one who wears her underwear outside of her clothes."

Paula looks disappointed. "Madonna's a flash in the pan," she says. "She'll never last."

We order Manhattans. None of us knows what they are, but they sound sophisticated. From across the room Humpty-Dumpty calls out to me. "Hey, 'Corner of the Sky,' you wanna sing?"

I don't feel much like singing, but my friends urge me on, clapping and cheering as I amble over to the piano.

"The usual?" he asks.

I shake my head no. "Do you know the finale from *Yentl*?" I ask.

He gives me a look like, "This is a gay piano bar; of course I know the finale from *Yentl*," and starts to play.

The song feels good in my throat and by the time I sing the final lines it's as if my whole body were singing.

> *What's wrong with wanting more?*
> *If you can fly, then soar.*
> *With all there is, why settle for*
> *Just a piece of sky?*

Why, indeed? I know I should be grateful if I can just stay alive and out of jail, but there's a part of me that simply can't stop dreaming, that can't abandon the idea of people lining up around the block to see me, that knows I'm supposed to do something important and meaningful with my life. The sky's the limit.

The crowd in the bar gives me a big hand. My tribe. My not-so-secret brotherhood.

Back at the table Paula requests a toast. "To Edward," she says.

"To Edward," everyone echoes.

"No," I say, "to all of you. To the best friends a guy could ever want."

"To best friends," Natie says.

"To best friends." We all clink glasses and once again tears surge out of me. I don't know what's wrong with me. Now that I've learned how to cry there doesn't seem to be any stopping me. I collapse in my chair. Doug puts his arm around me.

"This isn't right," Kelly says. "We've got to do something."

"It's because of that stupid Austrian bitch," I say, crumpling up a cocktail napkin. "Everything was fine until she came along."

Natie agrees. "Al always paid for everything before that." He takes a sip of his Manhattan and makes a face. "What the hell is this, lighter fluid?"

"Natie's right," Paula says.

"I'll have yours if you don't want it," Ziba says.

"No, I meant about Al," Paula says. "Sure, he made a lot of noise about business in the past, but that never stopped him from paying for acting classes and voice lessons and dance classes. Edward's right. Everything changed when Dagmar showed up. In fact . . . oh my God . . . I can't believe I never thought of this before."

I grab another cocktail napkin and blow my nose. "What?" I say.

"Don't you see? You've been going about this whole thing backwards. Instead of having gone to all this trouble to get the money for Juilliard, you should have just tried to get rid of Dagmar."

We all sit in silence pondering this thought while the group around the piano sings "Papa, Can You Hear Me?"

She's right. I can't believe I never thought of it before, either.

"So what's stopping us?" Kelly says finally. "Let's get rid of her now. She's, like, only going to make more trouble."

"No," I say, "I've given up my life of crime."

"It's not like we're going to kill her," Natie says. He looks around the table. "Are we?"

"Don't be ridiculous," says Ziba. "We'll just find a way to make sure she never bothers us again."

I shake my head. "But . . ."

"But nothing," Ziba says. She raises her glass. "I say reopen CV Enterprises and finish what we started."

Natie, Kelly, and Doug lift their glasses, too. All eyes turn to Paula.

"I'm not so sure about this," she says.

Ziba leans across the table. "You don't want to see Edward end up in prison, do you? Or me, or Nathan, for that matter?"

"No, of course not."

Ziba arches an eyebrow at her. "Well . . . ?"

Paula takes a deep breath, her boobs rising toward her chin, then exhales. "All right," she says, "I'm in."

Ziba turns to me. "Edward . . . ?"

I sigh and feel tears well up in me again. I nod my head.

"*Wunderbar*," Doug says.

✳   ✳   ✳

We spend the rest of the night formulating a plan and, for the first time in months, I feel the same heady thrill I experienced last summer when our only mission was to make the world safe from boredom.

The key to our plan is getting our hands on a narcotic that will knock out Dagmar for a few hours. Luckily, it just so happens I have a sister who works at a pharmacy. Or at least I thought I did. I call Karen the next day and she tells me in her rambling, incoherent way that she lost her job for doing exactly what I was about to ask her to do.

"I can hook you up, though," she mumbles. "I mean, as long as you can drive." I borrow the Wagon Ho and pick her up at her apartment, which she shares with some other burnouts above a Dollar Store in Cramptown.

Karen and I are not close. It's not like we hate each other; it's just that I'm repelled by everything she represents. But we're family and, when needed, we come through for each other, mostly by providing alibis or, in this case, black-market pharmaceuticals.

"Hey, bro," she says as she slides in the car. "Mind if I crank some tunes?" She flips on the radio without waiting for an answer and chooses a heavy metal station. Normally I'd protest, but I'm willing to do whatever it takes to keep her conscious.

"This guy I know gets the best shit," she says, drumming on the dashboard. I want to feel superior, but I've got to admit I'm grateful for her help.

We drive to Battle Brook, past the neighborhood where Kathleen's cryent lives and into a section that makes Hell's Kitchen look like Mayberry. I suppose I shouldn't be surprised (we are on a quest for illegal drugs, after all), but I've got to confess I've never given much thought about exactly where drugs come from.

We pull up in front of a dilapidated shipwreck of a house with moss on the roof and sheets of plastic lining the windows. An emaciated woman in a nightgown stands on the front porch hugging herself and rocking back and forth. I'm guessing she's not the Avon lady.

"Keep the engine running," Karen says.

I can well understand the wisdom in this decision, but I can't say I'm happy to be in a situation where that particular kind of wisdom is necessary. She doesn't get out of the car.

Over Karen's shoulder I see a skinny man amble down the front steps, but I can't get a look at his face from where I'm sitting. Karen rolls down her window. Guess we're getting drive-up service. Before you know it, drug dealers will be installing those pneumatic tubes, like at the bank.

I feel sweat gathering in the small of my back and I adjust so I don't stick to the seat. I think I'm perfectly justified in being a little nervous. When you consider how the cops treated us for stealing the Buddha, I don't even want to think about the consequences of buying drugs in this town.

The guy approaches the car and leans over to talk to Karen. He sticks his head in the window and my heart stops.

It's Alas Poor Yorick.

He's even more frightening in the light of day, the pale gray skin pulled taut over his skull, his hollowed-out eyes glazed and yellow. He smiles, revealing rotted teeth, and coughs what I suppose is his croupy version of a laugh. "Hey," he says to me, pointing a bony finger, "how ya' doin'?"

You know just how far you've sunk when you get recognized by your buddies from jail.

"Fine, thank you," I say, sounding way more like Julie Andrews than I intended. I turn away, hoping it will make me invisible. Karen gets on with the business at hand while I grip the wheel, eyes straight ahead, wondering whether Alas Poor Yorick is going to say anything else to me. But he just finishes the transaction quickly and Karen doesn't have to tell me twice to pull out. As I drive away I look in the rearview mirror and see Alas Poor Yorick waving his broomstick arms at the woman twitching on the front porch. I have to say I've never stopped to think how druggies like my sister actually got those drugs, so it's never occurred to me that I had any connection whatsoever with skeevy lowlifes like Alas Poor Yorick (I mean, beyond being cell mates for a couple of hours) or the poor junkie vibrating on the front porch like some highly caffeinated moth. Just the thought that I have anything to do with these people makes me shudder. I mean, I hate to sound like a snob, but *ick*.

Karen's bought a bag of pot in addition to the sleeping pills for Dagmar. She opens the baggie and takes a good, long whiff. "This is some good shit," she says. "You wanna smoke some when we get back?"

"Maybe another time," I say.

✳   ✳   ✳

A couple of days later I dash into English late as usual from my long lunch with Ziba.

Mr. Lucas peers at me over his glasses. "So nice of you to join us, Mr. Zanni." The fact that I have worked so closely with this man on some very emotional pieces of theater, run into him at a gay bar, and slept on his couch seems to make no difference to him. When it comes to the classroom, he's as formal as a butler.

"So, as I was saying before the prodigal son returned, now that the AP exam is over there will be no more reading assignments."

The class breaks out in spontaneous applause.

"There will, however, be writing assignments."

The class groans.

He holds up a copy of A *Portrait of the Artist as a Young Man.* "You've all read the book," he says, waving a crutch for emphasis and narrowly missing the head of Calvin Singh, a National Merit scholar in the front row. "Or, judging from your quizzes, perhaps I should say *some* of you have read the book."

I would be one of those people who hadn't. From the very first page when the moo cow came down the road and met the "nicens little boy named baby tuckoo" I thought to myself, "What is this crap?"

"Your assignment," Mr. Lucas continues, "is to write your own *Portrait of the Artist*—a portrait of yourself as a young person, minimum twenty-five pages . . ."

There's a gasp in the room.

". . . single-spaced."

This elicits a lot of conversation, even from the Ivy League early decision types. Assigning a twenty-five-page paper the month before graduation is like making the winner of the Boston Marathon walk home. I mean, enough already.

"Settle down, ladies and gentlemen, settle down," he says. "If you spent as much time writing as you do complaining, you'd be done in a week. It's not like you have to do any research. You already know who you are . . . pre*zoom*ably."

He says it the same way he says "*uh*bviously" and the class laughs. "This assignment is more for you than it is for me. Very soon you'll go your separate ways and your lives will be never the same again, so I want you to stop for a moment and reflect on who you are today. Right now. I don't want an autobiography with all the details of your lives. I want you to do as James Joyce does and describe for me what it's like to be inside your minds. And I want to know what made you that way."

Natie taps me on my shoulder. In the margin of his notebook he's written, "Saturday's the night."

"For instance," Mr. Lucas continues, "who can tell me why they think Joyce named his alter ego Stephen Dedalus?"

Underneath Natie's message I scrawl, "Are you sure?"

Natie nods. "He's going on a business trip."

"How do you know?"

"What do I look like, an amateur?" Natie says out loud.

"Mr. Zanni," Mr. Lucas says. "Perhaps you'd like to tell us. Why did Joyce name his hero Dedalus?"

"Daedalus is the Greek hero who escaped from prison by building himself wings," I say.

Hey, at least I read the Cliff Notes carefully.

"And what is Stephen Dedalus flying to?"

That's an easy one. What does any artist fly to? "To art," I say. Even without finishing the book I know that I am so like Stephen Dedalus, constrained as I am by bourgeois oppression. "And sex," I say.

The class laughs.

"Eggzellent," Mr. Lucas says. "Mr. Zanni makes a good, if slightly crude, point. Like Joyce, I want you uncensored. Don't be afraid to include whatever tawdry and sordid details of your adolescent lives you wish. No one's going to read this but me."

Some of us are going to need a lot more than twenty-five pages.

✳   ✳   ✳

That Saturday, a nun and a priest stand in the Nudelmans' darkened living room, their faces pressed against the picture window.

"Can you see anything?" Father Groovy asks.

Sister Natie shakes his head. "HEY MA," he shouts, "DO YOU KNOW WHERE THE BINOCULARS ARE?"

Fran screeches back, "IN YOUR FATHER'S STUDY."

Natie turns to me and shrugs. "He likes to watch the birds," he says. From the other end of the house I hear Stan shout, "WADDYA WANT 'EM FOR?"

"WE NEED THEM TO SPY ON THE ZANNIS' HOUSE SO WE KNOW WHEN IT'S SAFE TO GO OVER AND TAKE INCRIMINATING PHOTOGRAPHS."

Stan laughs. "YOU KIDS," he says.

Natie's just gone to hunt for the binoculars when I see another nun and priest leave Al's house carrying a large cardboard box, which they place in the back of the Wagon Ho. They cross the street, heading toward us. "They're coming!" I shout to Natie.

I open the door for them.

"Good evening," the nun says, "we're here on behalf of the Convent of the Bleeding Heart. Do you have any items you'd like to donate to our annual rummage sale?"

"Get thee to a nunnery," I say.

Sister Paula pulls off her wimple and shakes out her hair.

"She must have fallen for it," I say. "You filled a whole box."

"Yeah, but it's all your old stuff."

Stupid Austrian bitch.

Doug hands me Father Groovy's spectacles, then pulls off the mustache and goatee I glued on him. "I drank so much friggin' cocoa I thought for sure this damn thing was going to fall right off into my cup," he says. "Say what you want about your stepmonster, but she makes a kick-ass *Kakao mit Schlag.*"

Or in Doug's case, perhaps that should be *Kakao mit Schlong*.

Dagmar's pride in her cocoa with cream was the key element for our little plan to work. "It was so easy, man," Doug tells us as we sit on the back patio drinking lemonade and waiting for Kelly and Ziba to return. "The minute I said *Guten Abend* she was sweeter than a Sacher torte."

"What were you two going on about anyway?" Paula asks.

"Mostly how you can't get a decent cup of cocoa in the States, which is true. Actually, it was kind of nice to talk with her. It's too bad she's such a psycho."

"Well, you made a very convincing priest," Paula says. "It was an *inspired* performance."

Though certainly not divinely inspired.

Doug beams, "Ya' really think so?"

Paula reaches over with a tiny hand and twiddles his kinky hair, which has been slicked back into submission. "You might just be an actor, after all," she says.

Doug doesn't say anything, but I can tell he's pleased. A true Play Person at last.

Paula goes on to explain how, when she went to use the bathroom, she opened the shades on the window facing the street so we'd be certain to get the signal, and I tell them how excited Dagmar sounded on the phone when I pretended to be a dealer interested in her entire photo series of blow-dryers in bathtubs.

"It was perfect," Paula says. "You kept her on just long enough for us to get the sedative in her cocoa, but not so long that it cooled off. Excellent job." We all clink glasses of lemonade.

We have to wait for what feels like a very long time until Kelly and Ziba return from their own reconnaissance mission, or maybe it's just that I'm restless.

I sit listening to the buzz of cicadas in the air, wondering if something's gone wrong, when finally I see the silhouette of two nuns sneaking through the bushes at the back of the Nudelmans' property. I cross the lawn to meet them.

"What took you so long?" I say.

"We would have been here a lot sooner, darling, if you hadn't made us come around the back way," Ziba says. "Plus, she took this really long shower, which got us very worried. We were beginning to think she must have passed out and hit her head or something."

"Where is she now?"

Kelly laughs, a machine gun. "In the living room," she says. "She came back to turn off the lights but just sort of curled up on the floor right there and went to sleep."

"It was terribly undignified," Ziba says.

* * *

I make the six of us go around the back way again. After my brush with the law I'm determined that none of us get caught, and we might have a hard time explaining to the neighbors why a gang of nuns and priests keep going in and out of a house owned by Jews. Lucky for us we're all wearing black. We sneak around the side of the house as inconspicuously as half a dozen nuns and priests can and let ourselves in the back door. The house is quiet, naturally, but the lights are still on, which feels vaguely sinister to me, like in those old detective movies when they arrive at the scene of the crime and the needle on the phonograph is stuck on the end of the record while the victim lies splayed across the floor. We tiptoe to the entrance of the Museum of Furniture and peer in at our victim, who is also splayed across the floor, but more in the drug-induced comatose manner of Patty Duke in *Valley of the Dolls*.

"We should make sure she won't wake up," Paula says.

"Good idea," I say, and then call out Dagmar's name softly.

She doesn't stir.

"Hey, Dagmar," I say louder.

Still nothing.

I move closer. "Hey, Dagmar," I bark, "you're a gold-digging bitch who ruined my life."

She rolls over and starts to snore. I glance up at my friends. "It's showtime," I say.

* * *

The last official act of CV Enterprises is to take incriminating photos of my evil stepmonster in compromising sexual positions. As with Jordan, we realize that naked pictures of Dagmar won't be enough (there are probably a few of those floating around from her modeling days), so nothing short of an orgy will do.

Since Paula has actual onscreen experience going topless she's been cast as Dagmar's lesbian lover, Sister LaChance, who has risen from the grave for one final appearance. Doug and I are to be Juan and Jesús, two convent groundsmen we've invented (A) to give an excuse for there being someone else in the room to take pictures and (B) to make sure Al gets upset. We figure that seeing photos of his hot wife and a woman with big knockers might only succeed in livening up his sex life; but photos of her with a well-hung illegal alien are certain to piss him off.

Along with the photos, we'll send Al the following letter on Catholic Vigilance Society stationery:

> *May 19, 1984*
>
> *Dear Mr. Zanni,*
>
> *It is my sad duty to inform you of the horrible misdeeds of your wife with Sister LaChance Jones. Enclosed please find a letter we found in Sister LaChance's cell along with these shocking photographs.*
>
> *Regretfully,*
> *I am,*
> *Father G. Roovy*

Then, enclosed on perfumed stationery and forged in Dagmar's handwriting, will be this note:

> *Liebe LaChance,*
>
> *Thank you for bringing Juan and Jesús along for our night together. After all these months with Al I've forgotten what it's like to be truly satisfied.*
>
> *Here is the first installment toward buying our freedom. Soon, soon, we will both be free. I just need more time to transfer funds and we can finally be together.*
>
> *Patience, Liebchen,*
> *Dagmar*

Cecil B. DeNudelman takes over. "Okay, places everybody," he says.

"What places?" Doug says. "We don't have places."

"Right," Natie says. "Okay, first thing, we need to . . . uh . . . take off Dagmar's robe."

We all stare at each other. Okay, this is weird.

"Oh, for God's sakes, I'll do it," Ziba says. She kneels down and unties the terry-cloth belt and spreads open the robe. "Oh my," she says.

Dagmar's completely naked underneath.

"I hope my body looks that good when I'm her age," Kelly says.

I feel my mouth go dry. There was a time just a couple of months back when I would have been grateful for an erection, but the fact that my naked stepmother is getting me hard really disturbs me, particularly since I'm dressed as a priest. I turn to Natie to move things along, but he's just standing there with his mouth open.

"Okay," I say, clapping my hands together, "uh . . . Sis, if you wouldn't mind getting undressed, we'll start with you."

"Certainly," Paula says, the professional actress at work. She turns her back to us and undoes the snaps on her gown and lets it drop to the floor, revealing a silky lavender bra and panties. Paula reaches behind her and undoes the thick bra strap. Just as she hooks her thumbs under the elastic of her panties to pull them down she says, "Now I'm trusting everyone will be mature about this."

"Absolutely," I say. "Right, everybody?"

"Right," they say, except for Natie, who's suddenly auditioning for the role of Helen Keller.

Paula slides off her panties and turns around.

"Holy shit!" yells Doug. Her breasts are the size of milk jugs. Kelly gives Doug a smack.

"Doug, you *promised*," Paula says, covering herself up.

"I'm sorry, but, man, those are so . . ."

"Edward, make him stop."

". . . *beautiful.*"

Flecks of red dart across Paula's white-white skin.

"I mean it," Doug says. "You look like a woman in a painting or somethin'."

Paula runs her tiny fingers through her hair in the manner of Sophia Loren. "All right," she says, "let's get on with it."

She lies down on the floor next to Dagmar and I grab a chair to stand on so I can get the right angle for the pictures. Doug's right: Paula's breasts are magnificent. Her nipples are spread dark and large across the snowy landscape of her bosom, so pale you can see blue veins beneath the surface, like water trapped under ice. If these pictures weren't meant to be incriminating, they'd be considered quite artistic.

"This feels strange," Paula says, snuggling next to Dagmar.

"You'll get used to it," Kelly says and we all laugh. The atmosphere feels more relaxed now, as if taking blackmail photos were a party game. Natie joins the land of the living again.

"Make sure you don't get her face in the picture," he says.

"Got it," I say, clicking away. "Okay, Paula, just rest there a minute. Doug, it's your turn."

"Sure," he says, sounding as if he couldn't wait to be asked. As he starts to undress, Ziba and Kelly launch into the stripper theme and Doug responds by doing some Revolting Renée dance moves, the sight of which is rather unsettling when you consider he's dressed as a priest. He finishes by whipping off his boxers and revealing his best feature.

Now it's Paula's turn to stare.

I know I don't stand a chance with Doug, but that doesn't stop me from enjoying seeing him naked. "If you could just get on the other side of Dagmar," I say, "that'd be great. Paula, if you could . . . Paula? Paula?"

"Oh, I'm sorry," she says. "Did you say something?"

"If you could just move in closer again, thanks." I look through the lens. Doug's starting to get hard.

"Doug, I'm losing you," I say. "You're moving out of camera range."

"Sorry, man, I can't help it."

The guys at Toto Photo are going to love these.

"Okay, just scooch down a little closer toward Paula. Got it. One more. Perfect. All right, everyone relax. Paula, you're done. Thank you."

I'm tempted to say, "Don't call us, we'll call you," but there's such a thing as being too jocular.

Now it's my turn. "Natie, are you ready?"

"For what?" he says.

"To take these last pictures."

"Sure, sure," he says, wiping the sweat off his forehead.

I hand him the camera and begin to strip. "*Vámonos, Jesús,*" Doug says, much more alluringly than I can stand.

Natie tells Doug to kneel behind Dagmar's head and for me to kneel in front of her, straddling her thighs. "Now lean in," he says, "so it looks like you're screwing her." I lean in, trying not to graze her bush so I don't have to be in therapy the rest of my life. I look down at Dagmar's sleeping face and imagine her waking up at this very second and screaming bloody murder so I tilt my head up instead, only to be confronted with Doug's enormous member bobbing in front of my face.

"Arch your back just a little bit more," Natie says.

"Enough already, Scavullo," I say. "Take the fucking picture."

"I'm only trying to . . ."

He's interrupted by the sound of the doorbell ringing. Four nuns and two naked men freeze.

"What do we do?" Paula whispers.

"Nobody move," I hiss. "Maybe they'll go away."

"Who is it?"

"How the fuck should I know?"

The doorbell rings again.

I motion to Natie, who's dived behind the couch, to peek out the window and see who it is. He's about halfway up when there's a loud knock at the door, which makes him flinch so badly he knocks over a table lamp.

From outside a woman's voice says, "Hello? Is anybody there?" The door handle clicks.

If there's a God in Heaven, please let that door be locked. I'll go to church, I'll tithe, I'll never do anything bad ever again.

The door creaks open.

Where the fuck are my pants? I drop and roll onto the floor, grabbing my clothes and scrambling naked after a group of frantic nuns when I hear the woman's voice call out, "Edward, are you here?"

I stop. I know that voice. I know it as well as I know my own. And just as I reach up to cover myself, I turn around and see the body attached to that voice glide around the corner into the room, a tanned, ethereal vision in a gauze dress.

"Mom?" I say.

thirty-nine

My mother's being very Auntie Mame about the whole thing as we crowd into a booth at the Cramptown Diner, very I've-seen-it-all and you-can't-shock-me. As a result, everyone falls all over themselves trying to outdo each other with tales of our misadventures and misdeeds. No matter how unseemly or outright illegal the details are, Barbara reacts like the whole thing is just some big adolescent lark.

"Your mom is so cool," Doug whispers to me.

Everyone always says that.

Barbara is so cool, which is to say she is not like other mothers. Other mothers don't follow their yogis to India, or do past-life regressions at Stonehenge, or go to Baja a month at a time for silent retreats. ("Why can't she stay in New Jersey and be silent?" Al asked.) Other mothers don't walk on hot coals or read tarot cards or communicate with guides from the spirit world.

Other mothers stay home.

She's gotten thinner, traipsing all over South America. Her skin is tan and weathered, and when she relaxes her face you can see the places where the sun hasn't gotten into the wrinkles. Her graying hair has grown long, and she gathers it in a single braid down her back.

She is not wearing a bra.

"My *goddess*, Edward," she says, waving a turquoise-covered hand, "I go away for, what, four or five months and look at the trouble you've gotten yourself into."

"Eleven months," I say, pushing french fries around my plate. "This time you've been gone for eleven months."

"Time is an illusion," she says, addressing everyone at the table like this is a lesson worth learning. "I discovered that when I climbed Machu Picchu with Shirley."

Paula's Disney eyes go wide. "You climbed Machu Picchu with Shirley MacLaine?"

Barbara pats Paula's little hand. "Well, not at the same time, dear, but her presence was so strong that she acted as my guide. We're very connected, Shirley and I. Edward, dear, are you going to eat those fries?"

I shake my head "no."

Barbara scoops them onto her plate. "If you kids could see the kind of poverty I've witnessed, you wouldn't leave food on your plates. Ketchup, please, dear."

I grab the ketchup and plunk it down so hard the silverware jumps. Everyone looks startled, including the people in the next booth. "Would you like to talk about why you're so angry?" Barbara says in a low voice.

"I'm not angry," I say, taking a rather aggressive sip of my 7Up.

She sighs. "I thought we were beyond this," she says, "that you understood why I couldn't stay here."

I close my eyes in hopes it will make her stop. She always does this, gets all intense and personal in a public place. It's weird.

She continues. "Did you know that in some African tribes the boys are *forced* to leave their mothers when they reach puberty?"

I open my eyes so I can roll them at her. "Yeah, and some tribes wear that Ubangi lip thing. What's your point?" I glance around at my friends, searching for some encouragement. Everyone stares at their plates like there's something terribly fascinating there.

"Don't be smart," Barbara snaps. "I'm still your mother."

I feel my cheeks get hot, like she's just threatened to pull down my pants and spank me right here in front of everybody.

Barbara adopts a professorial tone, which frankly is annoying. "Other cultures understand that boys can't learn to be men until they're separated from their mothers," she says. She turns to the rest of the table. "I did my part. It's not my fault Al wasn't up to the task."

Those plates just get more and more interesting.

She sighs. "I find this anger very strange, Edward. You weren't angry like this the last time I saw you."

"That's because the last time you saw me was before my whole life went to shit, that's why."

"Then why didn't you get in touch with me?"

I bang my hand on the table in frustration. "How?" I shout. "You're never in one place long enough to have a fucking address!" My face grows hot all over and my eyes fill with tears. A few wiseguys and the women who love them turn and stare. Let 'em.

Barbara smiles like I'm being a silly child. "I meant on a psychic level," she says.

Oh, yeah, why didn't I think of that?

"You're enough of an intuitive not to have to rely on something as mundane as the postal system."

There's no talking to this woman.

"Come here," she says, opening her arms. She wraps her shawl around my shoulders and brushes the hair out of my face. Her fingers are rough and dry to the touch. "You just need a little mommy-ing, don't you?" She says it like it's something I should be ashamed of, like there's something wrong with me for not being as mature and evolved as pubescent boys in Africa. Well, I don't care. I'll take whatever mommy-ing I can get, even if it means I look ridiculous in public. I lean my head on her shoulder and breathe in the scent of Noxzema, a familiar Barbara smell since childhood. Tears roll down my cheeks and my nose begins to run, but I don't care. I'm just happy to snuggle.

Barbara closes her eyes and places a hand on my head, smiling that strange, beatific smile that's the hallmark of New Age mystics, born-again Christians, and the completely insane. "It's time for a vision quest," she says in that profound way that assumes I know what the hell she's talking about.

Actually, it's time for the check, which gets dumped in front of her rather unceremoniously by a gum-chewing waitress with no eyebrows. Barbara opens her purse.

"Oh, dear," she says. "Edward, do you have any cash? All I have here is Peruvian nuevo sols."

I pull out my wallet and laugh. I can't help myself.

She smiles at me. "What's so funny?"

"Vision quest, huh?"

"Yes," she says in a manner both definitive and defensive. "I think you'd greatly benefit from the Indian sweat lodges."

I hand Natie the check to figure out how much everyone owes. "Well, it's good to know I'll have something to do instead of college."

Barbara looks confused. "What are you talking about? Why aren't you going to college?"

My friends and I give each other shifty-eyed sideways glances, the Internationally Recognized Signal for "If this woman can communicate with spirits how come she can't communicate with us?"

"Haven't you been listening to anything we've been saying?" I ask.

"Not really," she says, digging into her fries. "Your energies are so scattered it's hard for me to keep balanced."

"Well, listen carefully," I say, wiggling my fingers like I'm interpreting for the deaf. "Al . . . refuses . . . to . . . pay."

She looks at me like I've just slapped her in the face. "What are you talking about? That's ridiculous."

"He won't pay for me to go to acting school."

"He can't do that."

"Well, he has."

"No," she says, "I mean, he *can't*. It's in violation of the divorce agreement."

Suddenly it feels like I'm looking at her through the wrong end of a telescope. Everything around me disappears—the clanging dishes, the little jukebox playing Sinatra in our booth, my friends—and all I can see and hear is my mother.

"What did you say?"

"Your father is in violation of the divorce agreement. It says very clearly: 'Albert Zanni agrees to provide for the children's education, both undergraduate and graduate, at the college of their choice.' I insisted on it."

Do you know that scene at the end of *The Wizard of Oz* when Glinda tells Dorothy she's had the power to go home the whole time? That she only needs to click the ruby slippers three times and say, "There's no place like home"? It always amazes me that Dorothy takes the news so well. If I were her, I would have taken one of those slippers off and clocked Glinda right upside her big, pink-crowned head.

"So what do I have to do?" I ask.

"That's simple," Natie says, plunking the bill back down in front of me. "You need to sue your father."

forty

I stand outside Mamma's, squinting as I look up and down the street, the bright setting sun shining right in my eyes. It's been one of those perfect June days where everything looks sharp and clean and somehow new and I feel the same way, my skin tight and tingly from having sat out in the sun today, my hair wet from a quick shower.

No sign of Al, though. I stuff a paperback copy of James Baldwin's *Go Tell It on the Mountain* in the back pocket of my chinos and go in. I'm also reading something Kathleen gave me called *The Peter Pan Syndrome*.

Inside, a guy with a bad comb-over (is there any other kind?) snaps his fingers at me and says, "Hey, waiter, could we have some more bread here?"

I look at his table. No entrées, no appetizers. I flash him a molar-grinding grin.

"Certainly, sir," I say, "but if you're hungry, why don't you try the antipasto plate? I can get one for you really fast."

"Yeah, sounds good," he says, as I top off his wife's wineglass.

There's no fucking way I'm going to let Mr. Comb-Over and his Wallingford Tennis Club wife fill up on free bread. People work here, people depend on these tips—I depend on these tips—and these two can fucking afford some goddamn appetizers if they're hungry. And none of this one-dessert-for-the-table crap, either.

Al shuffles in the door and gives a half-hearted hello to Ernesto, the maître d', who chats with him a moment then leads him to a booth in the corner. I pour a couple of glasses of water and bring them over.

He looks thin and he's got bags under his eyes.

"What happened to your jaw?" I say.

"She threw a goddamned coffee cup at my head," he says through clenched teeth.

"She what?"

His jaw is wired shut. "It's the steroids in her allergy medication. They make her crazy."

So that explains it.

"I had to get a restraining order against her," he says.

"Oh, Pop, I'm sorry." I really am.

"Eh, coulda been worse," he says. "The cup coulda been full of coffee."

Dominick Ferretti saunters over. "Hey, Mr. Z," he says.

Al nods.

Dominick turns to me. "You want me to cover for ya'?" he asks. He really is a nice guy once you get to know him.

"Thanks," I say.

"No problem. Youz guys want anything?"

Al shakes his head "no" and I make a mental note to remind Dominick later not to say "youz guys." If he's ever going to get anywhere in life he has to stop talking like he's one of the Bowery Boys.

I slide into the booth. "So what happened?" I ask.

Al sighs, like telling me is a big hassle. "I noticed somethin' was wrong as soon as I started getting my taxes ready," he mumbles. "Turns out that bitch stole over twelve grand from me."

My jaw drops. "No!" I say. It's not a subtle performance, but a convincing one.

"And would you believe she's actually got the balls to sue for alimony? Even though she knows I saw those . . ." He stops.

"Those what?"

"Never mind," he says.

I allow him his dignity. No man should have to tell his son that his wife had an orgy with a nun and two groundsmen.

We sit in silence. Al arranges and rearranges his silverware. I look around the room.

"House feels kinda empty now," he says.

"You should sell it."

"Ya' think?"

"It's an unhappy house. And you'll make a lot on it."

"The capital gains'll kill me," he says.

I ask him what that means and for a moment it's just like the old days as Al explains onetime exemptions. He becomes animated for the first time in the conversation. His eyes grow lively and he's able to move his mouth more. This financial stuff really gets him going. I guess what theater is for me, finance is for Al.

He clears his throat. "You, uh, wouldn't want to come back, wouldja?" he says, addressing the tablecloth.

"I don't know," I say. "Paula and I got jobs this summer as singing waiters down at the shore, and then . . . well . . ." I shrug.

Neither one of us wants to talk about then.

"You hear from your sister and your mom?" Al asks.

"Not since they left."

"What are they doin' again?"

"Indian sweat lodges," I say. I just hope Karen's not taking peyote.

Al grunts and shakes his head. Poor guy. Two wives and both are looney tunes.

A slice of the setting sun shines across the wall as the front door opens. A young guy in a shirt and tie, a kid not much older than me, says something to Ernesto, who points to our table. The guys crosses the restaurant.

I feel my mouth go dry.

"Are you Al Zanni?" the kid says.

"Yeah . . ."

The guy hands him a manila envelope. "For you, sir."

Al frowns and shakes his head. He pats his chest looking for his glasses.

"Try your jacket," I say.

The kid disappears. I curl my toes in my shoes.

Al rips the envelope open, unfolds the document, and scans the first page. He frowns, then flips through the rest of the pages quickly. He looks up at me.

"You wanna explain this to me?" he says quietly. Too quietly.

I'd love to, but I can't think of a thing to say. Not a thing. I open my mouth, hoping some words will drop out on their own, but it just hangs there like I'm Dominick trying to figure out the cash register.

Al tosses the agreement on the table and points a hairy finger right in my face. "There is nothing in that divorce agreement that says I hafta pay," he barks.

"Careful, Pop, you'll bust your stitches."

"Nothin', I tell ya'!" He swats the paper off the table.

I pick it up from the floor and smooth the pages. "Actually, Pop, there is . . ."

I flip to the place where it says he agreed to pay for the college of my choice and hand it to him.

Al reads the page slowly, massaging the vein on the side of his head, then takes off his glasses and rubs his eyes. "Son of a bitch," he says.

It's just an expression.

Al puts the document on the table, looks up at me . . . and smiles. Well, as much as a man whose jaw has been wired shut can smile.

"I can't imagine what I was thinkin' when I signed this dumb-ass thing," he says.

"But you did sign it."

He shrugs. "Yeah, I know."

"So?"

Al cracks his hairy knuckles. "So?" he says. "I guess it's your choice."

"Really?"

Al nods sadly. How sharper than a serpent's tooth is a thankless child.

I take a deep breath. "Then I choose Juilliard."

Al folds up the papers. "Juilliard it is, then," he says, his eyes glassy like mirrors.

I've been waiting for this moment all year, all my life, really, always imagining how elated I'd feel when this dream finally, finally came true. But now that it has, I'm more exhausted than anything else. This isn't a battle I wanted to fight.

Al twists one of his gold rings. "Y'know, son," he says, "I just want what's best for you."

"I know, Pop."

"When you have kids you'll understand." He snorts a half laugh. "And I hope you have ten just like yourself."

I laugh, too.

"What I mean is, when you see your kid headin' straight for a cliff, you wanna grab 'em and stop 'em like in . . . uh . . . what's it called . . . *Catcher in the Rye*."

"You've read *Catcher in the Rye*?"

"What do you think I am, stupid? I was a teenager once, too, y'know."

It may sound dumb, but it's never occurred to me that Al was ever a teenager. I always imagined he just sprang forth from the mind of Zeus, fully equipped with a briefcase and an ulcer.

"You *sure* you don't want to study business?" Al says. Hope springs eternal, I guess. I think back to last summer, a lifetime ago, when Al first brought Dagmar into this very restaurant. How could I have been so naïve? How could I not know Al wouldn't pay for acting school? All those frigging business dinners, and it never occurred to me he might want me to major in business? What was I thinking? He and I lived like strangers in that house, passing one another at the fridge or in the hallway, never noticing what the other was saying or doing. It must have been lonely for him.

I know it was for me.

I put my hand on top of his. The hair on his knuckles scratches against the soft flesh of my palm. "Pop, there are a lot of things I'm not sure of, but there's one thing I know for certain: I definitely do not want to study business."

He shrugs, the Internationally Recognized Signal for "Well, ya' can't blame a guy for tryin'."

I take his hand in mine. "Besides," I say, "I don't need a degree in business. I've got you to teach me."

Al grips my hand for a moment, then lets go to rearrange his place setting. "So," he says, blinking and sniffing, "waddya wanna know, kid?"

Aunt Glo was right. With Italians, you're not a man until you can beat up your father.

forty-one

I rub my hand over my head. I'm still not used to short hair. Everyone tells me they like it better, that I look more grown-up, but the fact is the only reason I cut it is so Laurel Watkins won't recognize me when I start Juilliard in the fall. Plus Paula tells me we're going to be running our asses off as singing waiters at the beach and there's no air-conditioning. Believe me, it gets really hot underneath all those curls. I put my mortarboard back on my head and wait for my marching orders.

The sky is a bright baby blue and we've got that kind of morning sun that makes people insist you turn around so it doesn't spoil the picture. All around me there's the buzz of excited chatter, but I stand by quietly, waiting for my signal to go. I've always assumed, having a name that begins with Z, that I'd be bringing up the rear at my high-school graduation, marching between Roger Young and Debbie Zimmerman, but since I'm starting off the ceremony by singing the national anthem I actually get to lead the class in. It's a real Pied Piper–Dr Pepper Guy moment and I feel a tingle across the back of my neck when the band begins playing "Pomp and Circumstance."

A cheer erupts from the crowd as we walk out onto the field; I know, of course, that it's not for me, but I can't help but smile, partly from the soothing, waves-on-a-beach sound of applause, partly from the delightful irony of being the person to lead the entrance onto a football field: me, the guy who never learned the rules of the game and got out of gym by faking a medical excuse. I wave to the crowd (I can't help myself), then climb the stairs to the platform to join Principal Farley, the Dork of the Universe, who is trying to look solemn and profound. He tells me to take off my sunglasses.

I stand and watch the rest of the class of '84 file in. There are more than five hundred students graduating, but even with the sun in my eyes I can still see my friends. There's Doug, flirting with the girl next to him. He and Paula say they have a committed relationship, but their commitment is really to having as much hot monkey sex as they can. ("It's a very *deep* commitment," Paula says.) Doug's staying in town this summer, playing Sky Masterson in the Summer Workshop's production of *Guys and Dolls* before starting community college in the fall. He also convinced TeeJay and a good number of the Floor Masters to be in the show, too. Revolting Renée is thrilled to finally have some guys in the chorus who can dance.

Ziba is easy to spot, of course. How could you miss a six-foot-tall Persian lesbian with a mortarboard slanted stylishly over one eye? She leans slouchingly on the folding chair in front of her, exhausted from a late night making last-minute alterations. She's taking this whole Fashion Institute of Technology thing very seriously; she's the only member of the class of '84 whose graduation gown is cut on the bias. She and her manicured mother (who still waves at me like she knows me but doesn't) leave next week for a month in the south of France. Ziba gets to bring a friend, so Kelly's going with her. I went bikini shopping with them and we kind of had a little three-way in the changing room of Saks. Don't say anything to Doug.

I don't know what to tell you about the sex thing anymore. Kelly and I have fallen into bed a couple of more times (don't say anything to Ziba), but with Kelly going off to Bennington in the fall, we both know it's not going to lead anywhere. We're friends—friends who screw around occasionally—but most of all, friends. I'm still adjusting to her new raunchy persona; she really is Sandy at the end of *Grease*, except she's got the good sense not to wear black eyeliner in broad daylight. When she saw I was voted "Most Likely to Succeed" in the yearbook, she crossed it out and changed it to "Most Likely to Suck Cock."

As for me, I got a second job working as a soloist at Father Angelo's church in Hoboken. Aunt Glo says it's my penance, but at $50 a pop, I think it's more like a gift from God.

I feel the same way about Mass as I do about Gilbert and Sullivan: it's a lot more fun to do than to watch. To actually be an integral part of the worship service, as necessary as the Holy Host and the wine, is an experience that's both heady and humbling, and every weekend I walk away from it feeling refreshed and invigorated. Plus, I've really hit it off with the organist, who is also a Juilliard student and moonlights occasionally at Something for the Boys.

What can I say? I'm a sucker for a guy with a big organ.

Oh, I forgot to tell you about Natie. Normally it's a cinch to spot his orange Afro in a crowd, but ever since TeeJay taught him how to use hair relaxer you'd hardly recognize him. He almost looks attractive, though without the extra boost from the hair, he's now about three inches shorter. Regardless, in a sure sign of the coming apocalypse, Natie landed his first date ever. TeeJay set him up with his cousin Margaret, the little lumpy one who looks like a Cabbage Patch doll. Apparently Margaret was equally eager to score because she gave Natie a discreet hand job while watching a community theater production of *How to Succeed in Business without Really Trying*. Natie leaves immediately for a summer internship in the office of Senator Jordan Craig. I don't know how he got it and I don't ask.

So we're all off on our separate ways. There'll be no more Creative Vandalism, no more su-hum-mer nights, no more days spent lounging by Aunt Glo's pool. (Not that there would be, anyway. Angelo finally convinced Aunt Glo to sell her place in Cramptown and take an apartment in Hoboken so she can be nearer to him.) Even if we do get together at the end of the summer to say goodbye, it will already be a reunion. I can't believe we're old enough to be re-anythinged.

The class president leads us in the Pledge of Allegiance, then I step up to the podium to sing the national anthem. There's a drum roll. I'm to begin a cappella. We've been saying for weeks that I could, if I chose, sing anything I wanted at this point ("Come Fly with Me" for instance, or the theme from *Green Acres*) and no one could stop me, but I take my civic responsibility seriously, even if I am a poor choice for representing our precious American way of life. Plus, if you've ever sung in a stadium you know how difficult it is because just about the time you're starting the third line you hear the echo of yourself singing the first line come back to you, a syndrome which invariably causes you to slow down and try to let your echo catch up. But despite concentrating on not singing a duet with myself I can't help but notice Al and Kathleen together in the picture-taking area. Al's been seeing Kathleen. As a cryent. He's decided he could use some help dealing with his relationship issues, like why he's attracted to mentally unbalanced women. Being a little unbalanced herself, Kathleen has a unique perspective on the issue. Al elbows somebody out of his way to get a shot while Kathleen shushes the people so she can hear me better. Seeing my father smack someone on my behalf makes me feel loved and I hold on to the high note until my echo catches up with me:

> O'er the la-hand of the freeeeee . . .

The crowd cheers for the note, just like they do at Yankee Stadium.

> . . . and the home of the braaaaave!

After the ceremony I weave my way through the crowd, accepting compliments from well-wishers and promising to stay in touch with people I could care less about and vice versa, when I find myself face-to-face—or face-to-chest actually—with a big tank of a guy in a too-tight suit. He's got a Cro-Magnon brow, which he wipes with a damp handkerchief, and a broad fleshy Italian face. He looks like Jabba the Hut wearing Armani.

"Hey," he says, shaking my hand, "that was some good singin'." His hand is the size of a catcher's mitt.

"Thanks," I say. This being New Jersey, I don't think much of it (there's no shortage of sweaty, Cro-Magnon-browed tank men in too-tight suits here) and I try to move on, but he throws a massive arm around my shoulder. It feels like a concrete pipe just landed on my neck.

"Come wid me," he says. "There's someone who wants to talk to yuz." His grip is too firm to be considered friendly and I'm immediately suspicious. He practically lifts me off my feet as he leads me away from the crowd.

I try to turn my head to catch someone's, anyone's, attention, but Jabba continues to steamroll me toward the parking lot. "Where are we going?" I say into his damp armpit, which smells like my third-grade lunch box. He quickens the pace and his breathing becomes more labored from the strain of dragging me along.

"Hurry up," he says.

I see that we're headed for a black stretch limousine parked at the far end of the parking lot, and it's in that moment I realize it: I'm done for. The yearbook should have said "Most Likely to Die an Agonizing Mob-Related Death." It's not enough I'm sorry for everything I've done, that I go to Mass every week and pray for forgiveness. No, I'm going to pay for my sins with my young, meaningless life.

The back window of the limo rolls down and I'm certain there's a gun with a silencer on the other side. Obviously Dagmar got in touch with Sinatra's people and, at this very moment, is probably in the backseat with her new boyfriend, a Mafia boss in a silver suit with oily hair pulled back in a ponytail. *Promising Young Actor Shot at Graduation! Film at Eleven.*

I shake free of Jabba. There's no point in struggling. It's over. My heart's beating so fast I'll probably drop dead of a heart attack right now anyway. When they make the movie of my life, there'll be a big close-up on a man's hand in the car window, the diamond in his pinky ring gleaming as he beckons me closer to the car. Oh God, it's going to be the wire around the neck. No, please, not the wire around the neck. I close my eyes and lean toward the window. Hail Mary, full of grace . . . its fleece was white as snow. Oh dear Lord, I promise if you let me live I'll learn the goddamn rosary.

"So you finally did it, huh, kid?" a voice says.

I know that voice. I know it like I know my own, as a matter of fact. I open my eyes and, be still my beating heart, there he is.

Frank Sinatra.

I must be dead already. I'm dead and I've gone to heaven and it turns out I was right all along: Frank Sinatra is God.

"Mr. Sinatra," I hear myself say, "I'm so sorry. I didn't mean to . . ."

"Don't sweat it, kid," he says, dismissing the thought with a wave of his diamond-studded hand. "You got balls. I like that."

"Thanks."

"It's me who should be thanking you. Without you, my cousin's grandkid wouldn't be going to Juilliard." He smiles and it feels like the earth just moved one step closer to the sun. He has the bluest eyes.

"You let me know if there's anything I can do for you," he says. "Us guys from Hoboken gotta stick together." He glances at his Rolex. "Now I gotta split. Sammy's waitin' for me in Atlantic City and he always panics when I'm late." He motions to Jabba that it's time to go and I stand back to watch the limousine slowly slide away, like a ship drifting out to sea.

The gods are definitely on my side. Or at least Frank Sinatra is, and that's close enough for me.

The fact is, I shouldn't even be graduating, and not just because of the underage drinking, reckless driving, illegal drug use (on federal property), unlocking and entering, embezzlement, fraud, forgery, blackmail, and grand theft Buddha. No, I shouldn't be graduating because I never handed in my *Portrait of the Artist* paper.

There was just too much going on, what with suing my father and all, but finally, at long last, here it is. Thanks for being so patient, Mr. Lucas. Turns out I did need a lot more than twenty-five pages. It ain't James Joyce, but I worked with what I had. It's not my fault I'm from New Jersey.

This is how I paid for college. This is how I misspent my youth.

acknowledgments

It takes a suburb to raise a writer and I was fortunate to have dozens of catchers in the rye who made certain I got out of adolescence alive.

So, thank you to all of my friends, teachers, and surrogate parents from high school, most particularly Amanda Burns and Mary Susan Clarke.

To my mother and friend, Megan Garcia; my talented brother, Neal; and, most of all, my amazing dad, Chase Acito, the best father a guy could ever hope for: thank you for not being like the Zannis.

Thank you to Dame Sinclair and Cool Neighbor Brooke for reading the manuscript; to Chuck Palahniuk for recommending it; to my manager, Frederick (of Hollywood) Levy, for opening doors; and, especially, to my agent, Edward Hibbert, for shepherding this story with such insight and intelligence.

Special thanks go to my eagle-eyed editor at Broadway Books, Gerry Howard; and his able assistant, Rakesh Satyal; Mike Jones of Bloomsbury Publishing; my British co-agent, Patrick Walsh; producer Laura Ziskin and her VP Leslie Morgan; and Shannon Gaulding of Columbia Pictures. Both the IRS and I thank you for putting me in a new tax bracket.

Beyond all else, my everlasting gratitude goes to my beloved partner, Floyd Sklaver, for his tender devotion to me and this book. I wish everyone could be as lucky in love as I am.

Finally, thank *you*, my dear reader, for getting this far. Be sure to tell all your friends.

about the author

Hailed as the "gay Dave Barry," Marc Acito is a syndicated humorist whose column, "The Gospel According to Marc," appears in nineteen newspapers, including the *Chicago Free Press* and *Outword–Los Angeles*. After being kicked out of one of the finest drama schools in the country, he went on to sing roles with major opera companies, including the Seattle Opera. He lives in Portland, Oregon.

His website is www.MarcAcito.com.